"An epic struggle between Light and Darkness . . . well paced, exciting and well researched."

—Mick Norman, author of
Forbidden Planet regarding *The Silver Hand*

"This graceful combination of Atlantean legend, Celtic myth, and Christian message [is] reminiscent of C.S. Lewis. Highly recommended."

—*Library Journal* review of
Taliesin: Book One of the Pendragon Cycle

"Lawhead's [*The Iron Lance*] displays the author's deep convictions as well as his storytelling expertise."

—*Library Journal*

"Rich in historical detail and peopled with a wide variety of believable characters, this novel of simple faith and high adventure should appeal to fans of Christian fantasy."

—*Library Journal* review of
The Black Rood: The Celtic Crusades Book 2

"Lawhead pulls off a genuinely moving parable of good and evil."

—*Publishers Weekly* regarding
Avalon: The Return of King Arthur

THE PARADISE WAR

SONG OF ALBION ~ BOOK I

THE PARADISE WAR

STEPHEN R. LAWHEAD

THOMAS NELSON
Since 1798

NASHVILLE   DALLAS   MEXICO CITY   RIO DE JANEIRO

To Ruby Duryea

Visit www.stephenlawhead.com

Published in Nashville, Tennessee, by Thomas Nelson. Thomas Nelson is a registered
trademark of Thomas Nelson, Inc.

Thomas Nelson, Inc., books may be purchased in bulk for educational, business,
fund-raising, or sales promotional use. For information, please e-mail:
SpecialMarkets@ThomasNelson.com

Publisher's Note: This novel is a work of fiction. Names, characters, places, and
incidents are either products of the author's imagination or used fictitiously. All
characters are fictional, and any similarity to people living or dead is purely coincidental.

ISBN 978-1-59554-890-0

Library of Congress Cataloging-in-Publication Data

Lawhead, Steve.
    The paradise war / Stephen R. Lawhead.
      p. cm. — (Song of Albion ; bk. 1)
    ISBN 978-1-59554-219-9 (softcover)
    1. Mythology, Celtic—Fiction. I. Title. II. Series: Lawhead, Steve. Song of
Albion (WestBow Press) ; bk. 1.
    PS3562.A865P3 2006
    813'.54—dc22

                                          2006014185

Printed in the United States of America
10 11 12 13 WC 5 4 3 2 1

contents

contents

PRONUNCIATION GUIDE

Many of the old Celtic words and names are strange to modern eyes, but they are not as difficult to pronounce as they might seem at first glance. A little effort—and the following rough guide—will help you enjoy the sound of these ancient words.

Consonants – As in English, but with the following exceptions:

c:	hard – as in *c*at (never soft, as in *cent*)
ch:	hard – as in Ba*ch* (never soft, as in *church*)
dd:	a hard *th* sound, as in *th*en
f:	a hard *v* sound, as in o*f*
ff:	a soft *f* sound, as in o*ff*
g:	hard – as in *g*irl (never soft, as in *George*)
ll:	a Gaelic distinctive, sounded as *tl* or *hl* on the sides of the tongue
r:	rolled or slightly trilled, especially at the beginning of a word
rh:	breathed out as if *h-r* and heavy on the *h* sound
s:	soft – as in *s*in (never hard, as in *his*); when followed by a vowel it takes on the *sh* sound
th:	soft – as in *th*istle (never hard, as in *then*)

Vowels – As in English, but generally with the lightness of short vowel sounds

a:	short, as in c*a*n
á:	slightly softer than above, as in *awe*;

e:	usually short, as in m*e*t
é:	long *a* sound, as in h*ey*
i:	usually short, as in p*i*n
í:	long *e* sound, as in s*ee*
o:	usually short, as in h*o*t
ó:	long *o* sound, as in w*oe*
ô:	long *o* sound, as in g*o*
u:	usually sounded as a short *i*, as in p*i*n;
ú:	long *u* sound as in s*ue*
ù:	short *u* sound as in m*u*ck
w:	sounded as a long *u*, as in h*ue*; before vowels often becomes a soft consonant as in the name G*w*en
y:	usually short, as in p*i*n; sometimes *u* as in p*u*n; when long, sounded *e* as in s*ee*; rarely, *y* as in wh*y*)

The careful reader will have noted that there is very little difference between *i*, *u*, and *y*—they are almost identical to non-Celts and modern readers.

Most Celtic words are stressed on the next to the last syllable. For example, the personal name Gofannon is stressed go-FAN-non, and the place name Penderwydd is stressed pen-DER-width, and so on.

Since all the world is but a story,
it were well for thee to buy
the more enduring story rather than
the story that is less enduring.

THE JUDGMENT OF ST. COLUM CILLE
(ST. COLUMBA OF SCOTLAND)

I

AN AUROCHS IN THE WORKS

It all began with the aurochs.

We were having breakfast in our rooms at college. Simon was presiding over the table with his accustomed critique on the world as evidenced by the morning's paper. "Oh, splendid," he sniffed. "It looks as if we have been invaded by a pack of free-loading foreign photographers keen on exposing their film—and who knows what else—to the exotic delights of Dear Old Blighty. Lock up your daughters, Bognor Regis! European paparazzi are loose in the land!"

He rambled on a while, and then announced: "Hold on! Have a gawk at this!" He snapped the paper sharp and sat up straight—an uncommon posture for Simon.

"Gawk at what?" I asked idly. This thing of his—reading the paper aloud to a running commentary of facile contempt, scorn, and sarcasm, well mixed and peppered with his own unique blend of cynicism—had long since ceased to amuse me. I had learned to grunt agreeably while eating my egg and toast. This saved having to pay attention to his tirades, eloquent though they often were.

"Some bewildered Scotsman has found an aurochs in his patch."

"You don't say." I dipped a corner of toast triangle into the molten center of a soft-boiled egg and read an item about a disgruntled driver on the London Underground refusing to stop to let off passengers, thereby compelling a train full of frantic commuters to ride the Circle Line for over five hours. "That's interesting."

"Apparently the beast wandered out of a nearby wood and collapsed in the middle of a hay field twenty miles or so east of Inverness." Simon lowered the paper and gazed at me over the top. "Did you hear what I just said?"

"Every word. Wandered out of the forest and fell down next to Inverness—probably from boredom," I replied. "I know just how he felt."

Simon stared at me. "Don't you realize what this means?"

"It means that the local branch of the RSPCA gets a phone call. Big deal." I took a sip of coffee and returned to the sports page before me. "I wouldn't call it news exactly."

"You don't know what an aurochs *is*, do you?" he accused. "You haven't a clue."

"A beast of some sort—you said so yourself just now," I protested. "Really, Simon, the papers you read—" I flicked his upraised tabloid with a disdainful finger. "Look at these so-called headlines: 'Princess Linked to Alien Sex Scheme!' and 'Shock Horror Weekend for Bishop with Massage Parlor Turk!' Honestly, you only read those rags to fuel your pessimism."

He was not moved. "You haven't the slightest notion what an aurochs is. Go on, Lewis, admit it."

I took a wild stab. "It's a breed of pig."

"Nice try!" Simon tossed his head back and laughed. He had a nasty little fox-bark that he used when he wanted to deride someone's ignorance. Simon was extremely adept at derision—a master of disdain, mockery, and ridicule in general.

I refused to be drawn. I returned to my paper and stuffed the toast into my mouth.

"A pig? Is that what you said?" He laughed again.

"Okay, okay! What, pray tell, is an aurochs, Professor Rawnson?"

Simon folded the paper in half and then in quarters. He creased it and held it before me. "An aurochs is a sort of ox."

"Why, think of that," I gasped in feigned astonishment. "An ox, you say? It fell down? Oh my, what *won't* they think of next?" I yawned. "Give me a break."

"Put like that it doesn't sound like much," Simon allowed. Then he added, "Only it just so happens that this particular ox is an ice-age creature which has been extinct for the last two thousand years."

"Extinct." I shook my head slowly. "Where do they get this malarkey? If you ask me, the only thing that's extinct around here is your native skepticism."

"It seems the last aurochs died out in Britain sometime before the Romans landed—although a few may have survived on the continent into the sixth century or so."

"Fascinating," I replied.

Simon shoved the folded paper under my nose. I saw a grainy, badly printed photo of a huge black mound that might or might not have been mammalian in nature. Standing next to this ill-defined mass was a grim-looking middle-aged man holding a very long, curved object in his hands, roughly the size and shape of an old-fashioned scythe. The object appeared to be attached in some way to the black bulk beside him.

"How bucolic! A man standing next to a manure heap with a farm implement in his hands. How utterly homespun," I scoffed in a fair imitation of Simon himself.

"That manure heap, as you call it, is the aurochs, and the implement in the farmer's hands is one of the animal's horns."

I looked at the photo again and could almost make out the animal's head below the great slope of its shoulders. Judging by the size of the horn, the animal would have been enormous—easily three or four times the size of a normal cow. "Trick photography," I declared.

Simon clucked his tongue. "I am disappointed in you, Lewis. So cynical for one so young."

"You don't actually believe this"—I jabbed the paper with my finger—"this trumped-up tripe, do you? They make it up by the yard—manufacture it by the carload!"

"Well," Simon admitted, picking up his teacup and gazing into it, "you're probably right."

"You bet I'm right," I crowed. Prematurely, as it turned out. I should have known better.

"Still, it wouldn't hurt to check it out." He lifted the cup, swirled the tea, and drained it. Then, as if his mind were made up, he placed both hands flat on the tabletop and stood.

I saw the sly set of his eyes. It was a look I knew well and dreaded. "You can't be serious."

"But I am perfectly serious."

"Forget it."

"Come on. It will be an adventure."

"I've got a meeting with my adviser this afternoon. That's more than enough adventure for me."

"I want you with me," Simon insisted.

"What about Susannah?" I countered. "I thought you were supposed to meet her for lunch."

"Susannah will understand." He turned abruptly. "We'll take my car."

"No. Really. Listen, Simon, we can't go chasing after this ox thing. It's ridiculous. It's nothing. It's like those fairy rings in the cornfields that had everybody all worked up last year. It's a hoax. Besides, I can't go—I've got work to do, and so have you."

4

"A drive in the country will do you a world of good. Fresh air. Clear the cobwebs. Nourish the inner man." He walked briskly into the next room. I could hear him dialing the phone, and a moment later he said, "Listen, Susannah, about today . . . terribly sorry, dear heart, something's come up . . . Yes, just as soon as I get back . . . Later . . . Yes, Sunday, I won't forget . . . cross my heart and hope to die. Cheers!" He replaced the receiver and dialed again. "Rawnson here. I'll be needing the car this morning . . . Fifteen minutes. Right. Thanks, awfully."

"Simon!" I shouted. "I refuse!"

⊲ ⊲ ⊲

This is how I came to be standing in St. Aldate's on a rainy Friday morning in the third week of Michaelmas term, drizzle dripping off my nose, waiting for Simon's car to be brought around, wondering how he did it.

We were both graduate students, Simon and I. We shared rooms, in fact. But where Simon had only to whisper into the phone and his car arrived when and where he wanted it, I couldn't even get the porter to let me lean my poor, battered bicycle against the gate for half a minute while I checked my mail. Rank hath its privileges, I guess.

Nor did the gulf between us end there. While I was little above medium height, with a build that, before the mirror, could only be described as weedy, Simon was tall and regally slim, well muscled, yet trim—the build of an Olympic fencer. The face I displayed to the world boasted plain, somewhat lumpen features, crowned with a lackluster mat the color of old walnut shells. Simon's features were sharp, well cut, and clean; he had the kind of thick, dark, curly hair women admire and openly covet. My eyes were mouse gray; his were hazel. My chin drooped; his jutted.

The effect when we appeared in public together was, I imagine, much in the order of a live before-and-after advertisement for *Nature's Own Wonder Vitamins & Handsome Tonic*. He had good looks to burn and the sort of rugged and ruthless masculinity both sexes find appealing. I had the kind of looks that often improve with age, although it was doubtful that I should live so long.

A lesser man would have been jealous of Simon's bounteous good fortune. However, I accepted my lot and was content. All right, I was jealous too—but it was a very contented jealousy.

Anyway, there we were, the two of us, standing in the rain, traffic whizzing by, buses disgorging soggy passengers on the busy pavement around us, and me muttering in lame protest. "This is dumb. It's stupid. It's childish and irresponsible, that's what it is. It's nuts."

"You're right, of course," he agreed affably. Rain pearled on his driving cap and trickled down his waxed-cotton shooting jacket.

"We can't just drop everything and go racing around the country on a whim." I crossed my arms inside my plastic poncho. "I don't know how I let you talk me into these things."

"It's my utterly irresistible charm, old son." He grinned disarmingly. "We Rawnsons have bags of it."

"Yeah, sure."

"Where's your spirit of adventure?" My lack of adventurous spirit was something he always threw at me whenever he wanted me to go along with one of his lunatic exploits. I preferred to see myself as stable, steady-handed, a both-feet-on-the-ground, practical-as-pie realist through and through.

"It's not that," I quibbled. "I just don't need to lose four days of work for nothing."

"It's Friday," he reminded me. "It's the weekend. We'll be back on Monday in plenty of time for your precious work."

"We haven't even packed toothbrushes or a change of underwear," I pointed out.

"Very well," he sighed, as if I had beaten him down at last, "you've made your point. If you don't wish to go, I won't force you."

"Good."

"I'll go alone." He stepped into the street just as a gray Jaguar Sovereign purred to a halt in front of him. A man in a black bowler hat scrambled from the driver's seat and held the door for him.

"Thank you, Mr. Bates," Simon said. The man touched the brim of his hat and hurried away to the porters' lodge. Simon glanced at me across the rain-beaded roof of the sleek automobile and smiled. "Well, chum? Going to let me have all the fun alone?"

"Curse you, Simon!" I shouted, yanked the door open, and ducked in. "I don't need this!"

Laughing, Simon slid in and slammed the door. He shifted into gear, then punched the accelerator to the floor. The tires squealed on the wet pavement as the car leapt forward. Simon yanked the wheel and executed a highly illegal U-turn in the middle of the street, to the blaring of bus horns and the curses of cyclists.

Heaven help us, we were off.

2
DOOM ON
THE HALFSHELL

There are worse things than cruising up the M6 in a Jaguar Sovereign with Handel's *Water Music* bathing the ragged aural nerve ends. The car tops ninety without a murmur, without a shimmy. Silent landscape glides by effortlessly. Cool leather imparts a loving embrace. Tinted glass shades the wayworn eye. The interior cocoons, cushioning the passenger from the shocks and alarms of the road. It is a fabulous machine. I would throttle a rhinoceros to own one.

Simon's father, a merchant banker of some obscure stripe and well on the way to a lordship one day, had bought it for his son. In much the same way, he was buying Simon a top-drawer Oxford education. Nothing but the best for dear Simey.

The Rawnsons had money. Oh yes, they did. Piles of the stuff. Some of it old; most of it new. They also enjoyed that singular attribute prized by the English above all others: breeding. Simon's great-grandmother was a duchess. His grandmother had married a lord who raised racehorses and once sold a Derby winner to Queen Victoria, thereby ensuring fame and fortune forevermore. Simon's family was one of those quietly respectable tribes that marry shrewdly and end up owning Cornwall, the

Lake District, and half of Buckinghamshire before anyone has noticed. All of which made Simon a spoiled brat, of course.

I think, in another day and age, Simon might have been sublimely happy idling away in a honey-stoned manor house in the Midlands, training horses and hounds, and playing the country squire. But he knew too much now to be content with a life of bag balm and jodhpurs. Alas, education had ruined that cozy scenario for him.

If any man was ever untimely born, it was Simon Rawnson. All the same, he could not suppress that aristocratic strain; it declared itself in the very warp and woof of him. I could see the lad as the lord of vast estates, as a duke with scurrying minions and a stately pile in Sussex. But not as an academic. Not for Simon the ivied halls and dreaming spires. Simon lacked the all-consuming passion of the great scholar and the ambition necessary to survive the narrow cut and thrust of academic infighting. In short, he had a genuine aptitude for academic work but no real need to succeed at it. As a result, he did not take his work seriously enough.

He wasn't a slouch. Nor was it a matter of simply buying his sheepskin with Daddy's fat checkbook. Simon had rightly won his pride of place with a particularly brilliant undergraduate career. But as a third-year doctoral candidate, he was finding it too much work. What did he want with a degree in history anyway? He had no intention of conducting any original research, and teaching was the furthest thing from his mind. He had no higher academic aspirations at all. Two years into the program, Simon was simply going through the motions. Lately, he wasn't even doing that.

I had seen it happening—seen the glittering prize slipping away from him as he began to shirk his studies. It was a model case of graduate burnout. One sees it often enough in Oxford and comes to recognize the symptoms. Then again, maybe Simon just aimed to protract his university experience as long as possible since he had nothing else planned. It is true that with money, college can be a cushy life. Even without money it's better than most things going.

I did not blame Simon; I felt sorry for him. I don't know what I would have done in his place. Like a lot of American students in Oxford, however, I had to justify my existence at every turn. I desperately wanted my degree, and I could not be seen to fail. I could not allow myself to be shipped back across the pond with my tail tucked between my legs. Thus, I had a built-in drive to achieve and to succeed that Simon would never possess, nor properly understand.

That, as I think of it, was one of the principal differences between us: I have had to scrape for every small crumb I have enjoyed, while Simon does not know the meaning of the word "strive." Everything he had—everything he *was*—had been given him, granted outright. Everything he ever wanted came to him freely, without merit. People made allowances for Simon Rawnson simply because of who he was. No one made allowances for Lewis Gillies. Ever. What little I had—and it was scant indeed—at least was mine because I had earned it. Merit was an alien concept in Simon's universe. It was the central fact of mine.

Yet, despite our differences, we were friends. Right from the start, when we drew next-door rooms on the same staircase that first year, we knew we would get on together. Simon had no brothers, so he "adopted" me as such. We spent our undergraduate days sampling the golden nectar of the vats at The Turf, rowing on the river, giving the girls a bad time, and generally behaving as well as anyone might expect untethered Oxford men to behave.

I don't mean to make it sound as if we were wastrels and rakes. We studied when we had to and passed the exams we had to pass with the marks we needed. We were, simply, neither more nor less serious than any two typical undergraduate students.

Upon graduation I applied for a place in the Celtic Studies program and was accepted. Being the only student from my hometown high school ever to attend Oxford, let alone graduate, was A Very Big Deal. It was written up in the local paper to the delight of my sponsors, the American Legion Post Forty-three, who, in a giddy rush of self-congratulation, granted me a healthy stipend for books and expenses. I hustled around and scrounged a small grant to cover the rest, and, Presto! I was in business.

Simon thought an advanced degree sounded like a splendid idea, so he went in for history—though why that and not astrophysics or animal husbandry or anything else is beyond me. But, as I said, he had a good brain under his bonnet, and his advisers seemed to think he'd make out all right. He was even offered rooms in college—a most highly sought-after situation. Places for undergrad students are scarce enough, but rooms for graduates are out of the question for any but the truly prized individual.

Privilege again, I suppose. Simon's father, Geoffrey Rawnson, of Blackledge, Rawnson, and Symes Ltd., no doubt had something to do with it. But who was I to complain? Top of the staircase and furnished with a goodly share of the college's priceless antiques—no less than three Italian Renaissance masterpieces, carved oak paneling, Tiffany tables, a crystal chandelier, two Chippendale desks, and a red leather davenport. Nor did the regal appointments end there; we had a meticulous scout, good meals in the dining hall fortified with liberal doses of passable plonk from the college cellarer's legendary cellars, modest use of student assistants, library privileges undergrads would kill for—all that and a splendid view across the quad to the cathedral spire. Where would I get a situation like that on my own?

Simon wanted us to continue on together as before, so he arranged for me to share his rooms. I think he saw it as three or four more years of bachelor bliss. Easy for him. Money was no object. He could well afford to dither and dally till doomsday, but I had my hands full just keeping up with the fees. It was imperative that I finish, get my degree, and land a teaching position as quickly as possible. I dearly loved Oxford, but I had student loans to repay and a family back in the States who had begun wondering loudly and often if they were ever going to see me again.

Also, I was rapidly reaching an age where marriage—or at least concubinage—appealed. I was tired of my prolonged celibacy, tired of wending my weary way along life's cold corridors alone. I longed for the civilizing influence of a woman in my crude existence, as well as a graceful female form in my bed.

This is why I resented taking this absurd trip with Simon. I was neck-deep in my thesis: *The Influence of Goidelic Cosmography in Medieval Travel Literature*. Lately, I had begun to sense fresh wind on my face and the faint glimmer of light ahead. Confidence was feebly sprouting. I was coming to the end at last. Maybe.

It is likely Simon realized this and, perhaps unconsciously, set out to sabotage me. He simply didn't want our good times to end. If I completed my degree ahead of him, he would have to face the cruel world alone—a prospect he sought to hold off as long as humanly possible. So he contrived all sorts of ingenious stratagems for sidetracking me.

This asinine aurochs business was just another delaying tactic. Why did I go along with it? Why did I allow him to do this to me?

The truth? Maybe I didn't really want to finish, either. Deep down, I was afraid—of failure, of facing the great unknown beyond the ivory towers of academia. After all, if I didn't finish, I wouldn't fail; if I didn't finish, I could just live in my snug little womb forever. It's sick, I know. But it's the truth, and a far more common malady among academics than most people realize. The university system is founded on it, after all.

"Move yer bloomin' arse!" muttered Simon at the driver of a dangerously overloaded mini. "Get over, you great pillock." He had been muttering for the last fifty miles or so. A six-mile traffic jam around Manchester had put us well and truly behind schedule, and the motorway traffic was beginning to get to him. I glanced at the clock on the dash: three forty-seven. Digital clocks are symptomatic of our ambivalent age; they provide the precise time to the nanosecond, but no greater context: an infinite succession of "You Are Here" arrows, but nary a map.

"It's almost four o'clock," I pointed out. "Why not take a break and get some tea? There's a service area coming up."

He nodded. "Yeah, sure. I could do with a pee."

A few minutes later, Simon worked his way over to the exit lane and we were coasting into an M6 oasis. The parking lot was jammed; everyone had rolled up for tea. And many of them were having it inside their cars. I have always wondered about this peculiar habit. Why would these people spend hour upon hour driving and then pull into a rest area only to stay locked in their cars with the windows rolled up, eating sandwiches from a shoebox and drinking tepid tea from a thermos? Not my idea of a welcome break.

We parked, locked the car, and walked to the low brick bunker. A foul gray sky sprinkled drizzle on us, and a brisk diesel-scented wind drove it into our clothes. "Oh, please, no," Simon moaned.

"What's wrong?"

He lifted a dismissive hand to the much-abused blue plastic letters affixed to the gray concrete wall facing us. The gesture was pure disdain. "It's a Motorman Inn—they're the worst."

We shuffled into the gents. It was damp and filthy. Evidently some misguided rustic had herded diarrhetic cattle through the place and the management had yet to come to terms with the crisis. We finished our business quickly and retreated to the concourse where we proceeded past a gang of black-leathered bandits loitering before a bank of screeching kill-or-be-killed arcade games. The cheerful thugs tried to beg loose change from us, but Simon imperiously ignored them, and we pushed through the glass door and into the cafeteria.

There was a queue, of course, and the cakes were stale and the biscuits shopworn. In the end, I settled for a Twix bar and a mug of tea. Simon, on the other hand, confessed to feeling puckish and ordered chicken and chips, apple crumble and cream, and a coffee.

I found us a table and, having paid, Simon folded himself into the booth opposite me. The room was loud with the clank of cutlery and rank with cigarette smoke. The floor beneath our table was slimy with mashed peas. "Too utterly grotesque," groaned Simon, but not without a certain grim satisfaction. "A real pigsty. The Motormaniacs strike again."

I sipped my tea. The balance of milk to brew had been seriously overestimated, but never mind; it was hot. "You want me to drive a while? I'm happy to spell you."

Simon dashed brown vinegar from a satchet over his chicken and chips. He speared a long sliver of potato; the soggy digit dangled limply from his fork. He glared at it in disgust before popping it into his mouth, then slowly turned his basilisk gaze toward the food counter and the kitchen beyond. "These subliterate drones have no higher challenge to their vestigial mental faculties than to dip overprocessed potatoes into warm oil," he said icily. "You'd think they'd get it right eventually—the laws of chance, if nothing else."

I didn't want to get involved, so I unwrapped my Twix and broke off a piece. "How much farther to Inverness, do you reckon?"

Writing off the chips as a total loss, Simon moved on to the chicken, grimacing as he wrestled a strip of woody flesh from the carcass. "Putrid," was his verdict. "I don't mind it being lukewarm, but I hate congealed chicken. It should have been chucked in the bin hours ago." He shoved the plate aside violently, scattering greasy chips across the table.

"The apple whatsit looks good," I observed, more out of pity than conviction.

Simon pulled the bowl to him and tested the contents with a spoon. He made a face and spat the mouthful back into the bowl. "Nauseating," he declared. "England produces the finest apples on the planet, and these malfeasant cretins use infectious tinned refuse from some flyblown police state. Moreover, we stand amidst dairy-land which is the envy of the free world, a land veritably flowing with milk and honey, but what do we get? Freeze-dried vegi-milk substi-tute reconstituted with dishwater. It's criminal."

"It's road food, Simon. Forget it."

"It's stupid bloody-mindedness," he replied, taking up the bowl and lifting it high. I was afraid he was going to fling it across the room. Instead, he overturned it ceremoniously upon the offending chicken and greasy chips. He pulled his coffee to him, and I offered him half of my chocolate bar, hoping to pacify.

"I don't mind the money," he said softly. "I don't mind throwing money away—I do that all the time. What I mind is the cynicism."

"Cynicism?" I wondered. "Highway robbery, perhaps, but I wouldn't call it cynicism."

"My dear fellow, that's exactly what it is. You see, the thieving blighters know they have you—you're trapped here on the motorway. You can't simply stroll along to the competitor next door. You're tired, need a respite from the road. They put up this façade and pretend to offer you succor and sustenance. But it's a lie. They offer swill and offal, and we have to take it. They know we won't say anything. We're English! We don't like to make a fuss. We take whatever we're given, because, really, we don't deserve any better. The smarmy brigands know this, and they wield it like a bludgeon. I call that bloody cynical."

"Pipe down," I whispered. "People are staring."

"Let them!" Simon shouted. "These scum-sucking slop merchants have stolen my money, but they do not get my calm acceptance of the fact. They do not get my meek submission."

"All right, all right. Take it easy, Simon," I said. "Let's just go, okay?"

He threw the coffee cup down on the table, got up, and stalked out. I took a last sip of tea and hurried after him—pausing in the parking lot to gaze in envy at the punters taking tea in the comfort and privacy of their automobiles. It suddenly seemed the height of prudence and taste.

Simon had the car running by the time I caught up with him. "You knew what it would be like when you went in there," I charged, climbing in. "Honestly, sometimes I think you do this on purpose, just so you can gripe about it afterwards."

"Am I to blame for their criminal incompetence?" he roared. "Am I responsible?"

"You know what I mean," I maintained. "It's slumming, Simon. It's your vice."

He threw the car into gear, and we rocketed through the parking lot and out onto the motorway. It was a good few minutes before Simon spoke again. The silence was merely the calm before the storm; he was working up to one of his tirades. I knew the signs well enough, and, judging from the intensity with which he grasped the steering wheel, the storm was going to be a doozey. The air fairly trembled with pent-up fury.

Simon drew a breath and I braced myself for the blast.

"We are doomed, of course," he said slowly, picking out each word as if it were a stone for a slingshot. "Doomed like rats in a rain barrel."

"Spare me."

"Did you know," he said, assuming my ignorance, "that when Constantine the Great won the Battle of Milvian Bridge in the year 312, he decided to put up a triumphal arch to commemorate his great victory?"

"Listen, do we have to go into this?"

"Well, he did. The only problem was that he could find no artists worthy of the project. He sent throughout the whole Roman Empire but couldn't find a single sculptor who could produce even a halfway acceptable battle frieze or victory statue. Not a man easily deterred, however, Constantine ordered his masons to remove statuary from other arches and attach them to his. The artists of his age were simply not up to the task, you see."

"Whatever you say," I grumped.

"It's true," he insisted. "Gibbon considered it the turning point of Roman history, the beginning of the decline. And it's been downhill for Western civilization ever since. Look around, sport; we have finally reached the nadir. The end of the line. Finis! Kaput! We are doomed."

"Oh, please don't let's start—" My plea was a paper parasol raised against a typhoon.

"Doomed," he repeated for emphasis, rolling the word out like a cannonball. "No doubt there was a curse placed upon our sorry heads from the cradle. You're an American, Lewis; you must have noticed— it's in our very demeanor. We British are a doomed race."

"You look like you're doing all right to me," I told him sourly. "You're surviving."

"Oh? Do we look like a surviving civilization to you? Consider our appearance: our hair is limp and greasy, our skin is spotty, our flesh pallid and scabby, our noses misshapen. Our chins recede, our foreheads slope, our cheeks run to jowl, and our stomachs to paunch; stoop-shouldered, bent-backed, spindle-legged, we are rumpled, shaggy, and unkempt. Our eyes are weak, our teeth are crooked, our breath is bad. We are gloomy, depressed, anemic, and wan."

"Easy for you to say," I remarked, seeing as how Simon displayed absolutely none of the physical defects he described. His own physique was blissfully free of blemish; his words were smoke and sizzle without the fire, all hat and no rabbit. As expected, he ignored me.

"Surviving? Ha! The very air is poisonous. And the water—that is poisonous too. And the food—that is *really* poisonous! Let's talk about the food, shall we? Everything is mass-produced by devious men in salmonella factories for the sole purpose of infecting as many consumers as possible and charging them for the privilege, before turning them over to the National Health, who give 'em the chop and a hasty, anonymous burial.

"And if, by some miracle, we should somehow survive our meager noonday repast, we are sure to be done in by the unrelenting meanness of our very existence. Look at us! We slog numb and shell-shocked through bleak, pestilential cities, inhaling noxious gases spewed from obsolete factories, clutching wretched plastic bags full of toxic meat and carcinogenic vegetables. The stinking rich amass wealth in tax-exempt offshore capital investment accounts, while the rest struggle along stark streets knee-deep in canine excrement to punch the time clock in soul-stifling sweatshops for the wherewithal to buy a rind of rancid cheese and a tin of beans with our overtaxed, undervalued pound.

"Observe any street in any city! You'll see us shuffling grimly from one hateful upmarket boutique to another, wasting our substance on obnoxious designer clothes that do not fit, and buying gray cardboard shoes made by slave labor in the gulags, and being routinely abused by blowzy, brain-dead shop assistants with blue mascara and chicken-fleshed legs. Overwhelmed by marketing forces beyond our ken and purchasing wildly complicated Korean appliances we neither want nor need with hologrammed plastic cash from smug, spotty-faced junior sales managers in yellow ties and too-tight trousers who can't wait to scuttle off to the nearest pub to suck down pints of watery beer and leer at adenoidal secretaries wearing black leather miniskirts and see-through blouses."

Simon had liftoff. I settled back for the ride as his cavalcade of horror rolled on. It was all about the Channel tunnel and a landscape awash in Eurotrash and French fashion victims and acid rain and lugubrious Belgians and Iranian language students and lager louts swilling Heineken and football hooligans and holes in the ozone layer and Italian playboys, and South American drug lords and Swiss banks and AmEx Goldcards and the greenhouse effect and the Age of Inconsequence, and so on and so forth.

Simon clutched the steering wheel with both hands and punched the accelerator for emphasis, bobbing his head to the cadence of his words and glancing sideways at me every now and then to make sure I was still listening. Meanwhile, I bided my time, waiting for an opportunity to toss a monkey wrench into his fast-whirling gears.

"We don't have any place to call our own, but we'll all have cold Guinness in cans and inscrutable Braun coffeemakers and chic Benetton sweatshirts and nifty Nike Cross-Trainers and gold-plated Mont Blanc fountain pens and Canon fax machines and Renaults and Porsches and Mercedes and Saabs and Fiats and Yugos and Ladas and Hyundais and Givenchy and Chanel pour Homme and Aeroflot holidays and Costa Del Sol condos and Piat D'Or and Viva España and Sony, and Yamaha and Suzuki and Honda and Hitachi and Toshiba and Kawasaki and Nissan and Minolta and Panasonic and Mitsu-bloody-bishi!

"Do we care?" he demanded rhetorically. "Hell, no! We don't bat an eye. We don't turn a hair. We don't twitch a solitary sedentary muscle. We sit transfixed before the Tube Almighty, lulled into a false Nirvana by a stupefying combination of pernicious banality and blather while nocuous cathode rays transform our healthy gray cells into jellied veal!"

As harangues go, it was one of Simon's better efforts. But his dolorous litanies could endure ad infinitum, and I was growing weary. He paused for breath and I saw my chance. "If you're unhappy," I said, throwing myself into the withering flow of invective, "why do you stay here?"

Curiously, that stopped him. He turned his face to me. "What did you say?"

"You heard me. If you're as miserable as you make yourself out to be, and if things are as bad as you say—why not leave? You could go anywhere."

Simon smiled his thin, superior smile. "Show me a place where it's better," he challenged, "and I'm on my way."

Offhand, I could not think of any place perfect enough for Simon. I might have suggested the States, but the same demons infesting Britain were running rampant in America as well. The last time I was back home, I hardly recognized the place—it wasn't at all as I remembered. Even in my own small, mid-American town the sense of community had all but vanished, gobbled up by ravening corporations and the townsfolks' own blind addiction to a quick-buck economy and voracious consumerism. "We might not have a Fourth of July parade down Main Street anymore, or Christmas carols in the park," my dad had said, "but we sure as hell got McDonald's and Pizza Hut and Kentucky Fried Chicken and a Wal-Mart mini-mall that's open twenty-four hours a day, seven days a week!"

That was the way of the world: greedy, grim, and ghastly. It was like that everywhere, and I was tired of being reminded of it every time I looked around. So I rounded on Simon, looked him in the eye, and I threw his challenge back in his face. "Do you mean to tell me that if you found a place that suited you better, you'd leave?"

"Like a shot!"

"Ha!" I gloated. "You never would. I know you, Simon, you're a classic malcontent. You're not happy unless you're miserable."

"Oh, really?"

"It's true, Simon," I declared. "If everything was perfect, you'd be depressed. That's right. You actually like things the way they are."

"Well, thank you very much, Dr. Freud," Simon snarled. "I deeply appreciate your incisive analysis." He punched the accelerator to the floor.

I thrust home my point. "You might as well admit it, Simon— you're a crap hound, and you love it. You are a connoisseur of misery: doom on the halfshell! Bring it on! The worse things get, the better you like it. Decadence suits you—in fact, you prefer it. You delight in decline; you revel in rot."

"Watch out," he replied softly—so softly I almost didn't hear him. "I just might surprise you one day, friend."

3

THE GREEN MAN

I had hoped to see Loch Ness. But all I saw was my own bleary-eyed reflection in the car window, made lurid by the map light in the dashboard. It was dark. And late. I was hungry, bored, and tired, aching to stop and silently cursing myself for being a party to this idiotic outing.

The things I said about Simon were essentially true. He came from a long line of manic depressives, megalomaniacs, and megalomaniac depressives. Still, I had only hoped to get him off his whining binge. Instead, my impromptu psychoanalysis produced a strained and heavy silence between us. Simon lapsed into sullen withdrawal and would speak only in monosyllabic grunts for the next seven hours. I carried out my navigational duties nevertheless, disregarding his sulk.

The map in my lap put us just south of Inverness. I turned from the window and peered at the atlas under my thumb. We were on the A82 approaching a village called Lochend. The narrow body of the famous monster-bearing lake itself lay a hundred yards off to the right, invisible in the darkness. "We should see some lights soon," I said. "Three or four miles."

I was still bent over the Bartholomew when Simon screamed. "Bloody hell!"

He hit the brakes and swerved. I was thrown against the door. My head thumped the window.

The car dry-skidded to a stop on the road. "Did you see it?" Simon yelled. "Did you see it?"

"Ow!" I rubbed my head. "See what? I didn't see anything."

Simon's eyes glinted wildly in the dim light. He jammed the gear-shift into reverse, and the car began rolling backward. "It was one of those things!"

"Things? What things?"

"You know," he said, twisting around to see out the rear window, "one of those mythical creatures." His voice was shaky, and his hands were trembling.

"A mythical creature—well, that certainly narrows it down." I craned my neck to look out the back as well, but saw nothing. "What sort of mythical creature, exactly?"

"Oh, for crying out loud, Lewis!" he shouted, his voice rising hysterically. "Did you see it, or didn't you?"

"All right, calm down. I believe you." Obviously, he had been driving far too long. "Whatever it was, it's gone now."

I started to turn away and saw, fleetingly highlighted in the red-and-white glow of the taillights, the ragged torso of a man. Rather, I saw the upper thigh and lower stomach and part of an arm as it swung away and out of sight. Judging from the proportions, the body must have been gigantic. I only saw it for the briefest instant, but my strongest impression, the thing that stuck fast in my mind, was that of *tree leaves*.

"There!" bellowed Simon triumphantly, slamming on the brakes. "There it is again!" He tore at the door handle and burst from the car. He ran up the road a few yards.

"Simon! Get back here!" I yelled, and waited. The sound of his footsteps died away. "Simon?"

Hanging over the seat back, I peered out the rear window. I could not make out a thing beyond the few feet of tarmac illuminated by the taillights. The engine purred quietly, and through the open car door I heard the sough of wind in the pines like the hissing of giant snakes.

I kept my eyes on the circle of light and presently glimpsed the rapid movement of an approaching figure. A moment later, Simon's face floated into view. He slid into the car, slammed the door, and locked it. He put his hands on the steering wheel but made no other move.

"Well? Did you see anything?"

"You saw it, too, Lewis. I know you did." He turned to face me. His eyes were bright, his lips drawn back over his teeth. I had never seen him so excited.

"Look, it happened so fast. I don't know what I saw. Let's just get out of here, okay?"

"Describe it." His voice cracked with the effort it took to hold it level.

"Like I said, I don't think I could—"

"Describe it!" He smashed the steering wheel with his fists.

"It was a man, I think. It looked like a man. I only saw a leg and an arm, but I think it was a man."

"What color was it?"

"How should I know what color it was?" I demanded shrilly. "I don't know. It's dark. I didn't see it all that—"

"Tell me what color it was!" Simon's tone was cold and cutting.

"Green, I think. The guy was wearing something green—rags or something."

Simon nodded slowly and exhaled. "Yeah, green. That's right. You saw it too."

"What are we talking about, exactly?" I asked. My stomach twisted itself into a tight knot.

"A huge man," he answered quietly. "Eight feet tall at least."

"Right. And wearing a ragged green coat."

"No." Simon shook his head firmly. "Not a coat. Not rags."

"What, then?" Tension made my voice sharp.

"Leaves."

Yes. He'd seen it too.

⊲ ⊲ ⊲

We stopped for gas at an all-night service station just outside of Inverness. The clock in the dash read 2:47 a.m. Except for a flying stop to fuel the car and grab some sandwiches in Carlisle, it was exactly eleven hours since our last real rest break. Simon had insisted on driving straight through, in order to be, as he put it, "in situ" by daybreak.

Simon saw to the gas while I scrubbed the bug juice from the windshield. He paid the bill and returned to the car, carrying two Styrofoam cups of Nescafé. "Drink up," he said, shoving one into my hand.

We stood in the garish glare of the overhead fluorescent tubes, sipping coffee and staring at each other. "Well?" I said, after a couple minutes of this. "Are you going to say it, or am I?"

"Say what?" Simon favored me with his cool, bland stare—another of the many little tricks.

"For crying out loud, Simon, you know perfectly well what!" The words came out with more force than I intended. I suppose I was still fairly upset. Simon, however, seemed to be well over it. "What we *saw* out there." I waved a hand to the highway behind us.

"Get in the car," he replied.

"No! I'm not getting in the car until—"

"Shut up, Lewis!" he hissed. "Not here. Get in the car and we'll talk."

25

I glanced toward the door of the service station. The attendant had wandered out and was watching us. I don't know how much he had heard. I ducked in and slammed the car door. Simon switched on the ignition, and we pulled out onto the road.

"Okay, we're in the car," I said. "So talk."

"What do you want me to say?"

"I want you to tell me what you think we saw."

"But that's obvious, don't you think?"

"I want to hear you say it," I insisted. "Just for the record."

Simon indulged me with regal forbearance. "All right, just for the record: I think we saw what used to be called a Green Man." He sipped some coffee. "Satisfied?"

"Is that all?"

"What else is there to say, Lewis? We saw this big, green man-thing. You and I—we both saw it. I really don't know what else to say."

"You could add that it's plain impossible. Right? You could say that men made of oak leaves do not, cannot, and never could exist. You could say that there's no such thing as a Green Man—that it's a figure of antique superstition and legend with no basis in reality. You could say we were exhausted from the drive and seeing things that could not be there."

"I'll say whatever you like, if it will make you happy," he conceded. "But I saw what I saw. Explain it how you will."

"But I *can't* explain it."

"Is that what's got to you?"

"Yes—among other things."

"Just why is an explanation so important to you?"

"Excuse me, but I happen to think it's important for any sane and rational human being to keep at least one foot in reality whenever possible."

He laughed, breaking the tension somewhat. "So, seeing something one can't explain qualifies one as insane in your estimation—is that it?"

"I didn't say that exactly." He had a nasty habit of bending my words back on me.

"Well, you'll just have to live with it, chum."

"Live with it? That's it? That's all you've got to say?"

"Until we figure out something better, yes."

We had come to a small three-way junction. "This is our turn," I told him. "Take this road to Nairn."

Simon turned onto the easterly route, drove until we were out of the city, and then pulled off the road onto the shoulder. He allowed the car to slow to a halt, then switched off the engine and unbuckled his seat belt.

"What are you doing?"

"I'm going to sleep. I'm tired. We can get forty winks here and still make it to the farm before sunrise." He pulled the lever to recline his seat and closed his eyes. In no time at all, he was sound asleep.

I watched him for a few moments, thinking to myself: *Simon Rawnson, what have you gotten us mixed up in?*

4

AT THE DOOR
TO THE WEST

I heard the deep, throaty rumble of a juggernaut and woke to find Simon snoring softly in the seat beside me. The sun was rising beyond the eastern hills, and the early morning traffic was beginning to hum along the road next to us. The clock in the dash read 6:42 a.m. I prodded Simon. "Hey, wake up. We've overslept."

"Huh?" He stirred at once. "Bugger!"

"It's cold in here. Let's have some heat."

He sat up and switched on the ignition. "Why didn't you wake me?"

"I just did."

"We'll be too late now." He rubbed his eyes with the heels of his hands, checked the rearview mirror, and then pulled out swiftly onto the road.

"What do you mean? The sun isn't even up yet. It's only a few more miles. We'll get there in plenty of time."

"I wanted to be there *before* sunrise," Simon told me flatly. "Not after."

"What difference does that make?"

Simon gave me a derisive look. "And you a Celtic scholar." His tone suggested I should be able to read his mind.

"The time-between-times—is that what you're talking about?" I was not aware that Simon knew any ancient Celtic lore. "Is that why we've busted our buns to get here so fast?"

He didn't answer. I took his silence as affirmation and continued. "Look, if that's why you've been dragging us all over the country, forget it. The time-between-times—that's just a folk superstition, more poetic device than anything else. It doesn't exist."

"Just like aurochs don't exist?"

"Aurochs don't exist!" And neither do Green Men, I might have added, but saved my breath. There was no need to bring that up at this hour of the morning. "It's just screwball journalism."

"That's what we're here to determine, isn't it?" Simon smiled deviously and turned his attention to the road. We were already in the country again, heading east on the A96 out of Inverness. The last sign I saw indicated that Nairn was only a dozen miles ahead.

I rummaged around on the floor of the car for the atlas, found it where I'd dropped it the night before, and turned to the proper page. The farm we were looking for was not on the map, but the nearest village was—a mere flyspeck of a hamlet called Craigiemore on a thin squiggle of yellow road which ran through what was optimistically called Darnaway Forest. Probably all that was left of this alleged forest was a hillside or two of rotting stumps and a roadside picnic area.

"I don't see Carnwood Farm on here," I said after giving the map a good once-over. Simon expressed his appreciation for this information with a grunt. Motivated by his encouragement, I continued, "Anyway, it's seven miles to the B9007 from Nairn. And from there to the farm is probably another two or three miles, minimum."

Simon thanked me for my orienteering update with another eloquent grunt and put the accelerator nearer the floor. The hazy, hillbound countryside fled past in a blur. It was already plenty blurry to begin with. A thickish mist hugged the ground, obscuring all detail beyond a thousand yards or so, and turning the rising sun into a ghostly, blood-red disk.

Scotland is a strange place. I failed to see the attraction so many otherwise sane people professed for this bleak, wind-bitten scrag of dirt and rock. What wasn't moors was lochs, and one as damp as the other. And cold. Give me the Costa Del Sol anytime. Better yet, give me the French Riviera and take everything else. The way I figured it, if one could not grow a decent wine grape within shouting distance of the beach, the hell with it.

Simon stirred me from my reverie with an impromptu recitation, as startling as it was spontaneous. Without taking his eyes from the road, he said:

> *"I am the singer at the dawn of the age,*
> *and I stand at the door to the West.*
> *Three fifties of warriors uphold me,*
> *whose names are lauded in the halls of chieftains;*
> *great lords make haste to do their bidding.*
> *Royal blood flows in my veins,*
> *my kinship is not humble;*
> *yet my portion is despised.*
> *Truth is at the root of my tongue,*
> *wisdom is the breath of my speech;*
> *but my words find no honor among men.*
> *I am the singer at the dawn of the age,*
> *and I stand at the door to the West."*

Well, knock me over with a feather. You live with someone for a few years, and you think you know them. "Where on earth did you get that?" I asked when I finished gawping.

"Like it?" He smirked at me like a naughty schoolboy.

"It's okay," I conceded. "Where did you find it?"

"Haven't the foggiest," Simon answered. "Must have tumbled across it somewhere in my reading. You know how it is."

I knew how it was, all right. Simon the dutiful scholar hadn't so much as winked at a book in months. "Have you any idea what it means?" I asked.

"Actually, I was hoping you'd fill me in," he replied diffidently. "It's a bit out of my line, I'm afraid. More in yours, I would have thought."

"Simon, what's going on? First this extinct ox business; then you get all bothered about the time-between-times thing; now you're quoting Celtic riddles at me. What gives?"

He shrugged. "It just seemed apropos, I suppose. The hills, the sunrise, Scotland . . . that sort of thing."

I would get more information from an oyster, so I changed the subject. "What about breakfast?" Simon didn't answer. He seemed stubbornly preoccupied with driving. "How about we stop in Nairn for a bite to eat?"

We didn't stop in Nairn. We whizzed through that town so fast I thought Simon might be trying for a land speed record. "Slow down!" I yelled, stiff-arming the dashboard. But Simon merely downshifted and drove on.

Coming out of Nairn, Simon picked up the A939 and we flew, almost literally, over the hills. Luckily, we had the road to ourselves. It unwound in a seamless, if convoluted, strip and we beat it along with respectable haste. Just beyond the Findhorn River we came to the village of Ferness located at the crossroads of the A939 and the B9007. "This is our turn," I told Simon. "Take a right."

The B9007 proved to be a narrow tarmac trail along the bottom of the Findhorn Glen, and the principal way into the remains of the Darnaway Forest, which, to my surprise, possessed all the earmarks of a proper forest. That is to say, hills thickly covered with tall pines, morning mist wafting among the trees, and little streams coursing down to the river below. After a mile we reached a tiny village called Mills of Airdrie.

I knew enough Gaelic to figure that the word *Airdrie* was a contraction for the ancient Celtic term *Aird Righ*, meaning High King. While there was nothing strange about a king having a mill on the river, I found it slightly peculiar that he should have been a High King. In antiquity, that title would have been reserved for only the most elite of royalty, and rarely in Scotland.

The village itself wasn't much: a wide spot in the road with an inn and combination grocer's-newsagent's-post office. We continued on another mile and reached an unmarked road. A weathered sign stood at the crossing; it had "Carnwood Farm" written on it in bright blue with an arrow pointing the way. We turned left and soon came to a stone bridge. We crossed the Findhorn once again and drove on deeper into the heart of Darnaway.

Carnwood Farm lay on the flat ground between two broad tree-clad hills. Small, neat, and spare, the place appeared efficient and prosperous. But it also had about it an air of . . . I don't know . . . emptiness. As if it were long abandoned. Not neglected, not deserted. Just untouched. Or, more precisely, as if the land were somehow resistant to human occupation. This was patently absurd. The buildings, the fields, and the tumbled ruin of an old moss-grown stone tower hard beside the farmhouse spoke of generations of continual habitation.

"Well," said Simon, "this is the place." He had slowed the car to a crawl upon our approach and now stopped on the shoulder of the road. A large gray stone house and outbuildings stood at the end of a long, tree-lined drive. A black-painted wooden gate separated the drive from the road. A tin mailbox bore the name Grant in bold white letters.

"So?" I wondered. "Are we just going to sit out here, or are we going in?"

"We go in."

He switched off the engine and took the keys. We got out and walked to the gate. "It's cold out here," I said, shivering. My poncho was in the car. Simon tried the gate; it wasn't locked and swung open easily.

A great floppy dog met us halfway up the drive. The animal did not bark, but ran to greet us, wagging its tail happily. It licked both my hands before I could stuff them in my pockets. Simon whistled the accommodating animal to him. "Hey, Pooch, is your master at home?"

"He's home," I said. "And here he comes."

From around the corner of the barn approached a man in a shape-less brown tweed hat, a black overcoat, and green wellies. He carried a long stick in one hand and looked as if he knew how to use it.

"Good morning, sir," Simon called, turning on the Rawnson charm. "Nice place you've got here."

"Mornin'." The farmer did not smile, but neither did he hit us with the stick. I took this as a good sign.

"We've come up from Oxford," Simon volunteered, as if this should explain everything.

"All that way?" The farmer gave a slight shake of his head. Apparently Oxford could not easily be compassed in his geography. "You'll be wanting to see the beastie, then."

I thought he meant the dog and was about to point out that we had already enjoyed that pleasure, when Simon said, "That's right. If it's no trouble, of course. I wouldn't want to put you out."

If it's no trouble! We've driven day and night to get here expressly to see this aurochs creature, and he wouldn't want to put anybody out. Give me a break!

"Oh, it wouldn't put me out," the farmer replied agreeably. "I'll take you now."

He led us out behind the barn to a small field. The frosted grass

33

crunched underfoot with a sound like eggshells. I scanned the field for any sign of the unfortunate ice-age relic but saw nothing.

Presently we stopped and the farmer thrust the end of his stick at the ground before us. "T'was here he fell," he said. "You can see the way he bent the grass."

I could see no such thing. I could see nothing at all, in fact. "Where is it?" I asked. Disappointment made my voice sharp. That, or desperation.

The farmer gazed placidly at me—much, I suppose, as one might regard the village idiot—pity and amusement mingled in equal parts. "But it's no here, is it?"

"I can see it's no here—not here. Where has it gone?" I didn't mean to be short with the man. But no one else seemed to think it mattered that we had driven eight zillion miles for the express purpose of looking at a bare patch in an empty field.

"They came and took it away yesterday afternoon," the farmer answered.

Simon crouched down and put his hand on the flattened straw. "Who took it?" he asked idly. "If you don't mind my asking."

"Ah dinna mind," the farmer replied. "The men from the university."

"Which university?" I demanded, feeling more of a dope with each passing second.

"Edinburgh," the farmer answered—as if there were only one possible institution of higher learning on the entire planet, and it was a wonder I should even ask. "Archaeologists they were. Had a wee van and trailer and everything."

Simon steered the inquiry back on course. "Yesterday afternoon, you say? About what time?"

"Quarter past four, it was. I was just going in for my tea when they came," the farmer said, crouching down beside him and waving the stick over the nonexistent body. "There, you can see how it fell. Ah reckon it rolled onto its side. The heid was there." He tapped the ground with the stick. "They took pictures and all. Said there'd be some other chappies along to set it down in writing."

"That's right," Simon confirmed, implying we were the very chappies. "We got here as soon as we could."

"You don't have a manure heap around here, do you?" I asked.

"Dung?" the farmer asked quizzically. "Is it ma dung heap you're after seeing now?"

Simon rolled his eyes at me. To the farmer he said, "Where did the university chaps take the carcass?"

"To the lab," the farmer said. "That's where they take them—to the lab. Tests and all. The things they do." He shook his head. Clearly, it was all beyond him. "Is it breakfast you'll be wanting?"

"Yes," I said.

"No," said Simon; he shot me a threatening look. "That's far too much trouble. If you don't mind, we'd just like to ask a few more questions and we'll be on our way. Now then, when did you first notice the beast was in your field?"

The farmer glanced at the sky. The sun had risen above the hills, burning off the mist. "Och, it would be no trouble," he said.

"Thanks just the same," Simon said, with one of his warm and winning smiles. "Still, it's awfully kind of you to offer."

"Will you no have a wee cup of coffee, then?" The farmer shoved his hands into his pockets.

Simon rose slowly. "Only if it's no trouble. We wouldn't want to take up too much of your time," he said. "I know what an intrusion all this can be."

The farmer smiled. "My Morag will have the coffee already in the cups. Just you come wi' me." He thrust out his hand. "Ma name's Grant—Robert Grant."

"I am Simon Rawnson," Simon said, shaking hands with the farmer. "And this is my colleague, Lewis Gillies."

I shook hands with the farmer and, having observed the ritual greeting, we fell into step behind our host. As we started toward the house, Simon grabbed me by the arm. "You can't come on to these people like that," he whispered tersely.

"Like what? He offered. I'm hungry."

Simon frowned. "Of course he offered—what'd you expect? But you have to let them coax you."

"Whatever you say, Kemo Sabe. This is your show."

"Don't screw up again," Simon hissed. "I'm warning you."

"Awright already! Geesh!"

We followed the farmer into the house and waited while he shed his coat. His wife, Morag, met us in the kitchen, where, as the farmer had predicted, she was pouring out the coffee as we trooped in. "These laddies are up from Oxford," the farmer told her. Something about the way he said it made it sound like we'd hopped all the way on one foot.

"Oxford, is it?" his wife said, visibly impressed. "Then you'd best sit down. The porridge is hot. How do you like your eggs?"

My lips formed the word "fried," but Simon beat me to it. "Please," he said sweetly, "coffee is enough for us. Thanks just the same."

The farmer pulled two more chairs to the table. "Sit ye down," he said. We sat.

"But ye canna keep body and soul taegither wi' just coffee," the farmer's wife said. "I'll no have it said you went from my table hungry." She placed her hands firmly on her hips. "I hope ye dinna mind eating in the kitchen."

"You're very kind," Simon told her. "The kitchen is splendid." He blessed her with his best beatific smile. I'd seen him use the same simpering smirk to remarkable effect on librarians and waitresses. Some people found it irresistible.

In moments we were all tucking in to steaming bowls of thick, gooey porridge. Eggs, toast with homemade gooseberry jam, thick-cut country bacon, farmhouse cheese, and oatcakes came next. Morag presided over the table with red-faced, fussy pride. Clearly, she was enjoying herself massively.

It wasn't until the dishes were being cleared away that talk turned once again to the absent aurochs. "It's very strange, you know," the farmer said, gazing into the coffee mug gripped between his hands. "I crossed that field but five minutes earlier. There was no a sign of the beastie then."

Simon nodded sympathetically. "It must have been something of a shock."

The farmer nodded slightly. His wife, who had been hovering over the table, broke in. "Oh, that's no the half of it. Tell them about the spear, Robert."

"Spear?" Simon leaned forward. "Excuse me, but no one said anything about a spear. There was nothing about a spear in the—ah, report."

The farmer permitted himself a slow, sly, prideful smile. "True, true. Ah haven'a told anyone else, have I?"

"Told them what, exactly?" I asked.

"The beastie in ma field was kilt wi' a spear," Farmer Robert replied matter-of-factly. "Clean through the heart." He turned his head to his wife and nodded. Morag stepped to a small nook beside the big stove. She reached in and brought out a slender length of ash-wood over five feet long. It was tipped with a flat, leaf-shaped blade of iron which was affixed to the shaft with rawhide. The blade, rawhide, and wooden shaft were much discolored with a ruddy brown stain that appeared to be blood.

She brought the ancient weapon to the table. I stood and held out my hands. "May I?"

At a nod from her husband, she gave it to me, and I held it across my palms. The weight of the thing was considerable—a stout, well-made weapon. I turned it over, examining it closely, butt to blade. The wood of the shaft was shaved and smooth and straight. The blade, beneath the patina of dried blood, was hammered thin and honed razor sharp. And it was decorated with the most intricate pattern of whorls imaginable; the whole surface of the blade to the very edges was covered with these precise, yet flamboyant, interwoven swirls.

A curious feeling drew over me as I stood holding the spear. I felt as if I knew this weapon, as if I had held it before, and as if holding it now was somehow the right thing to do. I felt a strange sense of completion, of connection . . .

Silly of me. Of course I had seen such a blade before, many times before—in countless photographs and more than a few actual specimens—and knew it well enough to identify: iron-age Celtic, La Tène Culture, seventh to fifth century BC. The British Museum has hundreds, if not thousands, of the things in its collection of iron-age artifacts. I had even handled a few of them in the research department at the Ashmolean Museum in Oxford. The only difference that I could see between this one and the rust-encrusted relics of the museums was that the weapon I stood holding in my hands looked for all the world as if it had been made yesterday.

5
THE CAIRN

It's all a prank. A hoax. And you're a stupe for falling for it. I bet they're laughing at us right now. Conned some city folk with the ol' vanishing aurochs stunt. How clever we are! What a great joke! Ha! Ha! Ha!"

Simon shifted the Jaguar into gear and the car rolled onto the road. "You don't believe Robert and Morag. Is that what you're saying?"

"Well, I didn't see any extinct beasties. Did you see any extinct beasties? No? Golly, what a surprise," I scoffed.

"What about the picture in the newspaper?"

"The rag probably gave him a hundred to pose for the picture and another hundred to keep his mouth shut," I rallied. "But *we* didn't see any aurochs, because there was never any aurochs to see."

"We saw a fine example of an iron-age spear."

"Grant made that up himself to make a good story better. Give me half a day in a machine shop and I'll make you one just like it."

"You really think so?"

"Oh, for Pete's sake, Simon. Wake up and smell the porridge! We've been conned. Let's give it up and go home."

He turned his head and regarded me placidly. "*You're* the one who asked about the cairn," he said. "Never would have occurred to me."

Simon *would* drag that in. "Okay, the excitement of the moment got to me. So what?"

"So it was your idea. We're going to see the cairn." He downshifted and we barrelled along.

"We don't have to do this on my account," I pleaded. "I've changed my mind. Look, it's barely nine o'clock. If we leave right now we can be back in Oxford by tonight."

"It's less than a mile up the road," Simon pointed out. "We'll swing by, take a look, and then we're off. How's that?"

"Promise?"

"Yes," he said.

"Liar! You don't have any intention of going home yet."

He laughed. "What do you want, Lewis? Blood?"

"I want to go home!"

Simon took his right hand from the steering wheel and pointed at the atlas. "See if you can find this cairn thingy on the map."

I retrieved the atlas and scanned the page quickly. "I don't see it."

Me and my big mouth. The cairn thingy in question had come up because, as we were sitting in Farmer Grant's kitchen, my head filled with thoughts of iron-age spears and extinct oxen and such, I suddenly blurted out, "Is there a cairn nearby?"

"Och aye," Farmer Bob had said. "Near enough. Used to be part o' this steading, but ma grandmother sold off the bit wi' the cairn. The Old'un was of a superstitious mind."

Then he had gone on to tell us how to find the cairn because Simon had immediately insisted that we should go and check it out since we were in the area. Farmer Bob seemed to think this a proper line of investigation and was only too happy to tag along. Simon cautioned him against that, suggesting that more university chaps might show up any moment, wanting to have a word with him. We had then made our farewells, promising to keep in touch and pop in again soon for a visit.

And now we were on our way to see this heap of rocks or whatever passed for a cairn in this dank hinterland, following one of those narrow, twisting, brush-lined farm roads built for head-on collisions. We met no one on the road, however, and in due course came to the gate Grant had told us to look for. Simon stopped the car and we got out. "It's across this field, in the glen." He pointed down the hillside to a line of treetops just visible above the broad descending curve of the field.

We stood for a moment gazing across the field. I heard the bark of a dog and swiveled toward the sound. Behind us, the way we had come, I saw a man approaching with three or four good-sized dogs on leads. They were still too far away to see properly, but it seemed to me that the dogs were white. "Somebody's coming."

"It's just one of Robert's neighbors," Simon said.

"Maybe we'd better go back."

"He won't bother us. Come on."

Without further ado, we climbed over the gate and jogged across the field. It felt good to work my legs and feel the crisp air in my lungs. At the lower end of the field we came to a stone wall, scrambled over it, and slid down a dirt bank into the glen.

It was little more than a crease between two hills, deep and narrow. A lively brook ran among the roots of the bare, twisted trees that lined the sides of the glen. Mist rose from the brook to seep among the trees. Away from the sun and light, the dim glen remained chill and damp.

In the center of this hidden pocket of land stood an earthen mound: squat, roundish, perhaps nine feet tall, with a circumference of thirty feet. But for a curious beehive-shaped protuberance on the west side, it would have been almost perfectly conical.

"How did you know there would be a cairn?" Simon asked. His voice sounded dead in the still air of the hollow.

"I guessed. With a name like Carnwood Farm, I figured there must be a cairn in a wood around here someplace, right?" I looked at the odd structure. "And here it is. Now we've seen it. Let's go before someone comes." I expected the man with the dogs to appear any moment.

Simon ignored me and walked closer.

A clump of holly grew on the north side of the cairn, and a thicket of something else on the south side. The exterior was covered with short grass. The air in the glen smelled of moldy leaves and wet earth. In the near distance I heard a dog bark.

"I don't want to be caught trespassing," I told Simon. He didn't answer but continued his inspection.

"What's the deal with these cairns?" he asked, after walking slowly around the odd structure.

"Nothing," I said. "Nothing whatsoever."

"Be a sport. I really want to know."

I took a deep breath and sat down on a rock while Simon undertook a second circumnavigation of the cairn. "Well," I began, "nobody knows for certain, but apparently people used to heap up stones and such into shapes like this to mark things."

"What sort of things?"

"Any old thing—a crossroads, a well or spring, the spot where something important happened."

"Like what?"

From the hilltop above the glen I heard a dog bark; I turned toward the sound and thought I saw a glimmer of white through the trees. "What do you mean—like what?"

"What important happenings did they want to mark?"

"Who knows? Maybe the place where somebody struck gold, somebody killed a giant, somebody carried off somebody's wife, somebody found religion—who knows? It's all conjecture, anyway. Maybe they just wanted to tidy up the landscape, so they tossed all the rocks into a pile."

"Then these cairns aren't hollow," Simon concluded, continuing his slow pacing around the turf-covered mound.

"Some of them are," I allowed. "What difference does it make?" I heard the crack of a broken branch from somewhere behind me. I whirled toward the sound and saw a brief flash of white flicker between the dark boles of close-grown trees. "I think someone's coming. We'd better get out of here."

"The hollow ones," he said, "what's in them?"

"There's no buried treasure, if that's what you're thinking." I watched him for a few moments. He seemed so intent on understanding this ancient monument, I had to ask, "What's got into you, Simon?"

He paused in his third circuit of the mound. "What do you mean?"

"Don't give me that."

"Give you what, dear boy?" He peered at me blandly.

"Don't 'dear boy' me. Why this sudden interest in all this Celtic stuff? What's going on?"

"*You're* the one who asked about the cairn, not me."

"Yeah, we already established that."

"You're as intrigued as I am," Simon concluded. "The difference is that I own up to it, and you, my friend, do not."

"Come off it, Simon. Don't play innocent with me. What's really going on? What do you know?"

He had disappeared from my line of sight around the back of the mound. I waited, and he didn't appear. "Simon?" My voice sounded muffled in heavy wool.

I got up from my rock and walked to the other side of the cairn. Simon was on his knees, fighting into the thicket at the base of the structure. "What are you doing now?"

"I think this one is hollow."

"Could be."

"I want to see inside."

"Do we have to do this? Why can't we just say we saw it and go home like you promised?"

"Just let me get a look inside; then we'll go."

I shook my head hopelessly. "All right. Have your look."

Breaking branches with his hands and wriggling like a snake, Simon pulled himself further into the thicket. I stood looking on and saw what he had seen—a small, dark opening at the base of the cairn, all but hidden by the undergrowth. Simon succeeded in pulling his head and shoulders into the mouth of the opening and then backed out.

"Satisfied?" I asked. More fool I.

"I need a torch," he told me. "There's one in the boot of the car. Be a good egg and get it for me, would you?" He shoved his hand into his jacket and withdrew the keys. "Here, you'll need these."

I grabbed them and climbed back up to the car, found the flashlight, and slammed the lid of the trunk. Just as I turned from the car, I glimpsed a flash of white out of the corner of my eye—as if something had dashed across the narrow road behind and disappeared into the brush on the other side. I watched for a moment, but saw nothing more, and made my way down to the cairn once more.

I returned to find that, in my absence, Simon had cleared away some of the brush and enlarged the opening of the mound somewhat. "Here you go, sport." I gave him the flashlight. "Knock yourself out."

"You're not coming in?"

"Not on your Nelly," I told him.

Simon doffed his driving cap. "Take this. I don't want to get it filthy."

I took the hat and put it on. "Be careful, okay? There could be a badger in there."

"I'll give you a yell if I bump into anything." He crawled into the brush and pushed himself into the opening in the mound, where he squirmed for a few moments. Then, with a last kick of his legs, he slid in.

I did not hear anything from him for a few moments.

"Simon? Are you all right?"

From inside the mound I heard him say, "Fine. Fine. It's dry in here. I, uh . . . I think I can stand up. Yes."

"What do you see?" I hollered. No reply. "I said—What do you see?"

"It's smooth—well, fairly smooth anyway," he answered. His voice sounded as if it were coming from inside a sofa. "Some of the stones look as if they have some sort of mar . . ."

"Markings?" I yelled. "Did you say markings?"

"Yes . . . ," came his reply. "Blue ones . . . mazes and hands . . . and . . ."

I waited. "Simon?"

No answer. I got down on my hands and knees and crawled to the entrance of the cairn. "Simon? What else do you see?"

I heard a low grating sound from inside the cairn—a sound like that of a stone being slowly pried from a wall.

"Simon?" I called. "Do you hear me? What are you doing?"

The strange sound continued. Over it, I heard Simon cry, "Blimey!"

"Simon!" I shouted back. "What's going on?"

A second later, Simon's head appeared in the hole. His face blazed with excitement. "Something's happening. It's incredible! Simply fantastic!" He disappeared again.

"Wait! Hold on—What's happening? Simon!"

His face bobbed into view once more, wide-eyed and breathless. "I don't believe it!" he said, shoving his jacket out through the hole to me. "It's bloody incredible, Lewis. It's paradise! I can't tell you. You've just got to see it. Come on! Come with me!"

"No! Wait!" I shouted desperately. "What is it? What's incredible? Simon, where are you going?"

"I'm going in," came his muffled reply. "Come with me!"

Those were Simon's last words.

6

THE BIG JOKE

I must have waited a good ten minutes—it seemed like as many hours—before I worked up nerve enough to go after Simon. I waited and listened, and every thirty seconds or so I'd call his name. I sat with my head near the hole, but I didn't hear a sound.

Tentatively, I pushed through the brush and stuck my head into the cairn. Pitch-dark, as I expected. I could see nothing. Thinking that perhaps my eyes would get used to the darkness, I lay down and wriggled, kicking myself through the opening as I had seen Simon do.

As Simon had indicated, the place was dry, and, to my surprise, a good deal warmer than the air outside. It smelled of must and mildew, like a cave. I sat hunched near the entrance and waited for my eyes to adjust. Even when they did, I could not see my hand in front of my face.

Still, I did not need to see to know that Simon was no longer there.

"Simon?" I called. My voice filled the stone beehive of the cairn. "Very funny, Simon! You can come out now. Simon?"

No answer.

I shouted louder. "I know you can hear me, Simon. Come out from wherever you are and let's go, okay? Come on, now. A joke's a joke, all right? Let's go."

I heard nothing but the hollow ring of my own voice pinging off the stone walls.

My first impulse was to leave. But on the off chance that he'd stumbled and hit his head on a rock, I crawled around the interior of the cairn to make sure he wasn't lying unconscious in the dirt. Starting at the entrance hole, through which a paltry light shone, I made a quick circuit, keeping my right hand on the wall. Then, just to make doubly certain I hadn't missed anything, I went back around the way I had come and finished by crossing back and forth through the center of the cairn a few times on hands and knees.

On my last shuffle across the center, I did find something. I struck it with my knee and felt it spin against my hand. I picked it up: Simon's torch. I switched it on and swept the interior of the cairn with the small spot of light. Every inch.

There was no unconscious Simon, no crack in the ground he could have fallen through, no hidden passage through which he could have escaped to the outside. He was simply not there.

I collapsed against the rough stone side of the cairn. "Simon, you bastard, don't do this to me!" I cursed him and pounded my right hand impotently against the dry earth. "Don't you do this to me. Don't you dare do this to me!"

Anger, quick and sharp, seared me. "I'm leaving, Simon!" I yelled. "You hear me? I'm leaving! You can rot here, for all I care!"

With that I struggled back through the narrow passageway and into the outside world. Simon's jacket lay where I had left it. And his hat. I picked them up and stomped up to the car.

I unlocked the car door, threw the jacket and cap in the back, and slid in behind the wheel. I jammed the key in the ignition, fully intending to drive off. But I hesitated.

Blast! I couldn't just leave him there. I gazed out over the field toward the hidden glen, expecting to see Simon skipping back to me, shaking with laughter at his brilliant prank. I could almost hear him: "Really had you going there, Lewis! Ha! Ha! Ha!"

I pulled the key out and swiveled sideways in the driver's seat with the door open. I settled back to wait.

⊲ ⊲ ⊲

I woke at half past two to find the late October sun diving toward the hills. The wind had picked up, tossing the bare branches of the nearby trees. Simon had not showed up while I slept, and my patience had long since run out. "This is nuts," I muttered to myself. "Tough luck, Simon. I'm outta here."

But, like a good Boy Scout, I decided to check one last time to see if I could find any sign of Simon. Pulling on his jacket, I started down to the glen. Halfway across the field, I saw him: the man with the dogs.

Where he'd come from, I don't know; he seemed to rise up out of the ground. All at once, there he was, with his three gaunt white hounds straining on their leashes. The dogs saw me the same instant I saw them, and started barking wildly. My first impulse was to run back to the car and drive away. But I stood my ground.

The man stopped a few yards ahead of me. He wore a dark coat and carried a long stick in one hand. In his other he held the leashes of the dogs. And what dogs! Easily the strangest-looking hounds I have ever seen: white, head to tail, but with bright-red ears. They were huge, rawboned beasts, thick through the chest, but long-legged and lean in the hindquarters. The animals appeared to be pulling the man along, and he restraining them, the leads taut in his hand.

"Hello there," I called to him, bluffing friendliness.

He did not reply. I took a few steps closer. "I'm waiting for my friend," I explained. The dogs went berserk. In the fading daylight, they seemed to glow, their pale white coats and blood-red ears shimmering in the twilight. Their long snouts flashed sharp teeth as they reared and jerked to get at me. Again I felt like hightailing it back to the car, locking the doors, and driving away very fast. But I fought down the impulse.

The man watched me impassively, his face all creased and wrinkled like a monkey's, his eyes glittering hard and bright. He did not speak, but with the unholy racket the dogs were making I would not have heard him anyway.

We might have stood there all night long, if I had not made up my mind that, dogs or no dogs, I had to check the cairn one last time. Raising my hand in wary entreaty, I stepped hesitantly forward. "Look," I shouted, "I'm just going to the cairn down there"—I pointed past him toward the glen and then turned toward the car— "and then I'm going to get in the car and leave—"

When I turned back, the man was stumping away across the field. I did not wait for an explanation but legged it down the hill. The glen was almost as dark as the inside of the cairn, but once down I had no difficulty finding the entrance hole in the side. I stuck my head in and hollered a few times and flicked the flashlight around inside. No answer. No sound. Nothing.

"All right, Simon, have it your way," I hollered, my voice falling dead at my feet. "This time you've gone too far. You've got no one to blame but yourself! You hear me, Simon? I'm leaving you here!"

I dug his wallet—bulging with cash, credit cards, various forms of identification—from the inner breast pocket of the jacket and pulled out a Barclaycard. I shoved the plastic credit card in a crack between two stones at the entrance to the cairn, where he would be sure to find it. "There you go," I shouted, my voice loud in the silent glen. "You're a smart guy, Simon. Find your own way home!"

I turned my back on the cairn, climbed from the glen, and returned immediately to the car. Halfway across the field, I saw a man in a long yellow coat hurrying along the road. At first, I thought of running to meet him and telling him what had happened. If he lived in the area, he would know about the cairn. Anyway, it seemed I should tell somebody.

As I got closer, the man slowed as if to meet me at the car so we could speak. When I got within shouting distance, I even lifted a hand and called to him. But at the sound of my voice, the man quickened his pace and hurried on. I reached the car just before he disappeared around a bend in the road, a few dozen paces further on.

I shouted again. I know the man heard me, because he turned. Even in the twilight, I could make out his face—if face it was. His features were large, exaggerated, masklike, with a long, hooked nose, a wide mouth, and absolutely enormous ears sticking out from under an uncombed mat of wild black hair. His eyes were wide and bulging beneath the single dark arch of a furry brow.

I beheld this singular visage, and all desire to speak to the man fled. My throat seized up and the call froze on my tongue.

He glanced once over his shoulder, then turned away again. Upon reaching the bend, the man disappeared. I do not mean that the bend of the road took him from sight. Strange as it is to tell, he actually seemed to vanish.

I say this because the man's clothing glimmered as he passed from sight. Now, it might have been a trick of the fading light, but I swear his coat shimmered, giving off a distinct flash as he departed. That, more than the sight of the man's hideous face, rooted me to the spot. I stood gaping after him, and the sound of the wind rising in the trees gave me such a chill that I jumped into the car and drove away.

On the drive back to Oxford, I had a good long time to think things through and convince myself a dozen different ways that

Simon deserved getting left behind for his idiotic practical joke. I don't know how he managed it, but I knew Simon. If anyone could pull off a stunt like that, he could. Who else would have the talent and the resources to waste on such foolishness? He'd probably spent months painstakingly setting up the whole thing behind my back. And it had surely cost him a bundle.

Well, funny joke, Simon. But I've got your car and your wallet, and you're freezing your beezer off in the gloaming. Who's laughing now?

I arrived in Oxford at six o'clock the following morning, red-eyed, exhausted, and quivering with fear lest anyone discover me driving Simon's car and raise the alarm. No one did. The garage where he kept the Jaguar was deserted; there was no one else around. Nevertheless, I retained his jacket and kept his hat pulled over my face as I parked the car and tugged the doors shut. Then I hurried through the gate and across the quad to our staircase.

The sight of Simon Rawnson skulking into college in the wee smalls was such a familiar pantomime, I reckoned, that even if I was seen, it would not raise alarm or comment—not that I cared one way or the other.

Exhausted, I flopped into bed without bothering to undress. I closed my eyes and fell asleep instantly, and would have stayed asleep the rest of the day if not for the telephone.

The first time it rang, I ignored it. But it rang again a few minutes later, and I knew that whoever was on the other end would keep on ringing until someone answered. Bleary-eyed and foul tempered, I raised myself up, shuffled to the living room, and picked up the receiver.

"Hullo?"

"Susannah here," chirped the voice down the wire. "Is that Lewis?"

"Oh, hello, Susannah. How's it going?"

"Fine, thank you. I'd like to speak to Simon."

"Simon? Uh, he's not here at the moment."

"Where is he?"

"Well, he's in Scotland, actually."

"Really?"

"Yeah, thing is, we went up there and he decided to stay, sort of."

I could hear the sprockets spinning in her head. "He decided to stay in Scotland," she repeated, her voice oozing disbelief.

"That's right," I insisted. "We went up Friday morning, you know—"

"I know he broke a lunch date with me," she said tartly.

"It was the trip, see? We drove up there and, well, he just decided to stay on a few days." I tried to make it sound like a spur-of-the-moment inspiration on Simon's part.

Susannah, of course, was not buying any of it. "Put Simon on this instant," she ordered. "Wake up the lazy lizard and put him on. I must talk to him."

"I would, Susannah, but I can't. He's really not here."

"What's going on, Lewis?" Her tone was glacial.

"What?"

"You heard me. What's going on over there? What sneaky little game are you two playing?"

"Nothing's going on, Susannah. I'd let Simon tell you himself, but he just isn't here."

"Let me get this straight," she said. "You and Simon drove all the way to Scotland on Friday, and he decided to stay—"

"Well, yeah, see—"

"—when he knew good and well that he had promised to go with me to early communion and then drive up to Milton Keynes for Sunday dinner with my parents?"

"Look, I know how this sounds, but it's the truth, Susannah. Really, I—"

Click! The line went dead.

I replaced the receiver and glanced at the clock. It was seven thirty in the morning. I was beat. I disconnected the cord on the phone and stumbled back to bed.

It took longer to get to sleep this time. But just as I was snoozing soundly, I was awakened by a loud thumping on the door. "What have I done to deserve this?" I whined, dragging myself from my warm nest.

The door rattled again as I lurched toward it. "Yeah, yeah. I'm coming. Keep your shirt on." I turned the key and opened the door. "Oh, Susannah, it's you. What a surprise."

She burst into the room as if launched from a catapult. "You needn't bother pretending," she stormed. I followed her to the door of Simon's room. She gave the room a quick once-over and whirled to confront me. "All right, where is he?"

"I already told you. He's not here."

Susannah was a firebrand. A long-stemmed beauty with radiant auburn hair and a figure that could, and regularly did, stop traffic. Bright as needles and twice as sharp, she was two or three notches too good for Simon. Or anyone else, for that matter. I don't know why she put up with an unregenerate rogue like Simon, or what she possibly saw in him. Their relationship seemed to me one long ordeal by fire—a venture more on the order of a military exercise than two hearts beating as one.

"You'll have to ask Simon when he comes back," I told her. "I really can't say."

"Can't or won't?" She stared at me, her dark eyes bright with anger. She was either deciding to dismember me where I stood, or calculating how much my dressed carcass would bring on the open market. "Is this somebody's warped idea of a joke?"

"I think it may be," I told her. And then I made the sad mistake of telling her about the aurochs in the newspaper, our hasty trip to Scotland, the cairn, and Simon's sudden disappearance. I tried to make it sound matter-of-fact, but succeeded only in making her more angry and suspicious with each word. "But I wouldn't worry," I ended lamely. "I expect he'll be back soon enough."

"When?" Susannah asked pointedly. Her usually exquisite features were scrunched up in an ugly scowl. I could see that she was only seconds away from pulling off my ears.

"Oh, he'll turn up in a day or two."

"A day or two." Extreme incredulity made her tone flat and husky.

"All right, a week or so—tops. But—"

"What you mean is, you don't really know when he'll turn up at all."

"Not really," I confessed. "But as soon as he realizes I'm not going to further this stupid practical joke of his, he's bound to come dragging home."

"A practical joke? You expect me to believe that?" She regarded me with a wounded yet supremely defiant look. "Well, I have news for you, mister," she said crisply. "I have had the brush-off before. But never like this. If Simon Rawnson does not wish to see me again, so be it. Why didn't he just say so—instead of sending his trained monkey along with some ludicrous story about going to Scotland to visit the Queen?"

"A cairn," I corrected.

"Whatever!" She spun on her heel and started for the door.

"Wait, Susannah! You don't understand."

"I understand perfectly!" she retorted. "Just you tell Simon that we are finished. I do not expect to see him again. And I am keeping the necklace!" She slammed the door so hard the walls shivered.

I hurried into the staircase after her. Susannah turned on me. She had reloaded both barrels and let fly. "And another thing! If I even so much as see Simon Rawnson in public again, I will cause the biggest stinking row he's ever seen. That man will wish he'd never been born. You tell him that, the creep!"

"Listen, Susannah," I said, reaching a hand toward her arm. It was a clumsy move. I almost lost my fingers.

"Don't you dare touch me!" She slapped my hand away. "I'm going home and don't either of you ever try to call me."

Feeling about as low as a garden slug, I watched her sail away, silk skirt streaming. Wrath had transformed her already considerable beauty into something magnificent and wild—a force of nature, like a hurricane or an electrical storm. Terrifying, but wonderful to behold.

I watched Susannah descend the stairs and then listened to the quick click of her heels on the flagstones as she crossed the quad and was gone. Then I turned and shuffled back to my room. I hated myself for deceiving her. But no, I hadn't deceived her; I had told her the truth. She had just assumed, for reasons of her own, that I was lying to her, and what could I do about that? Anyway, it was not my fault. It was all down to Simon—I had nothing to do with it.

Trained monkey, indeed!

7

MAD NETTLES

My plan, as far as I had one, was simply to carry on as if nothing had happened. Business as usual. If anyone rang up and asked Simon's whereabouts, I'd tell them he'd run off to Wolverhampton with a shop assistant from Boots. Serve him right, the toad.

The way I figured it, he was probably waiting until I panicked and blabbed to the police or something. He wanted to see his name in the headlines, and me looking like a fool explaining to reporters how he'd crawled into a cairn and disappeared. Well, he could just wait until hell froze over. I did not intend on giving him the satisfaction.

For the next few days, I carried on my life in the ordinary way. I behaved exactly as before. I took my meals, browsed at the bookstalls, loitered in the library, lounged in my adviser's office, chatted with acquaintances, pawed through my mail . . . In short, I sallied boldly forth into the frantic free-for-all of academic life I had come to know and love so well.

But work was impossible. How could I work? I could not, truly, ignore Simon's disappearance any more than I could ignore the nose on my face—however hard I tried. The days passed and Simon did not return. The phone did not ring. Doubt began taking a toll on me. I kept thinking: *What if it is no joke? What if something happened to him? What if he really is gone?*

Each day that passed brought a new worry. I lurched like a lop-sided pendulum between anger and anxiety. Anger at his absurd prank, and anxiety over his safety. Day and night, I suffered a relentless rain of questions: Where was Simon? What was he doing? Where had he gone? Why was this my worry? Why me?

"When Simon comes back," I promised myself, "I'll kill him. I'll cheerfully twist off his arms and beat him with the bloody ends. No, I won't. That wouldn't be civilized. I will, instead, sit him down and tell him calmly and rationally what a terrible, tasteless thing he has done. And then I will shoot him through his small, black heart."

As the days passed into weeks, I grew steadily more listless, disheveled, ill-tempered, and cranky; I yelled at the scout whenever she poked her nose in, until at last she got fed up and stopped coming by. I roamed aimlessly around the streets, muttering to myself and cursing a great deal. My socks didn't match. I didn't wash.

If anyone observed my increasingly debilitated state, they gave no sign. I could not have occasioned less comment if I were a dust ball under the bed. I found myself deeply tempted to grow a hunchback and start swinging from the bell in Tom Tower.

My rapid descent into the slough of despond was matched by an equally steep decline in mental stability. I did not sleep well. Odd dreams troubled me—visions of leafy green men and extinct oxen rampaging through my bedroom, of wandering lost in a dark forest and the ground opening up beneath me and swallowing me whole, of being hunted down and pierced through the thorax by antique spears, of wolves howling in a forest dark, and a hideous horror with a face of grinning death, pursuing me relentlessly over a cold and desolate land—disturbing images that melted upon waking, leaving me exhausted and all the worse for my night's rest.

I knew the cause of my slide into oblivion: my conscience was pulling overtime trying to attract my attention. From the moment I crawled into the cairn and realized Simon had vanished, my subconscious had begun hand-to-hand combat with my reason. The object? Getting me to admit to myself that what *might* have happened actually did happen, and that I had done absolutely nothing about it.

Still, it wasn't so much Simon's disappearance that hastened my decline. Unnerving as that was, the object of my inner conflict was not Simon's vanishing act; it was his destination. Where, then, *had* Simon gone? That was the sixty-four-trillion-dollar question. And I knew the answer.

But I didn't like to say it.

No, I would rather stew slowly in my own juices than admit what I knew to be true. Nature, however, has a subtle way of dealing with these amusing little dysfunctional games one enjoys so much. It's called a nervous breakdown.

I began seeing things.

The first incident happened very early one morning. I had spent another sleepless night and decided to take a walk along the river. I slipped through the quad and took the lane leading to the meadow and the riverwalk. That early in the morning I had the place to myself, and just as I was passing the field where the college's cattle are kept, I saw a large gray hound loping across the pasture, coming at an angle toward me.

At first, I didn't think anything of it. There are lots of dogs around, after all. But as it drew nearer, the size of the thing registered—the animal was seriously larger: almost as big as a pony. It had a short, curly coat and extremely long legs that ate up the ground at an astonishing rate. And it was coming right for me. I stopped and stared as it leapt the cattle fence without breaking stride. The dog landed in the lane a scant few yards away. Only then did it see me, for it turned as if startled and flattened its ears, baring its incredibly long teeth in a snarl.

I stood stock-still, my heart racing. The dog, if that is what it was, growled menacingly low in its throat and raised its hackles. But I did not twitch a muscle—I was too scared to move. The great hound, still growling, turned down the lane and dashed off. It vanished in the morning mist from the river. But in the instant it turned, I saw that it had an odd-looking collar made of iron chain—the antique kind with curious hand-forged square links.

Despite the fact that I had never in my life seen a dog so huge, I told myself that someone's pet had escaped from the kennel. Only that, and nothing more.

And then, a few days later, sitting by the window sipping tea on a rainy afternoon, I glanced out into the quad and saw something brown and hairy moving on the lawn. In the gloom of a thick over-cast, I could not be certain exactly what I saw. At the time I would have sworn it was a pig—but a different sort of pig from any I was familiar with. Long-legged and lean, with a thick, bristly coat of dark reddish-brown and two curved tusks issuing from the sides of his pinched and narrow face, it carried its tail in a comical flagpole fash-ion—straight up over its sloping back.

With my face pressed against the glass, the window quickly steamed up. When I rubbed away the fog, the creature had disappeared. And with it any certainty that I had seen anything at all.

The next day, I saw a wolf in Turl Street.

Tired of being cooped up all day, I had ventured out late and it was growing dark. The streetlights were lit and some of the shops were already closed. I had gone to the covered market for a loaf of bread and, returning, I turned down Turl Street, which bends so that you can-not see either end from the middle. I had just entered the narrow street when my scalp began to prickle—as if someone were watching me with evil intent. I walked a few yards, and the prickly sensation spread down the back of my neck and across my shoulder blades. I felt evil eyes boring into my back. Instantly frightened, I imagined I heard a faint scratching click on the pavement behind me. I walked a few steps further, listening to this strange sound, whereupon, utterly convinced I was being followed, I turned abruptly.

I had never seen a real live wolf before, and thought it another giant hound, but then saw its shaggy coat and its great pale yellow eyes. It walked with its head low, its long snout to the ground as if scenting a trail. When I stopped, it stopped, giving me the distinct impression that I was being stalked. The door of a camera shop stood not ten feet to the right of me, and I thought to run in the door and escape. I took one cautious step sideways. The wolf tensed. I heard a sound like gravel churning in a cauldron and realized it came from the animal's throat. We stood looking at one another across a distance of no more than fifteen or twenty feet. I decided to make a rush for the door, and was just working myself up to it when the door swung open and someone came out of the shop. I half turned, flung out a hand to the stranger to stop him. "Wait!" I said. The fellow grimaced at me—I suppose he thought me a beggar after loose change—and pushed brusquely past. When I looked again, the wolf was running up the Turl toward Broad Street. I saw its gaunt sides gleam silver in the streetlights, and then it was gone.

I told myself I hadn't actually seen it, that the episode with the giant dog had unnerved me. But the next morning the *Daily Mail* carried a story about a wolf seen running loose in the streets of Oxford. Numerous people had witnessed it. Police had been called out, and animal control, but they couldn't locate the beast. Speculation was that the wolf had escaped from someone's illegal menagerie and had fled to the open countryside.

I was afraid to leave my rooms for three days after that—afraid of what I might see next. And when I did screw up my courage to go out again, almost immediately I stepped off the sidewalk on the High Street smack in front of an Oxford Experience bus. I got knocked down, but not run over—those tourist buses do not move very fast and the drivers are skilled at bumping into unwary pedestrians.

It came to me . . . as I lay in the street . . . staring up into the ring of ripely disgusted faces gathered above me . . . that something had to give. A bus today, a train tomorrow. Or would it be a screaming free fall from one of the dreaming spires? More to the point: was this denial really worth my sanity, my life?

One gets a singular perspective on life while gazing up from the gutter. When the policeman who helped me to my feet asked, "You all right, then, son?" I was forced to consider the question in all its greater philosophical implications. No, I decided, I was definitely not all right. Not by any stretch of logic or imagination.

I spent the rest of the day wandering around the streets, aimless and sick at heart. I lost myself in the usual stream of shoppers and simply drifted. I shuffled here and there; I watched chalk artists and street musicians without heeding what they drew or played. I knew something was happening. I *knew* it had something to do with me. I knew also that I could not hold out against it much longer. But what was I to do? What was required of me?

These and other questions, barely formed, occupied me all afternoon. And when I finally gave up and headed back to my rooms, it was nearly dark and the weather had turned rainy. The streets were all but deserted. At Carfax I stopped for the traffic light, though there were no cars on the street. I felt silly standing in the rain, so I ducked under a nearby awning.

As I stood there, waiting for the light to change, a very strange feeling came over me. I was suddenly light-headed and weak in the knees, woozy and unsteady as if I might pass out any second. Perhaps getting knocked down by the bus had hurt me more than I knew, I thought. Perhaps I've injured myself after all. I grabbed my head with both hands. I gulped air, and my throat felt tight. I couldn't breathe.

The pavement beneath my feet seemed to buckle and heave. I glanced down, and my heart skipped a beat. For I was standing in the center of an elaborate Celtic circle drawn on the sidewalk squares with chalk. The street artists—I had seen them working earlier in the day and paid them no attention—had drawn a primitive maze pattern surrounded by a knotwork border of interwoven colored lines. I had often seen sidewalk portraits and landscapes. But never anything like this. Why had they drawn this particular design? Why, of all things, a Celtic maze?

I stood there, clutching my head, staring at the intricately interlaced lines and the dizzying pattern of the maze. I stood there for a long time, the traffic light blinking from red to green over and over, the rain pelting down on me. Staring, staring, unable to move, trapped in that charmed circle—inexplicably bound by those interlocking threads of bright-colored chalk. I might still be standing there but for the fact that my condition had not gone entirely unnoticed.

For I felt the light touch of a hand on my elbow and became aware of a kindly voice in my ear. "Let me help you," said the voice.

I swiveled my head toward the sound and found myself face-to-face with a white-haired old gent dressed like Central Casting's idea of an aging country squire complete with porkpie hat and black briar walking stick.

"N-no thanks," I told him. "I'm okay. Thanks."

But the grip on my elbow tightened. "Pardon me, but I think you need a hand," he insisted. He raised his walking stick before my face and then lowered it, pointing to the strange drawing on the pavement. He tapped the chalk with the tip of his stick three times. This simple action, deliberate and slow, gave me to know that our meeting was not mere happenstance and he was no ordinary passerby. He knew something.

"I had better see you home, I think," he told me. "Come along."

I looked helplessly at my feet, for I still could not move them. "There's nothing to fear," the old man said. "Come."

At his word, my feet came free, and I stepped easily from the circle. We crossed the street and, by the time we reached the other side, I was thoroughly humiliated. "Thanks," I said, stepping up on the sidewalk. "Really, thanks a lot. I'm okay. I just got a little dizzy, you know. I had a bump on the head earlier, but I'm okay now." The words just tumbled out. "I'll be fine. Thanks for your help . . ."

But the old gent did not release his grip on my arm. Thinking that he maybe didn't hear so good, I raised my voice. He stopped suddenly and turned to me. "You should have that bump looked at."

"Yeah, I'll do that. Thanks." I tried to disengage his hand from my arm, but he would not let go. "You've been a big help. I won't trouble you any further."

"Oh, it's no trouble. I assure you," he said airily. "I'm afraid I must insist."

"Are you a doctor?" I asked. I don't know why—something about his solicitous nature suggested it.

"I'm all the doctor you need," came the reply, and next thing I knew we were stumping along the all-but-deserted street, arm in arm. He seemed determined to have a look at my bump, and I seemed to have no choice in the matter. After the trauma of the last few days, my willpower was at low ebb, so I took the path of least resistance and went with him.

After much twisting and turning down this street and that, he eventually arrived at a low door in Brewer's Lane. A brass plaque proclaimed the residence of D. M. Campbell, Tutor. He put a key in the lock, jiggled it open, and ushered me in.

"Come in, please," said the old man. "Come in out of the cold, my friend. Make yourself at home. I'll get something warm on the hot plate. Put your coat there."

He peered at me myopically, patting his pockets absently. I stepped into the dim apartment. "Kind of you to invite me. But, really, it isn't necessary. I'm fine."

He smiled and bustled off into the dark interior, unbuttoning his coat as he went. His voice lingered behind him. "A pleasure. My load is light this term. As it is, I don't have enough visitors. Come, sit down. Won't be a moment."

I found an ancient, overstuffed chair and dropped into it, wondering why I was there. Well, I thought, I don't want to hurt his feelings. Just a quick cup of tea and I'll be on my way.

For his part, the old gent drifted in and out, snapping on lights here and there to no great effect. The room remained dark as before. At one point he came to stand before me, gazing down at me as if he had won me in a turkey shoot.

"Introductions," he said abruptly. "Professor Nettleton. Merton College. How do you do?"

"Not Campbell?" I wondered aloud.

"A former occupant," he explained. "I value my privacy."

"Oh."

"And you are?"

"Oh, right. My name is Lewis—Lewis Gillies."

"Glad to meet you, Mr. Gillies," he began. At that moment a kettle in another room whistled, and he bustled to attend it. He returned a moment later. "Best give it a moment," he said pleasantly and proceeded to clear off a table piled high with papers. It gave me a chance to study him.

Nettleton was the archetypal Oxford don. Shortish, baldish, sixtyish, slightly stooped, and nearsighted from deciphering the crabbed text of too many illegible manuscripts. What hair he possessed was wispy and white like candy floss; it floated over his head rather than resting there. His apparel was a subdued riot of mismatched tweed—all of ambiguous hue. He wore a Balliol tie, a bright-blue woolen waistcoat, and stout, brown Irish brogues on his feet.

The kettle sounded again, and while my host busied himself with practicalities—I could hear him clanking around in the dim recesses—I took the opportunity to examine my immediate surroundings. The professor's room was one of those immense Victorian caverns in which Oxford abounds, and no less eccentric than its occupant: twelve-foot ceilings; a forest of ancient dark oak paneling; mammoth carved mahogany sideboards, mantels, bookcases, and tables; a desk that could easily serve as the bridge of a battleship; great soft chairs one could get lost in. The dark oak floors were covered with about an acre of faded, threadbare carpet; the lighting apparently dated from the Dark Ages; and the heating system was older than Moses.

I glanced around at the various shelves, which were crammed with knickknacks and whatnots. Curiosity drew me from my chair, and I approached the shelves for a closer look. They supported a pack rat's museum of queer artifacts: odd-shaped stones; peculiar knobs of polished wood; tablet-sized slabs of slate with strange inscriptions scratched on them; gleaming nuggets of misshapen coins; a collection of carved-horn combs and buttons made from animal teeth. Bristling from a nook was a stuffed yellow cat the size of a cocker spaniel, and a gross black-feathered carcass I took to be a mounted raven.

So deeply engrossed in this inventory was I that I did not hear Nettleton creep up behind me. I felt a prickly sensation on my neck and swung around to find him gazing placidly at me, two steaming mugs of something in his hands. I say mugs—the vessels were tall and had no handles, and they appeared to be made of a sort of crude stoneware. I'd seen a similar style of pottery before—in the Ashmolean Museum next to a tag which read Beaker, Neolithic, ca 2500 BC.

My host handed a beaker to me, raised the other to his lips, and said, "*Slàinte!*"

To which I replied, "Cheers!" I took a large sip and nearly spewed the contents across the room. I managed to choke it down—but the corrosive liquid grated my throat like a wool rasp and produced an afterburn like an F16.

Nettleton smiled benignly at my discomfort. "So sorry, I should have warned you. There's whiskey in it. I find a wee dram on a day like this helps to drive out the chill."

Yes, and the will to live as well. "S'good," I gasped. I felt my tongue swelling rapidly to roughly the size of a summer sausage. "Wha—what is it?"

The professor dismissed the question with a flick of his hand. "Oh, roots, bark, berries—sort of a homemade concoction. I collect the ingredients myself. If you like it, I can give you the recipe.

I was speechless.

He turned away and led me across the room to a set of red leather chairs on either side of the only window. The sky was dark; the window panes appeared opaque. A small table that looked as if it had been assembled of driftwood stood between the chairs. The professor sat down in one of the chairs and placed his beaker on the table. He indicated the other chair was for me. I sat facing him and peered into my drink. Were those raisins bobbing around in there?

"So!" he announced suddenly. "Good to see you!" He enunciated this meticulously, as if I were an aborigine who might not speak his language. "I have been waiting for this."

His confession brought me up short. I could only stare and gulp. "You have?"

"Yes." He raised a hand quickly, "Please do not misunderstand—I mean you no harm. I intend to help you, as I said. And, if you don't mind my saying so, you look rather in need of help at the moment."

"Um, Professor Nettleton—ah, you seem to have me at a bit of a disadvantage here, I think."

"Nettles," he replied.

"Sir?"

"Why not call me Nettles? Everyone does."

"All right," I agreed. "But, as I was saying, I thin—"

"Not to put too fine a point on it, you've rather let yourself go, Mr. Gillies. You are distressed."

"Well, I—"

"No apologies, Mr. Gillies. I understand. Now then"—he folded his hands over his chest and leaned so far back into his chair that I could no longer see his face in the shadows—"how can I be of service to you?"

Nothing came to mind. I searched the shadows for a moment, and then suggested that he had already helped me a great deal, and that it was getting late and I was sure he had other things to do and that I shouldn't trouble him further, and that—

"Pish-tosh!" he replied calmly. "There's nothing to be embarrassed about. Come now, please be assured, your secret is safe with me."

My secret? Which secret? How did he know my secret? "I'm not sure I know what you mean," I told him.

Nettles leaned further forward. His eyes danced. "You are a believer," he whispered. "I can always tell."

"A believer," I repeated dully.

He smirked. "Oh, never worry. I'm a believer too."

I must have appeared as thick as a plank, because he explained: "The Faëry Faith, yes? Everyone thinks me mad, of course. What of it?" He became conspiratorial. "I have *seen* them."

"Fairies?"

He nodded enthusiastically. "Oh, yes! But I prefer to call them Fair Folk. I understand, the word *fairies* has taken on some unfortunate connotations in recent years. And even if that weren't so, *fairies* always makes them sound twee and diminutive. Let me tell you," he added solemnly, "they are anything but twee and diminutive."

I judged the conversation to have taken a peculiar turn, and attempted to steer it back. "Um, I saw a wolf in Turl Street. Maybe you read about it in the newspapers."

Nettles winked at me. "*Blaidd an Alba*, eh?"

"Excuse me?"

"Wolves in Albion," he replied. "Don't mind me. You were saying?"

"Just that. Nothing else, really," I lied.

"Is that all?"

"Well, yes," I confessed, slightly piqued at his insinuation that there might be more. "What else could there be?"

The professor chuckled dryly. "Why, appearances, disappearances, strange happenings—any number of things. People getting trapped in Celtic circles, for instance."

"You don't mean . . ." Was he talking about *me*?

"But that is precisely what I *do* mean."

I gazed stupidly. Mad? The man was dotty as a dodo. "But that is impossible," I mumbled.

"Is it?" The smile never left his face, but his eyes became hard and intensely serious. "Come now, sir! I asked you a question. I am wait-ing for an answer."

"Well," I allowed carefully, "I suppose it's not altogether impossible."

"Ha! You *know* that it is not altogether impossible. Come, Mr. Gillies, let us be precise." The ferocity with which this last was deliv-ered melted away as soon as the words were uttered. Instantly he was his merry self once more. "I told you, it's no good trying to get round me. I can smell a believer a mile away."

He leaned forward, reaching toward his drink, and froze in mid-motion. "Ah, but that's the difficulty, isn't it?"

"Pardon?"

"I've misjudged you." He remained motionless, his hand reaching out. "So sorry, Mr. Gillies. My mistake."

"I'm not sure I follow."

"Perhaps you are not a believer, after all." He collapsed back into his chair. "But then what are you, Mr. Lewis Gillies? Hmm? I become so accustomed to dealing with unbelievers that I often forget there is third category."

In order to mask my growing discomfort with this line of enquiry, I took up my drink and forced some of it down. This time, I actually enjoyed the taste.

"Believers and unbelievers," the professor said. "Most people fall into one or the other of those classifications. Yet there is a third: those who desperately *want* to believe but reason won't allow it."

He took up his drink and swigged it back. I followed suit and ended up gulping down more than I intended. "It does grow on one, does it not?" he said with a loud smack of his lips. "Mulled heather ale."

Heather ale? I stared into my cup. Folklore had it that the recipe for this ancient drink disappeared in 1411 when the English killed the last Celtic chieftain for refusing to divulge the secret of this legendary elixir. The beleaguered Celt leaped off a sea cliff rather than allow the hated foreigners to taste the Brew of Kings. How then did the professor tumble onto the recipe—if indeed he had?

My unlikely host rose and took himself to a nearby sideboard. He returned with a pottery crock and poured our beakers full of steaming liquid once more. "As I was saying—" He replaced the crock on the hot plate and returned to his seat. "You rather belong in the third category: one who wishes to believe, yet lacks conviction. Sympathetic, shall we say, yet skeptical." He nodded benevolently. "You have been out wandering in the Celtic miasma and you have caught the bug? Am I right?"

Bingo! "I think I could go along with that," I allowed cautiously.

"Now then, what has brought you to this impasse? This crisis of faith and reason? What has reduced you to stumbling around the city unkempt and unshaven, seeing things, and so easily ensnared by chalk drawings on the pavement?"

My lips began to frame an evasive answer, but the question was not for me. The barmy old gentleman continued: "What indeed? If I may hazard a guess, I would say that you have witnessed something for which you have no explanation, and for which you are struggling to discover a rational solution. One of these appearances you are speaking about? Or perhaps it was a *disappearance*? Yes! I thought so." He beamed with innocent pleasure. "I warned you—I can always tell."

"But how did you know?"

He ignored my question and asked one of his own. "Who is it? Someone you know? Of course it is. How foolish of me. Now you must tell me all about it. If I am to help you, I must know everything." He raised a bony finger in the air. "*Everything*—do you understand?"

I slumped in the chair, feeling the soft leather envelop me. I cradled the warm beaker to my chest and muttered, "I understand." How did I ever get myself into this? I wanted simply to sink so deep into the chair that no one would ever find me. Instead, I took a long pull of the mulled ale, closed my eyes, and began my dreary recitation.

Professor Nettleton did not interrupt. Twice I opened my eyes and found him sitting poised on the edge of his chair, as if he might pounce the moment I stopped. I rambled on and on until I had laid out the whole muddled episode, just as it happened. I told him everything—I did not have the strength of will to resist or play coy with the facts. I was too tired of keeping up the pretense, too weary of bearing the weight of knowledge all by myself. I just opened my mouth and the words tumbled out. I let my tongue flap on and on.

I told him about Simon's wild aurochs chase, about sighting the Green Man, about Farmer Grant, about the cairn and Simon's abruptly acquired interest in Celtic lore, about my disturbing dreams, about seeing things, about . . . everything that had happened before and after Simon's disappearance. And it was blessed relief to unburden myself. Twice blessed to have someone listening who believed me completely. I had no fear that he would betray me or think me insane. After all, everyone already thought *him* mad. He had told me so. My secret was safe with him; I knew that, and I made the most of it.

When I finally finished, I opened my eyes and glanced into the bottom of my empty beaker. Had I drunk it all? I must have guzzled away during my recitation. Now I was sorry not to have saved some. I placed the empty vessel on the table.

Through rain-streaked panes the sky glowed a sickly gray green from the city lights reflecting off the low pall of cloud. I glanced into the gathered gloom of the chair facing me. Professor Nettleton's white hair shone with a faint glow from the window. His eyes glittered in the darkness.

"Of course," he said at last. "Yes, I understand now."

"Believe me, I didn't intend wasting your time with all this."

He shook his head slightly. "On the contrary, it is why you came to me."

Misplaced pride flushed my cheeks. "Look, I don't know that this is any of your business. I just came along because . . ."

"Yes?"

"Well, because I didn't want to hurt your feelings."

"Pish-tosh, Mr. Gillies. Let us clear the air at once. If we are to work together, we must have no more of this false modesty and guile. We both know very well what we're talking about. It is the freedom of believers to shout aloud what doubters dare not confess."

"Huh?"

"You know what I'm talking about." The way he said it brooked no contradiction; I offered none. "Very well, let us put aside all inhibition and speak openly." He reached out a firm hand and tapped my leg. "I will make a True Man of you yet."

"I told you about Simon and everything else," I said, somewhat defensively. "But you haven't told me how you knew I was—" Words failed me. What was I?

"Troubled?" Nettles offered. "Since this began, I have been observing very closely."

"Observing what?"

"Why, everything. Quite literally everything. The signs are there for anyone with eyes to see them."

"I don't understand," I complained.

"No." He rose and stood over me. "But we have done enough for one day, I think. Good night, Mr. Gillies. Go home and get some rest."

"Uh, yeah, good night." I climbed slowly to my feet. "Thank you." I felt grateful in a nonspecific sort of way. I guess I was just glad he wasn't telephoning the men with the butterfly nets.

He propelled me quickly toward the door. "Come to me again tomorrow morning. I will explain everything."

Next thing I knew, I was standing with my coat in my hands in the gloomy half light of Brewer's Lane. I put on my coat and hurried into the chilly rain. The wind had risen, driving the fine rain before it. The relief I had enjoyed in Professor Nettleton's company quickly dissolved in the cold reality of wind and rain. "Mad as a hatter," I thought gloomily. "Old Nettles is crazier than I am."

I arrived back at the door to my rooms just in time to hear the telephone ring. I jammed the key in the lock and dashed to answer the phone, and instantly realized I'd made a big mistake.

8

SUNWISE CIRCLES

The clock read ten minutes past eleven. Who would be calling at this time of night?

"Hello, is that Mr. Gillies?" The voice sounded as if it were coming from a very great distance—the vicinity of Mars, perhaps. Still, it was one of those once-heard-never-forgotten voices, and I recognized it at once. My heart sank.

"Speaking," I said. "Good evening, sir."

"Geoffrey Rawnson here."

"Good to hear you, sir. How are things?"

"Oh, working too hard as usual. Haven't a minute to myself. Still, mustn't complain, I suppose," he replied affably enough. "Actually, I was wondering if I might speak to Simon."

"I'm sorry, Mr. Rawnson, but Simon isn't here at the moment."

"Not there? Well, where is he?" His tone implied that he thought it unlikely his son should be anywhere else but standing beside the phone, waiting for him to call.

"He's out for the, ah, evening, I believe," I lied, then added a corrective of truth. "As a matter of fact, I just got back myself."

"I see," he replied. "Well, I won't keep you. Would you just relay to Simon that I called?"

"I'll do that, sir—as soon as I see him."

"Fine," the elder Rawnson said. "There's just one other thing."

"Yes?"

"Tell Simon that unless I hear from him tomorrow before ten o'clock, I will arrive as scheduled to pick him up. Do you have that?"

"You'll be here to pick him up as scheduled—yes, I have it. Uh, what time would that be, sir—so I can tell Simon?"

"He knows the details, I should think," Rawnson said, and I detected an undercurrent of pique. He paused and, by way of explanation, added, "I don't mind telling you I'm a little put out with Simon just now. He was supposed to turn up for his grandmother's birthday celebration at the weekend. Never misses it. This year not a card, not a call, nothing. He'd better have a very good excuse. And I'll expect to hear it when I see him tomorrow. You can tell him that from me."

"Yes, sir," I agreed.

"Well, it's late; I won't keep you. Good night, Mr. Gillies. Best regards." The phone clicked, and the line went dead.

Sturm und Drang! Face-to-face with Simon's dad, and what was I going to tell him? Terribly sorry, your highness, but Sonny Jim has flitted off to La-la Land. Tut tut. Rotten luck, what?

I went to bed full of woe, and fell asleep plotting Simon's demise.

It may be that Professor Nettleton slept in his clothes. Then again, maybe he didn't sleep at all. When I arrived early next morning, he appeared exactly as I'd left him the previous evening, hip deep in research—there were piles of papers, pamphlets and journals, and stacks of books all over the floor. "Come in! Come in!" he called when I knocked, barely glancing up as I entered.

"Here it is!" he cried, waving a book over his head. "Sit down, Lewis, and listen to this."

Nutsy Nettles began reading at me from the book, pacing among the heaps of literature, running his hand through his wispy hair. I listened to him for a moment before I realized that I did not understand a word he was saying. I mean, the words I understood, but they made no sense. It was all a jumble of jargon: nexus this, and plexus that, and something about serial time and the infinite malleability of the future or some such thing.

I shifted a stack of papers onto the floor and sat down in the leather chair. The lamp next to the chair was the room's only light. He finished his reading and regarded me closely, his eyes pixie bright with excitement.

"Excuse me, Nettles," I said, "I'm not sure I got all that. I didn't sleep very well last night." Then I told him about my phone conversation with Simon's father.

The old prof clucked his tongue sympathetically. "It was only to be expected," he said. "People can't go missing and not be missed. Still, I had hoped for a bit more time. Never mind."

"Never mind? But he's coming to see Simon today—and Simon won't be here."

"We can worry about that later," the professor told me. "Would you like some tea?" He pottered off to his hot plate on the sideboard, saying, "The aurochs and spear—those are positive indicators. Likewise the Green Man, the wolf, boar, and hound. I expect there are scores of others—perhaps hundreds—but you wouldn't necessarily have noticed them." I could hear him rattling tins and filling a kettle. His voice drifted back to me as if from the outer darkness of the netherworld.

"Indicators," I repeated without enthusiasm. I yawned and rubbed my eyes.

"Now then, there are two things which puzzle me about your story. I must ask you to remember very carefully. Quite a lot depends upon it, I'm afraid." Nettleton returned to stand over me. "Think back to the cairn. Did you notice anyone nearby when you were there?" he asked, watching me intently. "Did anyone approach you?"

"No one." I shrugged. "Why?"

"An animal, perhaps? A deer? Or a bird of some kind? A dog?"

I sat bolt upright. "Wait a minute! There *was* someone. I remember seeing this guy and he had some dogs—three of them, funny looking. I mean the man was funny looking, not the dogs. Well, the dogs were strange, too, now that I mention it. White with red ears, big and thin—they looked like oversize greyhounds or something. They actually blocked my way to the cairn, but I just stood my ground and they left."

"When did you see him? Before or after Simon entered the cairn?"

"After," I said. "No, wait . . ." I thought back. "Before, too. Yes, I saw him before, too—Simon and I both saw him. Simon said it was probably just a farmer, and we went on to the cairn. I saw him again when I went back to the cairn after Simon disappeared."

Nettles clapped his hands and chortled with delight. The kettle shrieked from the sideboard, and the professor bustled over to it. I followed him. "Milk?" he asked.

"Please." I watched him pour boiling water into a large, tea-stained pot. He also poured water into two unwashed mugs. A fresh pint of milk stood on the sideboard; he took it up and pushed the foil cap with his thumb. "Have I said something important?" I asked.

He swished the water around the mugs and then dumped it back into the kettle. "Yes," he answered, splashing milk into first one mug and then the other. "Unequivocally."

"Good. I mean, that's good . . . right?"

"Oh, it's very good. I was beginning to wonder if you were telling me the truth." To my stricken look, he replied, "Oh, there is no doubt in my mind now. None at all. The presence of the guardian confirms it all."

"Guardian?" I asked. "You didn't mention anything about any guardian."

"We will let the tea steep a moment. Bring the mugs." He pulled a knitted tea cozy over the pot and carried it to the driftwood table, then nudged his chair closer to mine. "The guardian of the threshold," the professor said simply. "It might have been a stag, a hawk, or a wild dog—the guardian can take many forms. His absence puzzled me. And another thing puzzles me as well: why was Simon allowed to cross the threshold and not you?"

"That puzzles me too. No end."

"Was Simon perhaps more sensitive?"

"Sensitive Simon isn't," I said. "Not that sort at all. No way."

Nettles shook his head and frowned. "Then this becomes very difficult." He turned to the teapot and poured our mugs full. He handed a mug to me, and we drank in silence for a moment. Then he said, "Did he show any interest in the Otherworld before this business at the cairn?"

"None," I said. "Celtic studies is *my* thing, not Simon's."

"But it was his suggestion to go and view the aurochs, was it not?"

"Yeah, but—I mean, he just wanted an adventure."

The professor regarded me over the rim of his mug. "Did he indeed?"

"You know what I mean. Any excuse for a party, that was Simon."

"Of course. But you would say he was the adventurous type?"

"Sure. He liked a bit of excitement." I sipped some more tea and then remembered something else. "But you know, there *was* something weird that morning. Simon quoted poetry to me."

"Yes? Go on," Nettles urged.

"Well, I don't remember it, but it had to do with—I don't know."

"Please try to remember. It might be important."

"We were driving to the farm—this was before we'd even seen the aurochs—which we didn't see, because it wasn't there—and Simon all of a sudden rattles off this scrap of poetry. Celtic poetry. Something about standing at the door to the West," I said, trying to recall the exact details. "It was one of those Celtic riddle verses where the speaker gives all these clues and you're supposed to guess who he is."

"Standing at the door to the West," the professor repeated. "Yes, go on. Anything else?"

As with a jolt from an electric cattle prod, I remembered something else. "And before that," I said, excitement tightening my vocal cords, "when we were just waking up. We slept beside the road, like I said, and I woke up just before sunrise. Simon wanted to get an early start but we overslept—not much; it was still plenty early. But Simon got all upset because he wanted to be at the farm *before* sunrise—not after. When I asked him why, he sneered and said, 'And you a Celtic scholar.' It was the time-between-times—Simon knew about the time-between-times, see. That's why he had us rushing to get to the farm. I asked him and he didn't deny it. Simon *knew* about the time-between-times."

Nettleton smiled. "I see. Go on."

"That was all. I wasn't aware he knew about anything like that. It was odd, but that was Simon. He'd tear into anything that took his fancy."

"But you did not reach the farm or the cairn before sunrise?"

"No. We reached the cairn well before ten o'clock, though," I told him.

The professor rose and fetched the milk bottle. He poured milk into the mugs and topped up with hot tea, replacing the tea cozy. He rested his hands on the warm teapot and said slowly, "This is extremely interesting."

"Great, but what's it got to do with Simon's disappearance?"

As if he hadn't heard me, the professor got up and started rummaging through the pile of books on his desk. He found one and held it up to me. "I came across this last night," he said and began reading to me.

"On a day in August in the year 1788, I arrived in the chief village of
Glen Findhorn, a settlement of fair aspect called the Mills of Aird
Righ. I called first on the schoolmaster, Mr. Desmond MacLagan,
who kindly agreed to conduct me to the Cairn. MacLagan had been
raised in the region and indeed had heard stories of the Cairn from
his grandmother, Mrs. Maire Grant, who would oft times relate how
she and other youths of the village on bright moonlit nights were
wont to go to the Cairn. They seldom had long to wait before they
would hear the most exquisite music and behold a grand tower standing in the hollow there. The diminutive folk of Fairyland would issue
from the tower and perform their frolic and dance. Next morning the
tower would not be found, but the grandmother and her friends
would gather Fairy Gold from around the Cairn. This continued until
one of the youths, when questioned about the gold, told his father,
who then forbade any further excursions of this nature, saying that
from time to time people were known to have disappeared in that
vicinity.

"Upon reaching the glen, my guide and I dismounted and made
our way into the hollow to the Cairn on foot. I found the ancient
structure wholly unremarkable in size or proportion, and somewhat
dilapidated in appearance. The only distinctive feature is an oven-
shaped projection oriented west. Albeit, the farmers and uneducated
folk of the glen consider the Cairn a Fairy Mound and accord it wide
respect in their deliberations upon matters supernatural."

Nettles glanced up from his reading. "This document establishes
Carnwood Cairn as a site of Otherworldly activity," he announced.
"Although the author did not find the entrance—slightly puzzling,
that—still I have no doubt that the cairn described is the one you
have seen. The hill, the hollow, the bulbous protuberance on the side
of the structure, argue for precise identification."

I agreed. But the account was standard folklore stuff, and unremarkable at that. I had come across these same shreds and tatters of tales hundreds of times in my studies. It was the common grist of Celtic folklore, after all.

"The chronicle continues," Nettles said, "recounting several more sightings of wee folk, objects lost and found in the vicinity, and other benign disturbances. And then this . . ." He began reading again.

"MacLagan also introduced me to a farmer living at Grove Farm nearby, Mr. E. M. Roberts, who affirmed the reputation of the Cairn as a Fairy Mound, insisting that his father had once hired a labourer by the name of Gilim, who, returning home one Samhain Eve, espied a Fairy Cavalcade issuing forth from the aforementioned hollow. Directly he hid himself and, when they had gone, hastily made his way down to the mound which he discovered to be standing open. He entered the Cairn and found it bright daylight within and himself in the midst of a green meadow of great extent wherein other Fairy Folk were at labour preparing a banquet. He remarked to himself that the Fair Folk were no longer small, but well above normal stature and beautiful to behold. The most handsome women he had ever seen approached him and offered him to eat of their food, which he accepted, remarking that he had never in his life tasted anything so delicate on his tongue. He remained the whole day with the Fairy Women until at sunset the Fairy Riders returned from their errand and the banquet began, whereupon the prince of the Fair Ones gave him a silver cup of wine and a long yellow coat and asked him if he would stay. The unthinking labourer replied that he was expected at home in the morning, to which the prince observed, 'Then you must fly at once, my friend, lest your secret find you out!' Upon the instant, the Fair Company vanished in a golden mist and Gilim found himself in a hawthorn bush hard beside the Cairn, wearing the yellow coat and holding the silver cup which he had been given. Gilim used oft-times to display this coat and cup as a proof of his tale."

At this, the professor closed the book and lifted his cup as one who has driven the last nail into doubt's coffin. "What are you thinking?" I asked, already dreading the answer.

"I am thinking your friend Simon has left our world for the Otherworld."

Though Nettles spoke with simple frankness, the sick dread I had been holding at bay for the last few days swarmed over me at last. The room dimmed before my eyes. The coat . . . the yellow coat . . . I had seen it—and him who wore it.

"The Otherworld," I repeated softly, naming the fear that had pursued me since Simon's disappearance. I gulped air and forced myself to stay calm. "Explain, please."

"It is obvious that Simon manifested a distinct and lively interest in the Otherworld just before his disappearance."

"Lively interest—that's all it takes?"

"No"—Nettles sipped his tea thoughtfully—"not all. There would have to be some sort of ritual."

"There wasn't any ritual," I declared, snatching at the fact with a drowning man's tenacity. "I watched him every second, from the moment we reached the cairn to the instant he disappeared. He didn't do anything I didn't do. I mean, I sat down on a rock and he just walked around the thing, asking questions. He was all of a sudden interested in cairns and what was inside—that's true. But that's all. He just walked around it once or twice, looking at it. He only left my sight a couple times—when he was on the other side of the cairn."

The professor merely nodded indulgently. "But that's it. Don't you see it yet?"

"No, I don't see it yet. He didn't do anything I didn't do," I said flatly. I had invested so heavily in denying what had happened, I suppose I found it necessary to defend myself to the last.

"He walked around it! Of course, he did. He circled it. But you did not."

"That's right. So?"

The professor clucked his tongue. "Someone has sadly neglected your education, my boy. You should know this."

Realization broke clean sunlight through my wilful fog. Of course, it was the oldest ritual of all: sunwise circles. *Deosil*, the Celts called it. "Sunwise circles," I said. "You mean simply walking around the cairn a few times in the direction of the sun—that was enough to . . . you know, make him disappear?"

"Precisely," Nettles affirmed over the rim of his mug. "Representing the motion of the sun at an Otherworld threshold—at the proper time and under the proper circumstances, it is a very potent ritual."

"Proper time—like the time-between-times?"

"Exactly."

"But we missed it," I complained. "Sunrise was long past by the time we got there."

Nettles tapped his teeth with a finger. "Then the day itself . . . Of course! Late October, you said: Samhain!"

"Pardon?"

"Samhain—you *must* have heard of it."

"Yes, I've heard of it," I admitted glumly. Samhain—the day in the ancient Celtic calendar when the doors to the Otherworld opened wide. "It just didn't occur to me at the time."

"A day fraught with Otherworld activity. It would have fallen in the third week of Michaelmas term—on the day you viewed the cairn."

By now I was thoroughly distressed and disgusted. Distressed by Nettles's matter-of-fact assertions and disgusted by my own ignorance. You'd think after a few years studying this stuff I would have learned something, but no-o-o-o! "Look, you said you were going to explain everything. So far, you haven't explained anything."

Professor Nettleton set aside his tea. "Yes, I think I have all the pieces now. Listen carefully; I will explain."

"Good."

"First of all, you must understand about the way in which our two worlds are joined together."

"Two worlds—you mean the Otherworld and the real world?"

"The Otherworld and the manifest world," he corrected gently. "Both are equally real, but each expresses its reality in a different way. They exist in parallel dimensions, I believe some would say."

"I'll take your word for it."

"Now, then. The two worlds—or dimensions, if you prefer—are essentially separate, yet they do overlap slightly, as they must. It might help you to think about it in terms of islands in the ocean. As you know, the land mass beneath the ocean contains mountains and valleys. Well, where the mountaintop rises above the water, we call that an island."

"And the places where the Otherworld pokes through into our world—that's the island. Is that it?"

"For the purpose of our analogy, yes. It is, of course, much more complicated than that."

"Of course."

"Now then," the professor continued, "this island, or point of contact, is called a nexus—as I read to you when you first arrived. Among other things, the nexus functions as a portal—a doorway through which one may pass from one world into the other and back again. The ancients were well acquainted with these portals and marked them in various ways."

"Cairns," I said. "They marked them with cairns."

"Cairns, yes. And stone circles, standing stones, mounds, and other enduring markers. Whenever they discovered a nexus, they marked it."

"So that they could travel between the worlds," I said, feeling proud of myself.

But Nettles was not impressed. "Never! Oh, no. Quite the contrary, in fact. They marked the doorways so that people would stay away from them—much the same way as we might mark thin ice or quicksand. Danger! Keep out!" The professor shook his head. "This is why they used such large stones and built these structures to endure—they wanted to warn not only men of their own time, but generations yet unborn."

"I'm not sure I follow," I confessed.

"But it is very simple," Nettles insisted. "The ancients wanted these places to be distinguished clearly because they understood that it is very dangerous for the unwary to venture into the Otherworld unprepared. Only the true initiate may pass between the worlds safely. Stories abound of unsuspecting travelers stumbling into the Otherworld or encountering Otherworldly beings. These stories served to warn the unprepared not to venture into the unknown."

"But Simon was unprepared," I pointed out.

"So he was," Nettles agreed. "But there is more. I very much fear that there is a far greater danger involved. A peril which threatens us all."

Great. Really great. "What sort of peril?"

"Unless I am greatly mistaken, I fear the plexus has become highly unstable. It may already be too late."

9

†HE EПDLESS KПO†

P lexus? As in solar plexus?"

Crazy old Nettles clucked his tongue disapprovingly. "You weren't paying attention, were you? You didn't hear a word I said when I was reading to you."

"Sorry, I was a little preoccupied."

"I will explain once more," he sighed. "Please try to concentrate."

"I'll do my best." I centered my gaze on Nettles's round, owlish face, so as not to be distracted—and found myself wondering if he ever combed his hair. His glasses needed cleaning too.

"The nexus, as we have established, is the connecting point between the two worlds. Yes?"

"Uh, yes."

"Now then, the plexus is the fabric of their interconnection. For the two worlds are not simply joined but woven together." He interlaced the fingers of both hands by way of explanation. He spun around and snatched a scrap of paper from one of the stacks on the floor. "Recognize this?" he asked.

I looked at the paper and saw a pen-and-ink representation of a

85

distinctive intertwined lacework of Celtic design: two colored bands skillfully, dizzily interwoven; two separate lines, yet so cunningly conceived it was impossible to tell where one left off and the other began. "Sure," I told him. "It's the Endless Knot. Probably from the Book of Kells, I'd say."

"Not from the Kells, but close," Nettles replied. "It is from a Celtic cross on the Isle of Iona. Surely you've made your way to Iona, Mr. Gillies?"

To avoid disclosing the appalling shallowness of my education, I replied with a question of my own. "What does the Endless Knot have to do with all this nexus-plexus stuff?"

"I submit to you that it is a graphic illustration of the plexus. The Celts of old never tired of producing it. For them, the design represented the essential nature of earthly existence. Two bands—this world and the Otherworld—entwined in dynamic, moving harmony, each band dependent upon the other, and each complimenting and completing the other."

I gazed at the familiar design, following with my eyes the intricate patterns of loops and whorls and over-and-under crossings. "So that's a plexus, huh?"

"Yes," replied Nettles. "That is the plexus. In our analogy of the island, if you recall, the plexus is the shore of the island. The shore is neither completely land, nor is it all sea. The shore is that territory which bounds the island and separates the sea from the land, but is part of both. When you stand on the shore among the waves, you are effectively in both places at once—you have a foot in both worlds, as it were."

"The ancient Celts revered the shore as a sacred place."

"Aha! You didn't sleep through all your lectures!" Nettles cracked, and I reflected how poorly sarcasm suited him.

"Not all of them, no," I muttered. "As I understand it, the Celts venerated all sorts of plexus-type things: the seashore, dawn, dusk, the edge of the forest—anything that was neither here nor there, so to speak."

Nettles nodded approvingly. "Quite right. Still, we have been speaking of the Otherworld and the manifest world as quite separate places. The ancient Celts, however, made no such distinction; nor did they distinguish between the 'real' and the 'imaginary.' The material and the spiritual were not separate or self-limited states: both were equally manifest at all times.

"For example, an oak grove might be an oak grove, or it might be the home of a god—or both simultaneously. Such was their way of looking at the universe. And it inspired a great appreciation and respect for all created things. A respect born of a deep and abiding belief. The concept of one object or entity being somehow more *real*, simply because it possessed a material presence, would not have occurred to them.

"Interestingly, it is only modern man who makes such rash distinctions. And having made the distinction, he then calls the nonmaterial universe 'unreal' and therefore unimportant and unworthy of his regard. Children, on the other hand, do not discriminate between the material and the nonmaterial in this way. They can tell the difference, of course, but do not feel the need to assign relative value to one over against the other. Much like the Celts of old, children simply accept the existence of both realms—opposite sides of the selfsame coin, you see?"

"Okay, so where does that leave us?" I was beginning to grow a little impatient with all this philosophizing.

"I am coming to that," said Nettles in a tone that suggested he was not to be rushed. "Now then, while the nexus exists as a physical reality—albeit an invisible one, unless marked by a standing stone or a cairn or whatever—the plexus does not exist in the same way. It is, let us say, more the harmony created by the balance of the two worlds. Are you with me?"

"Barely," I admitted. "But do go on."

"Listen carefully. This is the crucial part: when the balance between the two worlds is upset, the harmony—the plexus itself, that is—becomes unstable. Like a strip of woven cloth, it unravels. Do you see?"

I took an impetuous leap. "Unstable plexus equals cosmic chaos and catastrophe—is that what you're driving at?"

"Essentially, yes." The professor rose and busied himself in a corner of the room. "In the light of this, it therefore becomes a matter of ultimate importance first to discover what has upset the balance, and then to set it right. Otherwise . . ." His voice trailed off as he began rummaging through boxes.

"Otherwise what?" I prompted.

He gazed into the air for a few moments and then said, "I greatly fear the Otherworld will be irretrievably lost to us."

"But I thought you said this was serious."

"It *is* serious," Professor Nettleton maintained. "I myself can think of nothing more serious that could befall humanity." He crossed to the other side of the room, opened a closet door, and began stuffing things into a faded canvas rucksack.

"Well, how about a nuclear holocaust? How about AIDS? How about war and pestilence and famine?"

"Those things are menacing, to be sure," Nettles allowed, taking up a tube of toothpaste. "But they do not threaten humanity at its very pith and core."

"I, for one, happen to think being blasted to a thimbleful of glowing protons is pretty darn threatening to *my* pith and core. I can think of one or two others who would back me up on that."

Nettles waved the observation aside with the toothbrush he was brandishing. "Death is death, Mr. Gillies. It has existed since man was born, and will continue until the end of time. It is, after all, part of life. Disease, pestilence, famine, and war, likewise. They are all the same in that respect—part of human existence."

"Spoken like a true academic. Here you are, snug in your little cocoon; the real world never touches you. How do you know anything about—"

"Allow me to finish!" he snapped, shaking the toothbrush at me. "You are speaking of something about which you know nothing! Less than nothing!"

My head ached and my eyeballs were dry and watery at the same time. I was tired and confused, and not in the mood to get yelled at. "I'm sorry. Go on; I'm listening."

The professor turned again to the closet and brought out a heavy wool cardigan. "Sometimes I wonder why I bother!"

"Please," I coaxed. "I mean it. I'll behave."

He was quiet for a moment, staring at the cardigan. "What difference does a Japanese vase make?" he asked unexpectedly.

"Pardon?"

"Or a Rembrandt painting, Lewis? Or a Tennyson poem—what difference do they make to us? I am asking you for an answer."

Nuts. The man was utterly nutters. "I don't know." I shrugged. "Art, beauty—stuff like that. I can't say, exactly."

Nettles blew out his cheeks and huffed in derision, rolled up the garment, and stuffed it into the pack. "If Rembrandt's paintings and Tennyson's poems suddenly ceased to exist, the world would be the poorer, certainly. But there are other paintings, other poems. Correct?"

"Sure."

"Ahh! But what if *beauty* itself ceased to exist?" he asked. "What if beauty—the very idea of beauty—ceased to exist?" He puffed out his cheeks. "Why, ten thousand years of human thought and progress would be instantly obliterated. The human race would have lost one of its primary endowments—the ability to see, value, and create beauty. We would descend to the level of the animals."

"Granted," I agreed.

"Very well." He brought out a pair of long wool socks, which he held up to check for holes. "Apart from pleasure, beauty also kindles imagination, hope, and encouragement. If beauty ceased to exist, we would, in a very real sense, cease to exist—for we would be no longer who we are."

"I'm familiar with the theory," I put in defensively.

"Good. We will continue." He folded the socks and shoved them into the pack, brought out another pair, frowned, and tossed them back into the drawer. "Now then, important as the idea of beauty is, the Otherworld is a thousand times more so. And its loss would be that much more devastating."

Ooops! Sharp turn. Lost me again. "This is the part I'm having trouble with," I said, breaking in.

"Because you're not using your head, Mr. Gillies!" the professor bellowed. He reached into the closet, brought out a thick-soled walking shoe, and pointed it at me. "Think!"

"I *am* thinking! I'm sorry, but I just don't get it."

"Then listen carefully," Nettles said with tired patience. "If you think of the Otherworld as a repository—a place of safekeeping, a storehouse, or treasury—of this world's archetypal imagery . . ." He must have seen from the frown on my face that he was losing me again, because he stopped.

"I'm trying, professor. But I'm a little fuzzy on this archetypal imagery storehouse stuff. It sounds Jungian."

"Forget Jung," Nettles admonished, placing the shoe on the desk and turning the whole of his attention on me. I sat up straight and tried to pay attention.

"Around AD 865, an Irish philosopher by the name of Johannes

Scotus Erigena proposed a doctrine which conceived of the natural world as a manifestation of God in four separate aspects, or discernments—that is, distinct divisions which are nonetheless contained in the singularity of God." He raised his eyebrows. "Anyone at home?"

"I'm here," I muttered. "Barely."

"Erigena's doctrine recognized God as the sole Creator, Sustainer, and True Source of all that exists—this is the first of God's aspects. Secondly, Erigena recognized a sort of Supernature, a separate, invisible *other* nature, wherein reside all primordial ideas, forces, and archetypes—the Form of forms, as he called it—from which all earthly or natural forms derived."

"The Otherworld," I murmured.

"Precisely," confirmed the professor with relief. "The meat of the matter," he continued, "is that, for human beings, the Otherworld performs several crucial functions. You might say that it informs and instructs our world in certain important lessons, mostly having to do with human existence."

"It supplies the meaning of life," I volunteered shakily.

"No," Professor Nettleton said. He pulled off his glasses, peered through them, and replaced them. "That is a common misunderstanding, however. The Otherworld does not supply the meaning of life. Rather, the Otherworld describes *being alive*. Life, in all its glory—warts and all, so to speak. The Otherworld provides meaning by example, by exhibition, by illustration if you will. Do you see the difference?

"Through the Otherworld we learn what it is to be alive, to be human: good and evil, heartbreak and ecstasy, victory and defeat. It is *all* contained in the treasury, you see. The Otherworld is the storehouse of archetypal life imagery—it is the wellspring of all our dreams, you might say."

"But I thought you said the Otherworld exists as an actual place," I pointed out, returning to an earlier point.

"It does," he replied, reaching into the closet for the other shoe, "but its existence in actuality is secondary to its existence as a concept, a metaphor, if you like, which informs, enriches, and illuminates our own world." He peered into the shoe as if looking for elves.

"Really, I'm not stupid," I insisted. "But I'm struggling here."

"We see our own world," Nettles explained patiently, "in large part only by the light cast upon it from the Otherworld." He placed the shoe next to its mate on the desk, turned, and stared into the closet as if it were the entrance to the Otherworld. "I ask you, Lewis," he continued abruptly, "where does one first learn loyalty? Or honor? Or any higher value, for that matter?"

"Such as beauty?" I asked, bringing up his previous point.

"Very well," he agreed, "such as beauty—the beauty of a forest, let us say. Where does one learn to value the beauty of a forest and to revere it?"

"In nature?" I gave the most obvious answer, which was most obviously wrong.

"Not at all. This can easily be proven by the fact that so many among us do not revere the forests at all—do not even *see* them, in fact. You know the people I am talking about. You have seen them and their works in the world. They are the ones who rape the land, who cut down the forests and despoil the oceans, who oppress the poor and tyrannize the helpless, who live their lives as if nothing lay beyond the horizon of their own limited earthbound visions." He paused a moment and recollected. "But I digress. The question before us is this: where does one first learn to see a forest as a thing of beauty, to honor it, to hold it dear for its own sake, to recognize its true value as a forest, and not just see it as a source of timber to be exploited, or a barrier to be hacked down in order to make room for a motorway?"

I knew what answer he wanted, and said it just to make him happy. "The Otherworld?"

"Yes, the Otherworld."

My brain hurt. "How," I asked almost desperately, "is this so?"

The professor brought out a wide leather belt and began threading it through the loops of his corduroy trousers. "It is so because the mere presence of the Otherworld kindles in us the spark of higher consciousness, or imagination. It is the stories and tales and visions of the Otherworld—that magical, enchanted land just beyond the walls of the manifest world—which awaken and expand in human beings the very notions of beauty, of reverence, of love and nobility, and all the higher virtues. The Otherworld is the Form of forms, the storehouse, yes? The archetypes reside there, you see.

"A fellow lecturer once asked me, 'How can you see a real forest if you have never seen a fairy forest?' Well? I ask you the same thing."

Remarkably, this made sense to me. Or perhaps I had parted with my senses altogether. "Because the Otherworld exists, we can see our own world for what it is," I said, almost panting with the effort.

"And for *more* than it is," Nettles added, buckling the belt. "That is very important. For it is chiefly by virtue of the existence of the Otherworld that we recognize the ultimate value of this one—a value which extends far beyond its literal elements."

"In the same way as the value of a forest extends beyond the value of the logs it produces?" I suggested hopefully.

"Very good, Lewis." Nettles seemed pleased. "You're making progress."

"Yeah, well, couldn't we do that by ourselves? Couldn't we recognize the value of this forest or whatever, whether the Otherworld existed or not? I mean, couldn't we just imagine it all?"

"God alone might. Human beings are not so gifted to create *ex nihilo*, out of nothing." I watched, uncomprehending, as the professor began unbuttoning his shirt. "No, human creations must be grounded in something actual, however elusive and subtle." He raised an admonitory finger. "Be assured, we do not come by this knowledge—this consciousness of higher things—naturally, Mr. Gillies. We must be taught. And the Otherworld is the principal instrument of our instruction."

He discarded his shirt, withdrew another from the closet, and began to put it on. The physique beneath was compact and remarkably fit.

"Fine," I said, "but what has it to do with this—this cosmic catastrophe you were talking about earlier?"

"I thought that would have been self-evident." He tucked the dangling shirttails into his trousers.

"Not to me, it isn't."

"Dear boy, anything which threatens the Otherworld threatens this world. It is as simple as that." He took up the backpack and placed it beside the door. Then he retrieved the hiking shoes from his desk and brought them to the chair opposite me. "When the Form of forms becomes corrupted, our world and all that is in it becomes corrupted at the root."

Good golly, this was tough going. I sucked in a deep breath, lowered my head, and slogged on. "All respect, Nettles, but I still don't get it. How—how is the Otherworld threatened? This plexus thing—you said it has become unstable, or is unraveling. What does that mean? What is this all about?"

"In simplest terms," replied Nettles, stuffing his feet into the shoes, "the Otherworld is leaking through into this one."

"And this world is leaking through into the Otherworld. That's bad, right?"

"Catastrophic." Nettles pursed his lips as he laced the right shoe. "A breach has opened between the worlds, and anything may stumble through."

"Anything—like an aurochs? Or a Green Man . . . ?" At last I understood. I felt my stomach tighten. It was *true*. All of it. True.

"The aurochs, the Green Man," Nettles echoed gently, "the wolf in Turl Street, and who knows what else?"

"Simon? Did he stumble through?"

"I think it likely, don't you?"

I pondered all he had said, desperately trying to take it all in. But there was too much; I bowed before Nettles's superior intellect and abandoned myself to his judgment. "Well, okay, so what happens now?"

"I think we must have a look at that cairn of yours, Mr. Gillies."

Another trip to Scotland. Super. On the whole, however, jaunting up to Carnwood Farm seemed a lot more fun than regaling an angry Geoffrey Rawnson with a cockeyed tale about prehistoric oxen and fairy mounds. "Sounds good," I agreed. "When do we leave?"

"At once. I'm packed." He indicated the backpack beside the door.

"I'll have to go back to my rooms and collect a few things," I said.

"That won't be necessary," the professor said. "What you have will suffice." He stepped to his closet and withdrew a spare toothbrush and washcloth which he stuffed into the pack. "There," he declared, "we're ready to go."

10

THE SERBIAN

The train from Oxford to Edinburgh left half an hour late and packed end to end and wall-to-wall with Oxford United devotees. I have nothing against British Rail—only that they let all the wrong sort of people ride on their trains. I don't suppose it's BR's fault, but it makes traveling by rail so tatty. At the end of four or five hours one would be hard-pressed to illustrate the difference between a second-class coach and a cattle car. Whoever esteemed the serving of alcohol to football hooligans in close confinement a good idea ought to be forced to endure a six-hour sojourn with the inebriate consequence.

By the time we reached Birmingham, I had pretty much had my fill of empty Sköl lager cans and rousing football songs. "'Ere we go! 'Ere we go! 'Ere we go!" can only divert a body for so long, I find, and then the lyrics begin to pall.

"Just once," I murmured wistfully, "I would like to travel first class. I think I'm ready for that."

At Birmingham the footballers cleared out, however, and we had the coach to ourselves. I tried to read a newspaper someone had left behind, but the words kept jumping around, and I couldn't make sense of what

I read. So I gave up and looked out the window at the drab countryside racing by in a dull blur outside. It was as if the focus knob had gone on the fritz and the picture was all screwed up—color drained away and image reeling by recklessly. A world sliding sideways out of control.

This is how it begins, I thought, and remembered Simon's impassioned harangue in the car the night before he vanished. Perhaps he *was* more sensitive than I gave him credit for. He felt it—felt the distress in his soul. I didn't, not then, at any rate. But I was beginning to feel something: if not the distress, then fear.

I closed my eyes on such uncomfortable thoughts and went to sleep.

In due course, the train arrived in Edinburgh. We retrieved our luggage and stepped onto the platform. It was cold. The air smelled of diesel oil and Casey Jones's hamburgers.

We tramped up the stairs to the shopping precinct above Waverly Station platform and jostled our way through throngs of cheerless shoppers. I noticed the spark and glitter of Christmas decorations in the shops and reflected that I would have to get some cards sent out before the rush. This time of year it could take three weeks for a holiday greeting to reach the States.

Last Christmas Simon had invited me home with him, but then cancelled at the last minute because Aunt Tootie had come down with the ague and his sister and her fiancé had gone to Ibiza and his mother had volunteered to produce the village pantomime and the staff had been given the hols off and the whole familial frolic had gone quite sour. So I ended up spending a rainy Christmas alone in my room. The thought made me sad.

Nettles hailed us a taxi. Edinburgh Castle, cold and forbidding on its high rock, loomed over us, eerily lit against the dark night sky. We piled into the taxi, and the professor gave the driver the address of a guesthouse he knew. "Inexpensive, but clean. And the food is good. You'll like it," he promised.

I didn't care if the place was filthy, cost a fortune, and the food was served by six-foot-tall cockroaches. I just didn't care. I was tired and sore oppressed by all the vexing thoughts Nettles had put into my head. All I wanted was to crawl into a warm, soft bed and forget everything.

The cab pulled up outside a narrow house, part of the sweeping arc of Carlton Terrace. A neon sign over the door formed the words "Caledon House." A sign in the window informed us that it was a Private Hotel, a term I have always considered slightly self-contradictory.

The professor and I climbed out of the car and assembled ourselves on the walk outside the guesthouse. "Ah, yes. Just as I remember it. Let's go in," he said. "Missus Dalrymple will be expecting us."

I hesitated. "Nettles?" I asked. "What happens next?"

"Dinner, I hope. I'm famished," he replied. "I could eat an aurochs."

Cute. It was good to see that at least one of us had retained a sense of humor. "I didn't mean dinner," I said, somewhat testily.

"We will check in first," the professor said, rubbing his hands eagerly. "Then we will take ourselves along to the Serbian."

The Serbian? What sort of restaurant was that?

⊲ ⊲ ⊲

"What sort of restaurant *is* this?" I demanded.

We stood outside a blank-faced brick building in the warehouse district. There was no window, no sign, no Egon Ronay plaque or VISA sticker on the exterior of the dour edifice to indicate that it was an eating establishment of any kind, let alone announce the fact to the world. A solitary lightbulb glowed under a rusted shade above a weathered wooden door. The doorknob was brass, blackened with age and use. On the doorpost was painted the number seventy-seven, one seven above the other, in white.

"Are you sure you've got the right address?" I asked, glancing along the dark street at our taxi's dwindling taillights.

"Yes, this is the place," Nettles replied—none too certainly, it seemed to me. He rapped on the door with his knuckles, and we waited.

"I don't think there's anyone here, professor," I pointed out. "Maybe we should go somewhere else."

"So impatient. Relax," the professor suggested. "You'll like this, Lewis. You need this."

He pounded on the door again, with the palm of his hand this time. Somewhere a cat yowled as it pounced on its long-tailed dinner. I could hear the wail of tires on the nearby overpass as the juggernauts sped toward the Forth Bridge somewhere in the dark distance. We waited. It was cold and growing colder. We would have to do something soon, or I, for one, would fall asleep and freeze to death on the warehouse doorstep. I was about to recommend we take our business elsewhere, when I heard a faint scratching on the other side of the door.

The door creaked open a crack. A bright dark eye surveyed us for a moment, whereupon the door was instantly flung back and a bearded giant lurched out at us, bellowing, "Professor!"

I stepped swiftly back, throwing my hands before me. But the poor professor was seized by this enormous man and crushed in a spine-popping embrace. He hollered something and the giant hollered back. Then he began kissing Nettles on both cheeks. Where *are* the police when you need them?

The great hulk released Nettles and, to my astonishment, the professor was not badly maimed. He turned to me, straightening his coat and grinning. "Come here, Lewis. I'll introduce you to our host!"

I sidled cautiously closer. The giant thumped himself on his vast chest and said, "I am Deimos!" He thrust a massive hand at me.

"Glad to meet you, Deimos," I said tentatively, watching my own hand disappear into his fist. Deimos was all of seven feet tall and solid as a Volvo tractor. A beard—thick, black, wild, and curly—wrapped the entire lower part of his face and spilled down his neck. He wore old-fashioned farmer's bib overalls and a plaid flannel shirt—the top two buttons of which would never meet their buttonholes. His hair, also gleaming black, formed a mane which was caught up and bound at the neck in a stubby queue. His eyes were lively and his smile wide and welcoming.

He was not satisfied with shaking hands. He grabbed me and crushed me to him, as if I were an only son who had been lost since birth. I felt my shoulder blades compressed and pummeled under his welcoming thumps. At least he didn't kiss me as he kissed the professor, so I counted myself fortunate to escape with minor contusions.

Nettles and the giant began chattering in something closely resembling a foreign language, and we were whisked inside all at once, just scooped in with one of Deimos's massive arms.

The interior of the building suited its gigantic occupant. It was an empty warehouse. Unlit, virtually unfurnished, and, from what I could tell, unheated. In fact, it was largely untroubled by creature comforts of any description. Deimos retrieved a candle from a table inside the door and led us along a narrow runner of ornate flowered carpet. I peered into the distance and saw, illumined by candlelight, a curious assemblage of castoffs thrown together in the middle of the empty space.

Closer, the mélange of junk turned out to be one long table with benches on either side and two smaller tables with chairs all around. Behind the tables rose a Persian carpet, draped like a collapsed tapestry over a lopsided frame. The carpet formed a wall, and several perforated wooden screens formed partitions. An absolutely mammoth oil painting of the Jacobite rebellion hung down from the ceiling on wires. A stuffed moosehead decked one of the partitions, and a fake medieval shield made of spray-painted tin graced another. A well-preserved piano sat nearby, on which a large portrait of the Queen held pride of place.

There were flowers everywhere. Flowers in baskets, flowers in urns, flowers in vases and jars and jugs, cut flowers and potted flowers, fountains of flowers, cascades of flowers on every available surface. In and among the flowers, I made out people actually eating at a long table; four of them. They glanced warily at us, speaking in hushed tones, as Deimos ushered us in.

Our giant host placed us at the opposite end of the long table, a good ten yards away from his other guests. "I saved this for you," he said, as if he had reserved, against all comers, the best seats in the house especially for us. "Be pleased to sit down." His voice boomed like that of an Olympian god in the empty space. I lowered myself onto a bench on one side of the table, Nettles sat across from me, and Deimos smacked a vase of flowers down between us. Then he disappeared, humming loudly.

"It's a fascinating place," Nettles said, pushing the vase aside. "Utterly unique."

"Yeah," I said, peering around. "Loads of atmosphere. How did you find it?"

"A friend introduced me. One must be introduced—*initiated*, you might say." He smiled mysteriously.

Deimos appeared out of the gloom with a crockery pitcher and two filmy glasses. He threw the glasses before us and splashed a frothy red liquid into them. Wine? An exploratory sip confirmed my suspicion.

Professor Nettleton raised his glass. "*Slàinte!*" he chortled.

To which I replied, "Cheers!"

I don't know a lot about wine, but the stuff in my glass was wet and fruity, with just a spicy hint of cinnamon in the nose. The deep-hued liquid tingled on my tongue, and its warmth spread through me. "Not bad," I allowed. "Uh, where are the menus?"

"Deimos will serve what he thinks we will enjoy," Nettles explained. "It depends largely on what he has found in the markets today."

As if answering the professor's remark, our whale of a headwaiter appeared with two big brass bowls in his hands. One bowl held a greenish mush, over which oil and paprika had been drizzled, and the other something swathed in a towel. "Bulakki!" he announced, and left.

Nettles unwrapped the towel to reveal a mound of warm flatbread. He withdrew a piece, tore off a hunk, and passed the remaining portion to me. The professor dipped the bread into the oily mush and scooped up a big glob. He popped it into his mouth, closed his eyes, and chewed.

"Food of the gods," he declared rapturously. "Do try some, Lewis."

I dabbed a bit of the stuff on a corner of bread and touched it to my tongue—and found it very tasty indeed. At least we wouldn't starve. The bread was good too—yeasty, buttery, with a slightly rubbery texture that suggested flour-dusted maidens kneading dough in troughs and singing lusty baking songs.

We tore bread, dipped bread, and ate bread, and we drank our good dark wine. And I, for one, was disappointed when the bottom of the bowl began showing through the bulakki. This hardship proved short-lived, however, for Deimos appeared at just the right moment with a platter of salad.

I think it was a salad. It might have been another floral arrangement. "Do we eat it or admire it?"

"Both," replied Nettles, reaching for a fistful of ripe olives. "You've no idea how I have missed this place. It is years since I've been here. I just had to come again."

The professor set to with a will. He ooohed over the olives, and ahhhed over the artichoke hearts. The fuss he made over the marinated beets and bulgar wheat was not to be believed.

Nettles was enjoying himself so much, it made me laugh just to see him. Or maybe it was the wine. Anyway, it felt good. I had not laughed like that in a long time. A *very* long time.

In the midst of this hilarity, Deimos appeared once more, bearing two heavy brass platters—one on either arm. These he placed before us with a genuine flourish of pride. "Eat, my friends!" he commanded. "Eat and be satisfied! Enjoy!"

On the meat platter, there was chicken, I think. And most of a duck, maybe. Part of a pig, certainly—or a goat. I don't know what roast goat looks like, so it may well have been goat. Or lamb. And there were *birds*! Whole cooked birds—complete with tiny little birdy feet and beaks sticking out. And there were some meaty joints of something else, I don't know what. Among the various meat portions there were bowls of sauces and condiments: creamy, sweet-flavored balms, and singe-the-hair-in-your-nose liquid flamethrowers; astringent herbal unctions, and soothing aromatic blends. The discovery process turned into a culinary adventure.

The vegetable platter was no less enigmatic. There were piles of potatoes and mounds of rice—these were the only familiars of my acquaintance, and even these had been boiled in a spice-laden liquor which rendered them unspeakably alien. Bulb-shaped tubers held center stage, boiled in nectar, I guess, for they were among the sweetest objects I have ever put in my mouth. There were several bowls of concoctions that looked and tasted like curries, each highly seasoned and spiced, but each distinct and peculiar in its own way. And all equally enjoyable.

We ate and talked and drank and ate and talked, filling the vast dark sanctuary of the warehouse with our ebullience and fellowship. Our meal was made more jovial, more exuberant, more cheerful and carefree, by the simple lack of plates or utensils. We ate from the platters with our hands, licking our digits like naughty schoolboys. Professor Nettleton showed me which hand to use, the proper way to hold my fingers, and I became, if only for the space of an evening, a sultan and potentate of exotic mien.

At last—too soon—Deimos appeared to clear away the debris. He brought a plate of flat almond biscuits and a large bowl of oranges. And he brought an urn of oily black scalding liquid which he said was coffee. We peeled oranges and sipped the coffee from tiny porcelain cups hardly larger than thimbles. Alas, I felt the blissful glow of my inebriation dissipating in the bracing surge of strong coffee.

I looked down the table to discover that the other diners had gone. I did not remember them leaving. But we were alone at the table all the same. When Deimos came to refill the coffee urn, the professor bade him sit with us. He brought himself a chair, took a cup—miniscule between enormous thumb and forefinger—and sipped delicately.

"Deimos," Nettles said, "your food is, as ever, worthy of kings—of the gods themselves! I cannot think when I have enjoyed a meal more."

"It was fabulous," I added, languidly lifting a segment of orange to my mouth. "I may never eat again, but it was magnificent. And these oranges are delicious!"

Deimos, inspired by our praise, toasted us with coffee, raising his dinky cup and saying, "To friends! Life belongs to those we love, and where love reigns is man truly king!"

A strange toast, but I heartily concurred with the sentiment. Then he and the professor reminisced about old times; their friendship went way back. When this ritual had been observed, our host asked, "Why have you come to me this night?"

"We are wayfarers on a journey, Deimos. We required nourishment for our bodies and our souls," Nettles answered happily. "You have served both gloriously."

Deimos nodded gravely, as if he understood all about the needs of wayfarers and their souls. "It is my happiness to serve you," he said, in a voice solemn and low.

And then our strange, wonderful evening was over. We rose, bade good night to our host, and were led to the entrance by candlelight. Deimos held the door for us, placed a huge, heavy hand on our heads, and blessed us as we passed before him. "May God go with you on your journey, my wayfaring friends. A thousand angels go before you; a thousand prayers for your return. Peace! Good night."

Stepping out into the night, we stood for a moment huddled under the lamp before striking out to find a taxi. As we turned to move away, the weathered door opened once more. Deimos ducked his head beneath the lintel and held out a white paper bag. "Please," he said to me. "For you."

I accepted the bag and opened it. "Thanks," I said simply. "Thanks."

Our genial giant bobbed his head and ducked quickly back inside. "Oranges," I told Nettles, reaching into the bag and bringing out a bright globe for his inspection. "He gave me *oranges*," I said, a little embarrassed by the man's peculiar largess.

"What an extraordinary place." Tucking the bag under my arm, I fell into step beside Nettles. "You brought me there on purpose, didn't you?"

"I thought you needed a night out."

"That's not what I mean," I said. "What was the point?"

"Nourishment, Lewis."

"Food for the journey—is that it?"

The professor only smiled and strolled away, humming to himself. I followed, too full of food and too sleepy to do anything other than let my feet fall where they would. Once, as we walked along a pitch-black street, I glanced up into the sky and saw a spray of stars, fiercely bright in the clear, cold air. The sight almost took my breath away. When had I ever seen a sky so vivid and alive?

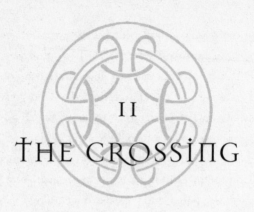

II

THE CROSSING

Getting to Carnwood Farm proved tedious, but not difficult. There was, it turned out, a train service from Edinburgh to Inverness, from Inverness to Nairn, and a bus from Nairn to the Mills of Airdrie. We could walk from there to the cairn. It was after four in the afternoon, and already dark, when we reached Nairn on the Moray Firth.

We stayed the night at a bed-and-breakfast place overlooking the sandy sweep of the bay. After a rousing breakfast of kippers, porridge, scrambled eggs, oatcakes, and coffee, provided by our plump and fastidious landlady, we bundled ourselves along to the bus stop in the town square. At ten past eleven in the morning, a maroon bus rolled up; we boarded and rode to the Mills of Airdrie. The driver dropped us off at the Carnwood Farm road; we stood beside the weathered sign, and the bus rambled on.

We walked through rich farmland, dusted now with a white powdering of windblown snow. The day was cold and misty, the wind crisp out of the north. A day to stay indoors by a fire. We spoke little. The professor seemed preoccupied with his thoughts, so I did not disturb him.

The chill silence unnerved me. It seemed as if we were trespassing, intruding in forbidden lands. The thick Scottish mist made everything appear broody and unearthly, and every step carried us deeper into this alien place.

Presently, the road led down and we descended into the small valley, arriving again at the stone bridge across the meandering Findhorn River. We crossed the bridge, continuing on into Darnaway Forest. The woods were quiet. The trees seemed sunk into winter hibernation.

Carnwood Farm appeared exactly as I had last seen it. The close-clustered buildings, the fields, and the broken, moss-grown tower beside the farmhouse—all exactly as before. This time, however, it seemed that the air of emptiness and abandonment I had noticed before clung more heavily to the place. In this serene and secluded part of the world, the silence was almost oppressive—a physical force gripping the land, choking off all sound. Even from a distance I could tell that the Grants were not at home.

Nettles insisted on knocking at the door, just in case. But no one answered; Robert and Morag were elsewhere. So we continued on our way to the cairn, following the deep-rutted farm road across the compact hills. As before, we met no one on the road—until we arrived at the gate leading to the field and glen which contained the cairn. And there, where Simon had parked his car, sat a gray van with the initials SMA lettered on the side, and some kind of logo.

Upon seeing the van, the professor stopped in his tracks. "What is it? What's the matter?" I asked.

Nettles turned and looked across the field toward the glen. "Is the cairn down there?"

"Yes," I told him. "It's just there—where you see the tops of those trees." I pointed out the line of treetops just visible above the broad flank of the hillside. "Do you wan—"

"Listen!" snapped Nettles.

"What? I don't hear anything."

"Quick! We don't want to be seen!"

"I don't hear anything," I protested. "Are you sure?"

"Hurry!" Nettles began running back along the road to a small rise where a stand of trees overlooked it. I followed reluctantly and joined the professor on hands and knees, peering at the road from behind a large ash tree.

I squatted beside him, listened for a moment, and decided we were being overly skittish. I was about to say so when I heard the soft burr of a car's engine and wheels on gravel. I rose up to look at the road below us. The professor grabbed my wrist and yanked hard.

"Get down!" he rasped. "Don't let them see you!"

I slumped down beside him. "Why are we hiding?"

The sound of the vehicle grew louder and then I saw it on the road below, not more than fifty yards from us—a standard-looking, gray van, with the same logo painted in white on the side: a representation of the earth with rings radiating outward from it like ripples or emanating vibrations. Beneath the logo were the letters SMA.

"Down!" rasped the professor as the second van rolled to a stop behind the first.

Two men climbed out of the vehicle, passed through the gate, and struck off across the field toward the glen. We watched them until they were out of sight.

"Well, they're gone. Now what?" I asked.

Nettles shook his head gravely. "This is not good."

"Why? Who were they?"

"For many years, different groups have been pursuing the secrets of the cairns and rings and stone circles, attempting to force entry into the Otherworld. The men we just saw belong to such a group, and a very dangerous one at that: the Society of Metaphysical Archaeologists."

"You're joking." I would have laughed if Nettles had not been so serious. "Metaphysical archaeologists, is that what you said?"

"They are scientists, for the most part—rather, they are men acquainted with scientific principles and techniques. I have run into them from time to time at various sites, conducting their 'researches.' They would love nothing more than to know what we know, and I have reason to believe they would stop at nothing to obtain this knowledge."

"You can't be serious."

"Entirely serious!" the professor exclaimed. "We've got to think this over very carefully. We can afford no mistakes at this juncture. Care for some chocolate?" He reached into a deep pocket, withdrawing a large bar of Cadbury's Dairy Milk which he unwrapped and passed to me.

"You think they know about the cairn?" I broke off a piece of chocolate and popped it into my mouth.

"I think we must assume that they do."

"But maybe they don't know. Maybe they're just looking around. Yeah, they're just looking around," I offered, trying to convince myself. "Anyway, we should go down there and find out if they've seen any sign of Simon."

"You're right, of course."

I climbed to my feet and scrambled down to the road. We approached the parked vans, walked around them to the gate, and would have started across the field to the glen—but Nettles thought better of it. "Let's go another way."

"What other way?"

He pointed up the road a little distance, to where I could see the line of the glen curve as the stream wandered among the hills. "We can follow the river."

"Whatever you say. Lead on."

A mile or so along, the road dipped to meet the glen. We found a sheep trail along the brookside and began making our way back toward the cairn. Almost at once, the trail entered a thick wood. Dark and silent, every step a creak or a crack—I thought we must sound like a mob of buffalo bulling through the bracken. In the gloom of the close-grown wood, the sheep trail disappeared, and we soon had our hands full, parrying low branches and preventing twigs from poking out our eyes.

We thrashed our way along, stopping every few minutes to listen—I don't know what for. What I heard was crows. Faintly, at first. But each time we stopped, it seemed that there were more crows, and louder than before. Judging from the racket, they were gathering in the wood for the night. Soon their raucous croaks and squawks were all around us, although I could not see any of the birds. We continued on, the day growing colder, the sky darker.

Carnwood Cairn stood in the center of the glen. As before, it presented an unassuming aspect to the world: no more than a hulking heap of earth and moss-dark stone, very nearly shapeless in the feeble light. I gave it a cursory glance, for the thing that commanded my immediate attention was not the cairn, but the crow: a big, black, spread-winged menace watching us with a baleful bead of an eye from a low branch, its sharp black beak open. I fought down the urge to pick up a stick to protect myself.

Preoccupied with the crow, at first I did not see the camp set up on the further side of the glen. Nettles nudged me with his elbow, and I looked in the direction he indicated. I saw a large canvas tent surrounded by the gear of what appeared to be an archaeological dig: lots of wooden stakes driven into the ground with white plastic flags on them, a gridwork of string overlaying a shallow excavation where the snow and dirt had been cleared away, shovels and picks standing in piles of fresh-dug earth. On a pole before the tent hung a blue flag bearing the words *Society of Metaphysical Archaeologists*, and the vibrating world logo in white.

Two men in khaki overalls hunched over their work at the grid, one sitting on a camp stool and holding a large drawing board, the other on his knees, scraping at something with a trowel. Their backs were to us, and, because of the crows' unearthly racket, they had not heard our approach.

"What now?" I asked softly.

"I'd like to examine that cairn."

I looked at the men, and something told me that they were not likely to let us, or anyone else, come near the cairn. "I don't think that's going to be easy," I muttered.

"No," Nettles agreed, his eyes narrow and sharp in the gloaming. "Nevertheless, we have come all this way."

Twilight comes early to Scotland this time of year. Still only midafternoon by the clock, the sun was already sinking toward the west. The time-between-times would soon be upon us. The realization filled me with dull alarm. My heart palpitated, lumping awkwardly in my chest. My stomach felt like a ball of worms. The professor stepped into the clearing of the glen. "What are you going to do?" My voice grated like the sound of the crows filling the trees around us.

"Hello!" Nettles called, stepping boldly into the clearing. "Hello, there!"

I watched him stride boldly toward the men, then plucked up my sagging courage and followed. "Hello, hello," he called, flapping his hands amiably, the very picture of a Hail-Fellow-Well-Met eccentric.

The two men's heads turned as one, their eyes automatically swinging toward the sound of the disturbance. Despite Nettles's kindly greeting, neither man smiled. Their faces remained expressionless and unwelcoming.

Together, Nettles and I trooped up to the digging site. The man with the drawing board put it aside and stood up. He opened his mouth to speak, but the professor did not allow him the first word.

"Oh, this is splendid," Nettles burbled. "I had not expected to find anyone here. It is so late in the year."

Again the man drew breath to speak, but the professor rushed on. "Allow me to introduce myself," he said. "I am Dr. Nettleton, and this is my colleague, Mr. Gillies." He placed his hand on my shoulder as I stepped beside him.

"How do you do?" I said.

"I was just saying to my friend here," Nettles continued, "I hope we don't come too late. I see that we haven't. Indeed, I think we have come just in time. You will be packing up soon, I should think, and—"

"What do you want?" the man with the drawing board asked bluntly. The crows in the treetops squawked loudly, shifting in the upper branches like wind-tossed rags.

"What do we want?" the professor replied, ignoring the man's rudeness. "Why, we have come to see the site, of course."

"It's closed," the man declared. "You're going to have to leave."

"Closed? I don't think I understand." Nettles blinked at me in apparent confusion.

"This is a private dig," the man replied. "The public is not allowed."

"The public!" Nettles reprimanded lightly. "I assure you, my good man, we are not the general public."

"We have a special interest in this site," I added. I could feel my armpits dripping inside my coat.

"Maybe you didn't hear," the second man said, pointing his trowel. He slowly stood. "The dig is closed. You don't have permission to be here. You'll have to leave."

"But we've come a very long way," the professor protested.

"I'm sorry," the first man said. He seemed about as sorry as a sackful of snakes. "You had better leave." He shot a glance at his partner, who tossed aside the trowel and took a deliberate step toward us.

Just then a head poked out from the flap of the tent. "Hello!" it called, and all four of us turned as a tall, distinguished-looking man with a nattily trimmed gray beard emerged. Unlike the others, he was dressed in a long, dark coat and Wellington boots. "Andrew," he said, stepping quickly over the tools and debris scattered around the site, "why didn't you tell me we had visitors?" To Nettles and me he said, "I'm Nevil Weston, project director. How do you do?"

"Pleased to meet you, Mr. Weston, I daresay," the professor replied, managing to convey a slight irritation at the way we'd been treated thus far. "Dr. Nettleton and my colleague, Mr. Gillies," he announced. "We have no wish to disturb you, but, as I was telling your friend here, we have traveled a very great distance to see the site. We have a particular interest in the history of this locality, you see."

"I quite understand," Weston replied. He nodded to his men. "Thank you, Andrew, Edward. I'll deal with this." He smiled at us, but the smile lacked any real warmth. "It's just that this is a privately sponsored project, so regrettably we cannot allow visitors without prior permission. It is the policy of the board of directors, I'm afraid. It's out of my hands."

As he talked, Weston stepped between us, turned us around, and began gently to escort us away from the cairn. It was smoothly done, but Nettles was not diverted. He stopped dead. "Oh, I know how it is, believe me. We wouldn't dream of interfering." He turned to the cairn. "But we've come all the way from Oxford, you see."

"Yes," Weston agreed sympathetically. "I'm sure we can work something out. Perhaps you would like to call again tomorrow. It's getting late; we'll be closing the site for the evening very soon."

Nettles stepped toward the cairn and put out a hand, as if imploring it to help him. "That's quite out of the question," he said. "We had no way of knowing it would be occupied, you see. We've made other arrangements."

"I'm sorry," answered Weston firmly, flashing his empty smile again. I could see him coming to the end of his tether.

"He's right, professor. It *is* getting late," I said, breaking in abruptly. "Maybe we should go."

Nettles sighed heavily; his shoulders sagged. "Yes, I suppose you're right," he said, but he did not move.

To Weston I said, "Perhaps you wouldn't mind if we just had a quick look around the cairn before we go? Wouldn't take a minute." I tried to make it sound as if this simple request was too reasonable to refuse. "We have a very long way to go tonight. Won't take a minute, and it would mean so much to us both."

I could see the refusal forming on Weston's lips. Whatever these metaphysical archaeologists were about, they were certainly a hard-hearted lot, secretive and hostile. It all added up to nothing good. Before Weston could answer, I played my trump card. "That way," I explained to Nettles—for Weston's benefit—"we wouldn't have to bother Robert and Morag with any of this."

Nettles, bless him, was as sharp as his namesake. "Yes," he agreed quickly, "I'm sure the Grants would rather not get involved in our trifling affairs. Mr. Grant is such a busy man. One doesn't like to disturb him unnecessarily."

I could see Weston weighing the risks his refusal would bring. He hesitated, and I moved to close the sale. "A quick walk around, and we're on our way. What do you say?"

"Very well," he said. "I really shouldn't allow it. But, as we're here at the Grants' guests, I definitely wouldn't like them disturbed."

"Oh, I couldn't agree more," replied the professor happily. "Come, Lewis, let's just take a quick look around the cairn before we go." He was already moving away from Weston as he said it.

We walked quickly to the cairn. At our approach a tremendous fluttering ruckus took place in the trees above us. I looked and saw dozens . . . scores . . . hundreds of crows flocking to the upper branches of the nearby trees. Their black shapes against the iron-dark sky gave me an eerie feeling. The birds raised an unholy racket as they hopped from branch to branch and flitted from tree to tree, scolding, shrieking, challenging.

On reaching the base of the cairn, Nettles pulled me close. "Ignore them," he said. I could not tell whether he meant the crows or the men. I fell into step beside him as we stalked around the cairn on the rough, overgrown ground. Weston watched us, his arms crossed over his chest and a pained expression on his face. As soon as we were out of Weston's sight, Nettles said, "What was it you said you left for Simon?"

"A bank card," I replied. "I left his Barclaycard—I stuck it in a crack at the entrance."

"We must try to retrieve it," he said. "It would not do for them to find it."

We rounded the cairn and came in sight of the tent and the excavation beyond. The two men had not moved. They watched us as we continued on around. Weston stood where we had left him, waiting for us to finish our circumnavigation of the cairn. As we drew near him, Nettles said, speaking loudly, "You see, Lewis, this is quite in keeping with cairns of this age. The stone is undressed; it will have come from the glen nearby—they used whatever came readily to hand . . ."

With a nod to the frowning Weston, we continued our inspection amid a raucous chorus of crow complaint. Their awful shrieking filled my ears. I gazed up into the branches of the circling trees and almost fell over backwards: every twig, bough, and limb of every tree in the glen was occupied by the ragged black form of a squawking crow. There were so many crows it was scary. Masses of birds! Fluttering, flapping, rippling over the branches. Crows by the treeful. And they were angry!

"What's with these crows?" I wondered.

"They are guardians of the threshold," replied the professor.

"I thought you said the man with the dogs was the guardian."

"Oh, there are any number of guardians. Their purpose is to daunt the unworthy. Ignore them, and you will pass by unharmed; fear them, and they will tear you to ribbons." Nettles's eyes scanned the cairn wall beside us. "Now where is the entrance? I have not seen it, have you?"

"No—but we should have passed it. That's strange . . ."

Continuing our circuit, we came upon the camp once more. The two men had joined Weston, and all three were standing in consultation together, watching us. Nettles made a show of pointing out something to me, waving his hand airily. "Don't look at them," he said softly. "I did not see the entrance you described."

"Neither did I. But there was one. I swear it."

"We will look again."

Once more around the cairn. The crows flapped and screamed, raising a horrific din. Scores circled the cairn, turning the air black with their darting wings. I kept stealing fearful glances skyward as we hurried around the base of the cairn. As a result, I missed the entrance once again. How odd. "It's got to be here," I insisted. "Simon went in—*I* went in!"

We came abreast of where the three stood waiting. "Well, that's fine. Good," Weston said, stepping forward. When we did not slacken our pace, he called, "Here! I think that's enough. Here, now! Stop!"

"Go on looking," Nettles instructed. "I will keep them busy for as long as I can." He continued beside me for a few more steps. I felt his hand on my arm. "Good luck, Lewis."

Then he stopped. I glanced quickly over my shoulder and saw that Weston was hastening toward him. Nettles raised his hand, as if in farewell, then turned to confront Weston. The cairn wall took them from view as I passed out of sight.

I hurried over the uneven ground, searching the cairn wall for the entrance we had somehow missed again. The sound of the screaming crows filled my ears, as scores of black shapes erupted from the winter-bare branches and took to the sky overhead. The crows! Of course, I thought, the crows were distracting me and trying to prevent me from finding the opening.

I hurried on, slipping on the long, wet grass that grew at the cairn's base, scanning the undulating mound beside me for the dark hole through which Simon had vanished. Awful shrieks assaulted the air. If I stepped one foot nearer the cairn, the birds would attack. They would swoop down and peck my eyes out. They would rip me to bloody tatters with their sharp beaks.

Again I rounded the side of the cairn facing the camp. I saw Weston and his henchmen clustered around Professor Nettleton. The one called Andrew had a hand on Nettles's arm and was attempting to lead him away. Nettles, hands waving wildly, voice lifted in rebuke, was doing his best to distract them. I put my head down and raced on.

As I drew even with them, Weston saw me. But I was already dodging away again, around the base of the cairn.

"Stop him!" Weston shouted, his voice sharp as a gunshot in the stillness. Andrew released the professor's arm, and he and his colleague leaped after me at once.

I ran on, my only thought to keep the cairn between me and my pursuers. But, pounding over the uneven turf, I caught my foot on a stone. I fell, sprawling headlong onto the wet turf. Instantly, the crows were on me, dropping from the sky like black buzz bombs. They flew at me, wings flashing, buffeting, glossy black beaks snapping like scissors. I threw my arms over my head to protect my face and wriggled through the long grass, struggling to regain my feet.

Ignore them, Nettles had said. With an effort of will, I lowered my hands and pushed myself up off the ground. The big, angry birds shrieked bloody murder as they swooped and dived, executing their mad challenge, but I turned my eyes away from the crow-filled sky and looked instead at the cairn wall. I heard the rustle and slash of their wings all around me, but I was not grazed by a single feather.

Bless you, Nettles, I thought. It works!

The thought had no more than crossed my mind when I heard a low grating sound next to me—the sound of stone grinding against stone. I had no time to wonder what it might be, for I looked at the section of cairn just ahead of me and saw the doorway. I do not know how I could have missed it before, but there it was—smaller even than I remembered and half-hidden by that wiry little thicket—a squat fissure at the base of the edifice.

Without a second thought or a backward glance, I threw myself at the hole, shrugging off the pack and tearing at the thicket with my hands. There! I saw the glint of blue plastic—the Barclaycard! Just where I had left it. I reached out to take it; I heard footsteps thudding behind me—and loud curses as the crows turned their attack on my pursuers. The dark entrance of the cairn yawned before me. I could smell the dry musty scent of the cairn's interior. I swallowed hard and lunged into the entrance, banging the top of my head as I tumbled into the deep blackness of the cairn. Little sparkly stars danced before my eyes. I squeezed my eyes shut against the pain and slumped back against the stonework to rub the throbbing goose-egg already rising on my temple.

When I opened my eyes, I was no longer in the world I knew.

12
PARADISE

One whole side of the interior wall of the cairn seemed to have collapsed; I could see through it to the hillside beyond. My first thought was to make a dash for it, before the metaphysical thugs caught up with me.

I stood, clutching my head, and lurched toward the broken wall. The moment I stepped forward, I heard a rushing sound behind me. It must be my pursuers. I glanced fearfully over my shoulder and saw the wall behind me inexplicably receding—as if I were striding rapidly away from it down a long, narrow corridor. And I felt a dark surge of air, a great churning, upswelling billow. In the same instant, the green hillside before me dimmed and disappeared from sight.

I stopped. It took me a moment to steady myself. My head was pulsing to an aching throb, as if I were being beaten rhythmically over the head with a brick. Each concussion brought bright pinpricks of light and angry red spots. Taking a deep breath, I carefully, cautiously placed one foot in front of the other and stepped forward. My clothes snapped and rippled in the upsurging air. With sickening dread, I realized that my first mistaken step had somehow set me upon the narrowest of spans over a vast, invisible chasm.

The bridge beneath my feet was thin as a sword blade. I could actually feel the sharp steel cutting into the leather of my shoes. I swayed dangerously, fighting to keep my balance on this ridiculously slender span. The slightest misstep and I would plunge into the unknown depths below, from which I could hear the restless echo of powerful forces shifting and colliding—like empty freightcars in a midnight train yard. Yet, with every nerve and sinew screaming *Fool!* I forced myself to take another step, knowing in my soul the step would be my last.

I teetered precariously as my weight shifted forward. Suddenly, the upswelling air blast stopped. All became quiet. But a moment later I realized that I could not breathe.

There was no air. I gulped and gasped, but my lungs could not draw. My mouth formed a yelp of surprise, but no sound penetrated the vacuum. I poised trembling on the sword-bridge, dizzy and light-headed with fear. I swayed precariously, but did not fall.

I forced my foot forward an inch, and then another. Only the solid blade beneath my feet seemed real. I could no longer see anything before me or around me. All was darkness—piercing darkness, and searing silence. And then arose the most horrendous gale of wind, shrieking out of nowhere, striking me full force, head-on. It felt as if the skin of my face was being slowly peeled away, as if my clothing was being shredded and my flesh pared to the bone.

Somehow, I found the presence of mind to take another step, and instantly regretted it. My foot missed the blade-span entirely and for a single, heart-stopping moment I felt myself balanced for flight—arms flung wide, head up, legs bent and loose . . .

I fell.

But instead of spinning headfirst into the fathomless void, almost at once my knee struck a solid surface and I pitched forward, sprawling on my chest in the soft dirt outside the cairn in the full light of day.

I still could not breathe. I lay on my stomach like a beached whale, mouth gaping, gasping, fighting for air. Breathe! Breathe! My lungs heaved in my chest, convulsing with the effort. My vision dimmed and I thought, *It is over—I am dying.*

I raised myself up on an elbow and rolled onto my back. The effort released something inside me, and I felt cool air gushing into my lungs. The air was raw and sharp; it burned my lungs like fire, but I could not stop inhaling the stuff in great gagging gulps. I lay on my side, panting and gulping, my limbs quivering, my eyes watering and fingers tingling. My heart beat a triple tattoo, and my head palpitated with the rhythm.

My first thought—I swear, even after all that had happened to me in the last few moments—the first thought that leapt to mind was: *It did not work.* The bump on my head, I thought, accounted for all the strange sensations. I had merely become disoriented in the dark and stumbled back through the opening by which I had entered the cairn. The trees, the hillside, the evening sky—it was all the same as before.

I had failed. And now the SMA goons would catch me and haul me away. At this thought I raised my head and quickly looked left and right. I saw no one. Maybe I could still get away. I stood shakily, swayed, and put out my hand to the wall to steady myself.

It was then I received my greatest shock. The cairn was gone. In its place stood an enormous grassy mound topped by a single, ragged standing stone. The low stone-lined entrance to the mound yawned dark and empty behind me. It seemed unlikely that I had crawled through it, but there was no other possibility.

I turned and looked again at the landscape around me and discovered further contradictions. The snow was gone. And the trees, for all their likeness to the wood surrounding the cairn, were *not* the same; they were taller, fuller, their branches more graceful. Everything that met the eye had a subtly altered appearance. Even the sky appeared brighter somehow, though it was still dusk—or was it sunrise?

Like a man in a dream, who realizes he *is* after all in a dream, I understood then that I had crossed over.

Oh, dear God, now what?

I sat down on the ground, drew my knees up, and hugged them against my chest. I rocked back and forth for a long time, my eyes closed, hoping, I think, that when I opened my eyes again the cairn would be there and I would be back in the place I had left.

My head ached. My throat burned. I felt miserable, lost, and utterly alone. And, as I sat nursing my misery, it occurred to me that the hillside had grown very quiet. No, not grown quiet—it had always been so. And not merely quiet; that is, not just silent—as in the absolute absence of sound—but still, hushed, and peaceful. I heard a world at rest with a deep and natural quiescence. As I sat there, with my arms wrapped around my knees, abject misery slowly metamorphosed into a tranquility that I had never, ever known in the world that I had left behind.

It was the serenity of a world that knew no mechanical thing; no planes, trains, or automobiles; no motors, no engines; no factories, mills, offices, or industry; no telephones, radios, televisions, and no satellites or rockets or space shuttles; no machinery of any kind.

I had never known such complete and perfect peace. In all my life, I had never experienced a single minute of such unblemished serenity. Until that moment, every single second of every single day of my entire existence had been bounded by and hedged about with a man-made, mass-produced noise of some kind.

Even in sleep, I had always sensed relentless engines droning away somewhere—the ticking of a clock, the squeal of wheels in the street, a siren's shriek, the distant shrill of a train whistle, or the subliminal hum of a fan or furnace. Years ago, I had hiked in the Rockies in southern Colorado, and even standing on the side of a mountain in that deep wilderness I had heard jet planes roaring overhead.

But here, in this place, in this other world, the incessant background noise that so loudly proclaimed mankind's frenzied endeavors simply did not exist. All was calmness and gentle repose.

This struck me as more miraculous, more incredible, than anything that had happened to me so far. I simply could not believe how immensely peaceful it was. Serenity beyond definition, tranquillity beyond words. The stillness beggared description.

It occurred to me that I had gone deaf—perhaps as a result of the blow to my skull. I cocked my aching head and listened . . . No, luckily I was not deaf. I could hear a gentle breeze sifting among the branches and, from somewhere nearby, the light trill of birdsong.

I rose, somewhat unsteadily, and began making my way down the hill. The air, though cool, was not uncomfortable. I passed among tall trees, walking on fine, new green grass as upon an endless, seamless carpet. Dew glistened underfoot with the gleam of emeralds. It appeared to be spring here, as the trees were leafless still. I stopped to examine some of the nearer branches and saw that they were budding; blossoms and leaves would soon appear.

By the time I reached the bottom of the hill, the sun had risen a little higher. And when the sun broke full above the hills, I actually fell down on my knees: the light was so keen and sharp and brilliant. Tears streamed from my eyes and I thought I might go blind. It was some time before I could see properly again—and then I had to shade my eyes with my hand from time to time, or simply stop and close them to ease the stabbing pain from the too-piercing light.

By dawn's clear light, I surveyed the land and stood transfixed with amazement: the grass literally gleamed, it was so green. Green!—that was too slight and inconsequential a word for what I saw: a shimmering citrine viridescence, breathtaking in its purity.

The sky was brighter and, I swear, a bolder, cleaner, more translucent blue than I had ever seen—a hue which had more in common with peacocks and lapis lazuli than atmosphere. I stood some moments just staring at the shining sky, drinking in that shocking azure.

In fact, everything I saw seemed brighter and fairer than anything I had known in the real world. It seemed *newer*—or perhaps more finely wrought, immaculate in form and crisply defined.

At the bottom of the hill, I found a brook. I knelt, dipped a hand into the ice-cold water, and lifted a mouthful to my lips. The water tasted alive!—clean and good and life-giving. I cupped both hands and plunged them in, greedily guzzling that sweet elixir down until my fingers became numb from the cold.

I stood slowly, wiping my chin with my sleeve, and gazed around me. I appeared to be standing in a glen surrounded by smooth hills—of which "my hill," with its mound and standing stone, was but one among many. I thought to go exploring, and thrilled to the thought. A whole world of wonders fresh for the plucking! I could not wait.

I struck out at once along the brookside. I do not know why, but it seemed like a sensible thing to do. Perhaps it would lead somewhere—a village, maybe. Did they even have villages in the Otherworld? I did not know. I knew nothing. Less than nothing.

The Otherworld! Every few seconds I would remember where I was and the awareness would jolt me like a bolt of lightning striking the top of my skull as if it were a weather vane. How was it possible? How could it be? I asked myself over and over. Who could have believed it? Who *would* believe it? I simply could not take it all in at once, so I gave myself over to a sort of slow-motion astonishment. Time and again the utter impossibility of my position exploded in my face; I lurched and staggered from one marvel to another, shell-shocked by sheer transcendent revelatory wonder.

Truly, this was Paradise! A virginal creation, fresh and unspoiled;

a world without blemish, whole and clean and undamaged by human-kind's insatiable appetite for destruction. Paradise! I wanted to shout the word from the hilltops. Nothing in my previous life had ever prepared me for this . . . this soul-dazzling harmony of beauty and peace, this fiery blaze of created glory. Like a tidal wave, the miracle of it whelmed me over, submerged me, pummeled me, and left me gasping for air. Paradise!

Despite my somewhat dazed and bedazzled condition, I made fair progress following the stream through the glen. As I walked, I began to make a mental list of everything I saw, a catalog of miracles. In doing so, I soon began comparing this list against everything I had learned of the Otherworld from the old stories and legends I had read in the course of my studies.

I worked at this systematically: animal, vegetable, mineral; people, places, things. Item by item, I built up a picture of the Otherworld as described in Celtic folklore. I do not say it was an accurate picture, or even a very complete one. Indeed, I simply assumed that it was the Celtic Otherworld I had arrived at; it did not occur to me to consider otherwise. Still, it gave me something to do. The effort occupied me a long while. It must have, because when next I stopped and raised my eyes to look around, I saw that the brook had widened somewhat, becoming rocky and shallow as the glen had spread to become a broad meadow between two massive grassy bluffs.

The sun now stood directly overhead. The stream continued on through the meadow to bend away to the west beyond the slope of a hill a few hundred yards further on. The hills on either side of me were wide and round; there were no trees or bushes. It occurred to me that it might be a good idea to climb the nearest hill and reconnoiter. Perhaps I would see something from the hilltop that I could not see from the valley. Wasn't that what explorers often did?

I turned away from the stream and started up the long, sloping hillside. As I turned, I noticed a smudge of thin, dark cloud in the sky. I stopped. That was not a cloud—it was smoke. Black smoke from a fire. Where there was fire, there were people: a settlement. Most likely I would be able to see it from the top of the hill.

Before I could even think these thoughts, my legs started to run. I hadn't run very far, however, when I heard a strange, unsettling sound—a rhythmic pounding, a drumming, steady and insistent. And it seemed to be coming from the very earth beneath my feet. It sounded like rolling thunder, or logs tumbling down a dirt bank.

I stopped again and listened. The deep throb grew louder, pulsing in the ground, drumming, drumming. I tried to think what could make such a sound. Horses? If so it must be a stampede—and a strangely orchestrated stampede at that. The beasts must be dancing!

The black smoke curled into the sky, drifting above the hilltop on the breeze. There was more of it now. I stood motionless: listening to the strange earth-borne rumbling sound, watching the smoke, absolutely mystified.

Then I saw something I had only read about in ancient texts: the sudden appearance of a bristling forest of ash saplings. Trees springing spontaneously into existence along the hilltop!

The image, though apt, was a poetic euphemism. I knew well what it was.

Before I could think what to do, the warriors themselves appeared. The throbbing pulse in the earth and air was the booming of their war drums and the pounding of their feet. The smoke trail in the sky was from the burning firebrands in their hands.

They ranged themselves all along the hilltop. There must have been a hundred or more. Some held huge oblong shields and swords, some flaming torches and spears, some rode horses, some advanced on foot, and others rode in chariots. Most were naked, or nearly so. They crested the hill and halted.

I figured they had come for me. I figured they would have me too. Here I was, a stranger in a strange land, lost, defenseless. I would not make much of a fight for a troop that large. But how did they know I was here?

I stood stock-still, stupidly trying to reason my way through this absurd situation, when there arose a tremendous bellow—as if a thousand mad bulls had begun to roar at once. A piercing, full-blooded clarion call; a sound to turn the bowels to water and scoop the hearer hollow. BWLERWMMM! BWLERWMMM! BWLERWMMM! BWLERWMMM!

The hideous clamor stung the ear and bludgeoned the brain; it twisted the nerves into limp threads, useless as soggy string. I pressed my hands over my ears and scanned the hilltop to discover the source of this phenomenal noise.

I saw twenty men holding enormous curving horns to their lips; these mighty instruments produced the sense-benumbing sound. It came to me then what these instruments were: the fabled battle horns of the Banshee. The *Beahn Sidhe*, the traditional dwellers of the Otherworld, were reputed to possess war trumpets of such terrible power that, when sounded, they could turn an enemy to stone. I understood now that this was a far from figurative boast. I myself actually felt as if I were cemented to the ground in catatonic terror. My legs were as dense and unfeeling as concrete posts.

This unearthly bellow continued for a few moments and was quickly bolstered by the clash and clamor of spear and sword on rim of shield, as all the warriors began banging away with their weapons. And the drums beat a steady thunder all the while. The clamor filled the air, filled the glen. In that once-serene world, it sounded as if the very hills were shaking themselves to dirt clods.

The din grew to a skull-splitting cacophony, whereupon it ceased.

The echo of its sudden cessation lingered long in the glen; I could hear it pealing away through the empty hills like the crack of doom.

The warriors stood poised on the rim of the hill in the unnatural calm created by their abrupt silence. Then they lofted their weapons and, with a mighty shout, flew down the hillside toward me.

It happened so fast, I stumbled back in fright and slid down the hill. I lay sprawling in the grass, scrambling backwards crablike over the smooth stones and into the cold stream.

The warriors raced screaming down the hill, swords and spears flashing, firebrands flaring, drums booming, battle horns blaring. They were still too far away for me to be able to make out their faces, but I could see the bright blue designs painted on their bodies in the manner of Celtic warriors of old—which, in a way, they were.

A preposterous thought thrust itself into my head: maybe I could hide. I glanced wildly right and left. Hope died before it could draw breath. Not one stone proved big enough to conceal me. I would have to run for it.

I leapt to my feet and thrashed across the stream to the other side, making for the hillside opposite. My only salvation lay in outrunning the pursuit.

Amazingly, I ran faster than I could have believed. My legs seemed longer, my stride swifter and surer, than ever before. I sailed over the ground, my feet hardly touching the earth. Wind in my face, my hair streaming. I flew!

And then I stopped. Directly ahead, flying down the slope in full plummet toward me, rushed another line of warriors—every ounce the equal of the first. These, like those behind me, advanced with staggering speed. Caught between two swift armies, like a fly between two crashing cymbals, I turned and dashed back to the stream where I hunkered down, breathless, beside the water. There was no escape.

The first warriors had nearly reached me. I could see their stern, manly faces now. If I had ever nurtured any notions of nobility, bravery, courage, dignity, or the like, these exalted qualities were embodied in the faces I saw. Clear-eyed, firm-jawed, virile, strong, and proud—they were the living embodiments of every red-blooded boy's childhood fantasy of glorious manhood: heroism incarnate.

That they were going to kill me seemed a thing of piddling consequence. Dear lord, but they were handsome!

Swiftly the battle line closed. I saw the glint of their bold eyes, the sweat on their firm-muscled limbs. I saw their teeth gleaming white, their dark braids swinging free. I heard their full-throated battle cries as they swept down upon me, and I cowered lower, hugging the stones, willing myself to disappear beneath them.

It worked. They did not see me. For even as the nearest combatant reached the place where I huddled, clutching my head and praying to keep it in closest possible contact with my shoulders, he dashed across the stream and all but leaped over me, without so much as a sideward glance in my direction.

The rest of the battle host likewise ignored my presence. They splashed across the stream and raced to meet the war band on the opposite hillside. Only then did I realize I was not the object of their desire.

This insight did not produce the relief it should have. Any comfort was all too quickly consumed by the fear that I would be killed in the confusion anyway. Dead by freakish mischance is still dead.

The two advancing battle lines closed on one another. The sound of their meeting shivered the air: spear clattering on shield, sword striking helmet, iron on bone, battle horns blaring, voices bellowing, drums pounding—all of it in the most horrific deafening clangor. I thought my eardrums would burst.

The impact of the initial collision threw the combatants apart. Some fell instantly, never to rise again. Most, however, swung into combat and the battle commenced in lethal earnest. Blood and spittle sprayed liberally. Horses reared and plunged, flinging dirt into the sky.

Men fought, hacking viciously at one another with wicked, blood-stained blades.

I could not watch! I could not keep from watching! I crouched at the water's edge, wide-eyed, yelping with terror as this or that warrior fell to his death with skull riven or throat slashed. I dodged this way and that, trying to stay out of the way. This became more difficult as the fight progressed, and the ordered lines became a ragged, rangy tangle. Men fought all around me. Just avoiding being trampled by a horse or stabbed by an errant spear, not to mention crushed by a falling body, occupied my utmost attention.

I thought to get hold of a shield to hide behind, and began scanning the nearby hillside. I saw several lying in the grass alongside the bodies of owners who would not longer need them. I ran to the nearest of these and tried to pull it free. The dead man's arm was still engaged, and his hand still clutched the shield strap tightly.

I knelt over the body and tore frantically at the binding. I was thus occupied when I felt a heavy hand on my shoulder.

I screamed and was jerked over backwards. I saw a spear waver in the clear blue sky above me. I threw my hands into the air to ward off the blow and lashed out with both feet at my attacker. I squirmed and writhed, shrieking. To my profound astonishment, a voice shouted, "Lewis! Stop it!"

I looked and saw that the form bending over me wore a familiar face. "S-Simon?" I stammered uncertainly. "Simon, is it you?"

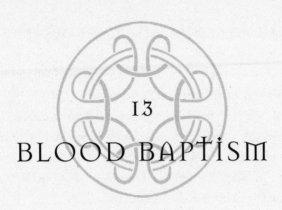

13

BLOOD BAPTISM

It was Simon, naked and painted for battle like all the others, and wearing a long, luxurious mustache. "Yes, it's Simon!" he hissed. "Stop kicking! I'm trying to help you!"

I ceased thrashing and sat up. "Simon! I've found you! What are you doing here? How—"

He grabbed me by the arm and yanked me to my feet. "Get up!"

"Simon, let's get out of here. We've got to—"

He stooped over the body of the dead warrior beside us and snatched the sword from the corpse's hand, shoving it into mine. "Here, take this."

"I don't know how to use this thing." I shoved it back at him.

"You'll learn." He began tearing at my clothes. "Get that shirt off."

"Hey! What—"

"You don't want to be seen like this," he told me tersely.

Reluctantly, I began unbuttoning the shirt. "Simon, I'm really glad I found you."

"Hurry!" Simon scanned the melée. The battle host of which he had been a member seemed to be overcoming their opponents, for the battle had quickly pushed beyond us. The heaviest combat was being waged higher up the hill.

I saw this as a perfect chance to creep away unnoticed. "Look, we've got to get away from here. We can—"

"Get if off!" he growled, snatching the shirt from me. "And get rid of this." He seized my arm and jerked the watch from my wrist. Then he turned and heaved my watch into the stream.

"Wait a minute! You can't—" The timepiece glinted in the air and disappeared among the rocks and the water.

"Follow me!" he cried, and, picking up his spear, dashed once more into the fray.

Reluctantly, I picked up the sword and tried once more, without success, to wrest the shield from the dead warrior. "Hurry!" cried Simon. "Try to stay with me!"

I followed without the shield, cursing every step. "This is crazy!" I cried. Simon did not hear me above the battle roar. "Bloody crazy!"

He gestured with his spear for me to follow, turned, and flung himself headlong into the fray. He was met almost the same instant by an immense warrior with a round, white-painted shield. The shield was spattered with blood, more red than white now, and the sword in his hand was notched and jagged. The warrior rushed at Simon, swinging the sword wide to strike, bellowing a brutal war cry as he came.

Simon did not hesitate but leaped to meet his adversary's attack, throwing the butt of the spear up and into the man's groin, ramming it hard. I winced. The warrior lurched back, swiping down with the blade, chopping off the end of Simon's spear.

"Run!" I screamed.

But Simon had no intention of fleeing. He drove into the staggering foe, swinging the spear violently against the bloodstained shield. Even above the tumult of the battle I heard the crack. The shield swung aside. In the same fluid motion, Simon turned the spear and thrust its slim, leaf-shaped blade deep into the man's bare chest. Blood spurted from the wound in a crimson torrent. The painted warrior fell dead to the ground, his mouth gaping in a silent scream.

Suddenly light-headed, black spots swimming before my eyes, I stumbled to Simon's side. "He tried to kill you," I mumbled, little knowing what I said. "Is he dead?"

By way of answer, Simon wrested the sword from his opponent's dead hand. Placing a foot on the man's chest and gripping the sword in both hands, he swung the blade high, then down, quickly, expertly. With a meaty crack, the dead warrior's head rolled free.

I yelped and jumped back. "Simon!"

He picked up the severed head and turned, raising his grisly trophy on high. I stared in perfect disbelief. Simon threw back his head and laughed. "Here," he called to me, "make yourself useful."

With that, he threw the head to me. It hit the ground with an ugly thump and rolled toward me down the hill, flinging blood from the amputated neck. It stopped at my feet where I regarded it with abhorrence, choking back the sour bile that suddenly filled my mouth.

"Pick it up!" shouted Simon. "Let's go!"

With difficulty I tore my eyes from the dead man's empty gaze. "What?"

"Come on," Simon snapped impatiently. "Pick it up! Let's go!"

I glanced down at the head and back to Simon. "I can't . . . I just—"

"Pick the wretched thing up!" he snarled savagely. "Now!"

I stooped and clenched a handful of hair. The head was warm and the hair was wet with sweat. I felt faint. My throat gagged. I thought I would throw up; my stomach heaved, and my knees went spongy. I stood retching, holding that hideous prize, dizzy and reeling with fear and revulsion.

Simon ran to join battle once more, but the fighting was over. The defeated were fleeing over the hill, and the victors—the war host I had encountered first—were throwing spears and hurling loud abuse at the rapidly retreating foe. The dead of both war bands lay scattered over the hillside like so many sun-bleached boulders. Crumpled and contorted, limbs askew, they lay in grass of the softest green I had ever seen, under that incredibly blue sky.

Even as I gazed numbly at the carnage around me, I heard a grating cry and looked up to see the carrion birds gathering. Already, they were flocking to their grim and ghastly feast. One big raven swooped low in front of me and landed on the headless corpse of the man Simon had killed. With a loud croak the big bird jabbed its black beak into the oozing chest wound, bit deep, and tore away a ragged strip of flesh. The raven tossed its sleek black head and gobbled the meat.

I had to look away. I stumbled after Simon, keeping my eyes away from the butchery in the grass.

Simon had joined the other warriors, who were setting the hills ringing with wild whoops of victory. Some leaped in the air and gestured with their spears to the obvious delight of their fellows, who barked with laughter. Simon laughed with them.

The merriment halted abruptly with the arrival of two young men on horseback: one looked to be a warrior and the other an adviser of some sort. But the warrior was dressed in bold checked trousers of gold and green, and a loose red shirt of shimmering satinlike fabric. He wore a large neck ring, or torc, of silver, and a wide belt of silver disks. The hilt of a golden dagger protruded from this belt, and he carried a spear with a silver blade. He, too, flaunted a great, spreading mustache. His hair—a long, full mane of tawny curls—gleamed in the sun.

The other youth was dressed more plainly: brown shirt and trousers of an ordinary cloth, a common leather belt. He wore no finery, and carried no weapons. His only adornment was a fine crimson cloak gathered at one shoulder with an immense silver brooch. He wore his dark hair scraped back tight to his scalp.

Both men were tall and striking, enjoying the ease and grace of youth. And both moved with a command and authority I imagined only Holy Roman emperors possessed: massive and benevolent, inspiring and daunting at the same time. They would have been at home in any of Europe's royal courts. Even their horses appeared more graceful, more powerful, more beautiful than any of the manifest world's much-vaunted thoroughbreds.

At the appearance of these two, the cheering and gyrating stopped, to be replaced by a general clamor of approval—a hailing of the chief, I reckoned. I crept next to Simon. "That's the king, right?" I whispered.

"No. It's the prince," he murmured. "Be quiet."

"Prince who?"

"Prince Meldron," Simon told me irritably. "Meldron ap Meldryn Mawr. The one with him is Ruadh—he is the prince's bard."

"Oh."

The prince halted amidst his gathered warriors and dismounted to the acclaim of all. Anyone would have thought he had won the battle single-handedly, though as far as I could tell he had not lifted a finger. Meldron beamed as his men exalted the victory; they began shouting and hugging and leaping onto one another and pummeling each other on the back. It reminded me of a locker-room celebration after a football championship match. All they lacked was champagne with which to douse themselves.

The cheering continued for a few moments, whereupon, by no sign or word that I could discern, it concluded. The prince issued a few brief words and everyone sprang into action, scattering across the hillside to the bodies of the slain. Their dead comrades were carried with all pomp to the stream and laid out beside the water. Stones were arranged over the bodies and a mound quickly, but carefully, raised.

The enemy dead were left where they had fallen. But each corpse was decapitated and the heads stacked neatly into a pyramid like so many ripe cabbages. Then their weapons were gathered, along with any ornaments—arm rings, torcs, bracelets, and the like. These were placed in a separate heap next to the severed heads.

Simon joined the others in these tasks, and I was left alone for the while. It was then that my presence on the battlefield was noticed and acknowledged for the first time. For, as the warriors were scouring the hillside for booty, one of them saw me standing apart, still holding the head of the man Simon had killed. The brawny fellow strode up to me and regarded me closely.

Not knowing what else to do, I offered him the head. The warrior behaved as if I had breached polite etiquette. His lips writhed back from his teeth in a grimace. He called over his shoulder to the bard, who turned, saw me, and joined the warrior in his scrutiny.

The bard spoke to me in a voice that sounded willowy and guttural at the same time. I could make nothing of the language, but realized that I had encountered it before—in a much altered form, at least. It had much of the same pattern and resonance as modern Welsh.

I stood grinning like an idiot, still holding the head. The bard turned abruptly and called to the prince, who came at once, striding down the hill. With him came several other warriors, and all at once I found myself under the stern examination of the prince and surrounded by naked, blue-stained bodies of powerful warriors—none of whom appeared particularly pleased to see me.

Prince Meldron, like his bard before him, spoke to me in his proto-Gaelic speech. I answered in my own tongue, which caused a small sensation—they murmured excitedly and pointed at my shoes and trousers. A few reached out to touch my bare skin with fingers extended gingerly. They stared at me and at the head I held, as if unwilling to believe their eyes at either curiosity.

Simon appeared in the press around me and came to my rescue. He stepped beside me and placed his hand on my shoulder; he pointed to me and to the dripping head in my grasp—jabbering all the while in their strange tongue. I was flabbergasted by his fluency. This was the same Simon whose linguistic prowess began and ended at the wine list on a French menu. Even more astounding, the bard addressed him solemnly. Simon answered quickly, unhesitatingly, keeping his hand on my shoulder all the while.

This colloquy continued for a short while, and then the bard nodded slowly, turned to the prince, and, I suppose, offered his learned opinion. The prince listened for a moment, then raised his hand. The bard fell silent. Meldron pulled on his mustache, scrutinizing me with sharp appraisal, as if making up his mind about me.

"What's happening?" I asked in a desperate whisper.

"Shh!" Simon warned, pinching the side of my neck to make me shut up.

Meldron concluded his rumination then, for he waved Simon aside and moved to stand before me, towering head and shoulders above me. I had no idea what to expect: A sharp dagger thrust in the ribs? A kiss of welcome? A slap in the face? A poke in the eye?

He did none of those things. Instead, he reached out to the hand that held the enemy's head, took hold of my wrist, raised it, and held it up. The head dangled grotesquely, dribbling blood from the raw neck stump. The prince spoke some words to all those looking on, which included the entire war host by now, and then he placed his free hand, palm up, beneath the obscenely dripping head.

Blood puddled in his palm. And when he had collected enough, he took it and poured it over me. Disgust and loathing churned inside me; I wanted to vomit. I wanted to die. But he held me fast by the wrist, so I stood in mute agony while he drizzled blood over my head. Then he lowered his hand and smeared my cheek with the residue.

My flesh crawled under his touch.

No sooner had the prince finished, than his bard, Ruadh, likewise marked me—reaching out, gathering blood and smearing it down either side of my neck, and over my heart in a bright, warm, crimson streak.

My repugnant baptism was far from finished. For I was made to endure the same appalling courtesy at the hands of the entire gathering, as one by one each warrior took blood and marked me with it. Some splotched my pale flesh with designs similar to their own; others simply left a handprint. When they had finished, my upper torso was well-nigh covered in congealing blood. Words cannot express the disgust and abhorrence I endured.

When the last of the warriors had smeared me, Meldron released my wrist, turned to the heap of weapons and ornaments, and selected an item—discarding two gold and several silver objects before settling on a big bronze armband, which he slipped over my hand and pushed onto my upper arm over my biceps. This done, the company erupted in shouts of approval, and I was treated to a solid thumping, as the warriors pummeled me with hearty backslaps. In all, it was a thoroughly disagreeable experience. If I could have melted into a crack in the ground, I surely would have.

Prince Meldron then began to divide the spoils and plunder among his men. Each warrior received something—an ornament or a weapon, some trinket of gold or silver. Everyone hoorayed and laughed and made merry over this, generally behaving like rowdy children on Christmas morning.

In no time at all the loot disappeared. Then the prince remounted his horse, cried for his war band to follow, and they all moved off at a run. Simon stepped beside me, grinning. "Well done, brother," he said, slapping me on the back. "You're in."

"Well done! It was awful. I thought I was going to puke." With a shock, I realized I still held the warrior's head. I let the gruesome memento drop to the ground and wiped my sticky hand on my trousers. I shivered with distaste. "I stink. I've got to get cleaned up."

"Pick it up," he ordered flatly.

"I'm not carrying that hideous thing around."

Simon's temper flared. "Stupid! That hideous thing saved your life just now. You are expected to bring it back with you."

"What?" I demanded shrilly. "You must be out of your mind!"

He pointed at the head, lying faceup in the grass. "That is the enemy tribe's champion you killed—"

"*I* killed! Wait one minute, buster. I never killed anyone! I—"

"And if you haven't guessed, you've been made a warrior in Meldryn Mawr's war band," he told me. "Now, pick up that head, and let's go before we are left behind."

He turned on his heel and, clutching a long spear the prince had given him, trotted off after the others. With supreme reluctance, I retrieved the hateful head and ran to catch up with Simon. "Where are we going?"

"Back to the caer," he explained. "It isn't far."

"The caer—what caer? What for?"

"I'll explain everything later," he promised. "Believe me, we don't want to be seen lagging behind."

He ran on and I followed as well as I could, clutching my life-saving trophy and cursing the day of my birth.

14

CAER MODORNN

The caer turned out to be a simple timber fortress atop a flattened hill. The hill soared above a placid river which meandered through a broad valley in a wide, slow sweep of shining water. As Simon had indicated, the king's stronghold was not far from the battlefield. All the same, I was breathless and exhausted with running by the time we reached the river.

The war band had drawn up at the water's edge to watch the prince, who continued into the river and halted halfway across, whereupon he withdrew a gold arm ring from among those he had collected as his share of the plunder. He held the arm ring to the sun, said something which I could not understand, and then heaved the golden trinket upriver as far as he could throw. I saw it flash in the air and plunge without a ripple.

The warriors cheered, and everyone splashed into the water at once. I floundered across the shallow fording place, climbed the far bank, and made my weary way up the steep hill track to the caer, last of the troop.

I expected something grand and imposing, but I was disappointed. Once we were past the narrow wooden gate, the caer turned out to be nothing more than an enclosed campsite. There were a dozen or so skin-and-pole tents scattered across the hilltop inside the encircling palisade. Numerous fire rings marked the various places where the warriors gathered to eat their meals and to sleep.

It was rude and crude, exhibiting none of the magnificence I believed existed in the Otherworld. As far as I could tell, this Meldryn Mawr, whoever he might be, was monarch of a modest wooden cattle pen.

Upon our arrival, those who had stayed behind to hold the fort gathered around to hear the juicy details of the day's exploits from their comrades. It was clear, by the exaggerated excitement of all concerned—listener and braggart alike—that the excursion had already taken on a rich luster of glory.

And I, owing to Simon's bald-faced lie, became the object of a considerable amount of this excitement. Killing a champion was powerful stuff, apparently. The way everyone behaved, what with all the shouting, laughing, and leaping around, one would have thought I, David, had beaned Goliath and routed the Philistines with my slingshot.

I was poked and prodded and generally slapped happily from one end of the camp to the other. My clothing was examined with curiosity, and the ghastly head in my grasp made much of. When at last a huge, brawny warrior, whom I took to be the king's champion, approached with spear in hand and, through pantomime, offered to spike the head for me, I gave up my dubious prize only too gladly.

With Prince Meldron looking on, the warrior expertly mounted the severed head upon the spear and drove the shaft into the ground at my feet. He then seized each of my arms in his crushing grip and kissed me on both of my blooded cheeks. This sealed my acceptance by the warrior band. All whooped and hollered as if some great deliverance had been performed among them. And I was treated to another round of backslaps and thumpings.

"You are in, my friend," said Simon, when the commotion died down somewhat. Everyone went about their business, and we were left alone for the moment. "We can relax now."

"Good." I regarded my gore-smeared torso with loathing. "Can I wash? Is that allowed?"

"Better not. Tomorrow, maybe," he said. "It's your initiation badge. Wear it proudly. Most of these men have trained for battle since they were infants, so you're getting off lightly. You should be grateful."

I cast my eyes upon Simon's blue-stained body. "But look at you, Simon. I would never have recognized you."

"This is just war paint," he explained, then extended his arms. "But these are the real thing." I saw that each inner arm had a bold blue tattoo in the distinctive Celtic design of intricate interwoven braided whorls. "This one is a salmon," he said proudly, indicating his left arm. "And this one is a stag." He lifted his right arm for my inspection. "I got them for killing enemy warriors—five each."

"You've killed ten men?" I gasped.

"I might have received a torc for my kill today," he said, somewhat peevishly. "A champion—that was my best one yet."

"Simon, what has happened to you?" I was still shaken by the battle, the scene still fresh in my mind.

"Happened to me?" He snarled and jerked his thumb at the nearby spear. "If I hadn't done what I did, it would be *your* head on the pole right now. Don't you forget it. I saved your life."

"And I'm grateful, believe me," I insisted. "It's just that—"

"Wandering out on a battlefield like that," he continued angrily. "If the Cruin hadn't killed you, the Llwyddi would have." Simon stooped to a cloth bundle at his feet, unwrapped it, and shook out a long shirt of fine yellow cloth.

"Who?"

"Clan Cruin," he said, putting his arms into the sleeves of the shirt.

"They are the enemy we fought today. We are the Llwyddi." He unrolled a pair of yellow and black checked trousers and drew them on.

"What was the fight about?"

"King Meldryn and one of the Cruin kings had a falling out over some hunting hounds." He sat down cross-legged on the ground and began pulling on soft leather boots.

"Dogs? Did you say dogs?" I plopped down beside him.

"The Cruin king said that Meldryn's hunting dogs stank."

"What? You mean to tell me that all that—that slaughter was over an insult to some dogs?"

"Don't be an ass. Of course it is more than that. There is honor at stake here."

"Oh, good. Glad to hear it. Dozens of men lost their lives today because somebody said King Meldryn has smelly dogs! I don't believe it!"

"Keep your voice down! You don't understand." He laced and tied one boot.

"Sorry, Simon, but I came this close to getting murdered out there, and I—"

"You did not," he said flatly, his lips drawing back from his teeth. He glared at me, then softened. "You should have seen your face," he said with a laugh. "I never saw anyone so scared! It was priceless."

"Yeah, thanks."

"Actually," he continued, more the Simon I knew, "you were lucky to find us at all. We are going home tomorrow." He laced and tied the remaining boot.

"Why? You mean this isn't the king's fortress?"

"This?" Simon dismissed it with an impatient flick of his hand. "This is just an overnight stopping place. Meldryn Mawr has hundreds of these scattered from one end of the realm to the other. This is just a small force made up of some of the younger warriors. We are only out here to avenge the affront to the king's honor; then we go back to Sycharth."

"We?" I heard the unmistakable note of pride in Simon's voice. I asked him again: "Simon, what has happened to you? What is going on here?"

"Nothing has happened to me. As you see, I am fit and happy. I have never felt better in my life." He turned the question back on me. "What are you doing here?"

"I don't know. I came to find you," I said and decided to skip a lengthy explanation of all I'd been through since his disappearance. "There's some trouble, Simon. We don't belong here. We've got to find a way to go back—you know, back to the real world."

Simon frowned. I could tell he did not like the idea. "That is not going to be easy, chum."

"Maybe not," I allowed, "but we've got to try. And the sooner, the better." I began telling him about the nexus and plexus and Professor Nettleton's notions about interdependent reality and all the rest. I finished with a much-abbreviated version of Nettleton's Unraveling Plexus Theory and the danger we were all in because of it.

Simon listened, staring at the ground the whole time, his eyes distant and cold. He did not say anything; he just nodded and pulled up a few blades of grass, which he twirled between his palms. I could not tell whether what I had said made any impression on him at all.

"Did you hear me, Simon?" I asked when I had finished.

"I heard." He glanced up at me and flung the grass away impatiently.

"What's wrong?"

"Nothing," he replied. "I told you, I'm fine. Never better."

"Then why the long face? I thought you would be glad to see me. Really, it's a miracle that I found you at all. I still can't believe I'm here."

"Do they miss me?" he wondered idly.

"Of course they do! Your parents are worried. They probably even have the police looking for you by now. You'll be an official missing person next. I'm telling you, the sooner we get back, the better for everyone."

Simon glanced away. I thought he would make some reply. Instead, he began to tell me about what he had been doing since crossing over. "It was rough at first," he said, and again I noticed that odd, distant look. "But it was late summer when I came here, so I could find fruit and berries to eat. When the Llwyddi found me, I had been wandering around the hills for—I don't know how long, weeks at least.

"A hunting party came upon me camped by the river. From my clothes and all that, they realized I was a stranger, so they hustled me off to the king. The Chief Bard took one look at me and declared me a visitor from the Otherworld. You can imagine the stir that caused . . ."

I nodded but could not actually imagine any such thing. I could hardly credit what had happened to *me* in the few short hours I had been in this strange world.

Simon continued. "I was given a place in the tribe—an honorary member. But I had no status, no name."

"No name? Why didn't you tell them your name?"

He shook his head slightly. "It doesn't work that way. You have to earn your name here. I'm well on my way to earning a great name."

I remembered the old Celtic practice of withholding a person's name until they achieved some great feat or special deed by which a name would be revealed and conferred. Also, a person's name was not common currency to be bandied about lightly. Many heroes of legend held their true name in secret, never revealing it to anyone lest an enemy get hold of it and cause them harm.

"So what do they call you?" I asked, fascinated.

"They call me Sylfenu. It must mean 'found,' because they found me by the river. Killing the Cruin champion today would have done the trick." He shrugged and added, "But never mind. I'll have another chance soon enough."

"They made you a warrior?"

"That was my choice," he said. "I reckoned the best way to get to the top was to become a warrior. A warrior has more status, more freedom to come and go and do as he pleases. Warriors are not expected to do anything but hunt and fight, and they get all the gold and glory."

"Sounds great," I said. "But they also get killed in pretty short order."

"Sometimes, if they are unlucky," he allowed. "But I have never been unlucky." He grinned maliciously. "*You* are a warrior, too, now, don't forget."

"Thanks for reminding me." I thrust the thought aside. I did not plan on staying long enough to see, let alone participate in, another battle like the one I had witnessed that day. I changed the subject. "Why did you throw my watch away?"

Simon simply laughed. "It would have been trouble if they had seen you with it. Time means nothing here."

"Where is *here*, Simon? Where are we? What is this place?"

"This is Caer Modornn," he said, climbing to his feet. He took up a wide woven cloth belt of green and black stripes and wrapped it around his waist, using it to close the front of his shirt. "Follow me; I'll show you around."

We walked across the compound, and I identified the missing element I had noticed earlier: there were no women at the caer. I mentioned this to Simon. "Of course not," he told me. "We are just a small raiding party. Women don't tag along on this sort of outing."

"Oh. Do they tag along other times?"

He arched his eyebrows. "You'll see."

We reached the entrance to the caer and proceeded along the narrow path which topped the steep-sided ditch outside the timbered wall. We walked around the perimeter of the hill a short way and stopped. Below us stretched the broad, shining length of the river we had crossed earlier.

"That is the Modornn River," he told me. "It forms the eastern boundary of Llwyddi lands. On the other side—where we fought today—is Cruin land."

He turned and continued on a bit further. When we stopped, I turned in the direction Simon pointed and saw, in the misty, hill-rimmed distance, the silver glint of a wide expanse of river. "Beyond those hills to the northwest is Myr Llydan, a gulf of considerable size."

We tramped a bit further around the circumference of the caer. I observed that the land changed, rising into ragged foothills and plateaus. Beyond these, sharp mountains towered—range after range, marching into the distance in ragged ranks until they were lost in cloud and blue mist. "That is Cethness," Simon explained simply. "In the heart of Cethness the Llwyddi maintain a fortress of stone which has no rival anywhere. It is called Findargad, and it is the ancient seat of the clan."

I peered at the solid ranks of mountains, blue and hazy on the horizon, and then we moved on. When we stopped again, I saw once more the gentle hills and the broad river basin and, behind these, the dark margins of woodland and forest. "To the south," he said, pointing along the curving waterway, "lies Sycharth, Meldryn Mawr's palace and stronghold. With Findargad in the north, and Sycharth in the south, he rules most of the West."

"The west of what?" I asked.

"Prydain," he replied. "One of the three realms. The others are Caledon, in the north, and Llogres in the south."

I knew these names from the old, old legends. "What is it called—the whole thing, all three realms together—what is it called?"

Simon scanned the vast landscape shimmering before us. "This," he said, lifting a hand to the grand panorama, "this is Albion."

"Albion," I repeated, thinking it extremely odd that Otherworld names were known in the manifest world as well. "But that is historical," I said. "Why should the Otherworld have a historical connection?"

"Who says it has?" Simon countered.

"Well, don't you think it's a little strange that a classical name should be known here?"

"You're the Celtic scholar," he informed me. "You work it out. I am merely telling you what the people here call this place."

The Britons of old called their island Alba—and to many it was Alba still. Old Nettles was right, and I was wrong—or, rather, backwards: the Otherworld did not have a historical foundation; the historical world had an *Otherworldly* foundation.

I grasped this truth, was made weak by the staggering weight of it; and then it slipped from me, elusive again and out of reach. But I knew that I had, for the briefest of instants, encompassed this revelation: Albion, the primal archetype of the Celtic world.

The web between the worlds was wide and many-stranded. If Nettles was to be believed—and he had not led me astray so far— then this place, this *Albion*, was the Form of forms, the original pattern for all that flowed into creation of the unique and magnificent wonder known as the Celtic spirit. I should not be overly surprised to discover other remarkable similarities.

Our circuit completed, Simon and I returned to the caer. Some of the warriors—not having had their fill of excitement for the day— had begun a wrestling match. A large circle had formed around the combatants, who stood inside the ring: seven pairs of wrestlers, each grappling with the other. The main idea seemed to be to lift one's opponent into the air by any means possible and body slam him to the ground. By some method I could not perceive, the losers were gradually eliminated and the winners brought to face each other. When the last two contenders were left standing, the wagering began.

The exchange was quick and lively, and everyone from the prince down placed a bet with one or another of his comrades. There was so much shouting and jostling, I thought the betting would come to blows. But, just as quickly as it had begun, the wagering ceased, and the wrestling began again.

The two in the ring squared off. They circled one another warily, walking on the balls of their feet, naked limbs glistening. I think they had oiled themselves to make gripping more difficult; it made them look as if they were carved of polished marble. Certainly, the finest Greek statues were never as graceful as the wrestlers in the ring. Flawless, I thought; perfection in motion. One dark-haired, the other fair—but each as impeccably formed as the other.

They revolved slowly, moving in tighter circles, nearer and nearer. All at once, the fair-haired man lunged at his opponent's knees, wrapping his arms around them and lifting them in the same swift motion. The dark wrestler clasped his hands and swung them down between his attacker's shoulder blades with a blow I thought would have stunned an ox.

Indeed, the fair-haired man went down on one knee, but did not release his hold. His dark rival raised his hands above his shoulders into his antagonist's stomach; the man let out a tremendous groan and doubled over. The lighter warrior stood, lifting his dark opponent off the ground—just a little, but enough to throw him off balance. They both fell, then. However, the blond wrestler landed squarely on the dark-haired warrior without touching the ground. The match was over just that quick, and the fair-haired warrior was accorded the victory.

Catcalls and jeers filled the air, and I gathered from the general demeanor of the wagering crowd that the blond man had been the underdog. The bets were settled: rings and armbands changed hands, brooches and knives and spears were relinquished to new owners. The winners were jovial, the losers gracious. Everyone seemed blissfully happy with the proceedings.

There was another match then—pitting seven more pairs against each other and narrowing the group to the two best—and then another. I feared it might go on all night but, as the third match finished, the crowd broke up and I saw the reason: the cooking fires had been lit and there was meat roasting on spits all across the camp. But before the food came drink: great draughts of a pale amber liquid I took to be ale, served in huge cups and bowls and horns and beakers—any sort of vessel, in fact, that could hold a quantity of liquid.

At several strategic places around the caer, large vats had been set up. The warriors clustered around these vats with their jars, which they filled by plunging them into the frothy brew. Simon led me to the nearest vat, where a copper beaker was thrust into my hand by a big burly fellow with long brown locks and a yellow leather apron wrapped around his waist. The man watched me keenly and made drinking motions with his hand.

"He is the brewer. He wants you to taste it," Simon explained. "Drink up!"

"Cheers!" I lifted the beaker to my lips. The liquid smelled pleasantly beery, and the taste was nicely sharp, if a bit sour. I swallowed a mouthful demurely—only to have it get up my nose. I sneezed and choked at the same time, spewing most of my mouthful at the brewmaster.

The brewer apparently considered this high affirmation of his subtle art. He laughed out loud and clapped me on the back with a heavy hand, jarring me so that I sloshed half the contents of my beaker over myself. The beer baptism combined with the dried blood spattered over my torso and ran down my belly in ruddy streaks. This made the jolly brewmaster laugh all the more. He threw back his head and guffawed loudly.

"Oh, well done," Simon crabbed. "I can't take you anywhere."

"You might have warned me," I muttered, shaking the liquid from my hands and arms. "What is it, ginger?"

"Spruce, I think," answered Simon. "It's an acquired taste."

"You're telling me."

"I suggest you acquire it as soon as possible. They drink it by the vat around here. You don't want to be seen stinting."

"God forbid," I murmured, gazing into my cup. The brewer took this to be a sign that I needed a top-up. He snatched away my cup and filled it to the brim, gave it to me, and made his "bottoms up" sign again. I lifted the cup and quaffed the cool ale, wiping my mouth on my bare forearm.

The brewmaster refilled my cup yet again, and Simon and I withdrew from the vat to sit down and nurse our drinks and wait for the food. "Is it like this all the time?" I asked.

"Like what?"

"Like this—you know, this crazy." I indicated the whooping, hollering clusters of revelers all around us.

Simon pursed his lips at my prudishness. "If you think this is crazy, just wait till you see a real victory celebration."

We tended our drinks in silence; I sipped mine slowly, as I was already beginning to feel a buzz from the ale—due to a combination of shock, exhaustion, spent adrenaline, and an empty stomach. We drank and watched the rosy dusk fade to a stunning twilight. I had never known such a brilliant evening; it seemed to me that my soul expanded to embrace the shimmering stars as they appeared in the radiant blue firmament. I saluted each in turn: "Hail, brother! And welcome. I recognize you."

By the time the food arrived, I was in my cups. My head all but flopped on my chest as I forced my jaws to chew the meat from a nicely roasted haunch cradled in my lap. The meat was savory and good, but I was too tired to eat much of it. I fell asleep clutching my empty beaker in one hand and my unfinished supper in the other. The last thing I remember was the bright fire leaping high into a night grown loud with singing and laughing.

15

SYCHARTH

I awoke to Simon's foot in my ribs. "Wake up," he said, prodding me with his toe. "We're leaving."

"What?" I came awake with a start—then experienced the sudden implosion of my skull into the empty space vacated by my brain. "Oooh! I drank too much!"

Simon favored me with his fox-bark laugh. "You'll get used to it—if you live long enough."

I opened my eyes and peered blearily around. My cup lay by my head, which rested on the unfinished haunch of meat that had been my supper. Someone had thrown a cloak over my bare torso, but otherwise I was as I had dropped the night before. I stank of ale and blood—my body was still daubed with gore. My face was rough; my eyes felt as if I had gravel sprinkled under my eyelids. My tongue seemed three times life size, furred and leathery. My bladder felt like a water balloon filled much too full—any movement would result in certain disaster.

"Kill me now and be done with it," I moaned.

Simon took me by the arm and lifted me to my feet, where I swayed unsteadily. "I feel like death."

"Come on. We can wash in the river."

The sun had just risen, and the camp was barely beginning to stir as we made our way out the gate and down the steep track to the fording place. A few warriors were already washing downstream where the water was deeper, standing hip deep in the ice-cold stream, scrubbing themselves furiously.

"Get those clothes off," Simon said, stripping quickly.

I folded the cloak and put it on a rock, then slipped out of my shoes, socks, and bloodstained trousers. The nearest warriors observed my underpants with interest—I guessed boxer shorts had yet to become a fashion force. I whisked these off as well and stumbled into the freezing water, slipping awkwardly over the round, loaf-sized stones.

Simon had waded out a fair way and was ducking and dousing himself with great gusto. Some of the warriors called out to him, and from the way they spoke to him, I could see that he was a favorite.

Meanwhile, I edged cautiously deeper into the river—the water pricking my flesh like ice needles. A nearby warrior waded over to me and, grinning and gesturing, handed me what I took to be a rock. It turned out to be a chunk of tawny soap, which smelled of tallow and some sort of herbal fragrance I could not place. He took the chunk back and showed me how to lather up. I suppose from the mystified expression on my face, he surmised I had never seen soap.

He washed himself thoroughly and with a zeal that approached fanaticism. When he'd finished, he rinsed himself, handed me the soap once more, and retreated to the riverbank. I had barely begun soaping myself when the warrior returned with a small curved blade that looked like a seashell. It was a razor. With much grimacing and gesturing he showed me how to shave with it. He rubbed the back of his hand against my disgraceful stubble and clucked his tongue, then pressed the slender blade into my hand and splashed away.

Once I got used to the water, I began scrubbing away, grateful for the luxury of soap to rid my hide of its odious markings. Watching my reflection in the water, I managed to shave without slitting my throat. I passed soap and razor on to a waiting warrior when I finished, and found myself much refreshed for a thorough scraping and scouring.

The horror of the previous day's battle disappeared with the rusty stain streaming from my limbs; all fear and disgust dissolved in the blessed bath and flowed away. In no time, it seemed as if the carnage of the day before had never happened, as if the slaughter was but a troubled dream that evaporated in dawn's clear light. I washed and felt absolutely reborn.

Indeed, I cannot remember ever spending a better time bathing: the air was crisp and clean, the day fresh as the first day of creation. The sun was warm and the western breeze soft and light. The clear water sparkled where the warriors sported and splashed, and the sound of their voices as they hailed one another filled me with contentment.

I lay back in the water and floated for a while, thinking: *This is me in the Otherworld, and I'm taking a bath. I'm swimming. I'm happy.*

Simon returned from his swim and said, "We should go up if we want something to eat. We'll be leaving soon."

I found my clothes and, though I loathed putting the filthy things back on, dressed, and followed Simon up to the caer. Breakfast was hard brown bread and cold meat from the night before, washed down with more ale. I went easy on the ale but wolfed down the bread and meat.

Then someone blew a long, sharp blast on a horn, and we decamped. Prince Meldron and his bard moved out first, followed by the other mounted warriors. The rest of us trailed along behind on foot. Three wagons bearing supplies and weapons came after. We did not move in ordered ranks, but ranged as we would—in clumps of two or three or more, tramping easily and rapidly through the low, wide valley along the riverside trail.

We walked a good while, and some of the warriors began to sing. Although I could not understand the words, I enjoyed their strong voices and the obvious pleasure they took in singing. The sun rose higher, and it felt good on my bare skin. As I walked, a contentment I had never known, and never would have believed could exist, drew over me, enfolded me.

What would I give, I asked myself, *to stay with these people forever?*

The thought was ridiculous, of course. I could not stay—*would* not stay a moment longer than necessary. I had come to find Simon, had found him, and now must find a way back to the real world.

"Where are we going?" I asked, falling into step beside Simon.

"We are returning to Sycharth."

"The king's place," I said.

"Yes, the king's place."

"Is it far?"

"Nine days," he told me matter-of-factly.

"Walking?"

"Walking," he confirmed.

"Oh."

"Something wrong?" He gave me a sidelong glance. "Another engagement?"

"It isn't that. But—"

"I suppose walking is beneath you."

"Give me a break! I'm new here, okay? I only wanted to know what's going on."

Simon frowned but did not reply.

"What's got into you, Simon? I thought you would be glad to see me. Instead, you act as though I was your kid sister with a bad case of smallpox or something."

"Sorry," he grunted but did not mean it.

"That's it, isn't it?" I told him. "You wish I'd stayed away. But now

I'm here, and you're afraid I'm going to spoil your good time. Well, too bad, but I'm here, and you'll just have to get used to it."

He stopped walking and jerked me around to face him. "Look!" he said through gritted teeth. "Get this straight: I did not ask you to come here. I did not ask anyone to rescue me. I can look out for myself. But now that you are here, I strongly advise you to take it easy. I saved your neck once; I may not be able to save it again. Got that?"

"Loud and clear."

"Good."

"But I'm not staying, Simon. Neither are you. We've got to go back—as soon as possible. The longer we stay, the worse it gets." I reminded him of our previous discussion about the dangers of messing about in the Otherworld. "It isn't safe, Simon. We could be doing irreparable damage."

"I see," he replied, nodding slowly. "You mean that just by being here, our presence could change things. If we change things here, it would change things in the real world."

"Right—and there's no telling what could happen." I was glad Simon understood so readily. "We have to find out where the next portal is, and when it's open."

"That might not be so easy," he said.

"Couldn't we ask what's-his-name—Ruadh, the prince's bard?"

Simon gave a slight dismissive shake of his head. "Look," he said reasonably, "leave it to me."

"But—"

"Just until we reach Sycharth. We can't do anything until then, anyway. Give it a few days, okay? In the meantime, take it easy. Have a look around. You might get to like the place."

"Well"—I paused, gazing at the bright world around me—"all right. I suppose it wouldn't hurt anything to wait a few days."

"Good," he said, flashing his famous smile. "Leave it to me."

"You'll take care of it?"

"I'll take care of it," he assured me. I felt the weight of responsibility lift from my shoulders. "Don't worry. It's really a fabulous place. It's paradise."

So we began our march through that shining valley, the silvery Modornn flowing in clear, glimmering ripples beside us. It was, as Simon said, a fabulous world—so fresh and unspoiled, immaculate and alive with beauty. The scenery moved me to rapture. As we walked along, I would catch a glimpse of mist-clouded hills, blue in the distance, or a stretch of sparkling silver water sweeping slowly around a stand of supple white birches. The sight of a brown speckled trout leaping in the water, or yellow lichen grown thick on a blue-black stone, or the sound of birdsong falling from the clear sky above . . . stopped me in my tracks.

I swear, more than once tears came to my eyes. My breath caught in my throat, and my heart was pierced time and again by pangs of longing—a hunger for completeness akin to worship. For, merely walking through that perfect glen, I was reminded of my gross poverty of spirit. That simple natural beauty could move me so, struck me as both a revelation and a shame. Was I really so bereft of wonder in my life that the sight of a sun-dappled hillside could provoke such powerful feelings?

In this radiant paradise of a world I felt deeply the privation of years of wandering through life blind to the beauty around me. And I regretted it bitterly. I was a blind man granted sight, and I both cherished the gift and lamented the waste and ignorance that it revealed. I walked as one drunk through a land at once alien and intimate in the smallest detail.

More than once, I caught myself muttering aloud: "This is it! This is how it is supposed to be." Although, if anyone had asked me what I meant by that, I could not have answered. The experience was still too new, too fantastic for me to make rational sense of it. I could only walk and wonder.

And, as I walked, I felt the ineluctable tide-pull of the Otherworld's allure begin to bear me away. It wielded an irresistible enchantment; and the more I saw of its splendors, the weaker grew my will to resist. I became a willing captive to its charms, and soon found the thought of returning to the manifest world intolerable. So much so that I stopped thinking about returning and simply gave myself up to the splendor and richness of all I saw around me.

For seven days we traversed the generous Vale of Modornn, following the river south, moving quickly, camping beside the river at twilight and hurrying on at daybreak. At the end of the seventh day's march, the valley spread and flattened to marsh and meadowland bounded by woodlands which covered the gently rolling hills. We left the river and struck off across country. At dusk on the ninth day, we came in sight of King Meldryn Mawr's southern fortress: Sycharth.

The settlement stood a little above the flat land, on a bluff overlooking the sea. The place was enormous; it could be seen from far away: a splendid crown surmounting the hilltop, glowing red in the fiery light of the setting sun like a city carved of gemstone. Even from a distance, it appeared the seat of a great and powerful king: imposing, grand, formidable. And yet, somehow, hospitable—as if the man who ruled such a place could be approached with some expectation of welcome.

The slopes leading to the caer had been cleared for fields, in which laborers toiled to ready the earth for spring planting. As the war band approached, the farmers downed tools and ran to greet us on the trail. From the warmth of the reception, I guessed that more than a few of the farmers were kinsmen to warriors.

We continued on up the trail to the caer, and had almost reached the entrance, when out through the wide-open gates rushed a welcoming party of women and children. The warriors on horseback dismounted and were instantly surrounded. Those of us on foot trooped along to join them and were accorded the same enthusiastic greeting—laughing embraces, children taking our hands, and garlands of spring flowers placed around our necks. It was the sort of homecoming one always imagines, but which never happens in real life.

"Is everyone so young?" I wondered, seeing no one above a robust and youthful middle age among the welcoming party. I turned to Simon with a sudden inspiration. "Doesn't anyone grow old here?"

Simon, winking at an arresting young lady with long chestnut tresses, confirmed my suspicion. "Not exactly. They seem to live forever—at least, they don't age like we do." Then he grew suddenly earnest, turned, and looked me full in the face. "You won't get any older, either, as long as you're here. Think of that."

Never grow old! Before I could ponder the implications of this staggering revelation, the crowd began moving. We were all but lifted up and carried bodily into the caer. I resisted the surge, staying well back to the last; and as others streamed around me, I turned away. The gleaming arc of a wide sea arm shone darkly to the south, now deep violet in the dusky light. *Yes, think of it,* I told myself. *Think long and hard, Lewis! What would you give to live forever in this shining land? Forever!* I stood dumbfounded at the possibility, trying to take it in, and Simon stepped beside me.

"That's Muir Glain," he informed me, mistaking my dazed expression for awe. "It is a sea estuary. The king's shipyard is in the inlet just there"—he pointed in the direction of the river—"between Sycharth and the Modornn."

He turned away quickly and hurried to join the festive crowd trooping up to the caer. I followed reluctantly, all at once a little uncertain of my reception. Simon's words reminded me how much a stranger I was after all. I bluffed away my uneasiness by scrutinizing the premises.

Two higher timber walls extended out from the towering palisade.

The track passed between these walls before reaching the gate, forming a perilous bottleneck for any attacking force. Though black with age, the timbers were stout and in excellent repair—a secure haven for a powerful monarch.

We passed through the tall timber gate and emerged onto a flat, grass-covered yard, large enough to hold an army. All along the perimeter of the yard stood low round stone houses with steep thatched roofs. Some of these houses were larger than others, but most were small, little more than sleeping quarters, I surmised. I also saw among the houses two large oblong structures, and, from the smoke rising through the central smoke hole, I guessed that these were cookhouses containing the kitchens and ovens and firepits.

Across this yard rose the high-peaked golden thatch of the king's hall: a massive barn of a building, easily dwarfing all surrounding it, made of oak beams and stone infill. The chinks were stuffed with green and orange moss, giving the walls a peculiar velvety appearance. Two doors large enough for horsemen to ride through two abreast stood open; and, before the doors, two great stone pillars from the top of which flamed two fires in huge iron baskets. The surface of the pillars were graven top to bottom with the most fantastically intricate designs—the heads and bodies of birds and beasts interlaced in endlessly elaborate knots and whorls.

We assembled in the yard before the fire pillars, where we were greeted by a happy throng of the king's subjects and by the king himself, no less, in a handsome chariot. He appeared at the far end of the yard and drove toward the throng, the spokes of the chariot wheels glinting and the plumed heads of the matched team of black horses tossing proudly as he came. From the moment he stepped down from the chariot platform, I could not take my eyes off him. Authority and dominance streamed from him; he moved with supreme confidence and self-possession—a mountain anchored to the center of the earth could not be more secure. His mere physical presence was a command: honor me; obey me.

Meldryn Mawr—his name meant Golden Warrior, as near as I could work out in my rudimentary Celt, and the epithet "Mawr" designated him "Great"—a great golden warrior king, much revered and honored among his people. And golden he was: the flashing torc on his neck was made from three thick strands of braided gold; his belt was a glimmering sash of golden disks woven in a cunning fish-scale pattern; his well-muscled arms sported wide rings of red gold in the shape of entwined serpents with glowing eyes of ruby; his cloak was yellow, with white emblems and edgework, shot through with threads of gold; the sword at his hip was gold-hilted. Behind the king stood a youth, bearing a round white shield, with a rim and center boss of white gold, and a long spear with a blade of burnished gold.

To observe this great king was to gaze upon the sun. His radiance dazzled and his magnificence burned. He was exquisite and awesome in his splendor: fair-haired, his long locks gathered in a manly queue, his mustache full and flowing, his dark eyes calm and grave. Meldryn Mawr's features displayed his noble bloodline: high handsome forehead, straight nose, firm jaw and chin, straight dark brows, and bold cheekbones.

And when he opened his mouth to speak, the voice that issued forth was the voice of a very god—deep and mellifluous, tinged with warmth and humor, and bold in the strength of its authority. I had no doubt that such a voice, when raised in anger, could command the very elements themselves. But then, I had not yet heard his Chief Bard, Ollathir, speak.

The king's bard stood close at his right hand, but a half step behind. Like Ruadh, the Chief Bard wore a simple garb of dun brown, although his cloak was rich purple and his brooch was gold, and he wore a slender torc of gold also. He was a tall, dour-looking man, who, alone among the citizens of the caer, seemed to have any age at all: not old, certainly not elderly, but possessing that air of immense gravity and dignity which sometimes comes to men of august age. Proud and solemn and wise, Ollathir stood serene beside the king, every inch as regal and imposing as any monarch. I had no doubt that here, truly, stood a champion among bards.

The king made a level, sweeping motion with his arm and the assembly fell silent. He spoke briefly; every now and then a word or two sounded familiar to me, and I guessed that he was issuing words of welcome. And then Prince Meldron approached; the two clasped one another's arms and embraced. The prince said something and turned to indicate the warrior band, whereupon the prince's bard stepped up before the king and, placing a fold of his cloak over his head, began singing loudly in a strange, jerky chant.

I saw Simon standing nearby, so, as unobtrusively as possible, I sidled closer. "What's going on?" I whispered.

"Ruadh is reciting the battle for the king," Simon answered.

"What does he know about it? He wasn't there," I said. "Neither of them showed up until it was over."

"Of course they were there. They watched the whole thing from the hilltop."

"What's he saying?"

"He's telling the king and the people that we are brave and invincible, that courage flows in our veins, that we are bears in battle—that sort of thing." He paused and the bard chanted some more. "Now he's describing the battle itself—what kind of day it was, the glen where it took place, how many enemy there were, all that."

I nodded. "I see." The bard chanted a good while longer and then stopped. The king spoke again, holding up his hands in a proclamatory way. "Now what's happening?"

"The king is declaring his honor restored, thanks to the admirable deeds of his warriors. He is calling for a feast to be held in our honor."

I liked the sound of that. I was hungry from walking all day. "Outstanding!" I whispered. "Lead me to it."

"The feast is tomorrow," Simon informed me sourly. "Tonight we rest."

Accordingly, after little more than a bit of bread and a swig of warm beer taken where we stood, we all shuffled off to bed. Those warriors who had wives and families went to their homes; the remainder of us found other places. Simon and I made our way to one of three long, low-roofed buildings—the Warriors' Houses, he called them—to wrap ourselves in woolen cloaks and lie upon pallets of fresh straw.

In the soft darkness, which ebbed and flowed with the sea swell of the warriors' breathing, I have seldom felt so sheltered and secure as I did that night, nor known so rich and deep a rest. Within the walls of the Great King's stronghold, among men who would give blood and life for one another without hesitation, I slept. And I woke before dawn, thinking: *What would I give to wake among such men always?*

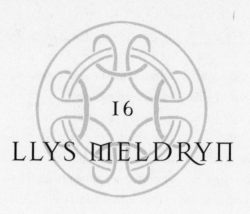

16

LLYS MELDRYN

With daylight the caer leaped to life. The soft night faded in a fiery dawn, and Sycharth's inhabitants shook off their languor and hastened to prepare the feast which their king had proclaimed. Simon had disappeared, and I didn't feel like sitting alone in the Warriors' House. So, wrapped in my borrowed cloak, I wandered where I would, making myself familiar with the lay of the land.

Wherever I looked I saw someone—man, woman, or child— bustling about some task. There was not an idle hand anywhere, except mine. No one gave me anything to do, or even seemed to take notice of me—although I caught some of the children gawking at me.

Sycharth was even larger than I first thought, sheltering perhaps a thousand people. There were three main sections: one of storehouses and granaries, one of livestock pens, one of artisans' and craftsmen's quarters. And, scattered throughout, the dwelling places of the inhabitants, huddled together in random clusters, usually three or more around a central cookhouse or kitchen. Threads of silvery smoke wafted up through the reed thatch of the cookhouses; the smells seeping into the air made my empty stomach grumble.

Every corner of the caer pulsed with sound and activity: from the dull chunk of wood being chopped to the sharp squeal of pigs being slaughtered, and always, everywhere, the voices of the laborers lifted in song—the fortress itself seemed to sing with a cheerful tumult. I meandered here and there, sampling the happy sounds, my fondness for the uncluttered simplicity of life in the caer growing with every step.

There were no streets as such, just a tangle of narrow lanes lacing several wider pathways together. All of the wider pathways were lined with a triple track of dressed stone, which at first puzzled me, until I tumbled to the fact that in seasons of rain the hooves of horses and the wheels of wagons would sink into the mud without this simple paving.

The various structures appeared to be in excellent repair; the livestock pens were full of fat pigs, sheep, and cattle; the artisans' huts were well stocked with goods—all indicating an industrious and prosperous tribe. Even after the most casual perusal, I could well believe Simon's boast that the Llwyddi were the preeminent clan in the land.

This informal survey of the caer occupied me until well past midmorning. Then my growling stomach got the better of me, and I returned to the Warriors' House to find Simon waiting for me—somewhat nervously. "Where have you been?" he demanded.

"Nowhere," I told him. "Just out walking around."

He turned and retrieved a bundle from a nearby pallet. This he placed in my hands, saying, "Put these on and be quick about it."

I untied the bundle and unfolded a pale blue shirt, a pair of dark green trousers with thin red stripes, a brown woven cloth belt, and a pair of the short, soft leather boots, or buskins, which the Llywddi wore. Every item was new and finely made. Glad to be free of my own filthy trousers, I shucked them off and prepared to pull on the new ones.

"The underpants too," Simon intoned. "Get rid of them."

"But—" I hesitated.

"They'll only make you miserable. Anyway, you don't need them."

Dubiously, I discarded my boxer shorts. True, I hadn't had a change of underpants for days, so it was no great loss; but I doubted Simon's assertion that I wouldn't need them. I was also a little sorry to see my good hiking shoes go. The soft boots, or buskins, looked comfortable enough, but I knew I'd miss a stout arch and good, hard sole.

Neither the shirt nor the trousers had buttons or laces of any kind, so Simon showed me how to wrap the long shirtwaist and cinch the trousers with the wide belt, which he wound around my middle twice and tied in front. The shirt and trousers—*siarc* and *breecs*, according to Simon—were on the billowy side, but the buskins fit as if they had been made to order for me.

When I'd finished, Simon stepped back and gave me a critical once-over. He pronounced the effect acceptable, if not exactly sartorially stunning. "That's better. You'll do."

Then he took up another bundle and shook out a bright orange cloak, which he proceeded to arrange about my shoulders. "You fold it like this," he said, showing me how it was done. "Then you pin it to hold it in place . . . like so." He passed a crude bronze pin through the folds at my left shoulder. "Sorry about the brooch."

"That's all right. I don't mind."

"Thing is, if you want a better one you have to earn it. Brooches are a sign of rank around here—the same with torcs and most other baubles."

"Gold for kings, silver for princes, copper for chieftains, and so on," I replied, reciting a bit of Celtic lore.

"That's right," he said with a satisfied nod, "but there are many subtle degrees having to do with size, design, workmanship, and so on. It isn't difficult; you'll catch on."

"Simon," I said seriously, "how do you know so much?" This question had been simmering at the back of my brain ever since I had clapped eyes on Simon on the battlefield. I had not been able to put words to it until just now. "How have you managed it in such a short time?"

He raised one quizzical eyebrow. "What *are* you babbling about?"

"Well, look at you—you're a warrior, you've fought in battles, you know everything about life here, you speak the language like a native. How is that possible? You've only been here a couple months."

"I have been with Clan Llwydd four years," Simon responded solemnly.

"Four years! You can't—" I began, and stopped short. Time in the Otherworld was not the same as time in the real world. Each world marked time differently, and there was no correspondence between them at all. Minutes might be years, years might be hours, might be decades, might be seconds, might be centuries. Who could tell?

This was a fact well documented in the literature of folklore, but I had not fully credited it until now. I felt a pang of dread at the thought that time was passing independently on the other side. What would await us when we returned?

Simon puckered his lips irritably. "Now what's wrong?"

Thrusting my anxiety aside, I grinned back at him. "Nothing. I feel like a real Celt now," I said. "This is great."

"Glad you think so."

I caught a slight undercurrent of waspishness to his words. "Why? What's up?"

"The king is holding court today, and he wants to see you."

"He does? Really?"

"You're high on the agenda, chum."

"I didn't know he knew I was even here."

"Oh, he knows," Simon confirmed flatly. "If Meldron hadn't told him, Ruadh would have. You killed the Cruin champion—remember?"

"Oh, that."

Simon fixed me with a stern and serious stare. "Look, let us have no misunderstandings, right? *You* killed the champion. You have to go along with that, do you understand? You will only embarrass yourself and the other warriors if you deny it now. And it could get you into a lot of trouble."

"All right, Simon. If that's the way you want it. But what's the big deal?"

"I'm not going to argue with you. You don't know the first thing about what goes on here. Just do as I say. This is for your own good, believe me."

"Fine. Wonderful. I'll do as you say."

I must have looked anxious, because Simon grinned suddenly and gave me a punch on the arm. "Don't worry. I'll be right beside you the whole time. Ready?"

"Ready as I'll ever be," I said, and then added, "There is just one thing."

"What now?"

"I know this probably isn't the time," I muttered hesitantly, "but we've got to talk about going back—back to the real world. You said to wait till we got to Sycharth, and—well, we're here. Maybe we should say something to the king."

"You're right," Simon replied. For an instant, I thought he was going to be reasonable. "This isn't the time. We'll talk to the king after the feast. Come on, enjoy yourself a little, Lewis. Relax, will you? We'll get this all sorted out."

"All right," I agreed reluctantly. "After the feast."

"Let's go, then." Simon turned and led me from the lodge. We made our way to the king's hall, retracing our steps of the night before, and I noticed that the nearer we came, the busier the bustle. In the yard before the king's hall, long boards had been set up on trestles, with benches flanking either side. A troop of men and boys was constructing a small pyramid of oaken casks in the center of the yard. Several dozen warriors lingered near the entrance to the hall. And there were a score or more horses tethered at the far end of the grassy expanse.

Simon saw me eyeing the horses and said, "Some of Meldryn Mawr's chieftains have come to the llys."

Llys is an old Briton word for court—designating either the place of meeting or the meeting itself. It was, I knew, often something of an occasion. Legal business was conducted, commerce and trade transacted, and personal squabbles and misfortunes set to rights. Anyone with a gripe or grievance could approach the seat of judgment and speak his piece before the king, who would mete out the required justice. A king's word was the law of the realm, the only law his people knew. Fortunes could be made or lost, lives forever changed, depending on the disposition of the king.

That I should be included in this high drama sent alternating waves of dread and excitement coursing through me: What did the king want with me? What would he say? What would *I* say? I found it difficult to abide by Simon's dictum to relax; enjoying myself was right out of the question. We paused at the entrance to the hall, and Simon cast a quick look at the sun. "They will begin soon," he said. "We'd better go inside and take our places." He checked my appearance one last time. "Too bad we didn't have time for you to shave."

"Oh, sure, now you tell me," I mumbled, rubbing my bristly chin, suddenly self-conscious and peeved at Simon for not taking better care of me.

We passed between the stone pillars, acknowledging the warriors loitering near the entrance—some called out to us, and Simon answered them. There was laughter all around. I guessed the joke was at my expense, but I smiled nervously and nodded. And we proceeded.

A huge, fierce-looking warrior stood in the entrance, imposing the proper reverence upon those who entered. At a word from Simon, the muscled giant moved aside to let us pass. There was no mistaking the glance of disdain he paid me as I passed beneath his sight; clearly he considered me no champion-killer. "That is Paladyr," Simon explained. "Meldryn's champion. Great chap."

The hall was cool and dark. When my eyes adjusted to the dim light which slipped fitfully through the slit windows, I saw what appeared to be a grove of trees—these were the great timber columns supporting the roof beams. Each column was carved with the endless knotwork of Celtic design. A gigantic hearth yawned cold and dark, like an open pit, taking up one end of the vast room. Opposite the hearth, a wooden partition enclosed the far end of the hall; this I took to be the royal quarters.

Before the partition stood a circular dais made of stone, around which stood seven iron poles from which seven torches flared. And upon the dais was a huge chair, which appeared to have been carved of a single massive piece of black wood. The wood was ornamented with innumerable gold disks bearing a spiral pattern. In the flickering light of the torches, the disks appeared to be revolving slowly. The illusion of movement made the chair seem a living thing—an animate object with its own power and will.

There were at least a hundred people gathered near the dais, standing together in small clusters, speaking softly. Some held objects in their hands—here a folded length of cloth, there an ornate weapon, elsewhere a fine bowl or dish—gifts for the king, I supposed. I wished I had brought something too.

I didn't have long to dither over this, for, as we took our places to one side of the assembly, a loud, blaring note—like the blat of a ram's horn—sounded in the hall. From behind the partition stepped the king's bard, who ascended the dais and came to stand before us. He took a fold of his cloak and placed it over his head, then raised his hands. I saw that he held a long staff, or rod, the head of which gleamed darkly in the torchlight. Holding the rod lengthwise above his covered head, he began to speak in firm, somewhat threatening tones.

I tossed a questioning glance to Simon, who answered, "The Chief Bard is reminding us that the word of the king is law and that his judgments are absolute."

When the bard finished, he took his place at the right hand and a little behind the king's chair. The horn sounded again, and Meldryn Mawr himself appeared, a very Sun King: his clothing was immaculate, and his countenance brilliant. He was dressed all in crimson—shirt, trousers, and buskins. His golden fish-scale belt flashed in every facet; the rings on his hands glinted with gems. In addition to his torc, the king wore a crown, which appeared to have been made of oak leaves and twigs dipped in gold. His dark eyes scanned the throng before him, confident and wise. The force of his presence filled the entire hall, drawing all attention to him; I could not look away.

When the king had been seated, Prince Meldron ascended the dais and draped a black bearskin cloak over his father's shoulders. The prince then bent to touch the instep of his father's foot, and withdrew to take his place with the other chieftains. I saw Ruadh step forward to stand beside Prince Meldron.

At a nod from the king, Ollathir raised his wooden staff and struck it against the stone three times. Then he pointed to the first of the petitioners—a tall, heavily built man of imposing mien, who stalked to the dais and stretched out his hands to offer his gift: a fine new bow and a quiver of silver-pointed arrows.

The king inclined his regal head in acceptance of the gift, and the man began stating his business. After listening a moment, Simon whispered, "This is Rhiogan of Caer Dyffryn, one of Meldryn Mawr's chieftains on the eastern border. He is asking for the king's permission to raid the Vedeii—that's a Cruin tribe—across the river." Simon paused and listened some more. "It seems the Vedeii raided last autumn and stole some cattle. He wants the cattle back, and an equal number in punishment."

The king heard this request, lacing his fingers from time to time. When Rhiogan finished speaking, Meldryn replied, asking a few questions which his chieftain answered simply, without elaboration. Then he turned to Ollathir, whispered something into his ear, and sat back.

Ollathir then spoke out the king's message to the chieftain. "What's he saying?" I asked, fascinated.

"He is relaying the king's judgment—permission to raid is granted, provided that the king receives a share of the spoils."

"Is that fair?" I wondered aloud.

"It is not a matter of fairness," Simon explained. "This way, if the king shares the plunder, he also takes responsibility for the raid—the blame falls on him. Then, if the Vedeii make trouble over this, they have Meldryn Mawr to answer to, not just Rhiogan."

"So the king is authorizing retaliation in his name."

"Essentially."

The lord seemed pleased with this decision and mounted to the dais. He moved to the king, knelt, and, leaning close, placed his head against the king's chest—like a child seeking comfort from its mother. It was, despite the curious posture, a most poignant gesture.

The next petitioner was not one of Meldryn's lords, but a bard from a holding in the north, who sought permission to attend a gathering of bards in a neighboring realm. The request was, I learned, a formality observed not so much out of deference to the king, but out of respect for Ollathir—who would be attending the gathering in any case.

The third supplicant was a farmer from Meldryn's own holding who sought the king's aid in clearing a patch of bottom land, a process which included draining a bit of marsh. This was clearly beyond the farmer's capacity as he would need a great deal of help to get the land ready by planting time, which was rapidly approaching.

The king, through his bard, blessed the enterprise—for a modest return in kind—and offered the labor of fifty warriors under the direction of a *Gwyddon* to accomplish the task.

"What's a Gwyddon?" I asked Simon, when he had explained the situation to me.

"It's a type of bard. There are several different kinds, degrees actually. From *Penderwydd*—that is the Head Druid, or Chief Bard—on down to *Mabinog*, which is a pupil or apprentice. The Gwyddon is an expert on anything to do with land or cattle; he's also the nearest thing to a physician around here."

Wheels within wheels, I thought. Even simple societies had bureaucracies.

The next claimant stepped forward and an audible hush fell upon the throng. Those in the foreranks moved aside from the man; from the way everyone behaved, he appeared to be a criminal. Simon whispered, "This should be good."

"Who is it?"

"It is Balorgain," Simon replied with wicked glee. "He is a nobleman of Meldryn Mawr's lineage. He killed one of Meldryn's kinsmen in a fight, so he's been exiled for the last few years."

"What's he doing here?"

"Watch and see." Simon's eyes glinted with keen, almost malevolent interest.

The king regarded the noble with obvious contempt, although for his part I thought Balorgain seemed genuinely contrite. He stood before the king with his hands at his sides. The Chief Bard said something, a question. The man responded in a low voice. I saw the king's face freeze; the line of mouth flattened; his eyes went hard.

"Balorgain's got guts, I'll give him that," Simon said. "He might have been killed on sight."

"What's going on?"

"He has claimed *naud* of the king," he explained. "It is—"

"I know what it is," I whispered back. I had encountered the word before: a legal term for asylum, or refuge. Among the ancient Celts, a nobleman had the right to claim naud, or sanctuary, excusing him from a punishment. Interestingly, the claim of naud carried with it a moral obligation on the part of the king to grant it. By some obscure logic, for a monarch to refuse naud when it had been asked would transfer the guilt for the crime to the king.

Apparently, Balorgain had returned and slipped unseen into the court of exile, seeking naud. If granted, the crime would be forgiven and plucky Balorgain would be free to return to life among his people. Of course, Meldryn Mawr, who had decreed the exile in the first place, was not happy about this. But, great king that he was, he simply whispered the words to Ollathir, who pronounced Balorgain's claim of naud granted. And Balorgain strolled from the hall a free man.

The next few cases were minor disputes between neighboring tribes—the most interesting of which involved an adulterous affair between a married woman from one holding and a single man from another. The complaint was resolved by requiring the single man to reimburse the cuckolded husband to the tune of three cows, or ten sheep, whichever the husband preferred. The wayward wife, however, did not escape punishment. For the husband was granted permission to take a concubine should he ever choose to do so.

Meldryn Mawr seemed to lose interest in the proceedings then and scanned the room for some diversion. His eyes turned to where Simon and I stood waiting. He inclined his head in our direction, and Ollathir beckoned us to the dais.

"That's us," breathed Simon. "Here we go."

Simon led me to the front of the dais. We had no gift, so we did not offer any. The king appeared not to mind. He gazed at me with,

I thought, lively curiosity. At least, his bored expression disappeared as he looked me over from head to toe.

As the others had done, Simon introduced us with a brief description of events. At least, I assume that is what he did. The king replied and asked questions. Simon answered briefly. The king nodded, and I thought the matter would end there, for he turned to his Chief Bard and whispered to him. Ollathir listened, surveying me all the while. I expected the king's pronouncement to follow.

Instead, the Great King turned to me and beckoned me closer. I stepped nearer the dais, and Simon moved behind me. The king spoke to me. I smiled pleasantly. "What's he saying?" I whispered out of the side of my grin.

"The king wants to know how you came here." Simon replied calmly. "He understands that you do not speak the language and has appointed me to interpret. You don't have to whisper; just answer him and I will translate."

"Okay, but what do I tell him?"

"Tell him the truth," urged Simon. "But whatever you tell him, do not hesitate. They consider even a second's hesitation the same thing as lying."

I swallowed hardly. The king examined me benignly. "Great King," I said, "I am a stranger here. I have come to your realm from another world—through a cairn on a sacred hill."

"Good answer," said Simon, who then proceeded to translate for me. The king nodded without surprise and asked another question, which Simon relayed. "He wants to know how you came to kill the Cruin champion."

"Great King," I said, "I killed the Cruin champion by, uh, accident. In the heat of battle, I found a spear and struck him when he attacked me."

Simon, without hesitation, answered for me and again relayed the

175

king's reply. "He wants to know if you are a great warrior in your world."

"Great King, I am not a warrior. I am the least among warriors."

At this, when Simon echoed my words, the king's eyebrows lifted in surprise. "If you are not a warrior, what are you? A bard?" Simon asked in the king's stead.

"Great King, I am no bard."

The king listened to Simon's reply, and asked, through Simon, "Are you an artisan, perhaps, or a farmer?"

"Great King," I answered, "I am neither an artisan nor a farmer."

Meldryn Mawr seemed genuinely puzzled by my reply. He said something to me in a tone of frank bewilderment. "What's he saying?" I asked desperately.

Simon translated: "You do not fight, you do not sing, you do not plant or reap. What do you do, stranger?"

"What do I tell him? What do I say?" I hissed at Simon.

"Just answer!" Simon hissed back. "Quickly!"

"Great King," I said, "I read and write. I learn."

"Oh, splendid," Simon muttered, "that's torn it." But he delivered my answer to the king.

Meldryn favored me with a frown of stern disapproval and turned to Ollathir and then to Meldron, who whispered something to him. Many of those around us murmured. "What's happening now?" I asked.

Before Simon could answer, the king spoke up. Simon interpreted: "The king says that he will not be mocked—even by a guest ignorant of Llywddi ways. You came to his court in a warrior's guise, a warrior you will become."

"I can't!" I rasped in a panicked whisper. "Explain to him. We're not staying. We're leaving as soon as possible—we *are* leaving, Simon. As soon as we find a way to return to our own world, we're gone." I

pleaded desperately. "You've got to tell him, Simon. Make him understand."

Simon said something to the king, who listened and then whispered into the Chief Bard's ear. Ollathir delivered the king's judgment
in a voice bold with authority and grave with finality. When he finished, he cracked the rod on the stone three times and the llys was
over. The king rose up from his judgment seat and withdrew. Those
of us gathered in the hall filed slowly outside, where preparations for
the victory feast continued.

"Well?" I said, as soon as we were out of the hall. "What did he
say? What happened in there?"

Simon was slow in answering. "He did not see fit to withdraw his
opinion," he said at last.

"Meaning?"

"You're going to become a warrior, boyo."

"He can't do that!"

"Oh, yes, he can do that," Simon insisted. "He is the king."

"But I don't know the first thing about being a warrior. I'll get
killed. Besides, I'm not going to be here that long. Didn't you tell him
we're leaving right away? We have to go back, Simon. You told him
that, right?"

Simon hesitated. "Not exactly."

"What *did* you tell him?" I was fairly shouting with indignation.
People around us were watching me with amused expressions, apparently much entertained by my hysterics.

"Keep your voice down," Simon warned. "They'll think you're
questioning the king's judgment."

"Darn right! I *am* questioning the king's judgment! That's exactly
what I'm doing."

"Don't," Simon warned. "Not here—not in front of the king's
hall."

"I'll holler anywhere I please! What in blue blazes is going on anyway?" I demanded. Simon grabbed me by the arm and steered me away from the hall.

"The king considers that anyone who can kill a champion by accident deserves a chance to prove himself a champion. Since you profess yourself good at learning, you will learn the warrior's craft. It is really an honor he is paying you. Quite high, considering."

"Considering what?"

"Considering you all but insulted him with your flippant answers."

"My flippant answers? What are you talking about?"

"Not a warrior, not a bard, not a farmer—you made him look foolish in front of his chieftains. That was a very chancy thing to do."

"I didn't mean to," I protested. "I was only trying to answer his questions, like you said."

"He knows that," Simon explained, "which is why he didn't have your tongue torn out where you stood. I told you, it's really an honor."

"Well, I won't do it," I insisted, crossing my arms over my chest. "You'll just have to talk to him. Explain things. Work it out. Maybe get his bard to help us."

"Too late," Simon replied. "You had your chance. The judgment is given. The king's word is law, remember?"

"Well, it stinks! Just what in blue blazes am I supposed to do now?"

Simon pointed across the grassy yard to where the horses were tethered. I turned to see Ollathir and a young man speaking to one another. The young man took the hem of the Chief Bard's cloak, raised it to his lips, and kissed it. Without a glance in our direction, Ollathir departed. The younger man quickly gathered the reins of two horses and proceeded toward where Simon and I stood looking on.

"He's coming this way," I observed. "Simon, what's he doing?" Apprehension crept over me like a swarm of ants. "What's happening?"

Simon put a hand on my shoulder. "Calm down, Lewis. It's for the best."

"What's for the best? Simon! What's going on here?" My voice scaled several registers. "You know—so tell me!"

"Listen carefully, Lewis," Simon explained, speaking as one would to a distraught child. "Nothing bad is going to happen to you. You are going on a journey."

"I don't understand. Where am I going?"

"You are going to Ynys Sci." He pronounced it Ennis Sky. "That's an island—where there is a school for warriors. There you will be taught how to fight, and, when you have learned, you will return here to serve Meldryn."

"Warriors' school! It's a joke, right?"

Simon shook his head solemnly. "It is no joke. Boys from all over Albion are sent to this school—the sons of kings and champions every one. I told you, it's a great honor."

I was too stunned to speak. I stood looking on in mute despair as the young man approached and greeted Simon. They exchanged a few brief words, and then the youth turned to me and touched the back of his hand to his forehead.

"This is Tegid Tathal," Simon told me. "He is a *Brehon*—that's another type of bard. He's Ollathir's right-hand man. The Chief Bard has chosen him to be your guide. He has also been given the responsibility of teaching you the language."

Tegid grinned at me and handed me the reins of one of the horses.

"Just like that—we're leaving?"

"Yes. Just like that." Simon moved to the side of the horse. "Here, I'll help you mount."

"This is crazy!" I muttered murderously. "I mean, this is *seriously* nuts! I don't belong here."

"Relax," Simon soothed. "Enjoy yourself. It is going to be an

179

experience you'll never forget. It is a wonderful gift you have been given. I wish I could go with you—and I mean that."

"Why can't you?"

"King's orders," Simon shrugged. "But don't worry. I'll be waiting for you when you return."

"Ha! *If* I return, you mean."

"Oh, you'll return, never fear," Simon assured me. "Tegid tells me the king has decreed that special care is to be taken—you are not to be killed in your training. There, you see? Nothing to worry about. Everything's been taken care of."

Simon cupped his hands and made a stirrup. I raised my foot and he boosted me into the saddle. I say "saddle"—but it was little more than a leather pad over a folded cloak with a strap to hold both in place. "Simon, listen to me. You've got to talk to the king. You've got to get him to change his mind. I mean it, Simon. We can't stay here. We've got to go back. We don't belong here."

"I'll see what I can do," he promised blandly. "In the meantime, try to take it easy. It's no use getting upset—just relax and enjoy it."

The moment I was settled, Tegid vaulted into the saddle, wheeled his mount, and began trotting away across the grassy yard. My own mount, an enormous gray beast, followed at a trot. "I can't ride a horse!" I hollered, clutching the animal's mane for dear life.

"Of course you can!" called Simon. "Good luck, Lewis!"

With that, we were off. People paused in their work and called out as we passed—wishing us farewell, I suppose. I turned and looked back when we reached the narrow gate of the caer and saw them waving us away. I frowned bitterly back and realized that, thanks to Meldryn Mawr's wonderful honor of a gift, I would miss the feast.

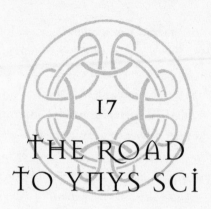

17

THE ROAD
TO YNYS SCI

I could not remain sullen in that fair land. We journeyed for days through the most beautiful landscape imaginable: every panorama breathtaking, each vista enchanting. I felt like stopping to admire the view every hundred yards or so. Had Tegid allowed it, we would still be on the road to Ynys Sci.

We traveled light; I carried nothing but the clothes on my back, and Tegid only his oaken staff and a large leather bag behind his saddle which contained a few provisions. Nevertheless, my guide assumed a slow, yet steady pace. For that, I was grateful. I had not ridden a horse since I was a small boy at the county fair, and then it had been a Shetland pony. Tegid allowed me time to marshal what rudimentary riding skills I possessed and master a few I lacked. He showed me how to lead the horse with the gentle pressure of my knees, leaving my hands free for holding a shield and sword or spear. And several times each day he urged the horses to gallop, so that I quickly learned how to stay upright on the broad, rolling back of the heaving beast beneath me.

The days were soft and bright, the nights cool and crisp as the land warmed to full spring. We traveled north and west through the wide lowlands above the Synchant River, following an old hill track which some Llwyddi king had made in an effort to link his further-flung holdings together: *Sarn Meldraen*, Tegid called it. According to him, the name commemorated one of Meldryn Mawr's celebrated ancestors. Tegid told me countless things, few of which I understood at first. But he was a tireless teacher, jabbering away at me from dawn's early light to well past the time when my eyelids closed for the night. By dint of Tegid's constant repetition and unflagging zeal, I began to gain a rough rapport with the proto-Gaelic the inhabitants of Albion spoke.

I recognized many of the individual words, of course; I had encountered scores of the older word-forms in my Celtic studies, and they were little changed. And why not? The bards of ancient Britain always maintained that their language emanated from an Otherworldly source. Most academics totally discount such stories, believing them to be nonsensical boasts on the part of a shabby tribe attempting to further itself by professed descent from an illustrious forebear. But hearing the language on Tegid's agile tongue, I entertained no such doubts. The native speech of Albion was strong and subtle, infinitely expressive, and rich with a wealth of color, sound, and movement. I could easily discern the root of modern Gaelic.

Since Tegid and I were alone on the trail, I tried my best to match my tutor syllable for tongue-knotting syllable, and vowel for elusive vowel. To his credit, he never laughed at my faltering, feeble efforts. He patiently corrected every gross mistake and lauded every small success. He made word games for us to play and pretended deafness whenever, in exhaustion or frustration, I lapsed into English. He seemed genuinely keen to have me master the brain-boggling intricacies of his speech, not merely salt away the odd word or phrase. And as soon as I gained a tentative foothold on a lower rung, Tegid was there, poking and prodding me to higher, more complex and sophisticated achievement.

Under such intense and imaginative instruction, I came to a flirting familiarity with what the bards called *Moddion-o-Gair*—the Ways of Words. And, as I learned, I began to see the world around me more clearly. A queer thing to say, I know. For the more words I had for things, the better I could frame my thoughts, the more vivid my thoughts became. Awareness deepened, consciousness sharpened.

I think this had to do with the language itself: there were no dead words. No words that had suffered the ignorant predation of a semi-literate media, or had their substance leached away through gross mis-use; no words rendered meaningless through overuse, or cheapened through bureaucratic doublespeak. Consequently, the speech of Albion was a valued currency, a language alive with meaning: poetic, imagaic, bursting with rhythm and sound. When the words were spoken aloud they possessed the power to touch the heart as well as the head: they spoke to the soul. On the lips of a bard, a story became an astonishing revelation, a song became a marvel of almost paralyzing beauty.

Tegid and I spent three weeks on the trail—I call them weeks, although the bards did not reckon the passage of days that way— three weeks, living and breathing the language of Albion: by the fire at night when we camped, in the saddle when we rode, by the cold-water streams and hilltop bowers when we stopped to eat or rest. By the time we reached Ffim Ffaller I was speaking like a Celt—albeit a somewhat laconic Celt.

I learned much about the new world around me. Albion was an island—which I had surmised on my own—occupying roughly the same place and shape in its world as the island of Great Britain occupied in the real world. Tegid drew a map in the dirt to show me where we were going. Though the similarities were many and striking, the major differ-ence was in size: Albion was many times larger in every way than the tidily compacted Britain I had left behind. Judging from the distances traveled, Albion was immense; both the land and the world that con-tained it were far more expansive than anything I could have dreamed.

I also learned something of wood and wildlife lore; Tegid proved a veritable fountain of information. Nothing escaped his notice—in the sky above or the earth below. No single detail was too minute, no occurrence so trivial it could not become a lesson. The man was indefatigable.

Yet, able teacher though he was, Tegid showed no interest in where I came from, or how I had come to be in Meldryn Mawr's court. I was asked nothing about my own world. At first, I thought Tegid's notable lack of curiosity strange. But, as the journey wore on, I became grateful for his indifference. I grew more and more reluctant to think about the real world. In fact, I forgot about it for whole days at a time, and found the forgetting liberating.

I gave myself wholly to Tegid's tutelage, and I learned a great deal about Albion—more than I would have discovered in years on my own. In the process, I learned much, too, about my guide and companion.

Tegid Tathal ap Talaryant was a bard and the son of a bard. Darkly good-looking, with eyes the color of mountain slate, a deep-clefted chin and a wide, expressive mouth, he looked like an artist's idea of the Brooding Poet. Tegid was of noble blood—and it showed in every line of his well-knit frame—born of a southern tribe which had produced bards for the kings of Llwydd for ten generations or more. In his company, I was conscious of my own undistinguished appearance: I must have seemed very ugly to such a handsome people—with my lumpen mug and weedy frame.

Although still a young man, by Albion standards at least, he was already a Brehon, only three notches lower than Penderwydd, or Chief Bard. Brehon was that phase of a bard's training in which he was expected to master the intricacies of tribal life—everything from the rules governing the choosing of a king and the orders of precedence in court, to the latest land squabble among farmers and how many cows should be paid for usurping a man's place in his bed. When he had become an authority on all matters public and private, the bard would become a Gwyddon, and then a *Derwydd*.

The degrees of bardship were elaborate and formal, their roles well defined through eons, apparently, of unaltered tradition. The candidate progressed from Mabinog—which had two distinct subdivisions, *Cawganog* and *Cupanog*—and proceeded up through the various degrees: *Filidh*, Brehon, Gwyddon, Derwydd, and finally Penderwydd, sometimes called the Chief of Song. There was also a Penderwydd over the whole, the Chief of Chiefs, so to speak. He was called the *Phantarch*, and was chosen by acclamation of his peers to rule over the bardship of Albion.

According to Tegid, the Island of the Mighty was protected by the Phantarch in some obscure way. The way he described it made it sound as if the Phantarch literally stood underneath the realm, supporting it on his shoulders. A quaint poetic image, I assumed.

All that first week I was saddle-sore and exhausted from the rigors of our journey. By the end of the second week, I was speaking to my horse again and optimistic about my chances of a full recovery. When the time came to exchange the horses for a berth aboard ship, I was sincerely sorry to see them go.

One afternoon toward the end of the third week, we halted atop a rocky headland on the western coast, and Tegid pointed out a settlement far down in the misty vale below. The sea inlet formed the valley floor between two towering headlands, creating a deep folded pocket which made for a nicely protected bay. The small settlement served the harbor there. "That is Ffim Ffaller," he told me. "There we will meet the ship which will take us to Ynys Scí."

"Will we have long to wait?"

"Not long. A day or two, perhaps a little longer. But I think not." He turned in the saddle to face me and put his hand on my shoulder. "You have done well, brother. The king will be pleased."

"And you have been a good teacher, Tegid. I am grateful for all you have done. You have given me eyes to see, ears to hear, and a tongue to speak. For that, I thank you."

He shrugged off the compliment, saying, "You would have learned it all sooner or later. If I have helped you, I am happy."

We started down the steep hill track to the settlement then, and said no more. The harbor at Ffim Ffaller was little more than a wooden jetty and a boatyard on the pebbled shingle. The jetty was large enough for three or four ships, with space in the bay for only half a dozen more. In short, the place appeared only what it was: a midway stopping place for ships bound further north and south.

The settlement consisted of an assortment of round wattled houses, a livestock pen, and a few outbuildings. Add to these the four brown huts on the shingle which formed the boatyard and that was all of Ffim Ffaller, home to perhaps thirty folk.

We ambled into the settlement and received a warm welcome, being the first visitors of the season. The headman of the holding confirmed that the ship was expected tomorrow or the next day, and gave us the use of the guesthouse and a woman to cook for us. Tegid gave him a bit of gold, broken off from one of the thin sticks he carried in a leather pouch beneath his belt. The headman accepted this payment, protesting that it was not at all necessary: they were only too glad for word of the realm.

I understood then how lonely such isolated places could be for a gregarious people. Word of events in the outside world was a precious commodity, and travelers were merchants of no mean status. Indeed, we paid for our lodging many times over before our stay was out, telling and retelling the tidings we brought with us.

That Tegid was a bard further heightened our popularity. The settlement had not so much as a filidh, or master of song, among its members. There had been no songs or stories all the long, cold winter—save those the people had told or sung themselves. This may not sound like much of a hardship, but winter nights are long and winter days dark. And the songs of a bard can transform life lived before the hearthfire into a sparkling enchantment.

It was in Ffim Ffaller that I first heard the true genius of a bard. Tegid sang for the settlement, and it is a wonder I will treasure forever.

We had all gathered in the headman's house, around the central firepit. It was after the evening meal, and everyone had come to hear Tegid sing. To my surprise, he had earlier produced a harp from his leather bag and taken it down to the jetty to tune its strings. The moment he entered the hut, a palpable thrill stirred the people.

He made his way to the far side of the firepit, where he took his place, standing straight and tall before us, his cloak falling in graceful folds from his shoulders, harp nestled against his chest, his handsome features illuminated by the flickering firelight. He bent his dark head and drew his fingers over the harpstrings, sending a shimmering cascade of sound spilling like a shower of silver coins over those huddled round about.

Then, drawing a long breath, he began to sing—simply, expressively. I followed the song as best I could, but lost much in the tight-woven tapestry of his words. What did that matter? What I gained far outweighed the loss. It was magic.

Tegid's story—a tale about a lonely fisherman who woos a woman from the waves, only to lose her to the sea—was sung in such an eloquent and compelling voice, and with such a poignant melody, that tears spilled from my eyes to hear it. I could comprehend but a fragment of all he sang, and none of the subtlety, yet the intensity of the song struck me with a power undiminished for all that. The haunting melody filled my soul with longing.

When he finished, the people sat in rapt silence. And, after a moment, Tegid began another song. But, like a poor man who has feasted on food far too rich for his humble appetite, I was glutted. More might have killed me. So I silently crept away and took myself off, alone, to walk along the water's edge.

There, in the deep-hearted darkness of the night, I strolled the pebbled beach, gazing up at the brilliant stars and listening to the play of the water on the shore. I was astonished. Never in all my life had I been so moved—and by a simple song about a mermaid. I could neither believe nor understand what had happened to me. For it seemed that something inside me had been awakened, some long-sleeping part of me had been roused to life. And now I could no longer be who I was before. But if I was no longer to be who I *was*, who was I to *be*?

Oh, this was a fearful paradise—full of fantastic raptures and alarms. Terror and beauty, undiluted, cheek-by-jowl—and me as defenseless against one as against the other. How could I ever go back to the world I had known before? Truth to tell, I no longer considered going back a possibility. Here I was, by some miracle, and here I would stay.

I walked for a long time along the strand, and I did not sleep that night. The thing in me that had been wakened to life would not let me rest. How could I sleep when my spirit was on fire? I wrapped myself in my cloak and walked again along the water's edge, as restless as the tide flow in the bay, my mind ablaze and dancing, my heart racing in an agitation of delight and dread.

Daybreak found me huddled on the jetty, watching the silver mist avalanching down the steep hillsides to spread across the cold blue black water of the bay. The early-morning sky was dull and hard as slate, but the clouds angling along the coast blushed pink with dawn. Out in the bay, a fish leaped. And the place where it splashed became a rippling ring.

The sight of that silver ring spreading on the peaceful water pierced me to the marrow. For it seemed to me an omen, a portent pregnant with meaning, a symbol of my life: a once disturbed surface stirred into a glimmering, ever-widening circle. The circle would expand until it was swallowed in the vastness of the bay—and then there would be nothing left, nothing to show that it had ever existed.

18

SCATHA'S SCHOOL

The spear in my opponent's hand had a smooth, rounded wooden head instead of a metal point. But it still hurt like fury when he poked me with it. I was bruised purple, head to heel, and I was growing mighty tired of getting jabbed every time I turned around. The smug little brute at the other end of the lance considered himself my superior in everything but age.

Cynan Machae was fifteen summers or so, large for his age, and already a formidable combatant. He was the very portrait of the spoiled royal darling: hair like a roof-thatch set to flame, small deep-set eyes of cornflower blue, a white skin lightly specked with rusty freckles. He wore his arrogance like the thick silver torc of which he was so insufferably proud.

And he had been getting the best of me, ever since we had been paired by our instructor, Boru—a tall, reed-thin genius with a javelin. Boru, himself a student under Scatha's tutelage, could throw a spear further than most people could see, and clip an apple from a tree as it fell. Most students listened well to Boru, whenever he deigned to offer instruction.

My problem, this particular day, was to save my battered pride—somehow to prevent another disgraceful drubbing at the hands of my pompous young antagonist. It was the same problem as every other day. But today I meant business. Things were not going my way, however, and time was running out. Spear practice would be over soon, and I had yet to ransom my self-respect.

Ten paces off, Cynan stood with the habitual haughty smirk on his freckled face. He held his lance across his body with both hands. Whoever initiated the last challenge, we knew it would end as it always ended: me on my backside with a sharp pain in the ribs or chest or shins or shoulders—or wherever else that little prig felt like poking me.

I glared at him—so smart, so cool, so pompous—and my blood boiled. I would, I vowed, wipe that insolent smirk off his face once and for all. As I hefted my practice spear, an idea thrust itself into my battered skull.

I took a step forward. Cynan squared off.

I took another step, and another. Cynan stepped forward to meet me—grinning now. "Another fall? Have you not had enough for one day?"

"One more," I told him, my voice flat. *Yes, just one more, you noxious creep.*

He moved closer, grinning with gleeful spite. He was cocky and cruel; he enjoyed knocking me around. Well, he had thumped me once too often, and now I had nothing left to lose. If I went down again, it would only be another in a long, sorry string of defeats. But if my plan worked . . .

I lowered my blunt spear. Cynan lowered his. I took a step closer. He stepped closer.

Boru, standing in the center of the field, raised his silver horn to his lips and gave a long, shimmering blast which signaled the end of the practice. But I ignored it. A look of surprise appeared on Cynan's ruddy face. Usually, I was the first to call it quits. "Not yielding?"

"Not today, Cynan. Make your move."

He edged forward, thrusting his spear in quick, short jabs, hoping to draw me. Instead, I stood motionless and let him come nearer. "You are obstinate today, Collri," he laughed. "I must teach you better manners."

Collri is what they called me—it is a play on a word that means "loser," which is what I was to my underage warrior comrades. "Teach, then, Cynan," I said. "I am waiting."

Others, sensing the tension between us, were gathering around. There were some jibes and jeers, but most were just interested in seeing who would get beaten. They offered inane advice and sniggered.

Cynan saw a chance to show off and made the most of it. He lowered his head and lunged. I lowered my lance and knocked his thrust down, as we had been shown. Anticipating, as the head of his spear fell, Cynan spun the butt overhand toward my head. It is a good move. Very good.

But he had used it before. And this time I was ready. I spread my hands and lifted my lance crosswise above my head to meet his crown-cracking blow. This left my stomach unprotected, to be sure. And Cynan saw this. He turned and aimed a kick at my vulnerable mid-section with his foot. As his foot came up, I slid my hands together quickly.

His spear connected with my upraised shaft. I let my spear shaft absorb the shock and spun it down, hard. I hit him a solid rap on the shin of his extended leg. He yelped—more in surprise than in pain, I am certain. Those gathered around us laughed out loud.

Cynan threw the head of his lance into my face to drive me back. But I dodged to the side and rapped a glancing blow on his knuckles. I thought this would keep him off balance and I could knock him down. Instead, he threw an elbow into my ribs, and I was the one to stagger.

Seizing the advantage, Cynan snaked out a foot, hooked my heel, and tripped me. I fell backwards onto the bare earth of the practice field, and Cynan thumped me on top of the head.

The insolent brat laughed, and those gathered around laughed with him. And there I was, yet again, rolling on my backside in the dirt. I saw his smirking face, saw his head turn to make some cocky remark to Boru, who was looking on with the others. He had bested me once again.

I heard the laughter, and rage boiled up inside me like lava. Everything went red. The sound of the surf pounded in my ears. Without thinking, I whirled the wooden spear at Cynan's knees and caught him a resounding crack across both kneecaps. He dropped his spear and pitched forward, his horselaugh becoming a strangled yelp in his throat.

He fell onto his hands beside me. I rolled onto my knees and brought the shaft of my spear down upon his back. He kissed the dirt. I leaped to my feet and thrust the butt of my spear down hard between his shoulder blades. Cynan shrieked with pain and passed out.

I lifted my spear and stepped away. The ring of jeering bystanders had gone utterly quiet. No one tittered now; no one laughed. They turned toward one another, wide-eyed.

Boru pushed through the crowd and bent over the inert Cynan. He rolled him over, satisfying himself that I had not killed the boy, and motioned for a cadre of Cynan's companions to carry him back to our lodge. Four young men stepped forward, lifted their fallen friend, and dragged him off the field.

When they had gone, Boru turned to me. "That was well done, Col." Boru always called me Col, stopping just short of the open insult, preferring the implied slight.

"I am sorry," I muttered.

"No, do not be sorry," he insisted, loud enough for all those gathered around to hear. "You have done well." He clapped me on the back in rare commendation. "It is not easy to bring down a foe with your back to the ground. You did not surrender to defeat—this is what separates the living from the dead on the battleground."

Boru turned to the stunned onlookers and dismissed them. They drifted off, mumbling to themselves. The incident would be well discussed at the evening meal. I wondered what Scatha would say when she found out about it.

I did not have long to wait, for no sooner had Boru and the others dispersed than I heard the light jingle of a horse's tack. I turned to see Scatha approaching, leading a black horse whose withers and flanks were lathered from a vigorous ride.

Scatha was our Battle Chief: a more beautiful woman could not be found, nor one more deadly. The hair beneath her bronze warcap was plaited into tiny beaded braids that gleamed like sunstruck gold; her pale blue eyes were cool beneath long golden lashes and smooth, straight brows; her lips were full, but firmly set. Her features were those which adorned the classic sculptures of an Athena or Venus. If there is such a thing as the poetry of battle, she was it: graceful and formidable, dazzling movement and terrible skill.

Scatha was renowned as the finest warrior in all Albion. And it was in Scatha's school on the Isle of Sci where I labored to learn the craft of war. Such labor! Up every morning at first light to run on the beach and swim in the cold sea, and then to break fast on brown bread and water before beginning the day's activities: practice with sword and spear and knife and shield, strategy sessions, lessons in combat of various types, more physical conditioning, sports and wrestling games, and on and on. When we were not running or climbing or wrestling, we were in the saddle. We rode incessantly: racing one another in the surf, hunting in the wooded hills and glens of the island, engaging in mock battles.

I had become accustomed to the regimen, and even enjoyed it for the most part. Alas, I had not greatly improved as a warrior. Apparently I still lacked some mysterious ingredient with which to bring all the skills together into a harmonious, effective whole. I was least and last among my fellows, and they were all younger than me. Boys barely eight summers old possessed skills I could only imagine, and they mercilessly demonstrated their superiority at every turn.

I swear by the tongue in my head, one has never learned humility until one has been bested by children!

I turned to meet Scatha, and understood from the sharply disapproving expression on her face that she had seen what I had done. "You defeated Cynan at last. You have taught him a valuable lesson," she said, adding pointedly, "though I would not await his thanksgiving."

"I did not mean to hurt him." I gestured vaguely toward the boys who were dragging my adversary's inert body across the practice field. Cynan's feet left two long tracks in the dirt.

"Of course you did," Scatha told me. "If your spear had metal at the tip instead of birch, you would have killed him."

"No, I—"

She raised a slender hand and silenced me. "You faced two today, and were defeated by one."

I did not catch her meaning. "Which two, Pen-y-Cat?" I used her preferred title: Head of Battle. She was that, and more: a canny and cunning adversary, endlessly ingenious, as shrewd and sly an opponent as one would ever care to face.

She replied, her voice low. "You were angry, Col. Your anger defeated you today."

It was true. "I am sorry."

"Next time, perhaps, you will not be sorry. You will be dead." She turned and began leading her horse to the stables. She motioned for me to walk beside her. "If you must always defeat two enemies each time you take the field of battle, you will soon be overcome. And of any two enemies, anger is always the stronger."

I opened my mouth to speak, but she did not allow me to interrupt. "Give up your fear," she told me bluntly. "Or it will kill you."

I lowered my head. She was right, of course. I feared ridicule, humiliation, failing—but, more than that, I feared getting hurt, getting killed.

"The feats you achieved against Cynan are yours, Col. You possess the skills, but you must learn to call them forth on your own. To do that, you must give up your fear."

"I understand. I will try harder," I vowed.

Scatha stopped walking and turned to me. "Is life so piteous where you come from that you must cling to it so?"

Piteous? Certainly she had it backwards. But then, the language still threw me sometimes. "I do not understand," I confessed.

"It is the poor man who clenches so tightly to the gold he is given—for fear of losing it. The man of wealth spends his gold freely to accomplish his will in the world. It is the same with life."

Suddenly ashamed of my conspicuous poverty, I lowered my eyes. But Scatha placed a hand beneath my chin and raised my head. "Cling too tightly to your life and you will lose it, my reluctant warrior. You must become the master of your life, not its slave."

I gazed into her eyes and believed her. I knew that she spoke the truth, and that she saw me for what I was. All at once, I wanted nothing more than to prove my worth in those clear, blue eyes. If largesse of spirit made a good warrior, I would become a spendthrift!

"Thank you, Pen-y-Cat," I murmured gratefully. "Your words are wise and true. I will remember them."

"See that you do." Scatha inclined her head in acceptance of my compliment. "There is no glory in teaching warriors to die."

Then she handed me the reins to her horse and walked away, leaving me to tend the animal. This was my reproof for losing my temper with Cynan.

I had been in Scatha's island school for over six months, by my reckoning. The folk of Albion did not go by months, but rather by seasons, which made precise time-keeping slightly difficult. But two seasons had passed since I had come to Ynys Sci, and two more made a year. At the end of the third season, *Rhylla*—the Otherworld equivalent of fall or autumn—most of the boys would return home to winter with their clans and tribes. But I would not. Always a few of the older youths, like Boru, stayed on through the dark, dismal northern months of cold and icy wind.

There were nearly a hundred young warriors in training on the island. The younger boys were trained apart from the older, although no strict age division was enforced. It mostly had to do with size and aptitude. I was sometimes put with the older boys and young men, even though I was rarely a match for their prowess—or even skillful enough to create much in the way of an interesting challenge. Consequently, I was the butt of their humor and the target of all their scorn.

Nor did I blame them. I was a hopeless warrior. I knew that. But until today, I had not really wanted to succeed. I wanted it now. And not only success, I wanted to win acclaim and honor. I wanted to cover myself in glory in Scatha's eyes . . . or at least to avoid further disgrace.

That evening, when I had finished watering and feeding the horse and settled it for the night, I joined my companions in the torchlit hall where we took our meals. But this night I was not greeted with catcalls and cheerful derision; this night I was welcomed with a silence approaching respect. Word had indeed spread about my contest with Cynan, and most, if not all, were on Cynan's side. They were annoyed with me for besting him and turned the cold shoulder. Still, their silence was more tolerable than their mockery.

Alone of all the rest, Boru came to sit at the board with me. We ate together but spoke little. "I do not see Cynan," I said, glancing from one to another of the long tables in the hall.

"He is not hungry tonight," replied Boru affably. "I think his head hurts."

"Pen-y-Cat believes I struck in anger," I said and told him about my talk with Scatha.

Boru listened to what I had to say, then shrugged. "Our War Leader is wise," he said solemnly. "Heed her well." Then he smiled wide, his thin face merry. "Still, I think you have earned a new name. It is no longer Collri—you will be Llyd from now on."

I warmed with unexpected pleasure. "Do you think so, Boru?"

He nodded and lifted a narrow hand. "You will see."

A moment later, he was standing on the table. He raised his silver signal horn to his lips and gave forth a loud blast which reverberated in the hall. Everyone stopped eating and talking, and all eyes turned to him. "Brothers!" he shouted. "Fortunate am I among men. I saw a marvel today!" Bards sometimes introduce an announcement in this fashion.

"What did you see?" came the expected response from the tables round about. Everyone leaned forward.

"I saw a stump grow legs and walk; I saw a clod of dirt raise its head!" Boru answered. Everyone laughed, and I knew they were laughing at me. They thought he was making fun of me. And, truth to tell, I thought so too.

But before I could hide my head, Boru thrust his open hand toward me and said, "Today I saw the spirit of a warrior kindled in the heat of anger. Hail, Llyd ap Dicter! I welcome you!"

Boru's words hung in the silent hall. I was grateful for his noble act, but it appeared in vain. The sullen faces lining the long boards of the hall were not about to let me escape their contempt so easily, nor yet release me from their scorn.

I glanced around and discovered the reason for their mute disapproval: Cynan stood in the entrance to the hall. He had heard Boru's speech and was frowning. No one wanted to shame Cynan by lauding me in his presence. So Boru's generous effort was stillborn. Cynan had defeated me again.

Cynan gazed haughtily at Boru and then at me. He stepped into the hall and marched toward me, his cheeks glowing red as his hair, his small eyes narrowed, his face hard. My stomach tightened. He was coming to challenge me—in front of the whole assembly. I would never live it down.

He walked directly to where I sat and stood over me. I tried to appear calm and unconcerned as I turned to meet his scowl. We gazed at one another for a moment. Boru, knowing full well what was about to happen, intervened, saying, "Greetings, Cynan Machae, we have missed your most agreeable company this evening."

"I was not hungry," the surly youth grunted. To me he said, "Stand on your feet."

Slowly, I rose from the bench, turned, and faced Cynan, desperately trying to think of some way out of this predicament. Boru stepped down from the table to the bench, ready to put himself between us.

Cynan clenched his right hand and slowly raised his fist in my face. With his fist almost touching my nose, he lifted his left hand and held the two fists together in angry defiance. Then he placed a hand to either side of his throat and slowly spread the knobbed ends of his silver torc and removed it—so that it would not be damaged in the fight, I guessed.

Then he reached out and slipped the silver ornament behind my head. I felt the clasp of encircling metal around my throat. Cynan pressed the two ends of the torc together. Then he jerked my arm up, holding it over my head.

He had given me his most cherished possession, the symbol of his royal paternity. He was not at all happy about it, but he was making the gift known before one and all. "Hail, Llyd," he grumbled threateningly. He released my hand and made to turn away.

"Sit with me, brother," I called after him. Of all the things I might have said, I do not know why I chose that. Cynan looked so wretched, I suppose I thought to placate him. In truth, I knew it was mere luck that I had won against him. Another day and I might not have fared so well. Besides, I now wore his highest treasure and could afford to be magnanimous.

He whirled on me, instantly furious, both fists clenched. Boru's hand shot out and gripped him by the shoulder. "Peace, brother. The thing was well done," he said soothingly. "Do not steal the honor of your noble tribute with an unseemly quarrel."

Cynan showed what he thought of Boru's suggestion with a murderously foul glare. "A warrior does not surrender tribute gladly!" he uttered in a strangled voice.

Boru answered lightly: "And I tell you that unless you give gladly, there is no honor in giving at all."

Cynan hesitated but did not back down.

"Come," Boru said gently, "do not disgrace yourself by squabbling over a gift once given."

I looked at Cynan's flushed and angry face and felt genuine pity for him. Why had he given the torc? He clearly did not want to do it. What compelled him?

"Is this silver trinket worth more than your honor?" asked Boru pointedly. Cynan's scowl deepened. Some of the onlookers began to murmur, and Cynan felt his support eroding. He was on the point of lashing out, because he knew of nothing else to do.

"You honor me with your gift, Cynan," I told him, loudly enough for those sitting at the far end of the hall to hear. "I accept it most humbly, for I know I am least worthy of any to receive it."

This brought a hint of puzzled agreement to Cynan's scowl. "So you have said," he replied, neither confirming nor contradicting my words.

"Therefore, in respect of your gift, allow me to give you a gift in return."

This was unexpected. Cynan did not know what to think. But he was intrigued enough to agree. "If you are determined, I will not prevent you."

"You are most gracious, brother," I said and carefully removed the silver torc from around my neck and replaced it on his.

Cynan stared at me. "Why have you done this?" he asked, his voice tinged with awe. "Do you mock me?"

"I do not mock you, Cynan," I said. "I only seek to honor your gift with one of equal value. And since I own but one torc, I give it to you."

This answer pleased him, for it allowed him to maintain his self-esteem and also reclaim his valued treasure. The scowl faded from his face, to be replaced with an expression of wary relief and amazement.

"What say you, Cynan?" Boru asked, pointedly.

"I accept your estimable gift," Cynan answered quickly, "lest I change my mind.

"Good," I said. "Then I ask you again, will you sit with me?"

Cynan stiffened. His pride did not allow him to bend so far. Boru stepped aside and indicated the bench.

"Come, brother," he coaxed. "Take my place."

Cynan fingered the silver ornament at his throat and then caved in. His broad cheeks bunched in a happy grin. "Perhaps I could eat something, after all," he said. "A place among warriors is not to be spurned."

We sat down together, Cynan and I, and we ate from the same bowl. And we talked, for the first time as something other than adversaries. "Llyd ap Dicter," Cynan mused, tearing bread, "Anger, Son of Fury, that is good, Boru. You should be a bard."

"A warrior bard?" wondered Boru in exaggerated interest. "Never has there been such a thing in Albion. Very well, I will be the first."

He and Cynan laughed at that, but I did not catch the joke. It did not seem to me such a peculiar union.

Talk turned to other things. I saw Cynan reaching now and again to his treasure—as if to verify that it remained firmly in place. "That is a fine torc," I told him. "I hope to have one like it one day."

"There is none like it," Cynan said proudly. "It was given me by my father, King Cynfarch of Galanae."

"Why did you give it to me?" I asked, seeking an explanation of the mystery. Obviously, the object meant a great deal to Cynan.

"My father made me vow to give it to the first man who bested me at arms. If I return to his hearth without it, I may not join the war band of my clan." Cynan stroked the ornament lovingly. "It is the only thing my father, the king, has ever given me out of his hand. I have protected it always."

He spoke the simple truth, without rancor or self-pity. But I could have wept for Cynan, forced to labor under the terrible burden of perfection. What must his father be like—giving his son a fine gift and then holding the boy hostage to it? It did not make sense, but at least I understood Cynan better.

And I understood that for Cynan to confide his secret to anyone amounted to almost as much of a sacrifice as his gifting of the torc. Yet he was willing to do it—just as he was willing to abide by a vow which only he knew, and which would have cost him his two dearest possessions. Had he simply broken the vow, no one would ever have known.

I could but marvel at Cynan's extraordinary fidelity. Though his cheek had yet to feel a razor's edge, he was already a man to be trusted through all things to the death. His loyalty humbled me.

"Cynan," I said, "I ask a boon of you."

"Ask what you will, Llyd, and you shall have it," he answered with careless amity.

"Teach me the spear feint," I said, making a swinging motion with my hands, as if cracking an enemy skull.

Cynan beamed with his pleasure. "That I will do—but you must guard the knowledge jealously. What benefit to us if every foeman learned its secret?"

We talked long into the night. When at last we rose from the table to make our way to our sleeping quarters, we parted as friends.

I9

SOLLEN

Winter on the Isle of Sci is windy, cold, and wet. The days are dark and short, the nights dark and everlasting. The land is battered by fierce northern winds, which blast icy rain and snow by day, and gust through the roof thatch by night. The sun rises low—if it rises at all—and hovers close to the horizon, barely skirting the hilltops before losing heart and sinking once more into the icy abyss of night. The season is called *Sollen*, a dreary time when men and animals must remain inside their huts and halls, safe behind protecting walls.

Yet, for all the dismal desolation of that bleak and cheerless season, there are interludes of warmth and comfort: endless fire burning bright in the hearth, embers glowing red in iron braziers, thick woolen mantles and white fleeces piled deep in the sleeping places, small silver lamps aflame with fragrant oils to banish the bitter gloom with sweetness and light.

Days are given to games of subtlety, skill, and chance—*fidchell* and *brandub* and *gwyddbwyll*, played on bright-painted wooden boards with carved pegs. And ever and always there is talk: an ornately woven garment of seamless speech, an unending fountain of heady oration, a merry bubbling cauldron of discourse on all subjects under heaven. As iron sharpens iron, my skill in conversation increased mightily in the good-natured cut and thrust of friendly debate. Time and again I silently thanked Tegid for teaching me so well.

Also during the dull Sollen season our simple fare of bread, meat, and ale was augmented to include pale yellow cheese, honey-sweetened barley cakes, steamy compotes of dried fruit, and the rich golden nectar of mead, the warrior's drink. To these luxuries were added roast duck and goose, fattened to grace the winter board.

The fellowship of hearth and hall was lavish and lofty—in part because few of Scatha's pupils remained through the winter. Most had returned to their tribes to winter with their people; those remaining—only a handful of the older youths, Boru among them—used the time to shape a bond closer than all but blood.

Our days were made the more enjoyable by the presence of Scatha's lovely daughters: three of the most beautiful young women ever to flower beneath fair heaven: Gwenllian, Govan, and Goewyn. They arrived on Ynys Sci with the ship which bore away the homebound students. They had returned to spend the long, somber Sollen season with their mother, each having served in the court of a king as *Banfáith*, or prophetess.

Fortunate the king who could boast a Banfáith; king among kings was he who retained one of Scatha's daughters for his court. None of them was married—not that it was prevented them—they rather chose loyalty to their demanding gifts. For on the day each gave herself in marriage she would cease to be a prophetess. A Banfáith was exalted among her kind. Like bards they could sing and play the harp, and like bards they were able counselors. But they also possessed an older, more mysterious power: the ability to search the woven pathways of the future to see what will be and to speak to the people in the voice of the *Dagda*.

They adorned the dank cold days with charm bright and warm, softening the generally savage tone of our military existence with feminine grace. Which was part of Scatha's education too. For a warrior must also master the intricacies of court etiquette and comportment in civilized society. This is why the older pupils stay. The final Sollen or two before a warrior completes Scatha's instruction, he is tutored in the gentler arts by Scatha's daughters.

Scatha's daughters, wise as they were beautiful, lavished affection on us all. It was the sweetest of pleasures merely to be included in the shining circle of their company. The long days in the hall were filled with enjoyable activities. I learned something of harp playing from Gwenllian, and spent many happy days drawing on tablets of wax with Govan; but my preference was playing gwyddbwyll with Goewyn.

What can I say of Scatha's daughters? That they were more beautiful to me than the fairest summer day, more graceful than the lithe deer frisking in the high mountain meadows, more enchanting than the green-shadowed valleys of Sci, that each was fetching, fascinating, winsome, entrancing.

There was Goewyn: her long hair, softly flaxen, plaited like her mother's in dozens of tiny braids, an exquisitely crafted golden bell at the end of each braid. When she moved, it was to a fine music. Her smooth, regal brow and fine, straight nose proclaimed nobility; her generous mouth with lips perpetually curved in a secret smile intimated a veiled sensuality; her brown eyes seemed always to hold a hint of laughter, as if all that passed before them existed solely for her private amusement. I very soon came to view our times together, head to head over the square wooden game board balanced on our knees, as a gift from a wildly benevolent Creator.

And Govan: with her ready laugh and subtle wit, and blue eyes, like her mother's, quick beneath dark lashes. Her hair was tawny and her skin dark, like a sun-browned berry; her body was well-knit, strong and expressive, the body of a dancer. On those few days when the sun lit the sky with its short-lived splendor—a radiance made all the more brilliant for its brevity—Govan and I would ride along the beach below the caer. The fresh wind stung our cheeks and spattered our cloaks with the ocean's spume; the horses splashed through the surf, rolling white on the black shingle. And we raced: she on a gray mare swift as a diving gull, I on a fleet red roan flying over the tumbled rocks and storm wrack until we were breathless.

We would ride to the far end of the bay where the great rocks of the cliff had collapsed into the sea. Then we would turn and thunder to the opposite headland, there to dismount and rest our horses. Their lathered flanks steamed in the chill air, and we trod the sea-slick stones, our lungs burning from the raw salt air. I felt the blood hot in my veins, the wind cold on my skin, Govan's ready hand in mine, and I knew myself to be alive under the Dagda's quickening touch.

The Dagda, the Good God they also called the Swift Sure Hand, for the infinite breadth of his creative feats and his ever-ardent power to sustain all that he touched. I learned of the enigmatic Celtic deity—and many another in the pantheon—from Gwenllian, who, in addition to serving as Banfáith to King Macrimhe of the Mertani, was also a *Banfilidh*—a female Filidh, or harper.

Gwenllian: beguiling with her dusky red hair and sparkling emerald eyes; bewitching, her skin like milk, and her cheeks and lips blushing red as if tinted with foxglove; graceful in every line from the bend of her neck to the curve of her foot. Each night Gwenllian wove the shimmering magic of the harp with her skilled fingers and sang the ageless songs of Albion: of Llyr and his sorry children, of inconstant Blodeuedd and her vile treachery, of Pwyll and his beloved Rhiannon, of fair Arianrhod, and mysterious Mathonwy, and Bran the Blessed, and Manawyddan, and Gwydion, and Pryderi, and Dylan, Epona, Don . . . and all the rest.

SOLLE∏

She sang their loves and hates, their strivings and peacemakings, their glorious feats and pathetic failures, their wisdom and folly, their wondrous lives and miserable deaths, their towering great goodness and their shocking evil, their mercies and cruelties and triumphs and defeats, and the eternal verity of the endless cycle of their lives. She sang, and the length, breadth, height, and depth of human life passed before me. When Gwenllian sang, I knew what it was to be human.

Each night after our meal we would fill our mead cups and gather around the flame-bright hearth to hear Gwenllian's song. She would sing, and time would take wing. Sometimes I would shake myself from reverie to see the dawn, rose-fingered, lifting the edge of night's black cloak in the east, my head filled with burning images, and the mead in my cup untouched.

To hear Gwenllian sing was to enter a waking dream of such power that time and the elements faded away. To hear that flawless voice lifted in song was to feel enchantment as a physical force. When Gwenllian sang, Gwenllian became the song. When Gwenllian sang, those who heard tasted of a higher life.

I could have lived the rest of my days listening to her, never tiring, never stirring for want of food or drink; her song was all the nourishment I needed.

This, then, was the pattern of my life on Scatha's island realm. As Llyd, I learned the warrior's art, toiling with dogged determination to master the craft of swordthrust and spear-throw, knife-feat and shield-skill. The hilt shaped my hand until sword and arm were one; the shaft of my spear became my faithful, unerring servant; my knife and shield grew no less intimate a part of me than teeth and nails. Gradually, painfully, my body honed itself to the strict authority of battle. I grew lean as leather and hard as the handle of my spear.

I labored long. Defeat taught me cunning; failure taught me resourcefulness. I became resolute, and my fear shrank away. I became relentless, and courage was born. I lived the life of a warrior, and a warrior I became. I strove until every nerve and every sinew, each bone, organ, limb, and tendon performed with fearful precision the warrior's art. And in time I won the icy detachment of the warrior who is free from either anger or fear, whose movements are purest joy, and for whom each blood contest is an exultation of skill.

Six years I labored. Six years of sweat and strain and struggle. Six years of friendly strife. Six years of *Gyd's* fair sun and Sollen's cold. Six years, Beltain to Samhain, and in the end I was not least among my companions.

The seventh year progressed like the others in most respects. But rarely a moment passed when I was not acutely aware that my time on Ynys Sci was coming to an end: soon I would return to Prydain to serve the Great King Meldryn Mawr. I counted the days and dreaded each day's ending—for it brought me that much nearer my time of leaving.

I did not want to leave the island: never again to enjoy Goewyn's gentle company, never again to ride with Govan, to hear Gwenllian's song no more. I could not bear that thought. The sisters had grown dearer to me than my own heart; I would sooner pluck it warm and beating out of my breast than leave them.

Yet, what could I do? My departure was ordained from the beginning. I would leave when the ship arrived in the spring.

But there was another reason for my dread. In returning to Meldryn's court, I would return also to Simon—and thus to my long-neglected task: we must return to the world whence we had come. The very thought filled me with despair. I wanted to go back to the manifest world no more than Simon. I understood him now. On Ynys Sci the ties which bound me to my own world had worn thin and fallen away. I did not feel them go; it was more an innocent forgetting. With each passing day, the manifest world had grown a little less real, a little less vivid, until it seemed a ghost world filled with gray vapors and shadowy existences. I, too, wanted to stay in the Otherworld—no matter what the cost.

At the end of the seventh year, Tegid came for me.

One chill morning I stood on the rock bluff overlooking the bay and watched the ship move slowly closer. I felt a pang of bitter regret that the ship which brought Scatha's daughters back to the island once more would bear me away in the spring—in Gyd, when Sollen's icy storms had ceased.

Through three unending seasons I had endured the harsh exile of their absence. Now they returned, and I was eager to greet them.

I climbed into the saddle and urged my horse down the switchback trail from the bluff to the strand, to await the ship. More than a few of the younger pupils were already gathered on the beach, eager for the ship to make landfall—to set sail for home once more. They sorely missed clan and kin; I could see the homecraving in their eyes. And I wondered if they could see the hopeless desire in mine.

Slowly the ship drew closer; each wave that dashed against the shore seemed to bring the square-sailed vessel nearer. Soon I could make out the comely forms of Scatha's daughters at the bow. I could see Goewyn, hand raised in greeting, her smile welcoming; Govan, laughing; and Gwenllian, her hair blowing in the sea breeze. And then . . . then I was standing in water surging around my knees, help-ing to pull the ship onto the strand, and reaching up to help the first of them down. Goewyn took my hands and came into my arms, kiss-ing me, her breath sweet and warm against my neck.

Govan, too, greeted me with a kiss. "I have missed you, Llyd," she said lightly. And then, holding me at arm's length away from her, "Let me look at you."

I gripped her hands tightly as she swung around me. "I have not changed," I told her. "Except that my hunger for you has grown with each day we have been apart."

"Rascal!" she laughed, delighted, and kissed me again.

Govan spun away, and, as she moved toward the strand, I saw Tegid striding through the swirling surf, his oaken staff raised high. "Now I know they have made a warrior of you," he called.

"Tegid!" I shouted. "Tegid, is that really you?"

"The same," he said. He came to me and clasped me by my arms in the greeting of kinsmen. "And I find a much different man from the one I left. Meldryn Mawr will be pleased when I present you before him."

Though he meant it as a compliment, his words gave me to understand why he had come. Elation at seeing my friend quickly faded. I swallowed hard. "When?" I asked, hoping against hope that we still might winter on the island.

"Tonight," Tegid answered. "We will leave with the tide. I am sorry."

Although the day was bright, I felt Sollen's desolation in my soul. The sun's warmth died in the melancholy of my leaving. I felt as if my most treasured possession had been stolen from me. On Scatha's island I had lived as I had never lived before. In the hard discipline of the warrior, I had learned what it was to be alive. Now it was over, and I felt as if my life—the only life I had ever valued—was over too.

"I would like nothing better than to winter here myself," Tegid told me. "But come, say your farewells. I will see to your things."

Those who had completed Scatha's tutelage must make formal request to leave. If, in Scatha's opinion, the warrior had mastered all that she deemed him capable of learning, the Pen-y-Cat would present him with his arms. Ordinarily it was a glad ceremony, but my heart was not in it. I did not want to leave.

Yet we made our way up to the caer and to the hall, where several of my fellow warriors were already gathering to entreat their leavetaking, Cynan foremost among them. He hailed me as we approached.

"Llyd! We are to go together, hey?" His ruddy face beamed with pleasure. He had worked long and hard for this day and could scarcely believe that it had come at last. "The ship is early this year. They are saying that there is trouble in Albion and we may be needed." He observed the glum expression on my face. "What is the matter with you?"

"I had hoped to stay a little longer," I replied, my voice bitter and low.

Friends though we were, Cynan could not understand the reason for my misery. "We will be battle chiefs! There is honor to be won, brother. Perhaps we will ride before winter! Meldryn Mawr is a great king; you will win much gold in his service. You will see."

Just then, the oxhide covering at the door was drawn aside, and Cynan was invited to enter. He ducked his head and stepped through. In the six years of our exile he had grown both confident and carefree. No longer a youth who must prove himself to the watching world, Cynan had become secure in his skill and settled in himself. He had gained some measure of peace from his father's awful, impossible demand for perfection. I liked to think I had helped him in this. Above all else, Cynan and I had become swordbrothers—a bond stronger than death and to be trusted above all others.

I did not care to wait with the others, so I walked a while around the caer, visiting for the last time the places I had come to know so well, lingering on the empty practice field which had absorbed so much of my sweat and blood.

Goewyn found me and wished me well, saying, "I will miss playing gwyddbwyll with you. You have become a worthy opponent."

"And it is you I will miss, Goewyn," I told her, hoping for a word of comfort.

She smiled but shook her fair head, setting the tiny bells jingling lightly. "Less than you imagine, of that I am certain. You have never wintered with the Great King. A glance from the maidens in Sycharth and you will forget you ever knew me."

"Yet I would have some remembrance of you."

"What would you have?" she asked, her lips curving in a sly smile.

I said the first thing that came into my mind. "A braid of your golden hair."

Goewyn laughed. "Take it then, if you will."

She stood before me, smiling, hands on hips while I cut off the end of a braid with my knife. Then she took it from me and wound the severed end with a bit of lavender thread pulled from the hem of her cloak so that the plait of hair would not unravel. "Come," she said, tucking the keepsake into my belt, "it is time for you to take your leave."

Drawing my arm through hers, Goewyn led me back up the stone-marked path to the round hut where Scatha received those who were sent to her and, their tutelage completed, dispatched them to their destiny. She drew aside the black oxhide covering and indicated that I should enter alone. I stooped low and stepped in. The room was dark, lit only by the sultry light of two iron braziers—one on either side of the three-legged camp chair on which the War Leader sat.

Scatha was wrapped in a scarlet cloak trimmed in gold and green, and fastened at her right shoulder with an enormous brooch of fine red gold and the glittering green fire of emeralds. On her head she wore a costly helm of burnished bronze, inlaid with gold and silver tracery; her unbound tresses spilled out from beneath her war cap to fall over her shoulders. Golden bracelets and armbands gleamed upon each wrist and arm—the gifts of grateful kings and princes whom she had served. Behind her, their shafts driven into the earth, were two silver-bladed spears, crossed shafts bound with a golden cord. Her feet were bare and resting upon a great round oxhide shield with a boss and rim of bronze engraved with the sea-wave spiral.

Gwenllian stood to one side in the shadows. She acknowledged me with a raised eyebrow when I glanced her way, but said nothing. I approached our beautiful Pen-y-Cat, touching the back of my hand to my forehead in the sign of reverence and respect.

"Why do you come here?" Scatha asked simply, beginning the ritual I had come to know well.

I replied, "I come here to request a boon, War Leader."

She nodded. "What boon would you have, son of mine?"

"I would have the boon of your blessing to go from your heart." The words clawed and nearly stuck in my throat.

"Where would you go, my son?" she asked gently, as a true mother might when looking upon her son for the last time.

"I would return to the hearth of my king, War Leader. For I am bound to serve him and swear fealty to him who succors me."

"If you would live as a warrior in a king's hall and bind your life to a king, you must first bind your heart to those who will serve you."

"Tell me who they are," I replied, "and I will do what may be done to bind heart and life to them that serve me."

At this, Scatha lifted a hand to Gwenllian, who stepped quickly to her side. I saw that she carried a sword in her left hand and a spear in her right. She placed the sword across Scatha's outstretched palms. Turning, Scatha held the sword out to me, saying, "Here is a Son of Earth, whose spirit was kindled in the heat of fire. Do take him, my son, and keep him always at your side."

With my right hand I reached out and gripped the naked blade and clasped it to my breast, the hilt over my heart. "I do take this one to serve me, Pen-y-Cat."

The War Leader inclined her head, turned to receive the spear from Gwenllian's hand, and said, "Here is a Son of Air, whose spirit was awakened in the darkness of the grove. Do take him, my son, and keep him always at your side."

With my left hand I reached out and gripped the ashwood shaft and held it close against me, saying, "I do take this one to serve me, Pen-y-Cat."

Scatha raised her hands, palms outward, as if in benediction. "Go your way, son of mine. You have the blessing you seek."

The ceremony was concluded with these words, but I felt the lack of something—I wanted something more. I knelt down and placed my weapons at her bare feet. "Yet I would have one thing more, War Leader."

At this, Scatha arched an eyebrow in surprise. "Ask what is in your heart, my son."

"The world is wide, Pen-y-Cat, and those who go from this place come not again. Yet I ask the boon of your blessing to return to your hearth as to that of a kinsman. For if I have any life after this day, it is because you have given it to me."

Our wise War Leader smiled at these words. "The world is wide indeed, son of mine. And it is true that those who go from this place come not here again. Yet my hearth is warm and there is room in my hall." She raised her arms and held them out to me. "Come to me, my son."

I bent forward and placed my head against her breast. She cradled me in her arms, caressing my cheek and running her fingers through my hair. "You are my son," she said softly. "Use the life I have given you wisely, and see that you acquit yourself with honor through all things. If nothing prevents you, return here when you will. You are welcome beneath my roof, my son." Scatha placed her hands on my shoulders, kissed me, and released me.

I took up my weapons and went out. I was Scatha's son now—one of her innumerable brood—with leave to come and go as I would. This pleased me, though I could have wished I did not have to go away at all.

I saw Goewyn again before going out to the ship. The day had turned chill and low gray clouds blew in from the east across the bay. The tide was already flowing, and some of the younger boys were waiting on the shore, eager to sail. They had been throwing shells at the gulls, who shrieked indignantly overhead. Goewyn walked with me upon the strand, clasping my hand tightly. I told her I would return but made no vow of it—we both knew better than to pledge vows we could not keep.

When the time came, I waded out to the ship, climbed aboard, and took my place at the bow to gaze my last upon Ynys Sci. Goewyn stood in the water, her yellow mantle bunched in her fists while the restless surf surged around the hem of her heather-hued cloak. The lowering sun flared briefly above the ridge, flooding the strand with red-gold light. The seawash turned all green and gold and seething, like molten bronze, its scattered radiance reflected in the shadowed hollows of Goewyn's face.

As the last passengers clambered over the low side and the ship moved slowly into deeper water, Goewyn raised her hand in farewell. I waved back, whereupon she turned and hurried across the strand to the path leading up to the caer. I watched her as she climbed the hill path; and, as she reached the top, I thought I saw her pause and cast a last look over her shoulder.

20

THE GORSEDD
OF BARDS

Mist and darkness stole Scatha's island from my view. Then, and only then, did Tegid reveal to me the reason for his coming to claim me a season early. He came to me where I stood alone at the prow. Our horses were tethered to the center picket behind us, and the other passengers and baggage were behind the horses around the mast. They had lit a fire on the ship's open grate and were cooking fish and talking loudly; no one was paying any heed to us. We could speak openly without fear of being overheard.

He began by apologizing. "I am sorry, my friend. If I had my way in the matter, I would have granted you a year and a day to take leave of your beloved island."

I could not tell if he was mocking me or not. "I do not blame you, Tegid," I said. "It was not to be. We will speak of it no more."

"Yet I would not have come without good reason." He turned from me to gaze out at the darkling sea, as if into a pit of despair.

I waited for him to say more, but a gloomy silence stretched between us. Finally, I said, "Well, am I to know this reason? Or are you to go on muttering in veiled hints all the way to Sycharth."

Without taking his eyes from the sea, he confided, "We do not go to Sycharth."

"No? Where then?" It was all the same to me; I would be miserable wherever I was.

"The Day of Strife is at hand," he replied by way of answer. "We go to see what may be done."

This sounded far more doleful and mysterious than I was prepared to accept. I tried to make light of it. "What? Do not tell me that King Meldryn Mawr's mead vats have run dry!" I gasped in feigned horror.

"Well," he allowed, cheering slightly, "it is not as bad as that, perhaps."

"What then, brother? Speak plainly, or I must think the worst."

"In three days' time this ship will pass Ynys Oer, and we will be put ashore," he told me, speaking quietly, earnestly. "We will ride across the island to the western side and take a boat across the strait to Ynys Bàinail, where we will join the *gorsedd* of bards. Ollathir has summoned the *Derwyddi* of Albion to a gathering on the Isle of the White Rock."

"This gathering of bards," I said, "am I to know the reason for it?"

"I have told you all that was given me. I cannot say more."

"I do not understand, Tegid. I am no bard. Why am I to be included?"

"You are to be included because Meldryn Mawr and Ollathir wish it to be so. I can tell you nothing more," Tegid replied. But he said it in a way that gave me to understand that he did indeed know more, but that if I wanted to hear more, it was my duty to pull it out of him. I had occasionally encountered this same reluctance in others. It seemed that the more delicate the situation, the less straightforward the talk. The purpose, as far as I could tell, was to protect the speaker from the blame of speaking out of turn. Also, being a bard, Tegid was no doubt under some kind of prohibition or taboo against revealing privileged information about affairs at court. But he clearly wanted me to try.

"How is Meldryn Mawr?" I asked. "Is he well?"

"The king is well," replied Tegid. "He is eager to see what manner of warrior you have become."

"If I remember correctly, Meldryn Mawr has no lack of warriors. Certainly, he can have no thought for me."

"Oh, but you are wrong. A king can never have too many warriors—just as a man can never have too many friends."

I knew how this game of cat-and-mouse was played, and it could go on for days. But I did not mind; we had a long sea journey ahead of us, and I had nothing better to do than unravel Tegid's riddle.

"A friendless man is worse than a homeless dog," I observed, quoting a local expression. "But Meldryn Mawr is a very great king, I am told. Were the stars in the sky twice as many, the friends of Meldryn Mawr would still outnumber them."

"Once, that could be said," sighed Tegid in overly exaggerated unhappiness. "Not now."

So, Good King Meldryn was unhappy because he had fallen out with some of his friends. Because of this, somehow, he had sent Tegid to fetch me a season or two early. Very well. I decided to leave that trail for the moment and try another. "Great is my distress to hear it," I said. "Still, it will be good to see the king again—and Ollathir. I have often thought of him." It was a slight overstatement, seeing that I'd never exchanged a word with the man.

"Oh, yes," allowed Tegid. "The Chief Bard remembers you with particular fondness." Even in the dusk I could see the corners of his mouth twitching. He was enjoying the way I played the game. "Of course, I would not expect too rich a welcome. Like the king, he has much to trouble him of late."

What could be troubling the king and his chief bard? I took a wild guess. "At least," I ventured, "Prince Meldron is an able leader. A man's sons can be a comfort to him in times of trouble."

Tegid nodded slowly, as if willing me to understand. "This is true. Would that Meldryn Mawr had more sons."

"Does he not?" I admitted surprise.

"Alas, no. Queen Merian was a most noble woman—a match for Meldryn Mawr in every way. It was joy itself to see them riding out in the morning. The queen loved to ride, so the king kept the finest horses. He obtained one for her from Tir Aflan across the sea—a magnificent animal, which he gave to his wife as a gift. The day she first rode that horse, that was the day of her death. The spirited beast threw her on stony ground. Queen Merian struck her head and died." He concluded his unhappy account: "The king vowed never to take another queen."

This only deepened the mystery. Sad though it undoubtedly was, what did it have to do with me? The answer seemed to dance around the person of Prince Meldron, though I could not imagine how.

"That is a very grave tragedy indeed," I remarked. "But at least the king was not without a son."

"That is so." Tegid's terse agreement was more condemning than an outright rejection.

So there was trouble in Meldryn Mawr's court, and Prince Meldron was somehow mixed up in it. Now what? I thought for a moment, but nothing more came to mind. "We are fortunate," I observed, slogging on. "The concerns of court are no concerns of ours. I would not want to be king."

"Perhaps we are not so fortunate as you believe," Tegid said ominously. "Soon the concerns of kings will be the concern of all." So saying, the moody Brehon slipped once more into his gray despondence. He moved away into the shadows, and I was left to puzzle over his parting words. But I was no longer interested in his puzzles. The

219

implied foreboding had soured me to the intrigue. I tired of the game. If he wanted to tell me something outright, well and good. If not, I was willing to put it out of my mind.

Two days of mist and rain made the voyage miserable, but on the morning of the third day, as the ship passed through the narrows between the mainland and Ynys Oer of the barren, looming hills, the clouds parted and the sun dazzled our eyes. Tegid and I disembarked on a rockbound strand. We led our horses to the inland track before mounting them. When I looked back, the ship was already putting out to sea once more.

The Isle of Oer is dominated by high black crags and deep-seamed glens with fast-running streams. It is a place of wild sheep and eagles, red deer, heather, gorse, and little else. The few hardy folk who live there shelter in the steep-sided glens, or on the flat land above one of the innumerable coves on the eastern side of the island.

The day stayed fair, so we made good speed, reaching the furthest western shore as the sun disappeared below the sea rim. In a sheltered cove of rock and sand we found many horses picketed outside a white stone hut, and several Mabinogi tending their masters' mounts. The boat Tegid expected was gone. Although, if we had been so inclined, we might easily have swum across to the small island which was our destination: Bàinail—the name means White Rock, and it was well-named. Except for the sparse green sea grass along the shore, the island seemed little more than a heap of chalky white stone tossed up from the seabed.

Why the bards should choose this place above all others for their gathering was a mystery to me. I could see nothing to recommend it, and much against it. But then, I was no bard. I asked him, as we stood looking across the narrow strait to the island, and Tegid explained it this way—simply, if obscurely: "Ynys Bàinail is the sacred center of Albion."

That the small rock of an island was in no way central—and was not even properly attached—to Albion apparently made little difference.

"Shall I see if I can find a boat?" I asked, looking around the rock-tumbled cove.

"We have come too late. The crossing must be made by daylight," Tegid explained.

Flipping a hand to the sky, glowing orange and pink in the full flush of sunset, I protested, "But the sky is not yet dark. We can easily reach the other side."

I might have saved my breath. "The boat will return for us in the morning. We will spend this night here on the shore."

Probably, it was just as well. I was tired from a long day's ride and, with the approach of night, the air was growing chill. I wanted nothing more than to wrap myself in my cloak before the fire with a bowl of broth in my belly. Indeed, we fared better than that. The Mabinogi were well supplied with mutton, bread, ale, and apples. And they had been instructed to care for those who, like Tegid and myself, were making way to the gathering.

They banked the fire high. We enjoyed a good night's sleep. And at dawn, as Tegid had said, a boat came for us.

The sea mist lay upon the still water, hiding the island I had seen the night before. The boat glided without sound or effort out of the fog, bearing a lone oarsman—a Gwyddon whom Tegid knew. They exchanged greetings while I settled myself in the center of the craft, my spear across my knees. The Gwyddon saw me and said, "No weapon is permitted on the sacred island. You must leave them here."

I hesitated, remembering my warrior's promise to Scatha. Tegid mistook my reluctance and sought to reassure me, "Please, have no fear," he said. "Nothing evil will befall us there, and your presence is required." He signaled to one of the young men staying behind, and I reluctantly gave over my sword and spear to the Mabinog's care. Tegid, his oaken staff in his hand, climbed in before me at the prow, and the oarsman took up his long oar at the stern. The Mabinog pushed us off the shingle, watched us away, and hastened back to the fire.

Once in deeper water, the Gwyddon turned the boat and propelled us across the water. The fog closed around us, cloudlike, thick as wool. It seemed to me that as the world passed from our sight it ceased to exist. I felt the uncanny sensation of traveling, not in distance, but through time—to another day, another age. With the slow dip and swish of the oar, the boat proceeded into a dim, mist-shrouded past, or a future veiled from view. The sensation made me dizzy, and I gripped the wooden sides of the boat with both hands.

Halfway across the narrow strait, the boat emerged from the sea mist. I saw the Isle of the White Rock before us and, turning my head to look behind, saw only the fog bank rising like a solid wall from the gray green sea. Nothing of the former world remained.

The boat seemed to take speed, shedding the last wisps of fog. A short time later, the prow touched the fine white sand of Ynys Bàinail. Tegid leaped out of the boat, pulled it onto the sand, and beached it alongside a few other vessels there. I climbed out of the boat to stand in water to my knees. To my surprise, the water was warm, palest blue, and crystal clear.

I splashed my way to where Tegid waited at the water's edge. I made to step ashore, but he stopped me. "This is a sacred place and you are not a bard. If it were not for Ollathir, you would not be allowed even this far. Do you understand?"

I nodded. Tegid, more solemn and serious than I had ever known him, took me by the arm and cautioned me tersely. "Do only what you see me do. Speak no word aloud while you are on this island."

I nodded again, and Tegid jerked his chin down sharply, ending my instruction. Then he turned and fell into step behind our oarsman, who was striding up the beach. I stepped onto the strand, walked a few paces and almost fell flat on my face—overcome by the weird and fantastic sensation that I could not touch the ground. That, or the ground beneath my feet was not solid, but fluid, like water or cloud. Alongside this, I had the bizarre sensation of growing very rapidly, expanding, towering above the landscape; it felt as if my head scraped the sky. The hair on my scalp and arms tingled, and my skin turned to gooseflesh. I could not move for fear of falling, certain that I would not be able to stand on the infirm ground, that it would no longer support me.

Seeing that I had become stranded, Tegid turned and hastened back to me. He placed three fingers on my forehead and uttered a word I did not understand. Instantly, the immobilizing sensation left me and I crossed the beach without difficulty. We very quickly reached a sheep-trail above the beach and followed it into the interior of the small island, toward the huge rock-stack of a hill which dominated the center of the islet, and from which it derived its name.

We walked for some time in silence and heard no sound: neither birds nor sea sounds reached the ear in that place. All was hushed and quiet beneath a heavy pall of dense haze—as if the hand of a god lay cupped over the island. Why this should be so, I cannot say. But I do not think it was a natural thing.

I followed Tegid, still a bit queasy, keeping my eyes to the uneven trail lest I catch my foot on a stone and fall down. When the sheep-track began to rise, however, I looked up to see the great hump of white rock soaring in front of me like an enormous bank of billowing cloud. The white rock formed a lofty promontory with three sides open to the sea. A narrow trail wound around the outer rim of the promontory. Without so much as a backward glance, the Gwyddon led us to this trail. At once the footpath became precipitous; one misstep and I would plunge headlong onto a scree-covered shingle far below.

I continued on, setting my feet to the path winding up and around the giant white rock. Upon reaching the furthest western extent, the track ended in a blank wall of stone. Pressing myself to the smooth rock face on my left hand, as I inched slowly closer, I saw the Gwyddon leading us into this wall of rock disappear. I almost remarked on this but remembered Tegid's warning and said nothing.

Tegid approached the rock wall, gave a quick sideways turn, and likewise disappeared. Following his example, I, too, stepped up to the wall, and then saw the narrow cleft—just wide enough for a man to pass through if he swung his shoulders to the side. I did as I had seen Tegid do and stepped through the opening into a short tunnel. The tunnel floor slanted sharply upward. I scrambled up the last few paces into daylight and onto a huge, flat, grass-covered plain. A scattering of sheep grazed over the green expanse, drifting like clouds across a wide green firmament.

In the center of the plain rose a vast conical mound with a flattened top. Whether the mound was a thing of nature or crafted in some ancient age by human hands, there was no way to tell. Perhaps it was a little of both. Atop the mound, a slender pillar pointed a tapered finger toward the sky. At the foot of the mound were gathered the bards in numbers amounting to nearly a hundred—three thirties and three, I later learned—some dressed in brown, others in gray.

The bards were milling about aimlessly, some carrying their wooden rods, others holding branches of hazel, rowan, oak, and other trees. They moved among one another, crossing one another's paths in random fashion. Every now and again, one of the bards would stop and strike his rod against the ground three times, or raise his branch and revolve it slowly in a circle around his head. Closer, I could hear the low murmur of their voices uttering unintelligible words.

As we approached the steep-sided mound, one of the bards saw Tegid and stepped out from among the others to meet him. Coming nearer, I recognized that it was Ollathir, King Meldryn Mawr's bard. He glanced at me as Tegid and I came to stand before him, and seemed pleased to see me. But he spoke only to Tegid. They conferred with one another head-to-head for a short while, whereupon they were approached by a third bard, emerging from the throng. I recognized him, although it took me a moment to place him—then I remembered him as Prince Meldron's bard, Ruadh. The discussion finished abruptly as Ruadh, smiling, joined the other two.

At the same moment, Ollathir whirled toward me. "Watch all," the Chief Bard said, clutching me by the shoulder as if compelling me to understand. "Watch well."

Then the three removed themselves to the company of the bards. I made to follow, but Tegid placed his hand against my chest and cautioned me with a curt shake of his head. I was left standing alone.

I gathered from Ollathir's cryptic instructions that I was to stay behind and act as some sort of observer, so I determined to find a good position from which to view the proceedings. I found no such place—not even a stone large enough to serve as a seat. I was still looking around when the bards, at some unseen signal, arranged themselves in ordered ranks and began walking around the base of the mound in a slow, sunwise circle.

Once, twice, three times they circled the mound, their voices murmuring in that strange, droning tongue. Upon completing the third circuit, they mounted the steep slopes of the mound to gather around the central pillar far above.

From my distant position below, I did not think I would see anything of interest. Certainly, I could not hear a word of what passed on the mound. What then was I to observe? I could, it seemed to me, but oversee the gathering itself. I could vouch for the fact that it took place, but little else.

Nevertheless, I trained my eyes upon the gathering atop the mound. A sonorous humming sound drifted down from above, which I supposed to be the bards chanting or singing. This stopped after a while, and all became silent—except that every now and then I would hear something drifting down from on high in gusts and bursts: a snatch of debate, mumbled agreement, grumbled disapproval, sharp choruses of affirmation and dissent. What these outbursts signified, I could not say.

The morning passed in this way: I watched restlessly, craning my neck toward the high moundtop, the cloaked bards muttering and murmuring. I began to weary of my chore. Since I did not know what I was watching, and nothing seemed to be happening in any event, I became bored. My mind wandered.

After a while the morning sun burned through the white haze, revealing a deep blue sky beyond. Despite the chill beginning to the day, the sun warmed the plain. I lay back on my elbows in the grass and soon grew drowsy. As my eyelids drooped, it occurred to me that Ollathir would not thank me for falling asleep on duty, so I dragged myself to my feet and began walking slowly around the base of the mound.

This is how I passed the day, sitting in a bored stupor, relieved only by an occasional ramble around the mound. All the while the bards held their assembly, or *gorsedd*, as Tegid called it. Nothing happened, as far as I could tell—nothing, except the long slow march of the sun across the empty expanse of sky.

Late in the day, I climbed to my feet for yet another of my restless circuits around the broad base of the mound. I made one circle, then another. On my third or fourth time around, the assembly concluded and bards began streaming down the sides of the mound. Most of the bards tarried in separate clusters; still others sat apart on the sides of the mound, their arms folded, gazing out across the grass plain to the sea. However, one small group of a dozen or so bards remained atop the mound, their heads together as if in deep and desperate conversation.

I stood apart from the groups, but no one took any notice of me. The Derwyddi, sour-faced and glum, all seemed preoccupied with weighty matters; at one point, however, I saw one of the Derwyddi steal away from the group and hurry across the plain toward the hill-track leading down to the strand. I noted it, since that was the only thing I saw the whole day.

As I did not see Tegid or Ollathir among any of the bards linger-ing on the hillside or plain, I supposed them to be among the group clustered around the standing stone atop the mound—and who, from the look of them, were ardently disputing some point. This palaver continued for a good while and then ceased abruptly. The bards lin-gering on the plain turned to watch their brothers coming down the slope, gazing, I thought, expectantly toward them.

But nothing was said, and no sign was given. Those who had been waiting took up places behind their leaders, and all moved in proces-sion across the plain to the hillside track and began the long descent to the beach below.

Tegid came and stood by me as the others departed, warning me yet again to remain silent. Ollathir, who had been the last to come down from the mound, walked to where we stood. He neither looked at us nor spoke, but merely passed before us and continued on his way to the path. Tegid took his place behind Ollathir, and I followed.

By the time we arrived at the beach, the boats were plying the nar-row channel between the islands. We waited as they worked back and forth across the strait, ferrying the Derwyddi to the larger island and the shore where their horses waited. We were the last to leave. Ollathir wanted it that way, I believe, though it made for a long, hungry wait.

The sun had begun sinking when we finally touched ground on Ynys Oer once again. The Mabinogi and all the other bards had gone; only our horses remained in the shelter of the hut. It was as if the gorsedd had never happened. I found my weapons stashed in the stone

227

hut, and a little bundle of food left behind. I retrieved my sword and spear, gathered up the food, and brought it to where Tegid and Ollathir stood in quiet consultation.

"We will stay here the night," Tegid informed me. "There is much to do yet, and daylight will not last."

Ollathir, grunting agreement, turned and walked away along the strand. Tegid watched him for a moment and, seeing my wondering glance, explained, "Yes, he is troubled. The gorsedd did not . . ." He paused, hesitated. "It ended badly."

I nodded. Tegid laughed at me. "You may speak now, my friend. Nothing prevents you."

Strangely, until Tegid released me from my ban, I had not felt that I *could* speak—yet I had noticed no impediment. I found my tongue now, however, and said, "Am I to know what is happening now? And why I have been brought here like this?"

Tegid put his hand on my shoulder. "It is for Ollathir to tell you what he will. When he returns, perhaps he will lay all before you." He let his hand drop, and as he turned away I thought I heard him mutter, "Knowledge is a burden—once taken up, it can never be discarded."

I watched him walk away, resenting the secrecy and guile. *Oh yes, knowledge is a burden,* I thought, *but ignorance is a burden too*—and one I was beginning to find extremely tedious. Someone had better tell me something soon, I vowed, or find himself another beast of burden.

21

CYTHRAWL

Ollathir did not return until the sun was well behind Ynys Bàinail across the water. I had occupied myself with fetching water and gathering firewood for our use through the night. For Sollen would soon be upon us and, despite the day's warmth, once the sun had disappeared we would feel the cold. Indeed, I was kneeling over a pile of kindling, ready to strike the flame for the fire, when the Chief Bard stood over me.

"Do not kindle the flame," he said. "Make ready a boat." He spoke calmly, but I could see that he was distracted. He kept his eyes downcast and his arms crossed, with hands hidden in the sleeves of his siarc. His face was gray, the pallor of illness, although his voice was strong and his eyes clear.

I put aside the metal and flint and proceeded at once to the strand where the ranks of boats had been beached. Tegid joined me and we dragged one of the boats over the sand and pushed it into the water. I took up the oar and passed it to Tegid, standing by the prow until Ollathir was settled in, his rowan rod across his knees. Then I pushed the boat out into the water and clambered in.

Tegid worked the oar with some urgency, and I realized what drove him: the time-between-times. The sun was already sinking behind the White Rock; we must hurry if we were to reach the mound before twilight.

We made the crossing to Ynys Bàinail quickly, and just as quickly reached the winding hilltrack leading to the grassy plain. Ollathir led the way and Tegid followed. I came last, and felt once again that strange sensation of expanding—stretching, growing, becoming larger with every step. It was dizzying and unnerving. Yet I did not stop. I lowered my head, gulped deep breaths, and plunged after the others. Heedless of my awkward stumbling, I hastened along as quickly as prudence allowed, dreading the entire journey—that tight trail would be treacherous to retrace in the dark.

We gained the grassy plain just as the sun sank beneath the rim of the western sea, flaming the wavetops, and staining the sky red violet and orange. The first stars gleamed in the east as the sky darkened at the advance of night. Ollathir and Tegid hurried to the mound and began climbing the steep sides. This time, since I was not prevented, I went up with them.

The cone-shaped mound was flattened at the summit, much as I had envisaged from below. A few paces in from the outer edge, the circle was marked with several hundred round, white stones—each stone buried in the earth with just the top protruding. Smaller stones marked the radials like the spokes of a wheel, one spoke for each of the four quarters. The tall pillar stone marked the hub of the wheel and was covered from its buried base to its tapering point with intricate whorls and spirals, and the curious, dizzying circle maze which was a Celtic commonplace—the entire surface covered in a richly patterned union of designs, all intertwining, all cut in sharp relief into the surface of the white stone.

Some of the departing had deposited their branches of hazel at the base of the pillar stone. Tegid retrieved one of these and handed it to me. "Hold to this. Whatever happens, do not let it go from your hand."

I was about to ask him what it was that he expected to happen, when he raised his hand and brushed his fingertips across my mouth. "This, too, is for your protection. See that you utter no sound."

At once the words forming on the tip of my tongue deserted me; all desire to speak fled. I merely nodded in mute agreement and clutched the leafless hazel branch more tightly. "Stand outside the ring," Tegid said, pointing to the outer circle of white stones. He glanced quickly at the sky, then turned, taking up his oaken staff, and hastened to join Ollathir, who had pulled his cloak over his head and begun pacing slowly around the pillar stone, his rowan rod clenched in his hands and held before him.

The two bards moved together around the standing stone, and the sun-flushed sky deepened into twilight. I looked to the east and saw the rising edge of the full moon just peeking above the sea rim. It was the time-between-times.

In that same moment, Ollathir, Chief Bard to Meldryn Mawr, stopped his pacing and raised his rowan rod to the sky, gripping it with both his hands. He called out in the secret language of the bards, his voice loud with the power of the *Taran Tafod*.

From the leather bag at his belt, he brought out a handful of the precious dust the bards call *Nawglan*, the Sacred Nine, a specially prepared mixture of ashes obtained from the burning of the nine sacred woods: willow of the streams, hazel of the rocks, alder of the marshes, birch of the waterfalls, ash of the shadows, yew of the plain, elm of the glens, rowan of the mountains, oak of the sun. This he scattered to the four quarters—and to the four quarters between the quarters—as he began slowly pacing once more in a sunwise circle around the pillar stone, which is the sacred center of Albion, the Island of the Mighty.

Tegid also paced, following three steps behind the Chief Bard, holding tight to his staff of oak, a fold of his cloak over his head. Ollathir spoke out a word, and Tegid echoed it. Around and around the pillar stone they marched, speaking out their strange, secret incantation.

How long this continued, I cannot say. I stood as one bereft of wit or sense, mute and staring at all before me, yet beholding nothing, understanding nothing. Time passed. Long or short the span, I did not attend it. I was caught up in the relentless flow of Ollathir's resounding voice and his peculiar words.

And then the words stopped.

All became quiet and still. It was but the peace before the storm. For, even as the thunder of the Taran Tafod faded into silence, I heard a sound like the rush of waters from a broken dam, or the sudden gush of a flood through a weed-dry riverbed: a boiling, bubbling tumult of sound, confused and striving, clashing, colliding, surging, breaking and forming, splashing and churning as it came.

I turned and saw that the plain below the mound was covered by a filthy yellow fog—inundating the land, whelming over all that stood before it like a plague. Seething, moiling, its ragged ropy tendrils curling ever and again upon itself, the foul fog began to swirl around the base of the mound. I watched, my skin turning cold and slick like clay, as the fog mounted up the sides of the sacred mound.

I lifted my head and looked to the sky. The stars seemed to streak and run together like molten silver. The new-risen moon burned red as blood. The darkness heaved and throbbed like the labored flanks of a beast in pain.

From out of the livid sky there came a thin, wailing shriek, bloodless and cold—like that of a Sollen wind when it howls down from the frozen northern heights. It grew louder, assailing the moundtop, drowning out the churning watersound, filling this worlds-realm with the sound of desolation and malice.

Even as I looked, I saw a ghastly form taking shape, monstrous as it was vast, and it was vast indeed. The thing seemed to come swimming out of the night air, out of the fabric of the sky itself, from out of the spaces between the streaming stars. From the heart of darkness was it formed, taking darkness as its flesh, and night airs and ethers as its blood and bones—screaming as it came, screaming with the agony of its own heinous creation.

The thing was no creature born of earth—it lived, and yet it was not alive; it moved, yet it was not animate; it cried out, yet possessed no tongue. Frightful to behold, it was a creature of the hell pit, possessing in itself not so much a body as a multitude of bodies, all of them forming and growing, separating and dividing, shriveling and decaying and melting into one another, always changing, yet ever presenting the same loathsome shape to view. A shape calculated to freeze the blood and to stop the warm heart beating in the breast.

I saw eyes—ten thousand glowing cats' eyes: baleful, slit-pupiled, bulging, and yellow. I saw mouths: gaping, sucking, mewling, and drooling venom. I saw limbs: gross, misshapen, writhing, thrashing—many-handed on the ends of convulsive arms; club-footed on the stumped shanks of wasted legs. I saw torsos: bloated and obscene, shrunken, skeletal, rotting and putrid with crusted excrescence. I saw hideous heads: faces ravaged by disease and disfigured, hollow eyepits burning, noses eaten away by cancerous lesions, white skull plates gleaming beneath scragged hair, wattled jowls jiggling, corded necks straining, blackened teeth bleeding pus from suppurating gums.

This hell-spawned creature loomed closer, driving down from on high. Cruel and ravening, it drove to execute our destruction. But something yet held it suspended between Earth and the nether regions of its abysmal habitation; held it still, but would not so hold it for long. The thing drew strength to itself, and its appalling power increased as it wafted ever nearer, spinning and hovering, its myriad bodies squirming in tortured motion.

I could neither watch, nor could I refrain from watching, as the demonseed reached out a great clawed hand toward the moundtop. The hand, leprous and scaly, stole swiftly across the empty distance which had seemed our only protection.

As the enormous hand closed over us, Ollathir raised his voice in an anguished cry and swung his rowan staff in a sweeping arc around his head. I heard it whir as it ripped through the air. Once, twice, and then . . . CRACK! He struck the pillar rock, breaking the stout wooden rod in half.

In the same instant, a bright light flashed from the pillar stone. The Derwydd fell to his knees, gripping the broken half of his rod between his hands, his face contorted in fearful agony. Instinctively, I made to dash forward, but Tegid whirled and raised a warning hand to stay me.

From deep within the mound there came a sound as that of an earthquake shifting rocks and tumbling rubble deep underground. Yet I felt no tremor, nor even the slightest quaver of vibration. I could feel the sound low in my bowels and in my knees. It seemed to rise up through the soil and into my very bones, traveling up my spine and rattling the top of my skull. I swayed, suddenly weak, my muscles losing strength.

Ollathir, using the broken rowan staff as a crutch, heaved himself to his feet, tottered, and fell back against the pillar stone, which was now glowing with a soft, pearly light. Yet I did not wonder at this, for my attention was trained upon the figure of Ollathir, whose features had undergone a terrible transformation.

He stood with his back hard against the weird-figured stone, arms stiffly raised, still gripping half the broken rod between his hand, and bawling with a mighty voice. Mouth gaping, nostrils flared, and eyes bulging horribly from his head, he appeared less a human being than an animal: a black-faced, bellowing bull.

The bull roar did not emanate from the bard's throat, but came up from out of the earth beneath us, through the pillar stone and thence through Ollathir who gave it voice. And such a voice! It was deep and dire, loud with sinewed strength, firm as rooted rock, and hollow as the mounded grave.

The sound became a wild, inchoate chant. At first I could not make out the words, but then I discerned a name—Ollathir was calling out a name. And the name was *Dagda Samildanac.*

The words of the name meant the Goodly-Wise Many-Gifted One. It was the secret name of the highest god known among the tribes of Albion.

"Dagda! Dagda Samildanac!" the resonant bull-voice boomed out. "Dagda! Samildanac Dagda!"

Again and again the eerie invocation sounded, taking shape and substance. Up it rose, spreading like a shield above us, enfolding us in a cloak of protection—a blessed lorica to hide us from the fell enemy of all living things.

"Samildanac! Dagda! Dagda Samildanac!" the great earth voice bellowed, louder and still louder until the very mound itself quivered and shook.

I could not stand before such a sound. I gripped my hazel branch and swayed dizzily on my feet. I squeezed my eyes shut, but that made the dizziness worse. I reeled backward and fell down on hands and knees, still clutching the hazel wand in my right hand. I could not breathe; I gasped for air. I tasted the salt-sweet taste of blood on my tongue and realized that I was grinding my lower lip between my teeth.

Fearfully, I turned my eyes toward the demon hand pressing down upon us. The lorica of Ollathir's invocation had halted the thing's advance but lacked the power to banish it. Not long could the Chief Bard endure the strain of his entreaty, for already I could see him tiring. He could no longer hold his head erect, and his arms began to sag.

Soon his strength would give out; the bull-voice of the Dark Tongue would falter. And the lorica of protection would fail. Then we would surely be crushed.

I dragged my feet under me and stood. Tegid lay before me on his side, bleeding from his nose and mouth, one arm flung over his head, the other stretched out as if trying to reach Ollathir. I saw Tegid's reaching hand and determined what to do: I would uphold the Chief Bard's hands; I would support his arms and keep them upraised. As long as the bard's hands gripped the rowan rod, we would be safe.

I lurched into the circle toward the pillar stone, stumbling over the body of Tegid. Instantly, I was battered by a force of blinding power which struck me like the heat blast from a fire, swirling around me like wind-driven flames. My sight dimmed. I could not see. I fought blindly onward, step-by-faltering-step, my heart thumping hard against my ribs. I could feel my flesh withering on my bones.

I struggled toward the pillar stone where Ollathir stood. His head slumped on his chest. His arms sagged.

I reached him just as his stamina failed and his hands, still grasping the broken rod, dropped. I seized the rod and lifted it. Ollathir raised his head, saw me standing over him, and recognition came into his bulging eyes. He opened his mouth and drew breath into his lungs.

"Dagda! Samildanac Dagda!" the Chief Bard bellowed. "Bodd cwi Samildanac!"

I felt once again the strange growing sensation in my hands where I touched the rod: my hands seemed to expand, to grow immense and powerful. I could feel a mighty strength surging into my fingers, palms, and wrists. Had I picked up a stone, I know I could have crushed it in my grip. The uncanny sensation flowed through my hands and into my arms, into my shoulders, neck, and head, into my back and chest and legs and feet. I felt as if I had grown huge, as if I had become a giant on the earth, possessing a giant's strength.

I lifted the rowan rod high. With a loud and terrible cry, Ollathir collapsed against the standing stone and slumped to the ground. Now I stood alone, raising the staff of power over us. Ollathir lay panting at my feet, feebly striving to rise.

Looking above me, I saw the immense clawed hand stretching itself above us, pressing down. My strength, great though it was, could not prevent it from crushing us. I was not a bard; I knew no words of power. I cried out to the Chief Bard: "Ollathir!" I shouted, my voice torn from my throat by the shrieking blast. "Ollathir, do not abandon us! Penderwydd, help us!"

He heard me and took heart at my words. He gripped my legs and pulled himself to his knees. I thought he meant to rise, but instead he beckoned me to bend near him. I thrust the rowan rod high, loosed a hand, reached down, and hauled him to his feet. He tottered, clutching at me, leaning on me for support, his limbs trembling with the effort to stand.

His jaw worked, his mouth formed words, but I could not hear them. I thought he wanted me to say the words he was saying. I cocked my head, placing my ear to his mouth. Ollathir crooked an arm around the back of my neck and turned my face to his. "Domhain Dorcha . . . ," he whispered in the secret language of bards. "The heart . . . in place beyond . . . the Phantarch sleeps . . ."

I understood nothing of what he said. "What are you saying? Speak plainly!"

But he was past hearing. "Llew!" he said in a tight, choked voice. "Llew . . . your servant greets you!"

I saw the sweat of death on his brow, and his eyes fierce and bright. Then he pressed his mouth to mine.

The Chief Bard held me in a desperate embrace. Before I could pull away, he breathed his dying breath into me. I tasted his breath hot on my tongue. My lungs swelled to bursting. With my free hand

I tried to break his stranglehold; I seized his wrist and made to pry his arm from around my neck. But he was already slipping away. The movement begun to loose myself from his grasp finished with a futile grab to save him from falling and striking his head against the pillar stone.

"Ollathir!" I cried, and my voice trembled the ground beneath my feet. "Ollathir, do not die!"

The Chief Bard was already dead.

That he should die, while I strove to save him, angered me. That he should die, leaving me to battle the hellborn beast alone, infuriated me. Instantly, I was overcome with a savage rage. "Ollathir!" I shouted. "Stand up! I need you!"

The body lay in a pathetic heap at my feet. "Stand you, Ollathir!" I cried. I kicked at him, but he did not respond. This angered me the more. In white-hot fury I struck him with the rowan rod. I struck him time and again, screaming at him to rise. But he did not rise.

Anger and frustration warred within me. I fell upon him, clubbing him with the broken rod. "Dagda!" I wailed, using the words I had heard him utter, "Samildanac Dagda, make him live!"

It came into my mind that I was beating a dead man—and that the hell spawn hovering over the mound was deriving pleasure and strength from this abomination. With an effort of will I pushed myself away from Ollathir's battered corpse. I stood and, with a mighty heave, slammed the rowan rod into the side of the pillar stone: once . . . and once more . . . and yet once more.

Then I threw the blood-smeared staff into the leering, smirking maw above me. The rowan rod spun up into the night sky, striking the creature of the pit. There came a sound like a terrible rush of wind as the lowering image splintered and flew into a vapor of fragments that vanished like the night's mist before the clear light of day.

The whole sky seemed to lighten at once, flashing forth in a blaze of crimson and gold. I looked and saw the flaming sun-rim touching the lip of the horizon. The time-between-times!

Within moments the plain below the mound was awash in golden light. The pillar stone shone like an earthstar, dazzling in the dawn light. I raised my eyes, shielding them with my hands from the new day's light. I saw only the morning stars gleaming in the paling firmament. The creature of the night was gone.

Great fatigue descended upon me, and I sank down on my knees beside the Chief Bard's body. Tears started in my eyes to see what I had done to that once-handsome head. Shame and sorrow flowed mingled in the hot tears that streamed down my face. "Forgive me, Ollathir," I wept. "Please, forgive me."

Tegid found me some little time later, still weeping over the body, holding Ollathir's broken head on my knees, bathing it with my tears. I felt a touch on my shoulder. "What has happened here?" Tegid asked.

I raised my head to make an answer, but the expression on Tegid's face stopped me. He stared at the body in stunned and bewildered silence, his hands shaking in utter agitation. His mouth formed words, but he could not speak. When he finally found his voice, it was a single astonished word. "How?"

I could only shake my head in reply. Was it the creature of the pit that killed him? Was it the Dagda? I did not know.

Tegid dropped to his knees beside me and pressed his hands to either side of Ollathir's head. He lowered his face to the Penderwydd's and pressed his lips to the now-cold brow. "May it go well with you on your journey hence," he murmured.

The Brehon lifted Ollathir's shoulders from my knees and set about straightening the crooked limbs and smoothing the rumpled clothing. When he had finished, he stood. "Where is his staff?" he asked.

"I threw it," I replied and glanced across the flattened top of the mound. I saw part of the broken rowan rod lying on the ground at the edge of the circle of white stones. I walked to it and stooped to retrieve it.

As my hand closed on the length of rounded wood, I felt once more the strange power of the rod. I stood holding the object before me as it were a snake. The sensation of strength overwhelmed me. It seemed as if my limbs were growing to the size of trees, as if my head touched the clouds, as if my hands could move the hills. I could hear the blood-rush pounding in my ears like the sound of wind-driven surf.

It seemed as if I held within myself the power to do all things. I had only to lift my hand and whatever I craved would be accomplished. Nothing was denied; nothing would be withheld if I desired it. At the sound of my voice, the earth and sky would obey. I held within myself the authority to accomplish whatever I sought. My very presence could heal or slay. No longer was I confined to tread the dust like normal men. Where other men walked, I would run; where they ran, I would fly.

I would fly.

Holding the rowan rod in my hand and gazing out across the plain from the moundtop, I knew I could fly. I had only to lift my foot and I would sail out upon the wind, borne by unseen wings. I walked to the edge of the mound and calmly stepped out into nothing.

22

LLEW

I do not remember sleeping. I do not remember waking. I remember only this: Goewyn softly singing, her voice like a silken cord gently tugging me back to my senses and to myself. Sight returned to me, and I saw Goewyn's fair face above me and felt my head cradled in her lap. I lay on a fleece-covered pallet in a small, rush-lit room, soft otterskin covering me.

I drew breath to speak, but before I could utter a sound she placed her fingertip to my lips. "Hush, my soul," she whispered. "Say nothing yet." She raised my head and offered a cup. "Drink this, and you will find your voice."

I sipped the warm liquid—tasting of honey and herbs—and it soothed my dry throat. I drained the cup, and Goewyn lowered my head to her lap once more. "What has happened?" I asked. "Why am I here?"

"Do you not know?" She held her head to one side, her long tresses slid from her shoulder to fall in a curling cascade above me. I smelled the scent of heather in her hair, and it made me ache with longing.

"I know only that I am where I always want to be," I replied. I spoke my heart without inhibition. And, taking a handful of her hair, I drew her face toward mine. Her lips were warm, her kiss sweet as the honeyed mead. I did not want the kiss to end.

"You have returned, indeed," Goewyn murmured. "I feared you had left us."

"Where am I?"

"Do you not remember?"

"I remember nothing, I—" Even as I spoke, I was assailed by a confused rush of images and sensations—but muted, as if dulled by great distance and greater time. I dimly remembered leaving Ynys Sci, the sea journey to Ynys Oer, the gorsedd of bards, and the fearful battle with the evil horror that took Ollathir's life. I remembered lying crumpled in the bottom of the boat, being tossed about on dangerous waves, and screaming—I remembered screaming unknown words at the top of my lungs, hurling garbled abuse at the four winds. I remembered, but it all seemed obscure and of little consequence compared with the look of love in Goewyn's dark eyes.

"Yes," I told her, "I remember now—some of it. But I do not recall leaving the sacred mound, or returning—if I *have* returned—to Ynys Sci."

Goewyn stroked my forehead. "You are with me in my mother's house. My sisters and I have been caring for you these many days."

"How many days?"

"Three threes of days since you came here."

"And how did I come here?"

"Tegid brought you."

"Where is he?" I asked.

"He is well. I will bid him come to you when you wish." She smiled, and I saw the fatigue behind her eyes. She had been watching over me day and night.

I attempted to rise, and found the effort greater than I had imagined. My muscles were stiff; my stomach, back, and legs cramped the instant I stirred. "Aghh!" I cried out in pain.

Goewyn carefully shifted my head to the pallet beneath me. "Lie still," she commanded, rising quickly. "I will bring help."

I bit the inside of my cheek to keep from screaming as the spasms racked my body. In a moment Goewyn returned with one of her sisters. Govan hurried to where I lay doubled over on the pallet and said to Goewyn, "Leave us. I will attend to him now."

Goewyn hesitated. "Go now," Govan insisted. "I will send for you when I have finished."

As soon as Goewyn had gone, Govan brought out a green jar which she placed amidst the burning coals of the iron brazier. Then she unwound the belt from around her waist, put it aside, and drew her arms through the neck of her mantle, pulling it off. Taking up the green jar once again, she pulled the clump of moss from its mouth and poured some of its contents into the palm of her hand. The room filled with the fragrance of scented oil. She replaced the jar in the brazier and rubbed her palms together. "Do not resist. This will soothe and heal you."

She stripped away my otterskin covering, took hold of my shoulders, and gently rolled me onto my stomach. My flesh warmed where she touched me, and in a moment I felt the same soothing warmth spreading across the knot-tight muscles of my back. Govan sang softly as she worked over me. Her strong fingers stroked the pain away, applying the healing balm, kneading life into my knotted, wooden flesh.

She massaged my shoulders and back, thighs, legs, and feet; then she rolled me over and rubbed my chest and stomach, arms, and hands. When she had finished, every part of my body felt loose and lank. I smiled through a lazy haze of pleasure, warm and relaxed from head to heel. I had no desire to rouse myself, and did not care if I never moved again.

Govan pulled the otterskin over me. "You will sleep now. And when you awake, you will be hungry. There will be food awaiting you." She dressed herself and departed. I was asleep before she left the room.

I woke again almost at once—or so it seemed. But I had slept, for someone had come in while I dozed and left me bread and ale and a little cheese. I drank some of the ale, and then, overcome by an almost ravenous hunger, tore the loaf in half and stuffed as much of it in my mouth as I could. I ate the cheese and the other half of the loaf likewise, and drained the cup.

Besides the food, someone had also brought clothing and left it folded neatly at the foot of my pallet. I rose slowly and climbed unsteadily to my feet. I took up the siarc and thrust my arms into the sleeves, admiring the color and quality: scarlet, the hue of winter-ripe nightshade berries; the fine-woven breecs were checked with shades of russet and brown. The leather of the wide belt and buskins was thick and soft, without blemish or mark, the color of sand; the cloak was feathery gray, the color of dove down, and the intricate knotwork of its hem bright silver. The brooch was silver, too, large and round, its surface inset with bright blue stones.

Never had I owned clothes so fine. It was the raiment of a wealthy chieftain. Why I should be so favored, I did not stop to consider. I dressed gladly, praising the generosity of my unknown patron—Scatha herself, no doubt. When I had arranged the cloak over my shoulders, I fastened the silver brooch and went out.

I was weaker than I thought, for the small effort of crossing the threshold made me light-headed and dizzy. I staggered against the doorpost and paused there until the house stopped spinning. The sun had slipped below a gray, hardcast sky briefly to illumine a dying day with a pale yellow light. Cold, with a raw wind off the sea, the air was sharp with the tang of salt.

Some of the older boys who were staying on the island through

Sollen had gathered nearby to play hurley. The low sun stretched their shadows long on the field. They stopped their game when they saw me, each one staring at me. None called out a greeting, though I knew them all and they knew me.

Goewyn appeared on the path outside my door. She saw me clutching the doorpost and hurried to my side. The brash sea wind caught her unbound hair and blew the long golden tresses across her face as she gathered my arm in hers. "I was coming to sit with you while you slept. I did not think you would rise so soon."

"I have slept enough. I want to walk," I told her. Supporting me, her arm beneath mine, she steered me past the gawking boys in the yard and out toward the sea cliff.

"How do you feel?" she asked.

"I feel new made," I said. At these words Goewyn hesitated—only a small falter in her step and a sidelong glance, both of which she covered instantly. But I noticed.

"Why do you look at me so?" I asked. "Is something wrong?"

She smiled but again I sensed the merest hint of indecision before she answered. "You looked like someone else just then," she replied. "It must have been the light."

Indeed, the fading afternoon light cast a golden glow over the sea and rocks below us and turned Goewyn's honey-hued hair to spun gold and her fair skin to finest amber. The wind was fresh off the sea, flinging waves against the rocks and kicking up a mist that glimmered in the air. Too soon the golden light began to fade. Overcome by a sudden urge to touch her, I stopped on the path and raised a hand to her face, cupping my palm to her cheek. She did not resist.

"Tegid is waiting," Goewyn said after a moment but did not draw away. We stood a little longer, then turned and made our way back to the cluster of dwellings.

We found Tegid in the hall and joined him at the hearth where he stood before a fire, holding a horn of ale. Upon seeing me, he affected an expression of indifference; but the relief in his voice was real enough. "So you walk the land of the living yet a little longer. I feared we had lost you, brother."

Goewyn refuted this happily. "He told us from the first that you would return," she said. "Tegid never doubted."

Embarrassed, Tegid gave a deprecating shrug and pressed the ale horn into my hand. "Drink! I will bring more."

He hastened away, and I turned to Goewyn, taking her hand and pressing it. "Thank you for . . . for watching over me, for caring for me—for saving me."

"Tegid is the one who saved you," she replied. "He endured much to bring you here. Compared to that, we did nothing."

"It was not nothing to me," I insisted. "I am in his debt, and yours. But it is a debt I look forward to repaying. Until then, accept my thanks."

"Truly," she replied, "there is no debt." She pressed my hand earnestly and stepped away. "You and Tegid will have much to talk about. I will leave you now."

She moved across the empty hall, and I watched her, surprised by the sudden surge of feeling for her. The hall seemed to grow visibly darker as she moved away, and I felt a chill creep into the air. I almost called her back to sit with me, but Tegid returned with cups and a jar of brown ale.

When we had seated ourselves at the hearth, I asked him to explain what he remembered of that freakish night on the White Rock. My own memory—so full of weird and frightening impressions and incredibly grotesque images—was not to be trusted. "I remember little of what happened," I told him. "And that which I do remember is not certain."

Tegid drank from his cup and then set it aside before answering.

"The Gorsedd of Bards failed," he said at last, beginning well before the events in question.

"The gathering—yes, I remember." And I remembered something else too. "Yes, but what I want to know is *why*? Why was I there at all? What was it all about?"

"As I explained to you aboard the ship—"

"Explained!" I scoffed. "You explained nothing. You said I was there because Ollathir and Meldryn Mawr wished it to be so. But you did not tell me *why* they wished me there."

"Ollathir intended to tell you after the gorsedd, but . . ." He shied from saying the words.

"But he died. So *you* must tell me, Tegid. Now."

Like a man composing himself, trusting his weight to an injured limb, Tegid paused, assessing the damage his words might inflict. "There is trouble in Albion," he said simply. "The three realms are divided: Prydain, Llogres, and Caledon—each looks only to itself and prepares for war with the others. The Day of Strife has come."

"Oh, yes, this mysterious Day of Strife. I remember. Go on."

"Even the noble clans are divided, royal houses are torn apart from within."

"Even the royal house of Meldryn Mawr?"

Tegid did not deign to answer, but I knew I guessed correctly. "You have lived in Sci these seven years," he continued. "You have been absent from Sycharth, so you could not have joined in the treacheries against the king. For this reason, you were chosen to attend the gathering. Ollathir and Meldryn Mawr determined to have you there to bear witness to all that happened at the gathering."

"But I did not attend the gathering," I reminded him, feeling cheated because I had not been better apprised and slightly insulted because I had not been fully trusted. "No one told me anything about this."

"To tell you beforehand," Tegid explained patiently, "would have poisoned your discernment."

"So you say," I grumped, remembering the cat-and-mouse game we had played aboard ship on the way to the island. Perhaps the bard had insinuated as much as he dared.

Tegid did not attempt to defend the judgment. He merely continued, saying, "Fear had already claimed the souls of many good men, bards among them. Ollathir suspected treachery among the brotherhood and planned to expose the traitors and purge them. But his plan failed. He had no choice but to conclude the gorsedd, lest he warn the traitors that he knew of their betrayals."

"So the thing I was watching for—whatever it was—did not take place."

Tegid held his head a little to one side, appraising me. "I do not know—but you do."

"Do I?"

"Did you see anything during the gorsedd?"

"I saw nothing. Everyone went up to the mound, and I stayed below. I waited, walking around the mound from time to time, and then everyone came down again. Nothing happened. Everyone left, and I . . . No, there was something."

Tegid leaned forward. "What do you recall?"

In my mind's eye I saw again the figure hurrying away across the plain, moments before the gathering concluded. "No doubt it is of little importance," I said slowly. "But just before the bards came down from the mound, I saw someone leaving the assembly."

"Was it Ruadh?"

"The prince's bard?" I thought for a moment, but I could not be certain. "It could have been Ruadh. I do not know."

"Ollathir would have known," Tegid said with conviction.

"Then why did he not ask me?" I demanded. This made no sense.

I hated these petty intrigues. I lacked the patience. Tegid looked away, his face closed as a slammed door. This was hard for him. It came to me that he loved Ollathir, his master and guide. I relented. "Why did Ollathir want to go back to the mound that night? Was it to do with this traitor?"

"Yes, and all the traitors," Tegid replied solemnly. "The Chief Bard sought knowledge of how far the treachery had spread." He halted, swung his eyes to me and then away again. He frowned into the deep-shadowed hall. "Ollathir believed the king was in danger," he said at last. His voice struck a hollow note in the empty hall. "That is why he returned to the sacred mound that night. He hoped by means of the Sight to learn whose hand was raised against the king. But he did not reckon on the . . . the . . ."

Tegid's voice trailed off awkwardly, and I knew why: the hellish creature on the mound. "Tell me, Tegid," I demanded, gently, but firmly. "What was it that we saw up there?"

Tegid's mouth twitched with revulsion. "The Dweller of the Pit of Uffern, the Ancient Evil, the Spirit of Destruction. You saw the force of death, decay, and chaos. *Cythrawl* is its name, but it is not a name spoken aloud save in dread."

I knew exactly what he meant. I felt my heart go cold within me as I recalled my unwitting rout of the monster. "Why did this thing, the Cythrawl—why did it attack us?"

"Ollathir summoned it—" began Tegid.

"What!" The ale nearly slipped from my fingers. "Are you saying he called it on purpose?"

"No," the bard replied. "He did not know that the Cythrawl was loosed, or he would never have gone up to the mound. He only thought to summon knowledge of the evildoers."

"And this monster answered instead?"

"Yes, and once the Cythrawl appeared, he had no choice but to force the confrontation. He hoped to bind it before its power in the land grew too great to defeat. He had no idea how powerful it had already become."

I could only shake my head in disbelief. "Was he insane? Why would he do such a thing?"

"We stood in the most sacred place in Albion. If the Cythrawl had succeeded in defeating us there, no force in this worlds-realm could prevent the destruction to follow. Albion would fall back into the void," Tegid added. "It would be as if our world had never existed."

Tegid became suddenly earnest. "But you drove the Cythrawl away before it could destroy the sacred center of Albion. Come the worst, some part of Albion will remain."

"Would that I could have saved Ollathir," I mused aloud. "I am sorry, Tegid."

"No doubt you did all that could be done," he replied unhappily. We lifted our jars to the Chief Bard's memory and drank in silence, whereupon Tegid put his aside. "Now you must tell me what happened up there on the mound."

"You know as well as I do what happened," I told him.

"I know some—not all. I was not with Ollathir when he died, but you were. You must tell me how it was. I must hear it all."

I made to answer, but could not. What had happened up on the mound? I hardly knew. I saw images—confused and grotesque—a bizarre flood of hideous impressions and nightmare sensations. I closed my eyes and tried to force the hateful vision from my mind. When I opened them again, Tegid was watching me expectantly. But how could I tell him what had happened when I did not know myself? "I cannot say," I said at last, shaking my head. "I do not know."

"You must tell me," Tegid urged.

"I cannot remember."

"Tell me," he insisted. "It is important!"

"I tell you I do not know! Leave it!"

Tegid stared hard at me, as if willing me to answer. He opened his mouth to speak, and then closed it, biting back the words before he uttered them. We sat for some moments at impasse while Tegid scowled at me. Then, all at once, he stood. "Come," he said quickly, motioning for me to rise. "Follow me."

"Why? Where are we going?" But Tegid did not answer; he was already moving toward the door.

He led us out from the hall. The sun had gone, and the wind with it. Still, the night would be cold. I regretted leaving the warmth of the hall and pulled my cloak more tightly around me as we hurried across the darkening yard.

We paused at the door of one of the small, round houses that stood within the caer. "Wait here," he said, and entered. I stood outside until he returned. After a while he emerged. "You may go in to her now," he said.

"Who?" I said, catching his arm.

"Gwenllian."

"Why? What is happening?"

"I think you should speak to the Banfáith."

"I do not want to speak to her, Tegid," I whispered harshly. "Why are you doing this to me?"

"You *must* speak to her," he replied firmly. "She is waiting."

"Come with me."

"No." He took my hand from his arm and drew aside the black calfskin at the doorway. "I will await you in the hall," he said and all but pushed me across the threshold. "Come to me when you are finished."

He turned and retreated across the yard. When he had gone, I stooped and entered the stone house. It was bare, like all the others, but Gwenllian had a low, iron brazier burning in the center of the room, and the floor was piled thick with reeds and covered with skins and fleeces of shaggy goats and brown sheep.

Gwenllian herself was sitting in the center of the dwelling's single room, her cloak gathered at the neck and spread around her so that only her head showed above it. Her long auburn hair, deep hued in the emberglow, fell unbound and smooth over her shoulders. Her large eyes were closed, her lips slightly parted. She seemed a sleeper on the verge of waking. I crept into her presence quietly, lest I disturb her meditations, and sat down cross-legged on the skin of a tawny calf.

After a moment, I heard her sigh—a long exhalation of breath, followed by an equally long inhalation. She opened her eyes and inspected me without utterance. I returned her gaze placidly, content to remain silent in her presence until she granted me leave to speak.

There came a movement from inside her cloak, and Gwenllian stretched forth a bare white arm toward the brazier. She held a cluster of dry oak leaves in her hand, and these she placed on the burning coals. The dry leaves smoldered and burst into flame, filling the small room with a sharp scent that reminded me of another time and another place, now far, far away.

Smoke curled into the air; she inhaled the scent, drawing air deep into her lungs. When she finally spoke, I did not recognize her voice. When Gwenllian sang, her voice was supple as a willow wand, sweet as summer's golden mead, passionate, eloquent, and charming. The voice that addressed me now, however, though serene, was somber and distant; yet the authority behind each word was absolute and infallible. It was Gwenllian the Banfáith, the wise prophetess, who sat before me now, watching me with fathomless green eyes.

She said: "The stranger's foot is established on Albion's Rock. Clothed in beauty, richly arrayed, is he who defends the Dagda's fair race. Hail, Silver Hand, your servant greets you!"

LLEW

I inclined my head in acknowledgment of her strange greeting, but gave no other sign, for I had not been granted leave to speak. Also, I was not at all certain it was me she was talking about. Silver Hand? The name meant nothing to me.

The Banfáith drew out from beneath her cloak a torc made of dozens of thick silver strands, each strand twisted and plaited. She placed the costly neck ring on the floor between us and intoned stiffly, "Ask what you will, the truth will be revealed to you. In the Day of Strife, nothing will be hidden from Samildanac's chosen." Then, in a softer voice, she added, "Speak your heart, Silver Hand; you will not be turned away."

Once more I inclined my head. There were so many things I wanted to know, so much I needed to ask, I was some time deciding which of the questions jostling one another on the tip of my tongue I should ask first.

"Banfáith," I blurted at last, "you have called me Silver Hand. I would know why I have been addressed by this name."

Although she had promised that nothing would remain hidden, her reply did little to enlighten me. "He who would wear the torc of a champion must a champion be. When the Cythrawl is loosed in Albion, Lleu Llaw Gyffes, the Lion of the Sure Hand, returns to defend Dagda's children."

"Banfáith," I said, "I am trying to understand. If nothing prevents you, please tell me how this came to be."

"Nothing prevents me, and I will tell you gladly: from time beyond remembering, the name Lleu belongs to the Dagda. Since the champion is raised by his call, therefore is the champion named Llew Llaw Eraint."

She answered my questions readily, but her answers only served to deepen the mystery and confusion. I tried again. "This champion," I said, "This Llew Silver Hand—how is he raised?"

"Goodly-wise is the Many-Gifted One," Gwenllian replied cryptically. "He sees all, knows all, establishes all with his Sure Hand. The Swift Sure Hand chooses whom he will."

"Wise Banfáith, do you think I am this champion?" I asked once more.

"The Dagda Samildanac has chosen. Now it is for you to choose what you will."

That made no sense to me either. However, not to appear contrary, I thanked the Banfáith for helping me understand and tried another approach. "The Day of Strife," I said, "is not known to me—I would gladly hear all you could tell me."

At this the Banfáith closed her eyes slowly and withdrew into herself. I heard the soft tick and snap of the charcoal in the brazier as she searched the secret pathways of the future for a word or sign she might impart. When she spoke again, her voice held a note of anguish that pierced my heart to hear it.

"Hear, O Silver Hand; heed the Head of Wisdom," she said, raising her hands, palms outward, in declamation. "The Destroyer of the North shall loose his rage on Three Fair Realms; with tooth and claw will he rend flesh from bone. His white minions will defeat the fair forces of Gyd. A pall of white lies upon the land; famine both young and old shall devour. The Gray Hound has slipped his chain; the bones of children he shall crack. The Red-eyed Wanderer shall pierce the throats of all who pursue him.

"Sorrow and be sad, deep grief is granted Albion in triple measure. The Golden King in his kingdom will strike his foot against the Rock of Contention. The Wyrm of fiery breath will claim the throne of Prydain; Llogres will be without a lord. But happy shall be Caledon; the Flight of Ravens will flock to her many-shadowed glens, and ravensong shall be her song.

"When the Light of the Derwyddi is cut off, and the blood of bards demands justice, then let the Ravens spread their wings over the sacred wood and holy mound. Under Ravens' wings, a throne is established. Upon this throne, a king with a silver hand.

"In the Day of Strife, root and branch shall change places, and the newness of the thing shall pass for a wonder. Let the sun be dull as amber, let the moon hide her face: abomination stalks the land. Let the four winds contend with one another in dreadful blast; let the sound be heard among the stars. The Dust of the Ancients will rise on the clouds; the essence of Albion is scattered and torn among contending winds.

"The Seas will rise up with mighty voices. Nowhere is there safe harbor. Arianrhod sleeps in her sea-girt headland. Though many seek her, she will not be found. Though many cry out to her, she cannot hear their voices. Only the chaste kiss will restore her to her rightful place.

"Then shall rage the Giant of Wickedness and terrify all with the keen edge of his sword. His eyes shall flash forth fire; his lips shall drip poison. With his great host he will despoil the island. All who oppose him will be swept away in the flood of wrongdoing that flows from his hand. The Island of the Mighty will become a tomb.

"All this by the Brazen Man is come to pass, who likewise mounted on his steed of brass works woe both great and dire. Rise up Men of Gwir! Fill your hands with weapons and oppose the false men in your midst! The sound of the battleclash will be heard among the stars of heaven and the Great Year will proceed to its final consummation.

"Hear, O Son of Albion: Blood is born of blood. Flesh is born of flesh. But the spirit is born of Spirit and with Spirit evermore remains. Before Albion is One, the Hero Feat must be performed and Silver Hand must reign."

Seized with a terrible sorrow, the prophetic voice broke. "The Phantarch is dead!" she sobbed. "Dead! . . . The Phantarch is taken from us and the Song is silent. The Cythrawl destroys the land!"

Gwenllian sat for a long time with eyes closed, weeping inwardly. I wanted nothing more than to slink away, to flee her presence so that I would not have to hear more of her pronouncements. But she opened her eyes and held me with her mournful gaze.

"Banfáith," I said, my own heart troubled with the torment of her terrible vision, "I know nothing of this Hero Feat, or how it may be accomplished. It seems to me a task more befitting a bard. Yet, what may be done, that I will do. Only tell me one thing more. How is the Cythrawl to be defeated?"

"Before the Cythrawl can be conquered, the Song must be restored."

"This song of which you speak—am I to know it?"

The wise Banfáith regarded me sadly, solemnly. "No one knows the Song, save the Phantarch alone. For it is the chief treasure of this worlds-realm and not to be despoiled by small-souled creatures or unworthy servants. Before the sun and moon and stars were set in their unchanging courses, before living creatures drew breath, from before the beginning of all that is or will be, the Song was sung. You have asked me to name the Song. Very well, know you this: it is the Song of Albion."

23

THE DAY OF STRIFE

I did not sleep that night. And I did not return to the hall. I stalked the cliffs above the restless water in the dark, little caring whether I struck my foot and plunged headlong to my death on the sea crags below. Then let the Dagda choose someone else. I wanted no part of it.

I stomped along the clifftops for a long time—anxious, fearful, tormented by the prophecy the Banfáith had given me, and angry at Tegid's goading. So I stormed the coast track, cursing to the wind and shouting my defiance to the surging sea. In the end, I perched myself on a rock overlooking the tide-washed shingle and settled to watch the sun rise. That was where Goewyn found me, watching the pearly sunlight seep into the sky and stain the sea with blood. She came so quietly to stand behind me that I did not hear her. I simply knew that she was there, and then I felt her warm fingers on my neck.

She stood for some time without speaking, pressing her body against my back, stroking my hair and neck. At last she said, "Tegid tells me you must leave."

"He is determined," I muttered morosely. "Determined to get us frozen to death and drowned."

"Sollen is not begun in force. You may yet sail with some assurance." She stepped around beside me and settled next to me on my cold rock.

"Nothing is assured," I muttered. "Nothing ever stays the same."

She leaned against me, resting her head lightly on my shoulder. "So gloomy," she sighed. "Yet you are strong, and life is yours for the taking. Why think the worst?"

Because the worst and the inevitable are often one and the same, I considered. But I did not want to provoke Goewyn, who was only trying to cheer me, so I said nothing, and we listened to the waves churn the pebbles on the strand. Four white gulls sailed low across the water, their wingtips touching the waves.

"When a bard like Ollathir dies," she said after a time, as if we had been discussing the subject at length, "he must breathe his *awen* into another, so that it will not be lost. Once lost, the awen is never recovered, and its light passes out of the world forever."

"Yes, and what else did Tegid tell you?" I snapped, regretting the remark at once.

"Tegid would have given his life to save Ollathir," Goewyn continued, ignoring my rudeness. "But it was not to be. Yet when the time came, you were with him to receive the Chief Bard's awen."

The awen . . . so that was on Tegid's mind as well. The awen, I knew, is considered the source of a bard's insight, the all-inspiring spirit of his art. It is that which nourishes, clothes, and shelters the people of his tribe. The awen is the breath of the Dagda which guides and instructs, and which sets a bard apart from other men.

"But why give it to me?" I demanded, my anger flaring again. "I am no bard! I do not want it. I cannot use it."

"It was given to you because you were there," Goewyn soothed.

"And I would give it to Tegid if I could," I declared sharply. "I want no part of it!"

I felt her hand on my cheek as she turned my face to hers. "You have been chosen for great things," she said, and although she spoke lightly her tone was edged with an iron conviction.

"You have been talking to Gwenllian too." I turned my face away.

"I know nothing of what Gwenllian has told you. But it does not take a Banfáith's vision to see it. When Tegid returned with you in the boat, I thought you dead. But one look, and I saw the hero light on you—and I knew that the Dagda had covered you with his hand."

"I never asked for it," I muttered bitterly. "I never wanted any of this!" I looked toward the rising sun. Already, the day's fresh light was fading behind black clouds, and the wind was lashing the waves to froth. Soon Tegid and I would set forth on that cold sea to return to Sycharth, and I would never see Ynys Sci again.

As if reading my thoughts, Goewyn replied. "The future is reached by many pathways. Who is to say where our ways may meet?"

We sat for a while longer, and then she departed, withdrawing quietly, leaving me to my selfish misery.

⊲ ⊲ ⊲

The boat that had borne us to Scatha's island was small. Without a pilot and crew, we would not have been able to handle a larger boat. So the small sturdy craft served us well, where another would have foundered in the Sollen swell. Indeed, our little black boat rode the wind-driven waves like a feather.

Still, it is tempting disaster to trust too much in the fickle and inconstant Sollen weather. One moment the sun can be warm and shining, the next an icy northern blast is slicing through your winter wool and freezing your flesh. We knew that we could not reach Sycharth by boat, though that would have been much the quickest way. Tegid was not intent on suicide; he only thought to reach the harbor at Ffim Ffaller where we could obtain horses and provisions to continue our journey overland. Or, failing that, to put in at Ynys Oer and make our way to the mainland from there—much the slowest way.

The weather was not a friend to us. The second day out, a storm swept down from the north, and we were forced to take refuge in a sheltered bay on the rock-bound coast of the mainland. We found a cave in the cliffside and managed to gather enough driftwood to make a fire. The cave was home to us for five endless days while we waited for the wild wind to exhaust itself.

The evening of the fifth day the wind fell, and as the moon rose we put to sea once more. The air was cold, but the sky clear and bright. Tegid had no trouble steering by the stars and by the softly silvered coastline. We sailed through the night, and through all the next day, and the next—taking it in turn to sleep.

My hand on the tiller was not expert, but I could spell Tegid long enough for him to rest and sleep. Nearly frozen by the constant lash of the wind and froth-churned waves, and almost out of food, we made for the western coast of Ynys Oer. I was not sorry to leave the boat and put steady land beneath my feet once more.

Our horses were put up in a dingle, where Tegid had left them to fend for themselves. They might have stayed there without harm through the season, for the steep sides of the dingle kept all but the foulest wind and rain away, and the grass grew thick on the valley floor. We stayed the night in the stone hut on the western shore—in sight of Ynys Bàinail and its sacred pillar-stone which now marked the place where Ollathir lay buried in his grave.

"I could not carry both of you down from the White Rock," Tegid explained. "As you had slightly more life left in you than Ollathir, I heaped the stones over his body and brought you to Ynys Sci."

"For that I am grateful, Tegid. You took a great risk. It could have been no easy journey."

"Far less risk than you took in facing the Cythrawl," he replied frankly. "I could in nowise leave you there, brother."

At dawn the next morning, we fetched the horses from their hidden glen. I say "dawn," although we did not see the sun that day, nor for many dark days to follow. Rain and wind whipped the coast; icy mist sheathed the high hills and filled the glens. We rode across the island in a misery of drizzle; wretched, cold, wet to the skin. We reached the eastern shore and paused to look at the expanse of gray, choppy water separating Ynys Oer from the mainland.

"What now?" I asked, gauging the narrow distance between the two shores.

"The farmers on the mainland swim their cattle to summer pastures on the island. And those on the island swim them to market on the other side."

"It sounds a wet undertaking."

"We cannot become more wet than we are," Tegid pointed out. Water dripped from us with every movement; our clothing lay heavy and sodden on our backs; our limbs were stiff from holding them close to our bodies.

"Then let us be done with it," I said, watching a sharp wind whip the wavetops. "The sooner we are on the other side, the sooner we will have a fire."

I knew the water would be cold, I just did not imagine it could be *that* cold. The distance was not far, and our horses swam well—but we nearly froze to death just the same.

We dragged ourselves out of the surf and across the beach, the wind slashing viciously through our sopping clothes. Behind the dunes we escaped the worst of the wind. Tegid knew where to find kindling and brush among the sandy hollows; much of it was wet, but it burned readily at Tegid's practiced touch. The Derwyddi know many secrets of earth and air and fire and water. I believe he willed the fire to catch by sheer enchantment. I know I could not have coaxed those few scant, soggy branches to burn.

"Take off your clothes," Tegid said, as the fire began to burn brightly. We had found a deep pocket between two dunes. It seemed utter madness to shed our clothing in that cold, but it was the only way to get warm.

We spread our clothing on surrounding sedge clumps and sea willow, and sat as close to the fire as prudence allowed. Even the horses edged as near as their fear would allow, drawn by the warmth.

Tegid fed the fire with twisted bundles of dry grass and blackthorn brush, keeping the flames alive. "When our cloaks have dried," he said, as I held a pair of thick woolen leggings before the flames, turning them to dry them more quickly, "we will ride inland."

I did not reply; there was more coming, and I could wait. In a little while he continued. "There will be game in the forest. We can hunt along the way. In a few days we will reach the Tyn Water and follow it south as far as Aber Llydan. From there it is only three or four days to Llwyddi land, and only a few more before we come to Nant Modornn. We will follow the river to Sycharth."

He made it sound as if we would be home and dry in no time at all. In fact, we were to spend many and many a frigid Sollen night on the trail and untold Sollen days along the cold empty trackways of Caledon. Snow had settled heavy and deep on the high hilltops before ever we came within sight of the Modornn valley.

Besides the cold, there was hunger. Hunting was poor, and we could not devote much time to it. Still, even when we could get nothing for ourselves, we made certain to find our mounts a mouthful or two to keep going. The cold made us lean and hard as stormblasted birches. I learned to sleep in the saddle and to find modest shelter in the most unpromising places. I learned to read a trail beneath a covering of snow. And I learned to find direction by the scent of the wind.

One day we passed Caer Modornn. The sight of the timber palisade on the hilltop above the river brought back a swift floodtide of memories. But, strange to tell, though I could remember those first glowing days of my arrival, I could not without intense effort recall much of my life before that—save in the most indefinite terms. Indeed, when compared to the intensely vivid life I knew in Albion, my life before coming to the Otherworld seemed almost unutterably remote and insignificant, little more than a vague pantomime acted out in a dim, colorless, half-light. That I could not remember did not concern me in the least, however. I thought it curious, yet felt no sense of loss. Clearly, I had the best of the bargain. I was content.

We went up to Caer Modornn for the food cached there: grain and fodder for the horses, dried meat and ale in sealed jars for Tegid and myself. Firewood had been stored in the caer as well, so we stayed one night in the fortress, more for the warmth than the rest—though both were equally welcome.

Next day we proceeded on our way. Still weary, still stiff with cold, and whipped by every wind that bawled down the soggy vale, we journeyed on in better heart, for we were in known lands and the end—though still far off—could be seen.

We followed the wide Vale of Modornn, keeping close to the ice-edged river until we came to the marshland. There we turned from the river way in favor of firmer footing on the wooded trail. Two damp, drizzly days later, a little before sunset, we reached Sycharth.

"There is no smoke," Tegid observed. Weary from our long sojourn, we had paused to rest before continuing to the caer.

I scanned the sky above the caer. The clouds had cleared at the last of day, leaving the sky a frail blue—against which it would have been easy to see the white smoke smudge from the king's great hearthfire and from those of the kitchens and lesser hearths as well. But there was no smoke, and therefore no warming fire.

What can it mean? I wondered. I could think of no good reason that we should have come all this way to face a cold hearth and a cheerless welcome.

"Something is wrong." Tegid urged his horse to speed and hastened down the hillside into the glen separating us from the hill on which stood the caer.

I admit my own heart pricked with apprehension as the hooves of our horses pounded across the valley floor, drumming on the frozen earth, hastening toward the silent caer. But even before we passed along the narrow palisade and entered the wide-flung gates, I knew that Sycharth was abandoned. One glimpse of the charred remains of the Great King's hall confirmed our worst fears: Meldryn Mawr's fine fortress was a burned-out ruin.

The Day of Strife had dawned.

24

TWRCH

Deserted by the living, peopled only by the dead who lay unmourned and unburied amidst the destruction, once-proud Sycharth stood as a pillaged tomb—cold and desolate, broken. The mighty stronghold appeared itself a corpse, forsaken and forbidding.

The eye met atrocity at every glance: women bludgeoned to death still clutching their frozen babes to their breasts; children with hands and feet cut off and left to bleed; dogs and warriors decapitated and their heads switched; cattle roasted alive in their pens; sheep slaughtered and their entrails pulled out to bind and then strangle their herdsmen . . . Everywhere the marks of fire, filth, blood, and outrage.

The stink of death permeated the misty air, just as the thickened blood stained the rain-sodden ground. Tegid and I lurched from one abomination to the next in dazed disbelief. Bile bitter in our mouths, sick and numb, we muttered ever and again the same two questions: How could this have happened? Who could have done such a thing?

Still more mysterious to us was the absence of any sign of battle. For we did not find the king or his war band, although we made a thorough search of all that remained of the hall and the royal quarters.

Aside from those few warriors struck down outside the hall, we discovered none of the battle host. By this we presumed that the king had fled the fight with his war band virtually intact, or else that he was away when destruction overtook his stronghold, and perhaps even now did not know it.

Any suggestion that the king had fled the fight, Tegid considered repugnant. "He would sooner cut out his own heart," Tegid murmured darkly. "He would sooner be food for ravens than see his people slaughtered like pigs and his fortress laid waste. Nor would he allow himself to be captured while he drew breath."

We stared dismally at the devastation. There was no telling when it had happened. The cold and snow preserved the bodies as they had fallen. If the king and his war band had been there, we would have seen them.

"He must have departed before the destruction took place," I said. This seemed equally unlikely. Yet there seemed no other explanation. "Meldryn Mawr is not here."

Surely the Great King must have been absent when disaster fell upon Sycharth. But in the season of ice, when all the worlds retreat inward, what would induce him to leave? "Where would he go?" I wondered aloud.

"I do not know, brother," Tegid answered ruefully. "We will not find the answer here, I think."

"Where else, then?"

"We will go to the settlements and holdings round about. We will ride the circuit of the land and see what may be found."

We left the caer. Stupid with grief and sick with dread, eyes staring, hands shaking, we mounted our horses and rode directly to the king's harborage on the nearby Muir Glain estuary. We rode fast to outrace the fading light and reached the shipyard in the dim twilight, as dark clouds closed overhead.

We did not even bother to dismount but sat in our saddles and scanned the wreckage: ships burned to the waterline, every sail and mast destroyed, every hull stove in.

The sheds and houses had been torched, and with them the stacked timber. Even the earthen banks of the sea mouth were burnt and blackened. Nothing escaped. The destruction was utter and complete. All was charcoal and ashes. "It must have burned for days," Tegid muttered. "The blaze would have been visible halfway to Ynys Sci."

Our horses jittered nervously, blowing and stamping, as we searched here and there with our eyes for any sign of survival. I touched my weapons—carefully wrapped against the weather, but close to hand—grimly grateful for their cold consolation.

"There is nothing here," Tegid said at last. "We will go on."

Night overwhelmed us as we struck off across the wooded hills—a longer way to go, but we could not traverse the marshlands in the dark. So we took the hill track, riding the ridgeways and hunting runs which joined Sycharth with neighboring settlements. As we approached the first stronghold, the cloud cover thinned somewhat and the moon shone briefly; not long, but enough to see the settlement: black against the blacker hills beyond the river.

Caer Dyffryn was built on a flattened river knoll, home to perhaps two hundred Llwyddi clansmen. All two hundred had fled, or were murdered. We did not stop to count them. There was no need—no living thing remained within the circle of charred stumps that had been the timber ringfort. This we could see before we even dismounted. Yet, out of respect for kinsmen, we did dismount and walked among the blasted ruins of their homes.

"We cannot stay here," I said, when we had concluded our futile survey. I spoke softly, but my voice sounded loud in the unnatural silence. Tegid made no move or sound. I touched him on the arm—his flesh was rigid and cold beneath my fingers. "Come, brother, let us go from this place. We can camp by the river and return here in the morning if you wish."

Tegid made no reply but turned and mounted his horse once more. We left Caer Dyffryn but did not stop. We did not rest that night at all and paused only once, long enough to water the horses before moving on. Gray dawn found us standing, red-eyed and weary, in the ruins of Cnoc Hydd. Once a pleasant settlement nestled in a fair fold of the vale, it was now, like Sycharth and Dyffryn, a scorched husk. Here, most of the inhabitants had been burned, but whether before or after death could not be told.

While Tegid sifted among the soggy ashes of the hall, I inspected the blackened, fallen beams of the Warriors' House. Using the butt of a broken spear, I poked here and there amidst the debris, searching for I know not what. The acrid stench of smoke and charred corpses brought the tears to my eyes, but I persisted. And in a corner of the collapsed hearth, my efforts bore fruit.

I had been stirring the rubble to no purpose and made to move on. A furtive movement caught my eyes as I turned away. I thought I heard a dry rustle. I spun on my heel and stared into the shadows of the firepit. At first I saw nothing . . . but then, hidden in a crevice beneath the tumbled stone, I saw a small huddled shape.

I took the butt of my spear and nudged the cringing form gently. It made no sound but cowered deeper into its hole. I shifted some of the fallen timber and stone, and carefully opened the crevice to the light. Peering into the hole I saw the scorched carcass of a bitch hound and, quivering beside it, her pup.

The slate-gray coat was matted and singed in a dozen places; a wicked gash, red and raw, laid open one small shoulder. The creature lay shivering with fright and cold, curled next to the stiff body of its dead mother. There were three other pups, all dead; the bitch had died protecting her litter, her teeth still bared in a frozen snarl. The pup appeared old enough to be weaned—though still round as a ball of butter with its baby fat, it showed several fine white teeth when I reached down to pick it up.

The kindest act would have been to kill it outright and end its suffering. But after all the waste and destruction that Tegid and I had witnessed, finding this lone survivor—though it was only a half-starved hound pup—I could not bring myself to add even this small, wavering life to the death around me. I determined to let it live, to make it live.

It did not whimper or cry out when I took it by the scruff of the neck and lifted it from its den. But the little beast nipped at me when I tried to pet it. And as I made to cradle it in the crook of my elbow, it snagged the side of my hand with its sharp new teeth, and held on. "Be still, *Twrch!*" I scolded it with a tap on the nose, blurting the first word that came to me.

Tegid heard me speak; he turned at once, expectantly. He saw the pup in my hands and smiled sadly. I carried the dog to him, and he took it and held it up before him. "So! One yet remains in the land of the living." He glanced at me. "What did you call it?"

"Twrch," I said.

"Boar?" wondered Tegid. "Why that?"

"He tried to bite me when I held him," I explained. "It put me in mind of the way an old boar will keep fighting on when it is beaten and will not give in to death." I shrugged, adding, "It was nothing. You name it, Tegid. This one should have a good name."

But Tegid would not hear of it. "You have already given a good name. So let him be called." He held the dog aloft. "Little defiant one, Twrch, may you be to us a Boar of Battle indeed."

He gave the pup to me and said, "This ruin is like the others. We will find nothing here. We will move on."

"We need rest, Tegid. Rest and food. Our horses are near-dead with exhaustion. We should stop a day at least. There is a place near the river—we passed it on the way here. Let us stop there for today and decide what to do when we have slept."

Tegid was not for it, but his horse stumbled to its knees in the muddy track as we rode down from the caer, and he was forced to admit that I was right. If we did not stop, we would likely go the rest of the way on foot. And since we did not know how far we might have to go to find our missing king and kinsmen, it did not make good sense to squander our horses.

So we returned to the refuge beside the river—nothing more than a stand of young alder trees and willows, with a place cleared among them for a fishing hut overlooking a weir. The trees offered shelter from the wind, and the hut kept the rain off our heads. Grass grew long on the bank of the river, and enough green remained for the horses to graze. We let them drink their fill from the river and then tethered them among the bare trees.

Inside the low, wicker hut we found a small supply of firewood, a little charcoal, goatskins, and several sealed jars. The skins were filthy, but the firewood was dry, and, best of all, the jars contained good sweet mead. The keeper of the weir knew well how to ease his cold vigil.

I made a nest for Twrch in a corner of the hut with one of the skins. He sniffed it cautiously, then settled down. Likely the weir keeper's dog used the goatskin for a bed, and the pup took some small comfort from a familiar scent, for, after licking his wounded shoulder, he tucked his nose between his paws and went to sleep.

While I was about this trifling chore, Tegid had inspected the weir. He returned to the hut with four sleek brown trout. In no time he had the fish gutted, and I had a fire burning in the pit outside the hut. We skewered the trout with sharpened willow wands and set them over the fire.

The sweet, oily scent of the roasting fish mingling with the dry, oaky smell of the silvery smoke brought the water to my mouth and pangs of hunger to my stomach. We had not eaten well for many days. Tegid opened one of the jars, and we passed the mead back and forth between us while we waited for the fish to cook.

We sat on either side of the fire, turning the willow skewers from time to time in silence. There were no words for what we were think-ing and feeling. We were too tired and hungry to make sense of any of it—wiser to eat and sleep before trying to understand what we had seen and deciding what to do about it.

Though the day remained gray and cold, the trout warmed us inside. I savored each succulent bite, licking my fingers before pulling off the next morsel. Although I could have eaten my weight in trout, I saved a portion for Twrch. I did not know if he would eat it, but thought it would do no harm to try.

The hut was cramped, but the shelter welcome. We slept.

I awakened some time later, feeling a cold, wet spot on my throat. Twrch had crept near while I slept and curled himself in the hollow of my throat with his nose pressed beneath my chin. I rose, taking care not to wake Tegid, picked up the pup, and carried it outside. The day had not improved. If anything, the fitful wind out of the northeast was colder than before, and the clouds lower and darker.

"I have something for you, Twrch," I whispered. "Taste this, and tell me if you like it."

I offered the pup the bit of cooked fish I had saved for him. He sniffed at it, but would not eat it—though I held it against his closed mouth. He would, however, lick my fingers. So I rubbed the fish on my fingertips and let the pup lick them clean. After he had done this a few times, I tried the fish again. He gobbled it down as only a starv-ing pup can, and then cleaned my fingers to get every last morsel.

"There will be more later," I told him. "We will find something more to your liking—a deer, perhaps, or a fat partridge." In saying this, it occurred to me that we had seen no signs of game. Excepting the fish we had eaten, we had not seen any wild creature since entering the Vale of Modornn.

"Is it possible," I wondered aloud to Tegid when he joined me a short time later, "to drive all wild game from the valley? Could such a deed be done?"

He merely shook his head and said, "It is not possible—but neither is it possible to destroy three fortresses without any of them alerting the others. Clearly, there is a greater mystery here than I can fathom."

That ended the matter for the moment, as neither of us cared to dwell on it further. Tegid undertook to water the horses and move their tethers, while I looked to the nets in the weir. There were no fish in the nets, and, as I set about replacing the nets on the poles, Twrch began yipping fiercely from the bank. I waded from the water to find him digging into a hole in the bottom of an earthen mound the shape of a large beehive.

The mound was half-hidden among the trees, but a few paces from the riverbank. I would not have noticed the mound at all if Twrch had not called it to my attention. Seeing the pup so excited by his discovery, I decided to have a look myself. I thought he might have found an otter's den, or that of a badger. But I soon saw that the mound was made of turf, newly cut and stacked carefully. I lifted off the top few turves and knew at once why the dog had become so eager, for the pungent smell of oak smoke met my nostrils the moment I looked into the round hole I had made in the top of the hive.

The Many-Gifted One had smiled upon us! Inside the mound were wooden stakes with crosspieces—each crosspiece bending under a splendid weight of smoked salmon.

"Good dog, Twrch!" I said, reaching in at once and seizing the first fish I saw. I stripped a chunk of smoke-browned flesh from the silvery side and give it to Twrch as a reward for his good service. I stroked him and praised him lavishly while he ate it.

Then I restacked the turves and carried the remaining portion of the fish back to Tegid. "Whatever else befalls us, we will not starve," I said, handing him the smoked salmon. "We will grow weary of eating them long before we've seen the last of them. Twrch located the smoke-hive and led me to it."

"Once again we are indebted to the keeper of the weir."

"And to Twrch's nose," I added.

Tegid tasted the fish. "He knew his craft, this weir master." He offered me the last morsel. "This was bound for the king's board."

At mention of the king, I felt a twinge—as if an icy hand had clutched my shoulder. "What are we to do, Tegid?"

"I do not know," he answered softly. "But I think it is time to consider what has happened."

"What *has* happened?" I could think of no good explanation for any of it. "Whole settlements laid waste, the people murdered without raising a hand to their own defense, even the cattle slaughtered where they stand—and all else burnt to ash. Yet nothing is carried off or plundered. Such meaningless destruction is insane."

Once I started, it all tumbled out in a rush. "And how could it happen?" I demanded. "One caer might be attacked—two at most—but then the others would know. They would see the smoke from the fires, if nothing else, and they would sound the alarm. The king would raise the war band against the invaders. There would have been a battle, and we would have known about it; we would have seen the signs at least."

Tegid looked thoughtful. "Not if the attack had come by night," he replied. "No one would have seen the smoke."

"The glow from the fire, then. Someone would have seen *something!*" I was all but shouting now. "Still, who is it that can attack in the night? What enemy can strike three fortresses at once—and who knows how many others—without warning any of them and without losing a single warrior? Who is it that can destroy all without leaving a trace?" Anger and outrage made my voice tremble. "I am asking you, Tegid. What enemy can do these things?"

A strange expression had come into the Brehon's eyes as I spoke. I stared at him. "What is it? What have I said?"

"Your questions are better than you know," he answered in a thin, tight voice. "There is one who can do the things you describe."

"This person, this monster—who or what is it?"

Tegid halted me with a sharp gesture, as if he feared I might blurt the answer before he could tell it. Or as if the telling of it would bring the fiend down upon us. "You are right to call it a monster," he said softly, "for such it is. Yet it goes on two legs and takes the form of a man."

"Will you name this creature to me?" I dreaded the answer, but I had to know.

"I will. It is Nudd, Lord of Uffern."

25

THE PARADISE WAR

The lord of the Underworld? That Lord Nudd?" I asked, thinking I must have heard wrong. I remembered Gwenllian mentioning a figure by that name in some of her stories—according to which Lord Nudd was a shadowy, furtive figure who ruled the nether realms as chief of the damned. Surely Tegid did not mean *that* Lord Nudd?

Grave and wary, the Brehon extended the fingers of his left hand in the sign against evil. "It may be that in the days to come you will wish you had never allowed that name to cross your lips. I will tell you what little is known—yet that little will chill the warm heart in your breast."

"So be it. My heart is numb already from the outrage of all I have seen of this dread lord and his handiwork. Nothing you can say will abuse me more than that."

"Well said, brother," Tegid approved. "Sit you down and hear me, if you will."

The day had worsened. Already the murky light we enjoyed was failing and it would soon be dark. So, while Tegid built up the fire against the cold night, I fetched skins from the hut and placed these at the fire ring. I took my place cross-legged on the goatskin, and Twrch came to me and climbed into my lap.

Tegid busied himself with the fire, but I could see that he was ordering his tale in his mind. I pulled my cloak around my shoulders and sat stroking Twrch, waiting for Tegid to begin.

"Few there are who have heard this song," Tegid said at last, seating himself on the pelt across from me. "Fewer still those willing to sing it. There are some tales that cause the words to clot on the tongue and harpstrings to fall silent. This is such a song."

"Yet I will hear it gladly," I said, "if some good may come of it."

"Hear then the tale of Nudd, Prince of Uffern." So saying, Tegid began. "In elder days, when the dew of creation was still fresh on the earth, twin sons were born to Beli, Great of Renown. The first was Nudd, and his brother was Lludd. And this is the way of it:

"Beli ruled long and wisely, gaining much honor through his just and honorable ways. In all the time that Beli held the Island of the Mighty, there were no wars, no plagues, no troubles. The peace of Beli was such that Albion became the fairest realm that is in all the world. Men and women spent their days searching for knowledge of every kind and learning the truth of all things. They increased in knowledge and truth and in all the pleasing arts, and forgot the craft of war. Far easier in those fortunate times to hear a graceful song than the clash of swords, far easier to see poetic champions compose than chiefs of battle mount their chariots. So wonderfully did the sons and daughters of men wax wise and gather themselves the bounty of the land of every good thing under heaven, that they were called *Tylwyth Teg*, the Fair Family, and their abode was Paradise.

"Now, it happened that one day Beli was seized by a powerful *taithchwant*, a wanderlust intense and strong. Such was his longing to journey through his realm, to see for himself the marvelous things that were coming to pass under his rule, that he could not eat from his golden bowls, nor could he sleep in his fine featherbed. This taithch-want beset him most fiercely, each day more pressing than the day before. 'Alas and woe!' the Great King said to himself. 'Most miserable among men am I if I continue on this way even one more day.'

"So saying, he sat down on his silver throne and bethought him-self what he might do. 'I will give the kingship to one of my sons, who will rule in my place while I take my leave. Then I will journey through my lands and see for myself the happiness of my people, and share their joy.' All that remained was to choose which of his two sons was most worthy to rule in his place.

"Great Beli, Most Astute, Pillar of Judgment, Soul of Wisdom, sat on his throne and thought long and deep. He thought and thought, but at the end of all his thinking he was no closer to a deci-sion than when he first sat down. And the reason for his dilemma was this: between Lludd and Nudd there was not the least bit of differ-ence on which to make a choice. As one son was fair and able, so was the other; as the second was gracious and friendly, so was the first. Each was as generous in his giving as the other. Neither was the bet-ter, nor was either the worse. So alike in every way were these two that only by the color of the hair on their heads could they be told apart: for Lludd had hair like the sun's bright dawn, whereas Nudd had hair like night's glorious darkness. Sunbright yellow the first, black as pre-cious jet the second.

"Beli, Monarch of High Renown, called his two sons to him and he said, 'Full many a day I have longed to journey through my realm and see for myself how the people enjoy the great good that has come to them through my rule. Know you that the taithchwant is on me, so I cannot stay here even one day longer. Indeed, were I to stay even one night more in this house, my heart would burst from yearning. I must leave this very day.'

"The two sons looked at one another and agreed that their father's plan was a good one. 'A most excellent wish, Great King,' they said. 'Only allow us to accompany you and share your joy at contemplating the good fortune you have brought about through your wise and noble rule.'

"Beli Mawr gazed at his two sons and answered them, 'It is not for you to accompany me, but to hold the realm in my stead while I am away.'

"The two sons answered, 'So well have you ruled, father, that the lowest man among us could hold the realm in your stead, the most innocent child could prove himself adept at kingcraft. Choose who you like, that person can but increase the honor of your name.'

"These words did not fail to please Beli. His great heart swelled in pride and delight. Still, he was not moved. For once Beli had set his mind on a thing, that thing would he have and not another. And he had set his mind on roaming his realm alone: alone he would go, alone would he fare, alone would he savor the sweetness of his renown. Alone and unknown by any, lest his people discover his presence and make much over him. For he ever sought the truth of all things, and he knew that men will sometimes alter their conduct when a king approaches. Thus he replied, 'As ever, your desires do you credit, my sons. Yet I have resolved to go my way alone, and alone will I go.'

"The two sons saw how the matter stood. 'Go your way, father,' they said. 'And all blessings attend you while you are gone from us.'

"Nudd approached his father, and, laying his head against the king's chest, he said, 'May it go well with you; may you find all you seek to find, and nothing you do not seek.'

"Lludd then drew near, placing his head against his father's chest, and said, 'And may your kingdom flourish, so that you return to a better realm than the one you left behind.'

"Beli raised up his sons and spoke his mind to them. Many things he told them about the right ruling of a realm, and about how a king serves his people. And then he said, 'I am going now. But one of you must rule in my place while I am gone.'

"'Must it be so?' the sons asked. For neither wanted to rule over the other.

"'It must,' replied Beli. 'For I see the path stretching out before me, and indeed I see my feet already upon it.' Then he asked them which would consent to rule in his place.

"Nudd answered, 'My brother is more worthy than I. Choose him.' To which Lludd replied, 'Of we two, Nudd is more worthy. I insist you choose him.'

"Beli heard their words and, being a king of some discernment, peered into the empty places between the words and saw a way to discover at last which of his sons was the more worthy. He told them, 'You have asked me to choose. Therefore, I choose Lludd.' He rose from his silver throne and gave the sovereignty of Albion into the hands of Lludd. 'Fare you well, my sons. May you grow in grace through all things.'

"Thus the Great King left his realm, and his people saw him no more for a time. But they saw his sons, and what they saw did not please them. No, not at all.

"At first they were pleased, for Lludd was as wise and good as his father. But Lludd had not reigned as much as from one moon to the next when a dispute arose between the prince and his brother. And the source of the disagreement was this: Nudd became jealous of his brother's good fortune.

"In truth, it was no greater thing than that. But it was enough and more than enough to bring suffering most terrible to the paradise of Albion. Suffering so great that from that far-off time to this, Albion has never been the same. For, although there had never been so much as a harsh word between the brothers, from the moment Nudd saw the golden torc of kingship around his brother's throat and not his

STEPHEN R. LAWHEAD

own, and saw the rod of sovereignty in his brother's hand and not his own, he began scheming how best to seize the kingship for himself. Day and night he paced the high ramparts, pondering how best to steal the throne. Day and night he turned his mind to thoughts of treachery and deception. And one fair night it came into his mind how he might trick his brother into giving him the kingship. And this is what he did:

"One bright night, not long after their father the king's departure, Nudd and Lludd were making a circuit of the caer. Nudd looked up into the wide, star-washed sky. As they lingered on the gatewalk, Nudd declared, 'Look yonder and see what a fine, far-spreading field I have.'

"'Where is it, brother?' asked Lludd, thinking no ill.

"'Why, there it is above your head, and as far as your eye can see,' answered Nudd, throwing wide his arms to the star-filled heavens.

"Lludd looked up at the sky. 'But see how many fine, fat cattle I have grazing in your field!' he replied.

"'Where are these cattle of yours?' asked Nudd.

"'Why, there they are—all the shining silver stars of heaven, with the moon as their bright cowherd,' laughed Lludd.

"This answer annoyed Nudd, who heard in it the sound of his brother's superiority. 'You would do well to remove your cattle from my field,' Nudd muttered. 'For I say they shall not graze on the field I have chosen for my own.'

"'Why so vexed, brother?' Lludd asked. 'It means nothing to me where my cattle graze.'

"'Yet it means something to me,' Nudd insisted. 'You take unfair advantage of me.'

"'How so?' asked Lludd, bewildered by his brother's strange behavior.

"'I would not expect you to understand,' replied the sullen Nudd. 'For you have never been made to endure the shame of living in another's shadow.'

"Lludd understood then why his brother was unhappy. 'Only tell me what I may do to make amends,' he told Nudd. 'And you may be certain that the sun will not set before it is accomplished.'

"Nudd frowned mightily. 'I have already told you! Remove your cattle from my field!' Then off he stomped, secretly singing to himself, for the task he had demanded of Lludd was impossible to perform.

"But Lludd took himself to his hall and gathered his bards to sing before him. He ate and drank the whole night and went to his bed and slept soundly. Nudd saw this and gloried in his heart, for he knew that his brother would not succeed. 'No man can chase the stars from the sky, and Lludd has not even tried. He has already failed; I am as good as king.' He, too, went to his bed and slept soundly.

"In the morning, Lludd rose and went at once to the rampart outside the hall. 'Wake you, Nudd!' he cried in a loud voice. 'Come out to me!'

"Nudd woke and went out. 'What is this unseemly noise so early in the morning?' he asked. 'I can see no reason for it, unless it is to give me the torc of kingship from around your throat.'

"Lludd smiled and clapped a hand to his brother's shoulder. 'There is no need, brother. For I have done all that you have demanded. I have removed my cattle, and your field is restored as you asked.'

"Nudd could not believe his ears. 'How can this be?' he wondered.

"'You have only to look at the sky to see that what I say is true,' Lludd told him.

"Nudd turned his eyes to the sky and saw the fair blue heavens spreading clear and bright above him as far as the eye could see. And there was not so much as one glimmering star to be seen. The sun had chased them all away.

"Lludd said to his brother. 'I have done as you asked. Let us have no more disagreement between us but continue as we lived before.'

"But Nudd would not. He saw how easily his brother had bested him, and he appeared small and foolish in his own eyes. Nudd imagined that Lludd was mocking him, and he scowled. 'You have tricked me once, but you shall not trick me again. From this day you are no brother of mine.'

"When Lludd heard this, his heart broke. 'Great is your name in the land, and greater may it yet become. Tell me what I can do to make peace between us and that I will do.'

"Nudd crossed his arms over his chest and said, 'Deliver to me the kingship of the realm, and remove yourself from my sight.'

"'Would you had asked anything but that,' replied Lludd sadly. 'For this I cannot do.'

"'Why not?' demanded Nudd.

"Lludd answered, 'Because the kingship of the realm belongs to the one who gave it to me. It is not mine to give as I please.'

"'Yes it is,' insisted Nudd.

"'No, it is not,' Lludd maintained. 'And that is the end of the matter.'

"'Very well,' shouted Nudd, 'since you will not give me what was promised me, I have no choice but to take it for myself.'

"Lludd told him, 'Though you tear the torc from around my throat and place your haunches on the silver throne, that will not make you king. I tell you the truth, a man may not make himself king; only the blessing of him who holds the kingship can elevate a man to that high place. For sovereignty is a sacred trust that may not be bartered or sold; still less may it be stolen or taken by force.'

"Lludd spoke the truth. Nudd heard it and liked what he heard not at all. He fled the hall; he fled the caer. In far-off lands he gathered to himself those who were like him: greedy, grasping men, inflamed by haughty desires and cravings for wealth and rank beyond their rightful shares; men from Tir Aflan across the sea who were lured by high-sounding promises of easy plunder.

"Lludd ruled well. The people adored him and sang his praises wherever they wandered in the world. Each word of praise became a dagger blade in the heart of Nudd. And as Lludd's light grew bright in the land, so did Nudd's jealousy harden into hatred—fierce, stiff-necked, and proud.

"He summoned his war band and said, 'You see how it is. My brother's portion grows greater while mine is diminished. It is not right that I should live as a hound cast out from the hearth. The king-ship of Albion should have come to me, but does Lludd consider this? Not at all. He goes his way with impudence. I am not lying when I say that I have endured the outrage of his arrogance long enough. The time has come to set this matter right.'

"Thus did Nudd take up his spear against his brother. Nudd and the men of his war band raised war upon Lludd. Warriors were armed. Battle hosts were gathered. And the Island of the Mighty—where not so much as an angry shout had been heard—echoed to the loud thunder of the carynx and the clash of sword on shield, of spear on helm.

"Great the battles between them, greater still the slaughter. The blood that flowed upon the land became a river which reached to the fetlocks of the horses and to the wheelhubs of the chariots. From dawn to dusk, the fair sky above Albion was rent with the clash of weapons and the pitiful cries of the wounded and dying. The land was laid waste; no man's life was safe. The practice of war became para-mount in Albion. Black the day; war had come to Paradise.

"War bands fought and warriors died. More war bands were amassed, and more were killed. Yet, for all the fighting and killing, nei-ther brother could claim victory over the other. Indeed, the warriors of Nudd and Lludd would still be waging war each upon the other to this very day, had not their father suddenly appeared one day at the place of battle. The Great King approached where the hosts were drawn up waiting for the sound of the battle horn to attack; he came riding a wayward horse, passing between the two battle lines.

"He halted in the center of the battleground and summoned his two sons to him. 'What is this that I am hearing?' he asked them. 'To and fro have I roamed from one end of this worlds-realm to the other, and nowhere have I heard that sound which is most hateful to my ears above all others. All I have seen and all I have heard has pleased me until now. And what do I behold? What do I hear? Morning to night there is no sound but that which I cannot abide; there is no sight but that which is an abomination to me: the sound of the battleclash and the sight of red blood spilled upon the earth and life snuffed out. Explain this, if you can. For I tell you truly, unless I know the reason why this has come to pass, though you are my own beloved sons and dearer to me than my life, you will curse the day of your birth.'

"With these and other stern words, Great Beli addressed his sons. Both were moved with shame and grief, but only Lludd lamented his part in the evil he had helped bring to the fairest realm that ever was in the world. 'The fault is mine, father,' he cried, stretching himself upon the ground before the king. 'I am not worthy of the gift you have given me. Take away the torc of kingship, and cast me out of your kingdom. Better still, kill me for the fool that I am. For I have placed right before mercy and honor before humility.'

"King Beli heard these words and knew the truth of them; his great heart broke. He turned to Nudd and asked, 'What do you say to this?'

"Nudd thought he saw a way out of his plight, so he answered, 'You have heard Lludd say that the fault is his. Who am I to disagree? He is king, after all. Let his blood be shed for the evil he has practiced against you, your land, and your people.'

"Beli, Wise and True, heard these words, and they pierced him through his great good soul. With tears in his eyes, Beli drew his sword and struck off Lludd's head. Lludd quivered once and he died.

"Nudd saw this and, though it frightened him, he still did not own the blame of starting the quarrel which led to the war. 'Do you yet having nothing to say?' Beli asked his son. But Nudd made no reply. And his silence stung his father more than his false words had hurt him before.

"The Great King did not want to lose two sons in one day, so he asked Nudd yet again, 'It takes two to wage war, my son. Am I to think that this wrong was Lludd's alone?'

"Nudd, whose heart had grown cold as stone, still believed that he might win the kingship now that Lludd was dead. So he replied, 'Think what you wish, my father. Lludd held the kingship, as you well know. He has paid the blood-price for the wrong practiced upon the land. Let us end the matter there.'

"Beli Mawr heard this and gave a long and terrible groan—the first of the Three Grievous Laments of Albion. Taking the edge of his cloak in his hands, he covered his head in his sorrow and wrath. 'You are right when you say that Lludd has paid the blood-debt he owed. With my own hand I have killed him who stood in my stead, my servant and my son. Lludd it was who would have held Albion after me, who would have reigned in my place, whose flesh and blood is my own—him I have sacrificed for the justice that I created. I have sacrificed myself to myself. This I have done so that righteousness will once more flourish in Albion.

"'Lludd is dead. But his death is nothing to the punishment you will receive for your part.'

"'Punishment?' sniffed Nudd. 'Justice is satisfied. What wrong have I done to you?'

"'You let your brother accept the punishment which you earned, and which you alone deserved,' said Beli. 'You are right when you say that the debt has been paid, for Lludd has paid it in full with innocent blood.'

"'If the blood-debt has been paid,' Nudd argued pitiably, 'let that be the end of the matter. There is no need to kill me.'

"'Listen well, Nudd,' replied Beli, Keen of Knowledge. 'Had you answered truthfully, you would have been spared. But by your own words I know that the truth is not in you. Lludd is dead, but in his death he will become greater than any who ever lived. He will be raised up, and you will be brought low.'

"'But you said you would not kill me!' cried Nudd.

"'You shall not die, Nudd. You will live to hear the name of your brother acclaimed wherever men revere justice and honor. You will endure to hear your own name as a curse upon the lips of all men everywhere. You will live and never die, and your miserable life will be worse by far than Lludd's noble death.'

"'You cannot do this to me!' cried Nudd. 'I am your only son!'

"But Beli would not hear any more of Nudd's twisted words. 'Depart from me, Wicked One,' he said. 'Go you from my sight. Wherever you find anyone to receive you, let that be your home.'

"Nudd flew from the field of battle and traveled throughout the length and breadth of Albion. Never did he find a friend to greet him; never did he find a hearth to warm him, or a welcome cup to quench his thirst. His cold heart hardened and grew still colder in his breast. At last he came to himself and said, 'All men hate me. Every hand is raised against me. I am an outcast in the land I might have ruled. So be it. If I cannot rule here, I will go where I can rule: I will go down into the Pit of Uffern, where no man dares go, and there I will reign as king.'

"So Nudd turned his cold heart against every living thing that enjoys the light of day and took himself down into the deep, black Pit of Uffern, where there is nothing but suffocating darkness and fire.

"Meanwhile, Beli, All-Wise King, gathered up the body of his beloved son and carried it to the highest hill that is in Albion. He raised the gorsedd of a hero over Lludd and established bards to praise

Lludd's virtues at all times and all days. From the heart of the hero-mound there grew a silver white birch tree. Beli cut the birch, made a fire, and burned the slender tree. Sparks from the fire leaped high into the sky. These became the Guide Stars by which men find their way in the darkness. Next, Beli gathered up all the embers and ashes from the fire and threw these into the sky also. These became the radiant belt of silver light known as the Sky Path. Lludd himself, Bright Spirit, nightly treads that shining starpath, ever gazing down upon the fairest island that is in the world. Those who look upon that wonder are ever moved with awe and reverence for its matchless beauty.

"But Nudd, Cold-hearted Enemy of All, gathered to himself every evil of every kind. The wretched spirits infesting the nether regions of the world thronged to him and called him lord. These became the *Coranyid*, the Host of Chaos, the inhuman minions of the Cythrawl, who delight in misery and exult in death: vicious in hate, ferocious in malice, brutal in spite, infinitely resentful of order and right and goodness.

"Endlessly resourceful in depravity, obscenity, and every iniquity, the Coranyid abide their darksome halls, gnawing out their poisonous souls, until through escape or release they are loosed upon the world, then they fly on the wings of the storm behind their dread monarch: Nudd, Prince of Uffern and Annwn, King of the Coranyid, Sovereign of Eternal Night, who wears the Black Serpent of Anoeth for his torc and carries Wyrm's fang for his weapon. At Lord Nudd's command they fly to destroy all that is good and right and beautiful."

Tegid raised his eyes from the fire and looked at me. I saw the fear in his glance and knew that the words he had spoken contained a truth too potent to impart in any other way save the veiled meaning of a song. He intoned softly, "Here ends the tale of Lord Nudd, believe it who will."

I did believe his tale. There are those who would not, I suppose, but they had not seen what I had seen. Unbelievers enjoy the security of their unbelief; there is great confidence in ignorance. But I had seen the Cythrawl.

I did not doubt that Lord Nudd and his Demon Host had been loosed and now roamed Albion in a savage spree of death and destruction. Once more, Nudd was free to wage his ghastly war of evil on Albion. The Day of Strife had dawned, yes. The Paradise War had begun anew.

26

THE BEACON

We stayed seven days at the fisher's hut by the river. The weather grew steadily worse all the while. Each day brought cold, gusting winds from the freezing north, rain, and sleet. We banked the fire high and sat huddled near it most of the day. When we grew hungry we ate from the salmon hoard.

I spoke little, and Tegid less. As each day passed, he seemed to withdraw more into himself. He sat staring into the heart of the fire, his eyes narrow and sad, round-shouldered with grief. He did not sleep well—neither of us slept at all soundly, but I would wake at night to see him sitting hunched in his skins, staring at the embers of our night fire.

I grew concerned for him. I tried to talk to him, but my attempts at drawing him out were met with silence and mute resignation. Each day passed in a gray blast of cold, and Tegid grew more remote and despondent. It was a knife in my heart to see him slipping away before my eyes, so I determined to do something about it.

On the morning of the eighth day I rose and went to the river to fetch drinking water in a leather cannikin. When I returned, I found

Tegid sitting before the spent embers of the previous night's fire, his head bent, his chin resting on his chest. "Tegid, get up!" I called loudly.

He did not stir when I spoke his name. "Tegid," I called again, "stand up on your feet; we must talk together. We can no longer sit here like this."

Again, my words brought no response from him. I stepped near and stood over him. "Tegid, look at me. I am talking to you."

He did not raise his head, so I lifted the leather cannikin and poured the ice-cold water over him. That roused him. He jumped up spitting and spewing and glaring at me. His face was pale and wan, but his eyes were red-flecked with anger.

"Why did you do that?" he demanded, shaking water from his sodden cloak. "Leave me alone!"

"That is the one thing I will not do," I told him. "We must talk."

"No!" he muttered darkly and made to turn away. "There is nothing to say."

"Talk to me, Tegid," I replied. "We must decide what to do."

"Why? This is as good a place to die as any other."

"It is not right to sit here like this. We have to do something."

"What would you have us do?" he sneered. "Speak, O Soul of Wisdom. I am listening."

"I cannot say what is to be done, Tegid. I only know we have to do something."

"We are dead men!" he said savagely. "Our people are killed. Our king is gone. There is no life for us anymore."

He collapsed once more on the ground—sinking beneath the weight of his despair. I sat down opposite him, more determined than ever to draw him out. "Look at me, Tegid," I said, seizing on a sudden inspiration. "I want to ask you something." I did not wait for his surly reply but forged ahead. "Who is the Phantarch?"

Tegid sighed, but answered lifelessly. "He is the Chief Bard of all Albion."

I remembered this from my early lessons. "Yes," I replied, "so you have said. But what is he? What does he do?"

He stirred enough to lift his eyebrows and look at me. "Why do you ask?"

"Please—I want to know."

He sighed again and hunched his shoulders, and I thought he would not answer. But he was thinking, and after a while he said, "The Phantarch serves the Song. Through him, the Song is given life; through him, all is held in order."

"The Song," I said, recalling what Gwenllian had told me. "The Song of Albion?"

Again he raised his eyes to me. "The Song of Albion—what do you know about the Song of Albion?"

"I know that it is the chief treasure of this worlds-realm; it upholds all and sustains all that exists," I told him, recalling the words the Banfáith had used in her prophecy. "Is this so?"

"Yes," Tegid replied flatly. "What else did the Banfáith tell you?"

I hesitated, feeling again the dread inspired by the torment of Gwenllian's prophecy—a dread deepening to fear. Yes, what else did the Banfáith say? Tell him—Tegid should know.

Something in me resisted; I did not want to reveal all the Banfáith had said. The prophecy carried with it a duty—a great and terrible duty I did not want to accept. But Tegid had a right to know at least a part of it . . .

"She said—" I began, hesitated, and then blurted, "she said the Phantarch was dead and that the Song was silent."

At this, Tegid lowered his eyes to the cold ashes of the dead fire. "Then it is as I have said." His voice was sorrow itself. "There is no hope."

"Why? Why is there no hope? What does it mean?" I challenged, but he did not respond. "Answer me, Tegid!" I picked up a charred stick and threw it at him, striking him on the shoulder. "What does it mean?"

"It is the Phantarch who prevents the Cythrawl from escaping the underworld abyss," he said softly, lifting a hand to his face as if the light hurt his eyes. "The Phantarch is dead," he groaned. "Albion is lost, and we are dead."

"Why?" He did not respond. "Tell me, Tegid! Why is Albion lost? What does it mean?"

He glared at me. "Must I explain what you see before you with your own eyes?"

"Yes!"

"The Phantarch is dead," he muttered wearily, "otherwise the Beast of the Pit could not escape, and Lord Nudd would not be freed."

At last I understood what the Banfáith had told me. Since the Phantarch alone held the power to restrain the evil of the Cythrawl, the Phantarch's death must have released the Cythrawl, and now Lord Nudd was free to roam where he would, destroying all in his path. I was beginning to understand, but even so I could not share Tegid's despair.

"Then let us go down fighting," I said, climbing to my feet. "Let us summon Lord Nudd and challenge him and his vile Coranyid to do their worse."

Tegid frowned and mumbled, "You are talking foolishness. We would be killed straightaway."

"So be it!" I spat. "Anything would be better than sitting here watching you gnaw at your bowels."

He scowled and balled his fists as if he might strike me. But he lacked the will, and his halfhearted anger gave way to misery once more.

"What? Are you afraid to die?"

He gave a mirthless laugh. "Why speak of fear? We are dead already."

"Then let us go to our graves like men."

He observed me for a moment, trying to determine whether I meant what I said.

"Well?"

"What do you suggest?" he asked finally.

"Let us build a beacon fire," I said, speaking out the first notion that sprang into my mind.

Tegid did not laugh in my face. Neither did he embrace the project. Instead, he grunted and returned to his dismal survey of the sodden ashes.

I pursued him, strengthening my resolve. "A beacon fire. Think of it, Tegid. If any are alive in the land, they will see it and come to us. If not, we will summon Foul Nudd and defy him to his wicked face. Let him come! He can but kill us. We are no worse off either way. What do you say?"

"I say you are a fool," he grunted. Nevertheless, he slowly unfolded himself and stood. "But it is true, we cannot live like this."

"Then you will help me?"

"I will help you," he agreed. "And we will build the biggest beacon fire ever seen in Albion. Let come what may."

With that, Tegid Tathal became as active as he had been lethargic. He threw the bridles and skins on the horses and pulled up the tether stakes while I wrapped some fish in a bit of cloth and kicked dirt over the fire. I called Twrch to me and mounted my horse, and, with the hound pup before me in a fold of my cloak, we started off.

"Where shall we build the fire?" I asked as we turned our horses onto the track.

"In Sycharth," Tegid called back over his shoulder. "It is a high

293

fortress. We will defy the enemy at the place of his most fierce destruction. The beacon will be seen from Llogres to Caledon! Any who see it will know that we did not go to our graves without a fight."

The change in my gloomy companion was swift and complete. He had resigned himself to dying, and now raced to embrace death lest that, too, elude him.

I, for my part, was less eager to die. But I followed Tegid willingly, because I feared death less than empty, wasted life.

Upon reaching the ruin of Meldryn Mawr's fortress—a more forlorn and desolate place I never want to see—we set about our task. Through the stench of rotting corpses, Tegid and I steeled ourselves to our work, gathering together whatever we could find and dragging it into a heap. Our hearts were as stone and our hands were unflinching.

"We will make of this once-splendid stronghold a pyre without equal," Tegid said, through clenched teeth. "Our ashes will mingle with those of our people."

Still, in the end, there was not enough dry fuel to kindle a decent pyre, let alone to make one. Almost everything that would burn had already been consumed by the flames that had destroyed the caer, and the rest was wet from the rain and snow. Tegid surveyed the sorry pile of wooden objects we had heaped together in the place where the Great King's hall once stood. "There is not enough," he said flatly. "We will have to go to the shipyard."

We worked until well after dark, dragging the unburnt ends of timbers from the shipyard up to the caer. "There is still not enough," Tegid declared, surveying the heap in the dying light.

"We will have to find more," I agreed. "But that must wait for tomorrow."

We did not sleep in the fortress. Having plundered their tomb and disturbed their rest, we did not care to intrude further on the unburied dead. So we camped by the river near the shipyards.

The next day we cut long birch poles for our horses and rode to the wooded hills across the marshes to gather dead wood and timber to add to our beacon. We worked quickly, despite the treacherous trackways through the marshes, a sullen rain, and the ceaseless wind that whipped at us in icy gusts. By day's end we had amassed a sizable addition to our beacon pyre, but Tegid said it still was not enough. Exhausted, we curled up in our damp cloaks, slept, and rose to repeat the labors of the previous day.

Beneath a looming, leaden sky, we heaped brush, branches, and logs upon the slender birch poles and hauled them from the woods, across the watermarsh, and up the trackway to the caer. All day long, without food or rest. When I suggested stopping to water and rest the horses, Tegid only laughed and replied that soon we would obtain our fill of rest. He was certain that the beacon fire would do its work and the Lord Nudd would see us settled in our graves before the night was through.

But I became more determined than ever to fashion some plan of escape. My mind whirled; my thoughts ranged far and wide. As I lashed the last clumsy bundle of brushwood to the birch poles, I tried desperately to think of a way to forestall the lighting of the beacon. The last days, spent in the company of corpses, had brought a change in me. As I smelled, shifted, and stepped over the rotting dead, I came to understand something fundamental: I was alive, and I wanted to go on living. I did not want to be killed by Lord Nudd. I did not want to become yet another hideous, grinning, bloated lump of putrid flesh. I was not ready to die; I wanted to live.

As we splashed back across the marshland and floundered up the muddy track to the ruined caer, my mind raced, seizing one pretense after another to stay Tegid's determined hand. Even as the last fitful light of day faded and Tegid held the wad of pitch-soaked cloth to the embers he had carefully conserved to start the fire, I still believed I would think of some way to prevent him lighting it.

I did not. Nothing came to me. Instead, I stood mutely by and watched as he blew gently on the blackened rag, touching an edge to the bright-glowing coals. As the first white wisps of smoke curled into the mean, dusky sky, I swallowed hard, believing that I saw my life spiraling upward in that slender thread of smoke. One gust of wind and the smoke scattered and dispersed. Thus would my life end when Lord Nudd appeared with his fell host of demon Coranyid.

Tegid's cheeks puffed as he coaxed the tiny flame to sprout. An instant later it caught, and the rag blossomed into orange flame. Tegid raised the pitch-soaked cloth on the end of the stick and offered it to me. "Here, brother," he said. "Will you light our pyre, or shall I?"

"You light it, Tegid," I said, still trying to discover how I might prevent the beacon from catching fire and announcing our presence to the enemy.

And, even as the first bright flames began licking along the lower edges of the huge jumble of timber and brushwood, I still imagined that somehow I would think of something to rescue us . . . even as the flames passed from branch to branch, climbing through the tangled latticework of wood, I thought I would prevail . . . even as the larger logs sizzled, throwing off steam from the rain that had soaked them, I believed I would discover a way of salvation for us . . .

Even with the night full around us, and the flames leaping high into the black vault of heaven, I thought I would yet catch hold of that which had all day escaped my grasp.

And when I stood on the ruined rampart and gazed out on the night-dark plain below Sycharth and saw the kindled torches of mounted warriors racing toward the caer and knew that I saw death flying toward us and heard the dull thunder of their horses' hooves drumming on the ground, even then, I still believed we would not die.

"See how swiftly our beacon summons them!" exulted Tegid. "Come, Lord Nudd! We defy you!"

Tegid's voice was harsh and his face rigid with a strange excitement. He lofted the torch in his hand, waved it in a wild arc above his head, and jeered at the onrushing enemy. Picking up Twrch, I turned from the rampart and ran to retrieve my weapons. I tied the pup with the loose end of the horse's tether. I unlaced the oiled skin and withdrew my sword, and then I pulled the covering from the honed head of my spear. I took up my shield and ran back to the place where Tegid stood.

"Take this," I said, putting the spear into his hand. "Come, we will meet them at the gate."

The gates were battered to splinters and burned, but the narrow passage of the trackway offered some protection. I did not know if demons fought like other warriors—or if they might pass through walls of stone to wound a mortal with a single deadly glance—still, I resolved that if strong metal could strike a blow against such a foe, any who raised hand against us would feel the bite of my blade. We took our places side by side, Tegid and I, and we watched the glimmering torches drawing near.

The flames hot on our backs, the blazing beacon casting our shadows long upon the track before us, the roar of the great fire loud in our ears, we watched and waited. I gripped the sword hilt easily, feeling its familiar weight fill my hand. Tegid stuck the burning brand into the bank and held the spear across his body, his face livid in the guttering firelight.

My thoughts were not on the death that awaited us, nor even with the burned and battered bodies of our kinsmen that littered the caer. My thoughts were on the length of sharp metal at the end of my arm and the practiced movements of the fight. This was my first real battle since becoming a warrior, and, though it would likely be my last, I welcomed it, eager to try my hard-won skills.

"Whatever happens," Tegid cried above the beacon fire's roar, "I count it an honor to die beside you."

"There is no honor in death," I said, repeating what Scatha told her students. "Rather let us count it an honor to send a few of the Coranyid back to the darkness of the hell they so richly deserve."

"Well said, brother!" replied Tegid. "So be it!"

The first horses had reached the trackway at the base of the caer. I knew the enemy could see us silhouetted against the beacon fire at our backs. They hesitated. Circled.

I heard a sharp cry. Then the first of the warriors entered the narrow trackway and flew up the long ramp toward us. I lifted the blade and crouched behind my shield. I could not see my attacker, but followed the surging path of the torch in his hand. Even as the first demon warrior entered the trackway, another sprang up behind him, and another. The three came at us, one at a time, and the rest stayed behind—as if unwilling to chance the ruined walls which bounded the path leading up to the gates.

The first rider reached the crest of the hill. I dashed forward to the place where his horse would strain to gain the hilltop. There he would be momentarily unbalanced as he shifted his weight forward to keep us from sliding back over the rump of his mount. And there I would meet him with my blade.

Tegid saw what I intended and moved into position to take the second warrior before he could aid the first.

The blood rushed in my veins and my heart leapt, but my thoughts were cold and precise as my movements.

I was ready for the face of my foe, for the grotesque manifestation of my most loathsome imaginings. I was ready for the face of death in any of its most hideous revelations. But I was not ready for the sight that met my eyes as the enemy advanced into the glare of the beacon fire. One moment the demon was a shadow in motion; an instant later, he took flesh in the light.

Seeing the form of my attacker, I dropped my arm.

For I was prepared for any sight but that which met my eyes: Meldryn Mawr's champion, Paladyr, the chief of battle I had met at the Great King's court.

My hesitation almost cost me my life. For, as my swordpoint wavered, the warrior thrust at me with his spear. With a shout I jumped back. Paladyr's spearpoint flashed. In the shattering firelight I saw his lips draw back in a snarl of rage. His mount, guided by the pressure of his master's knees, turned and drove toward me, eyes wild, nostrils flaring, sharp hooves biting the earth.

I raised my shield to meet the blow. My blade came up under the shield, ready to flick out the instant the shield lifted clear. Even as I readied to strike, my mind was struggling to find the meaning of this strange turn of events: Paladyr. Here. Attacking me!

Was it Paladyr indeed? Or had a cunning demon taken the great warrior's form to confound and defeat me?

Though the enemy before me might not be human, the rage in his eyes was real enough. Human or not, he meant to kill me. His spear shaft crashed against the iron rim of my shield. The shock shivered the bones in my arm, and my knees buckled. But I raised the sword and cleanly deflected the thrust which followed. The spear swung wide, and I saw the great man's chest exposed.

In his rage, he had left himself vulnerable. I might easily have pierced his heart with the point of my sword. But I stayed my hand. This was no demon.

"Paladyr!" I shouted. "Hold!"

The fierce snarl of rage that curled his lips relaxed. In the fire glare I saw bewilderment softening those stony features. He glanced to either side and saw that Tegid and I fought alone. His eyes noted the ruin around him, exposed in the light of the beacon flare. His confusion deepened.

I called to Tegid. "Hold, Tegid! These are our kinsmen!"

Tegid left his attack on the second horseman and raced to my side. "Paladyr!" he cried. "Do you not know us, man?"

Recognition dawned in the huge warrior's eyes. He raised a hand in salute, but the spearpoint remained leveled at our chests. "Tegid?" he said. "How come you to be here, brother?"

Tegid thrust his spear into the ground at his feet. The king's champion threw down his spear in turn and called for the other warriors to put up their weapons. He dismounted and came to stand before us.

He glanced at the beacon fire and then at the ruined stronghold. He looked long upon it and was shaken by the sight. When at last he found his voice, he spoke. "What has happened here?"

The simple question held a world of anguish. Those with him sat on their horses and mutely contemplated the devastation, stunned, bereft of words.

Tegid stepped toward Paladyr. "Sycharth is destroyed," he replied. "Our kinsmen are dead. Search where you will, all have entered death's dark hall and will no more be found in the land of the living."

Paladyr passed an enormous hand before his eyes. He swayed on his feet, and his jaw muscles worked, but he did not fall or cry out. I saw then how tired he was. They must have been riding for days.

"We saw the beacon," the champion said. "We thought . . . we thought the caer was . . ." He straightened himself, turned, and mounted his horse. "The king must be told."

He rode back down the trackway and disappeared into the darkness.

"The king is alive, then," remarked Tegid. And, indeed, it was Meldryn Mawr himself who appeared before us but a few moments later—haggard and red-eyed from lack of sleep, but it was he. With a small escort of warriors, he appeared at the ruined gate, dismounted, and proceeded to make a circuit of his desolated fortress.

In the lurid glow of the beacon fire, I watched as he moved slowly through the ruins alone. He bore the outrage bravely at first, but the devastation was too great. When he reached the scorched and broken timbers of his hall, he staggered to the ravaged hearth and fell upon his knees, filled his hands with sodden ashes, and flung them over his head. A ragged cry ripped from his throat—a single heartrending shout of unutterable grief and anguish and pain. The warriors, who had begun loudly clamoring for revenge, were shamed into silence by their lord's distress.

After a time we went to him. His face was smudged with filth, except where his tears had washed twin trails down his cheeks. He stood as we approached. The sadness in his eyes, and in his voice, broke my heart. "Where is Ollathir?" he asked quietly. I think he already guessed the answer.

"He lies under a grave mound on Ynys Bàinail," Tegid answered.

The king nodded slowly and turned his eyes to me. "Who is this man?"

He did not recognize me from our one brief meeting. I would have answered him, but the question was not for me. "He is the wanderer you sent to become a warrior," Tegid answered. "He was with Ollathir when he died."

Despite his shock and sorrow, the king welcomed me and said, "Ollathir is gone, thus Tegid Tathal is become my Chief of Song. Therefore, you are become his sword and shield. Never depart from him. We will all have need of a bard in the days to come. Guard him well, warrior."

"With my life, Great King," I pledged.

The king raised his hand to Tegid. "You, Brehon, are all that is left to me of your kind. From this night you will be my bard and my voice. As the voices of my people are silent, so I will be silent. For I tell you the truth, until the voices of my people are heard again in this place, I have no voice."

The king lifted his head and scanned the black ruin of his once-great stronghold. He stood for a moment, contemplating the horror of death and devastation, as if to fix it in his mind. Then he turned abruptly, swung into the saddle, and started down the track.

As the remaining warriors filed slowly down the trackway, Tegid and I returned to our horses. "Take heart, Tegid," I told him. "We have held off death a little longer."

"We have exchanged one grave for another," he grumbled. "That is all."

"So gloomy," I told him and heard Goewyn's soft words in my ear. "We are still alive. Why think the worst?"

The bard grunted his disdain but stirred himself nonetheless. We pulled up the tether stakes and mounted our horses. Twrch, shivering from the excitement of the fight and fire, barked lustily as I gathered him to me and rode from the caer.

27

THE FLIGHT
TO FINDARGAD

Together with his war band the Great King made the circuit of his lands: Caer Dyffryn, Cnoc Hydd, Yscaw, Dinas Galan, Caer Carnedd. In each settlement and holding he viewed the wicked destruction with the stone-hard silence of a mountain, remote and impenetrable in his grief. None could tell the king's thought, for he spoke to no one, but viewed the carnage and waste with an unflinching eye.

The warriors howled for justice; they screamed for revenge. They raged. At each place of destruction, at each atrocity of desolation, they renewed their cries for vengeance. Like frenzied hounds baying for blood, they filled the air with their bellowing, shouting taunts and curses, urging the king to ride in pursuit of the enemy. They imagined the enemy could be fought with sword and spear.

But the king knew better. When he had seen enough, King Meldryn turned away from the desolation of his lands and, much to his warriors' dismay, rode for Findargad, his ice-bound fortress in the vast heart of the high northern peaks of the Cethness Mountains. There the Great King would gather the ragged remnant of his people. For, by some fabulous chance, there were survivors. A few settlements had escaped annihilation: smaller, hidden holdings where the Demon Host did not come. Perhaps these were overlooked in the frenzy of destruction, or were deemed insignificant. However it was, when Meldryn Mawr turned his back on the lowlands and set his face toward Findargad, six hundred souls followed in his train.

Of those six hundred, nearly one hundred and fifty were mounted warriors. The rest were farmers and craftsmen from the holdings. At each settlement where people endured, we gathered only those provisions we could carry easily and moved on. We needed food and warm clothing in order to survive the journey north. Yet we were compelled to travel swiftly and silently lest we attract the notice of Lord Nudd. We could not be burdened with heavy baggage, nor slow our pace for ox-drawn wagons. If we went hungry, at least we went quickly.

At Yscaw on the banks of Nantcoll, the river whose headwaters issued from the snowbound heart of Cethness, Tegid erected an ogham tree: an oaken post squared on one side and carved in ogham letters revealing to any who came after us that we had survived.

Then we proceeded along the banks of the swift-racing water northwards into the highlands of the Cethness Mountains. Sollen, most cruel of seasons, showed no mercy—save in one regard: the cold froze the water marge and allowed us to travel at pace along the banks, leaving little evidence of our passing.

We were all kept busy, morning to night. Moving so many people quickly and quietly is arduous work. "It is impossible," growled Tegid. "Sooner herd a shoal of salmon with a willow wand!" He had reason to complain. The brunt of the chore fell to the bard, for the king would speak no word to anyone except Tegid, who remained by Meldryn's side at all times. And as I was pledged to Tegid's aid, I, too, was busy.

Owing to my duties and my vow to watch over Tegid, it was not until the evening of the third day after turning north that I learned that Simon was still alive. In truth, I had not thought about him since leaving Ynys Sci. So much had happened since then that I had scarcely a spare thought for myself, let alone Simon.

But I caught sight of him among the retinue of warriors in Prince Meldron's band. And the shock of seeing him again brought with it the sharp realization of where I was and why I had come. In that instant, I understood exactly how Simon had felt that day when he discovered me on the battlefield. I deeply resented the reminder that I was a stranger, an outsider, and I lived in a world not my own.

Simon did not see me, so I was able to observe him for a few moments before going to him. He moved in the company of Prince Meldron, who, I quickly learned, maintained an elite force among the warriors—his Wolf Pack, he called them. These had been given the task of guarding our escape, riding at the rear of our procession to challenge any pursuit, which is why I had not seen him sooner. And Simon had won pride of place in the prince's Wolf Pack. One had only to look at the way the others deferred to him to know it.

He had added some weight to his athletic frame—all of it muscle, especially through the upper arms and shoulders. His back was broad and his legs powerful. I watched him move among his swordbrothers and recognized the old assurance and easy confidence—now heightened by the many victories he had won in Meldryn Mawr's service. He was a chief of battle, and looked it, with his hair grown long and bound in a queue at his neck. His breecs were fine blue linen, and his siarc was bright yellow; his cloak was green and blue checked. He wore no torc, but boasted four broad armbands of gold and golden rings on the fingers of each hand.

Disagreeable as was the shock of seeing him, I was glad he was alive and well—despite the changes wrought in him during our time apart. For he was no longer the blithe young man I had known, but a Celtic warrior through and through. He might have said the same of me, for I had undergone a similar transformation.

When I had finished my scrutiny, I went to where he sat on a red calfskin beside a small twig fire he shared with three others. "Simon?" At the sound of his name his head swiveled toward me. His eyes played over me for a moment, and recognition broke slowly over his features. "Lewis!"

"So you do remember me, after all."

He rose to stand before me but did not grip my arms in a kinsman's greeting. "It is good to see you, friend. I heard you had returned." Though his tone was light and welcoming, I felt the restrained coolness of his greeting and knew that he was not at all happy to see me. "I have been meaning to find you."

He was lying, but I let it pass. "You look well, Simon."

He cocked his head to one side as if trying to decide what to do with me, then laughed softly. "It seems an age since I saw you last," he said. "How was the island? I hear Scatha has very lovely daughters." Simon laughed again. His friends smiled and nudged one another.

"That is true," I replied. "How have you been, Simon? Rising in the world, I see."

His face clouded suddenly in a frown, and he glared at me for a moment. "I am Siawn Hy now," he replied quietly, pride and scorn blending in his gaze. His jaw bulged menacingly. I looked at the face of the man I had once known well, and now knew not at all. He had changed—in more than name. "You seem to have done well for yourself."

"I am still alive."

Simon accepted this explanation readily. "You always did surprise me."

"We have all had a few surprises the last few days," I told him. "I did not mean to disturb you."

The tension went out of him, and he became expansive in his pardon. "Think nothing of it," he said loudly. "It was nothing. Less than nothing!" This was said more for his friends' sakes than for mine. "Here, sit with us; share our fire. We are always glad to have a sword-brother."

The other warriors heartily concurred, expanding their circle to make room for me. I settled among them, feeling instantly a part of their fellowship. I wondered at how quickly they welcomed me, and then realized that they must have seen me with Tegid and the king and speculated about my exalted position. "They say you were with Ollathir when he died," said the warrior sitting across the fire from me. It was the accepted way of fishing for information: by indirect statement of fact, usually attributed to someone else.

"I was there," I replied tersely. It was a subject which I had no wish to discuss openly.

"He was a great bard," put in the warrior next to Simon. "A king among his kind. His counsel will be keenly missed."

"That is true," said another. "If he had been there, Sycharth would not have fallen."

I could feel the sadness of the warriors; it was no greater than my own, but the horror of devastation was still fresh for them, and they were struggling to imagine the enormity of the loss.

One of them turned to me. "They say you and Tegid lit the beacon. Were you there when the destroyer came? Did you see it?"

The question carried with it the mild insinuation that Tegid and I should have done something to save the stronghold. "No," I told them. "Like you, Tegid and I came after. But as to that, why were you not there to protect your kinsmen?"

There I had probed the raw wound of their regret. They all winced and gazed sullenly at the fire. One of their number, a warrior named Aedd, spoke for all of them. "I would gladly die a thousand deaths to save even one of my kinsmen."

"Ten thousand," added the warrior sitting next to him. "If we had only been there . . ."

I could not take away their grief, but I could ease their pain. "It would not have mattered," I told them. "I have seen the enemy, and I tell you the truth—you would have been slaughtered with all the rest."

"Who is it?" they wanted to know, suddenly angry. They leapt up as if they meant to seize their weapons and ride away at once. "Who has done this?"

Before I could answer, Simon spoke up. "Sit!" he commanded. "You have seen Caer Dyffryn and Yscaw and Dinas Galan. We could have done nothing."

"It may be as you say," Aedd replied, slowly taking his place once more. "But a warrior who fails to protect his own is worse than a coward. Better that we should have died with our kin."

"Your presence there would have made no difference," I repeated with as much conviction as I could muster. "There is no virtue in useless death."

"Well said," agreed Simon quickly. "Dead we can do nothing. But alive we have a chance to avenge our kinsmen."

They all agreed heartily with this and voiced their approval with solemn vows to kill as many of the enemy as possible when the day of retribution came. They still did not comprehend the hopelessness of our predicament. I did not have the heart to disappoint them; they would learn the truth soon enough.

The warriors accepted the small comfort I offered. "The blood debt to be repaid is heavy indeed," Aedd observed. "Still, it is shame to me that I was not with my kinsmen in their time of travail."

"That is what we thought to prevent," Simon reminded him.

"When Tegid and I arrived at the caer," I said, returning to my question, "we thought you dead. We could not imagine what had taken you from the stronghold."

"We rode to the summons," Aedd replied and went on to explain how word about a coming invasion had reached them from the south-west coast. Thinking to forestall the assault, the king had raised the warriors of his hearth and left the caer. They ranged far in protection of the realm but sighted no invaders, and after many days with the weather growing worse, they had turned back.

"When we saw the beacon fire, we thought—" Aedd halted abruptly, unwilling to go on.

The soft splutter of the twig fire and the sigh of the rising wind made a melancholy sound in our ears. After a moment, Simon said, "Hear me, brothers. The blood debt will be repaid. We will avenge our dead. The enemy will be crushed into dust beneath our feet."

Despite Simon's brave words, the warriors' sorrow was too great to shrug aside easily. Given time, bold words would again ignite the spark of their valor; they would rise up and clasp courage to their hearts. But not now, not this night. This night, and for many more nights to come, the lament for the lost would fill their souls, and their hearts would remain heavy with mourning.

I left them to nurse their grief and returned to my place with Tegid and the king. Prince Meldron was there, too, vainly trying to pry some word of explanation from his father. At last he yielded to the king's stubborn silence and stormed away, saying, "You talk to him, Tegid. Perhaps he will listen to you. Tell my father that we cannot reach Findargad like this. It is too far and too cold. The high mountain passes will be filled with snow. We will lose half our people before we ever come within sight of the towers. Tell him that, Tegid!"

"I have already told him," Tegid mumbled, when Meldron had gone. "He will not listen."

"Is it really so dangerous?" I asked.

Tegid nodded slowly. "The mountains of Cethness are high, and the Sollen winds are cold. The prince speaks the truth when he says that many will die before we reach the stronghold."

"Then why are we going?"

"There is nothing else we can do," Tegid replied dismally. "It is what the king has ordered."

I saw how the matter stood, so I did not bother asking the most obvious, and most disturbing, questions. If mighty Sycharth could not protect her people, why believe the stone walls of Findargad would fare any better? What good were swords and spears against an enemy that felt neither pain nor death?

As Tegid had morbidly suggested, we might as well have stayed in Sycharth and saved ourselves the hardship and distress of a cold mountain journey, for one grave is very like another, and when Lord Nudd came for us there would be no stopping him wherever we happened to be.

And yet . . . and yet, an elusive glimmer of hope danced at the edge of my awareness like a firefly floating just out of reach. It was there, and then it was gone. I gave chase and it disappeared; I stood still and it drew close. But, try as I might, I could not capture it.

Yet I could not rest until I had seized that hope, however small. That night I withdrew from the comfort of the king's fire and stood alone in a nearby grove, holding vigil until I should succeed. All through the night I stood, wrapped in my cloak, leaning now and then against one of the alder trees of the grove, listening to the branches clicking in the thin, cold wind while the knife-bright stars turned slowly in the black Sollen sky. All through the night I waited. And when the moon sank from sight below the hills, I was no closer to achieving my purpose.

Then, even as a sullen, gray green dawn lifted night's curtain in the east, the evasive quarry I sought drew near. It came, slim and fragile, in the form of a question: if Lord Nudd was so powerful, why remove the king from his stronghold before laying waste to the fortress?

The Coranyid had not moved against Sycharth and the other settlements of the realm while the king remained in his stronghold. The destruction came only after Meldryn had been drawn away through deception. It seemed to me that some power had prevented Lord Nudd's awful attack while the king remained with his people. Despite all the terrible Coranyid had done, the annihilation was not complete. And even now it might be avoided somehow. But how?

As the first faint rays of daylight spread a sickly glow into the sky, I heard again the voice of the Banfáith, clear and strong as if she were before me once again: *Before the Cythrawl can be conquered, the Song must be restored.*

Was this the hope I sought? It seemed unlikely, for she had also said: No one knows the Song, save the Phantarch alone. How could the Song of Albion be restored if no one knew the Song but the Phantarch, and the Phantarch was dead?

It was a riddle and it made no sense.

I worried at it through the mist-shrouded day and the long hours of the freezing night, as we sat huddled in our cloaks before our twig fire. But the riddle turned inward upon itself, and I could make no sense of it.

"Tegid," I said softly, "I have been thinking." Twrch slept at my feet, the king rested fitfully on his white oxhide nearby, and Tegid sat beside me, staring into the shimmering flames, brooding in silence.

The bard grunted but did not turn his eyes from his contemplation of the fire.

"Where is the Phantarch?"

"Why speak of it again?" he muttered. "The Phantarch is dead."

"Hear me out," I insisted. "I have pondered this in my mind and do not speak just to amuse myself with the sound of my voice."

"Very well, speak your mind," he relented.

"The Banfáith told me many things," I began and was quickly interrupted.

"Oh yes, the Banfáith told you many things. And you have told me little." He was sullen in this observation. "Have you now decided to part with some of your treasure hoard?"

The words of the Banfáith were still a mystery to me, and I still feared them and all they might mean. But as the days passed and the hopelessness of our plight became ever more apparent, I grew less concerned for myself. This was no time for the selfishness of secrets. Tegid was Chief Bard now; he must be told what I knew.

"You are right to rebuke me, Tegid," I told him. "I will tell you everything." So I began to relate all she had told me regarding the Phantarch and the Song of Albion—reluctantly at first, but then more readily as the words sought release and tumbled out. I described the prophecy as well as I could remember it. I told him about the destruction and upheaval of the days to come, and the looked-for champion. I told him about Llew Silver Hand and the Flight of Ravens and the Hero Feat at the end of the Great Year and all that I could remember, just as the Banfáith had given it to me. When I finished, Tegid did not raise his head but sat staring morosely into the fire.

"It seems to me that despite all the prophecy portends, there may yet be some future for us."

But Tegid took no comfort in what I told him. Instead, he shook his head slowly and said, "You are wrong. What future there may have been, now can never be. The Cythrawl is too strong in the land; Lord Nudd has grown too powerful."

"Then why give the prophecy at all?"

Tegid just shook his head.

"I do not understand you, Tegid. You moan because I would not tell you the Banfáith's prophecy, and when I do tell you, all you can do is complain that it is too late. Before the Cythrawl can be conquered, the Song must be restored—that is what she said. It seems to me that we have to find the Phantarch."

"The Phantarch is dead, as you well know."

"And the Song with him?"

"Of course the Song with him. How can it be otherwise? The Phantarch is the instrument of the Song—there is no Song without the Phantarch."

"But where is he?"

"*You* have Ollathir's awen," he snapped, "not me."

"What does that mean?"

He muttered something under his breath and made to turn away, but I held him.

"Please, Tegid, I am trying to understand. Where is the Phantarch?"

"I do not know," he answered and explained how, in order to protect the Song, the Phantarch's chamber was hidden and the location kept secret. "Only the Penderwydd knows where the Phantarch hides. Ollathir knew, and Ollathir is dead."

"And he died before he could tell you the secret?"

"Yes! Yes!" Tegid rose to his feet and raised his hands in clenched fists about his head. "Yes, Llyd! You have finally grasped this important truth: the Phantarch is dead; Ollathir is dead; the Song is dead; and soon we will be dead too." The king stirred in his sleep. Tegid saw that his outburst had disturbed the king and dropped his fists.

What a cruel deceit, what a pitiless ruse this prophecy. I felt the fragile hope I had held so lightly begin to disintegrate. There could be no defeating the Cythrawl without the Song, and no Song without the Phantarch. But the Phantarch was dead, and, as if to make matters worse, the only person who knew where to find him was dead too.

"Tell me now that there is still hope for us," said Tegid, his voice a choked whisper. The fight went out of him, and he sank once more to the ground.

"The king is alive," I replied. "How can we be without hope if the king is alive? You are alive, too, and so am I. Look around—there are hundreds of us here, and we are ready to fight once more. Why has Lord Nudd been unable to kill our king? Why has he only attacked the unprotected villages?"

Even as I spoke, my own words began to convince me that there was still something or someone keeping Nudd from his ultimate victory. "Listen, Tegid, if I were as powerful as you say Nudd is, I would first kill the king, and the kingdom would be mine. But why has he not done this?"

"I do not know! Ask him—ask Nudd when next you meet!"

"The Coranyid attacked only after the king had been removed—why?"

"It is not for me to say! Perhaps Nudd wishes to prolong his enjoyment with the rich spectacle of our futile efforts at escape."

"We live only at Lord Nudd's pleasure? I do not believe that."

"Believe it! We live at Lord Nudd's pleasure. And when it pleases him to kill us, he will kill us—just as he has killed all the rest."

"And it is our king's pleasure to die at Findargad?" I challenged.

"That is the way of it! It is the king's pleasure to die in Findargad, and I serve the king."

These were Tegid's final words. But as I lay sleepless by the fire that night, these few words of the Banfáith sustained me: *Happy shall be Caledon; the Flight of Ravens will flock to her many-shadowed glens, and raven-song shall be her song.*

And as I stared into the shimmering flames I saw, framed in the molten red and gold of the embers, a vision: I saw a green oak grove and, under spreading branches of clustered leaves, a grassy mound. On this mound stood a throne made of stag antlers adorned with the hide of a white ox. And perched on the back of the throne an enormous raven, black as moonless night, with wings outstretched and beak open, filling the silent grove with a bitter, stringent, yet strangely beautiful song.

28
THE HUNT

As if maddened by our escape, the Season of Ice pursued us down the valleys and riverways, filling the world with its ravening roar. Sollen became an enemy to be battled, a foe growing from strength to strength while we slowly weakened. Yet we journeyed on. By the time we reached the foothills of the high peaks, everyone agreed that this year's Sollentide was by far the worst that any had ever known for wind, rain, snow, and fierce, stinging cold. Not a day went by that the sky did not shed snow; the winds wailed and raged from dawn to dusk; the streams and rivers froze hard. As the snow rose about us, our progress slowed to a crawl.

Finding enough fuel to make the night's campfires became an obsession. Often we had to stop well before nightfall—sometimes even before midday—in order to find and gather enough firewood to keep us through the night. Any extra was carried along with us. Food supplies held good, but only because we began eating less. To fill our empty stomachs we ate snow as we stumbled along the trail. The warriors now walked, giving their horses to the children and mothers with infants, who could not flounder through the snow. We took to wrapping the horses' legs—and our own as well—in rags and skins to keep their feet from freezing, and walked two by two on either side of a horse lest anyone fall away unnoticed.

I carried Twrch beneath my cloak when I walked—the snow was too deep for him—and more than once blessed the warmth of his small furry body. I fed him from my own portion, or obtained meat scraps for him from those given to the other hounds. At night he slept next to me and we kept one another warm.

"I have never been so cold," I observed to Tegid one day, as we stopped to chop holes in the ice of the river to water the animals.

"Save your breath," he told me bitterly. "The worst is yet to come."

Hoping to lighten his mood, I replied, "Then the worst will be wasted on me, brother. I am numb from head to heel—I will not feel the difference."

He shrugged and continued chopping. When we had made a large enough hole in the thick ice, I scooped the ice chips from the hole with my hand to clear it. The water made my hand feel warmer for an instant, and then my fingers grew numb again. We brought our horses to the hole and, while they drank, I asked, "How much farther, Tegid? How many more days on the trail before we reach the fortress?"

"I cannot say."

"You must have some idea."

He shook his head gravely. "I do not. I have never attempted the journey in the snow. Our pace has slowed from when we first began, and even then it was not quick. As our strength begins to fail in the high passes, we will move even more slowly."

"Perhaps it will clear soon," I observed. "If we had even a few good days, it would help."

He cocked an eye to the sky—dark, as it had been for days on end, the clouds thick and gray with shut-up snow. "No," he said, "I think that will not happen. Indeed, I am beginning to think that the Season of Snows will not end until Lord Nudd is defeated."

"Is that possible?" The notion of never-ending winter would have seemed ludicrous, if not for the evidence mounting around us with each passing day.

The bard's voice was solemn when he answered. "Great evil is loosed in Albion. Anything is possible."

Though I hated to admit it, I knew in my heart that he spoke the truth. Lord Nudd and his Demon Horde had seized Albion, and the hatred of Nudd's cold heart now inundated the land—howling in the cruel, cutting wind, and raging in the stinging ice and blinding snow.

"Have you told anyone this?"

Tegid busied himself with the horses but made no reply.

"You should tell the king, at least."

"Do you think he does not know this already?"

After watering the horses we moved on, but with heavier hearts for the bleak prospect ahead. Day followed day. The land became steeper, the trail narrower and harder to follow. Our pace slowed accordingly—though we rose earlier, we were forced to rest more often, so gained no benefit there. Still, all was not against us. For, as the hills became more rugged and rocky, the sparse brushwood of the empty upland hills gave way to forest. We were able to find as much firewood as we needed, and, for the first time since leaving ruined Sycharth, we were at least warm at night.

Also, the game which had fled the lowlands seemed to have taken refuge in the forests. We began to see signs of animals among the forest runs, and sometimes the gray flicker of a wolf loping silently through the trees. Prince Meldron formed a hunting party, which he led. At first, the hunters were luckless. But as the forest became more dense and the game more plentiful, the prince's efforts began meeting with some success. More and more often, we had the roast meat of wild pigs and deer to fill our stomachs.

One day, as we set about making camp, a small hunting party rode out in search of game. The hunters had not long left the camp when one of their number came riding back. "Hurry!" he cried. "We need six more warriors to follow me."

"What is it? What has happened?" inquired Tegid.

"We have found an aurochs," the hunter explained. "The prince has sent me to bring six more men to join the hunt."

"I will go," I offered, feeling a strange tingle of excitement as a long-forgotten memory awakened. An aurochs . . .

"Choose five to go with you," Tegid told the rider. "I will remain with the king."

He did not lack volunteers, and in a moment we were mounted and flying after our guide. We rode along a hunting run cut deep into the forest. Because of the trees, the snow had not drifted to much depth, so we were able to ride with good speed. In almost no time we joined the prince and his party: four companions—Simon and Paladyr among them—and three hounds.

"Here is where we raised the trail," Prince Meldron said, pointing to the snow with the butt of his spear.

I saw from the enormous tracks in the snow that a huge and heavy creature had wandered into the hunting run. And next to the first set of tracks was a second, slightly smaller set. Two animals. I looked in the direction indicated by the tracks, but the trail turned and the forest grew close, so I could not see far.

"The tracks are new," the prince observed. "The creatures can be but a little distance ahead of us. We will loose the dogs. Ready your spears." He turned his horse and shouted, "Release the dogs!"

Freed from the leash, the three hounds—all that were left of the king's hunting pack—raced after the quarry. We lashed our horses to follow. The cold wind bit our hands and faces as the horses' driving hooves kicked up a spray of snow. Along the trail we flew, spears level, slicing the chill air.

The narrow corridor of the hunting run turned, and we rounded the bend to see that it ended at an outcropping of stone a short way ahead. Tumbled slabs of moss-covered stone thrust up from the level ground, forming a toothy, jagged wall atop a small mound. And before this gray green mounded wall stood two aurochs, enormous beasts, an adult and a youngster—a cow and her calf, I guessed—by the look of them, exhausted.

The smaller animal was a young bull, huge and sleek and black, its enormous shoulder hump rising like a dark hill above the broad plain of its back. Its mother was even larger—a massive mountain of flesh and hide, hoof and horn. Separated from their herd, the beasts had grown weak with hunger and thirst. They had stumbled into the run and lacked the wit to realize the danger. These great creatures know few predators; lords of the forest, they are seldom challenged—even by the wolves which will only attack an old or enfeebled animal.

At first glimpse of the beasts, the dogs sounded. Their long, qua-vering cry pierced the air and echoed down the run. At the first shiv-ering note, the aurochs made to bolt, but saw that they were trapped by the close-grown pines and blackthorn thickets on either side. As the dogs raced swiftly toward them, the larger aurochs trotted forward and stopped stiff-legged to await its attackers. The young bull remained behind its mother, safe for the moment.

On Ynys Sci I had taken part in many hunts, but never hunted an aurochs. Indeed, I had never before seen one of these secretive beasts in the flesh. Seeing one now, even from a fair distance, I marveled at its size. Closer, it made our horses seem small, foolishly delicate crea-tures—more like deer than the mounts of warriors.

I thought the beast would charge us. But it remained steadfast, with stiffened legs and lowered head. The wide-sweeping horns, sharp as spearpoints and strong as iron, tilted toward us. One misstep and both horse and rider would be impaled; those gracefully curved weapons would rip the belly of a horse wide open, or pass like an arrow through the body of a man. One mistake and the unlucky hunter would not live to make another.

Heedless of the danger, the hunters raced ahead, raising the hunting cry, flying full-voiced down the run. Like keening eagles we swooped toward our prey. The aurochs stood like a massive black boulder in our path, waiting patiently. Not a muscle twitched, not a nostril quivered. Likely, the animal had never been attacked, and even now did not sense the peril hurtling down upon it.

Our horses sped closer. The dogs bayed, their necks stretched low and teeth bared. The first riders were almost within striking distance. Yet the cow did not move. Far better if the beast takes fright, turns tail, and flees—then it can easily be ridden down from behind. A quick spear-thrust behind the shoulder and into the heart, and the hunt is over. The kill is quick and clean.

But the aurochs did not easily surrender or retreat. The beast stood its ground, forcing its attackers to maneuver in close around it. At such close range the chances for a misstep multiply.

The hounds reached the cow first. Most creatures succumb to terror at the sound of a hound's hunting cry, and the sight of a pack closing for the kill sends most prey into a fatal panic. Not the aurochs. The bold black beast merely lowered its head still further, protecting its throat. The dogs circled, barking and snarling in a frenzy of rage and frustration, yet keeping well out of range of those long, lethal horns.

We halted a short distance away to assess the situation. "We will drive the animals apart," said the prince. "You four distract the cow." He pointed at Simon and three others. "The rest come with me. We will take the young bull first."

The small aurochs was welcome, to be sure, but the larger animal was the more desirable, for it would feed that many more. The prince thought that without its offspring to protect, the cow would be easier to kill. And at first the plan looked likely to succeed.

As it happened, the seven who were to take on the calf had the more difficult task. And as for driving the animals apart—they seemed to have taken root where they stood or been frozen to the spot, for neither so much as lifted a hoof. Nevertheless, Simon and his group went to work, whooping and shouting, dodging and feinting, in an effort at diverting the aurochs cow.

Meanwhile, the rest of the hunters joined Prince Meldron in forming a large circling ring, riding around and around the young bull, waiting for a chance to strike. One look at that vast, thick-muscled shoulder and that massive neck, and I knew that nothing save a direct, plunging thrust would kill it, and even then I doubted that a single spear could bring it down.

The young bull gazed placidly at us with calm black eyes, wagging its immense head from side to side. With each sweep, its horns described a killing arc which only a fool would ignore. And there were no fools among us this day.

But the prince and his men had hunted aurochs before. After circling the beast long enough to establish a predictable rhythm, the prince, who had been holding his spear aloft, lowered the spearpoint and, in the same motion, turned his horse, driving toward the aurochs, approaching it obliquely from the rear.

Those of us opposite the prince shouted at the animal. The spearhead flashed nearer its mark. The prince leaned forward to plunge the spear deep, the full weight of horse and rider behind the gleaming blade.

Just as the prince tensed to deliver the blow, however, the young bull turned, raising its head at the last moment. If I had not seen it, I would never have believed a creature that large could move so fast.

In a shattered instant, the great black head jerked and the wide-spreading horns struck the prince's horse just behind the left foreleg. With a quick, effortless toss of its head the horse was caught.

The same moment, swift and certain, the prince struck with his weapon, driving the spearhead deep into the shoulder. Thinking to turn the beast, I heaved my spear as hard as I could. My throw glanced harmlessly off the aurochs' hump and made no serious wound. But the aurochs spun toward me, thus freeing the prince. Meldron threw himself from his mount just as the screaming, flailing horse toppled backwards.

My action spared the prince a nasty wound, or worse. But now I had no weapon and the prince had no horse. I continued the circuit around the aurochs and called to Meldron. As I came upon him, I reached down a hand; he caught it and vaulted up behind me in the saddle.

Meanwhile, the dogs, seeing the beast's head rise, sprang to the attack. One of the hounds succeeded in getting close enough to sink its teeth into the soft skin of the aurochs' throat. The dog bit and held on. The aurochs lowered its huge jaw, catching the hound's head between its jaw and chest. Then it simply knelt and crushed the dog.

The two remaining dogs smelled the blood and rushed upon the aurochs. The young bull turned to meet the attack with a sweep of its horns and caught one of the hounds, piercing it through the neck and lifting it high. The hapless dog whined hideously and thrashed to free itself, but only succeeded in working the smooth horn deeper. The aurochs tossed its head to shake the dog loose.

The hunters saw their chance and took it. Three riders turned as one, and three spears sliced the air. Two spears found their mark in the aurochs' neck, and another bit deep into the swelling side between two huge ribs.

The last two riders drove in and two more spears penetrated the exposed neck; one of these severed an artery. Blood spewed in a sudden fountain and gushed from the great beast's mouth and nostrils, steaming in the cold air.

The aurochs fell to its knees in the snow, and one of the hunters rushed upon it. In an instant he threw himself from the saddle, plucked a spear from the fallen beast's side, and drove it in again, thrusting the spearhead into the base of the skull behind the horns. The young bull stiffened and then rolled onto its side, dead before its body stopped quivering.

We paused but a moment—just long enough to retrieve our spears, and for the prince to mount another's horse—then turned to join the assault of the larger aurochs. But the cow must have seen what happened to her calf, for the larger beast broke from the circling riders and hurtled toward us. None of us was in position to meet the charge, and we all scattered to get out of the way. This gave the wily creature a wide-open path of escape.

The cow ran to the rock mound behind us, and those of us closest gave chase. I was one of the nearer hunters, and Simon was another. Four of us flew after our retreating prey, and the prince began shouting orders to the others to take up positions on the near side of the mound to seal off the beast's escape. We would chase the aurochs around behind the mound and into the waiting spears of our fellow hunters.

I saw the enormous beast reach the curving slope of the mound and start around the base. As the aurochs turned, Simon, who was slightly ahead of me, saw his chance for a clean throw. I saw the spear streak to its mark, burying itself deep in the upper chest behind the foreleg, very near the heart.

Then the animal disappeared behind the rocks littering the slope of the mound. Simon and I, with two others close behind, pursued the animal around the far side of the mound. We could not have been more than fifty paces behind. Yet, when we came around the rocks, we could not see the aurochs.

Thinking it had climbed the mound, Simon urged his mount up the slope between the rocks. I reined in and wheeled my horse to scan the short distance between the mound and the thick-wooded ridge beyond. But the beast was nowhere to be seen.

"Where did it go?" yelled Simon, lashing his horse back down the slope. "Did anyone see it?"

"It must have run ahead of us," said one of the other hunters. From the odd expression on his face, I could see that was not what he thought at all. Then again, where else could such a large creature go?

We each gazed this way and that for a moment but caught no sign of the huge animal—no hoofprints, no trail of blood in the snow. Simon turned his horse and lashed it to speed. We three followed and proceeded the rest of the way around the mound to meet the prince and the others waiting on the other side.

They had not seen the aurochs, either.

"It must have escaped into the forest," observed Paladyr.

"Then it cannot have gone far," Simon told the prince. "I had a clean throw. I know I wounded it."

"Aye," agreed one who had ridden with us. "I saw it. A clean throw into the shoulder."

Some of the hunters urged giving chase and prepared to do so right away. But the prince cast an eye to the darkening sky and said, "No, it is growing late. A wounded aurochs is too dangerous, and we could not hope to attack it in the forest. We will have enough to do, getting the calf back to camp before dark."

The hunters did not enjoy letting their prey escape but could not gainsay the prince. So we returned to where the man whose horse the prince had taken was already hard at work. The wounded dog had been lifted from the horn that impaled it, and the poor hound's agony ended swiftly and mercifully. The same had been done for the prince's horse.

At our approach, the hunter took his knife and slit the aurochs' throat, to let the meat bleed. He caught some of the blood in a small wooden cup, and the cup was passed from one hunter to the next. I tasted the thick, hot, salty blood, and gave the cup quickly to the next hand.

This ritual observed, the hunters, with a wild whoop of jubilation, fell upon the aurochs with their knives. One began opening the belly to gut the carcass. Another made an incision around the neck, while two more made similar cuts around the lower legs so that the fine black Sollen-thick hide could be stripped from the body in one piece.

Two other hunters hastened to the nearby forest to cut birch poles on which to drag the quartered carcass back to camp. They worked deftly and efficiently, each hand busy. I remarked at the speed with which the men set about their tasks. The prince nodded. "They have good reason," he said meaningfully.

"Darkness?" I wondered, for the sky was now the color of iron and the light was failing fast.

"Wolves."

I looked at the spilled blood, crimson upon the snow. The scent was even now spreading on the wind and soon—if not already— every wolf within reach of the gusting wind would be hastening to the place of slaughter.

"I have lost one horse today; I would rather not lose another to wolves," remarked Meldron. He turned to me. "You saved me from injury or worse. I will not forget you. When we come to Findargad you will have your reward."

"A portion of that haunch would be reward enough," I answered, watching the dog greedily gulping down a bit of liver while the hunters set about cutting up the carcass.

"Well said!" Prince Meldron laughed, slapping me on the back. "Tonight you will receive the hero's portion from my hand."

The flesh-side of the hide was scrubbed with snow and the skin rolled up, bound, and placed on the back of a horse. The carcass was cut into four pieces and the quarters washed with snow to remove as much blood as possible. Then each quarter was lashed to birch poles and the poles tied to ropes and hauled away behind the horses.

When we turned our horses toward camp, all that remained of our exploit was a mound of offal amidst a faded red patch in the well-trampled snow. Ordinarily, the two dead dogs and the prince's horse would have been removed from the hunting run, but these were left where they lay. "For the wolves," the hunter who rode beside me explained. "Perhaps they will content themselves with that."

The way back to the camp proved much longer than I remembered. It was fully dark by the time we reached the river, and we crossed the last expanse of snow guided by the fireglow from the numerous campfires. Word of our success went before us, and within moments of our arrival, throngs of people gathered to view the kill—and to claim a portion of the meat.

Speaking solely through Tegid, the king gave instructions for the meat to be divided equally among the various family clans. And though it was a massive amount of meat, it disappeared at once. True to his word, Prince Meldron rewarded me with the hero's portion, though it meant that he himself received less than anyone else. I would have shared it with him gladly, but to do so would have shamed him.

The meat had scarcely been shared out among the clans when the ghostly howl of wolves came snaking down the wind. Twrch, who had been prancing playfully around the fire, scuttled back to sit between my feet. Frightened by the strange sound, the pup peered warily from side to side and shivered nervously. I had on several occasions heard the cry of wolves, but it had always seemed mournful to me, rather than fearful—a sound full of longing and lament, a sad, lonely sound. I said as much to Tegid.

"That is because you have never been chased by wolves," Tegid replied when I offered my observation. We were sitting before the fire, watching the meat roast on spits of forked alder. "They are only gathering. Wait until they catch scent of the trail and raise the hunting cry, and tell me then if you think it a lonely sound."

"Will they come here?"

Tegid pinched a bit of meat, tasted it, and turned the spit. "Yes."

"Soon?"

"When they have finished with the horse you left them."

"Is there anything to be done?"

"Move the horses nearer to the fires, and keep your spear close to hand."

As if in fulfillment of Tegid's words, there came a long, feral, full-blooded howl. It made my skin prick up in gooseflesh and raised the hackles on Twrch's back. I knew at once that no one would sleep this night.

29

NIGHTKILL

King Meldryn appeared from out of the gloom and approached the fire; he had been walking alone through the many camps of his people. He stood a little apart and gestured for Tegid to join him, and they conferred for a moment. I did not hear what passed between them; but I watched the king. This journey was clearly changing him.

The man I saw before me was not the man I had seen in Sycharth. Meldryn appeared drawn, haggard, and drained. He was tired, yes; we were all tired. But it was more than fatigue. It was as if the journey itself, or the bitter Sollen wind, was bleeding him of his spirit and strength. His eyes no longer held their spark; he no longer held his head erect, nor his shoulders square. The Great King Meldryn was like a mighty tower beginning to crumble inward upon itself, and it was a distressing thing to see.

When they had finished their talk, Tegid returned. I rose to offer the king my place at the fire, but Meldryn motioned me to remain seated. He walked away once more, continuing his restless circuit of the camps.

So far as I knew, Meldryn Mawr had not uttered a word to anyone save Tegid since turning his back on Sycharth. All that he wished known, he told his bard. Tegid then acted or instructed others in the king's command.

"Why does the king not speak?" I asked, handing a spit of roasted meat to Tegid.

"He has taken a *geas* upon himself," he explained simply. "The voices of his dead kinsmen are silent. Therefore will the king remain silent until he either joins them or until the voices of the people are heard in Sycharth once more."

I remembered Meldryn Mawr saying as much the night we left Sycharth, though I had not realized he meant it literally. "The king speaks to you," I pointed out.

"Kingship comes to the lord through the Chief Bard, who holds the power to grant or withhold sovereignty. It is the bard alone who approaches the king without bending the knee. Therefore may Meldryn speak to his bard without violating the geas."

I had heard of these strange taboos. But I had never seen one in action, and I wanted to know more. "I do not understand," I said, stripping meat from the alder spit and sucking the hot and savory juices. I pulled off a strip of meat and gave it to Twrch—still huddled between my feet, though the cries of the wolves had ceased for the time being. "You make it sound as if the bard is greater than the king."

Tegid lifted some meat to his mouth and chewed thoughtfully. Finally, he swallowed and said, "It is not a question of who is greater. The bard is the voice of all the people—the living, the dead, and those yet to be. It is through the bard that the king receives wisdom; and through the bard the king's judgments are dispensed. The king's word is law to his people, who must submit to him, but the king must also submit to a higher authority—that of the sovereignty itself. It is the bard's duty to hold the law of kingship for the people, lest the king become haughty and forget his place."

"So talking to a bard is not like talking to an ordinary clansman," I said. "It is more like talking to yourself—is that what you mean?"

Tegid smiled, and it was good to see him smile. "The things you say, brother."

"Well, is it?"

"For a king, talking to his bard is like talking to the source of his kingship. It is like taking counsel from his soul and from the soul of his people. The bond between a king and his bard is not like any other."

"I see," I said casually. "Well, if I were king, I would want a bard just like you, Tegid."

I meant it as a compliment, but Tegid lowered the meat from his mouth and stared at me.

"What have I said now?"

He did not reply, but his gaze took on a disturbing aspect—as if he were seeing through me, or seeing me differently somehow. His scrutiny made me uncomfortable. "Listen, Tegid, I meant nothing. If I have spoken amiss, forgive me."

"You may have cause to regret those words," he replied slowly.

"I am sorry," I told him. "I tell you I meant nothing by them."

Tegid relaxed and began eating again. I was itching to know what I had said to upset him, but I did not like to probe the wound again so soon. We finished our meal in a somewhat strained silence, and I reflected on another lord who had gone down into death without a sound: the aurochs we had killed that day. Even as its life spilled out upon the snow, the young bull did not bellow or cry out. The beast went silent to its death. Now its flesh nourished us and kept us alive.

This meditation brought to mind the other aurochs—the one that had disappeared, almost before our eyes. Where had it gone?

I wondered about this as I gnawed at the last of the meat. And the more I thought about it, the more certain I became that I knew where it had gone. This conviction induced a queer feeling in the pit of my stomach, and a tremor of excitement like that which I had experienced at the first mention of the aurochs. I told myself that it was preposterous, that I could not know, that there had to be another explanation.

Still the odd feeling and the bewildering certainty persisted. I heard a voice—my own voice, maybe, but coming from a faraway place—as if whispering down a distant corridor, saying, *It is true, Lewis. You know it is true. You know where the aurochs has gone. Say it! Speak the words!*

I pushed the uncomfortable thought aside and lay down upon my calfskin before the fire. Tegid had strewn armfuls of pine needles over the snow for us to sleep on. I stretched out before the fire with my cloak over me. Taking Tegid's advice, I had my spear ready to hand and my sword was at my side. Twrch curled beside me, his nose resting on my arm. It was a chilly bed, but more or less dry.

I closed my eyes, but sleep remained far off. I knew I would find no rest until I admitted to myself that what I had imagined might actually be true.

But how to acknowledge such a thing? It was ridiculous. Absurd. And yet . . . what if? I rolled over and pulled my cloak more tightly around me.

Say it!

I sat upright, throwing my cloak aside. The mound, the spear—Simon's spear, in fact—and the wounded aurochs itself . . . It all made sense, and none of it made sense. Yet, what if? What if?

Stumbling to my feet, I left the campfire, snatching up my cloak as I strode away. Tegid called after me, but I did not answer him. Instead I walked out along the perimeter of the camp, my head throbbing with the question: How could this be? The thing I was thinking was impossible. How could it be?

As I stumped along, another voice assailed me: *A breach has opened between the worlds, and anything may stumble through.*

I stopped in my tracks and admitted what I suspected: the wounded aurochs, in its terror and pain, had stumbled through an open portal into the other world—the world I had left behind and all but forgotten.

But how could this be? How could the aurochs we had chased that day be the same one that had brought Simon and me to the Otherworld in the first place? How could the spear I had held in my hands at Farmer Grant's breakfast table be the very same spear Simon had thrown?

I did not know. But I was certain of one thing: I loathed being reminded that—no matter how I tried to forget, no matter how I pretended otherwise—I was a stranger here, an interloper, a trespasser. When all was said and done, I did not belong in the Otherworld. And, as much as I might want to—and I desperately wanted to—I could not stay. The thought filled me with despair. For I could no longer conceive of any other life than the one I had come to know. *The day I return to my own world*, I told myself, *will be the day I die.*

When I grew cold, I turned my footsteps back to the campfire. Tegid was waiting for me. He fed more wood into the fire as I wrapped myself in my cloak and sat down. "Meldryn Mawr is a very great king, very wealthy," he said abruptly.

"That is true," I replied. I did not know this for a fact, but I believed it to be so, for I had seen much evidence of his wealth.

"Have you ever seen his treasury?" the bard asked.

"No," I answered.

"He does not keep one."

"No? Why not?"

"It would be an offense against sovereignty," Tegid told me flatly, and at last I understood that we had returned to our previous conversation regarding the nature of kingship.

"But he does amass wealth," I said, feeling some pressure to defend

NIGHTKILL

my assumption, though I had no idea why. "There *is* gold and silver; there are jewels and such. I have seen them."

"The wealth exists for the king," Tegid intoned. "And the king exists for the people. A king uses his wealth for the good of all, to the increase of his clan. He looks only to the welfare of the clan, never to his own."

"The people take care of the king," I mused, "and the king takes care of them." It seemed a tidy arrangement. What could be better?

"Do not dismiss it lightly," Tegid warned, breaking a twig between his hands and throwing it into the fire. "The king does not belong to himself. His life is the life of the tribe. A true king lives out of himself, owning no life but that which he gives to his people."

I considered this for a moment. "And Meldryn Mawr is a true king." Indeed, I had never doubted it.

"Yes." Tegid's affirmation was solid and assured. "He is that."

I had no idea why Tegid felt it necessary to make this point to me. And he dropped the subject as brusquely as he had begun. We turned to our sleep then, but not for long. It seemed I had only closed my eyes when the howling began.

I was awake and on my feet, spear in hand, before I knew what had awakened me. I glanced around quickly. Tegid sat nodding before the fire. He raised his head. "They have finished with the horse," he said. "And their scouts have been watching us. Now they have returned to tell what they have seen."

Wolves are canny creatures, quick-witted and aggressive. The cries resounding through the forest around us were of a most unsettling kind—not at all like those we had heard earlier. These howls were sharp-edged and keen, cutting the cold night air like knives.

"In the mountains," Tegid said, "the wolves grow larger."

"Why have we not heard them before tonight?"

"They have been following us for several days, waiting for this time."

333

"Will they attack?"

"This is a hard Sollen. It is cold, game grows scarce, and they are hungry. When their hunger overcomes their fear, they will attack."

The howling increased, growing louder as more wolf-voices joined the weird nightsong. Rapacious, insatiable, savage, and feral—it was a sound to terrify, to unnerve, to paralyze. I felt the sound in my bowels and fought the urge to flee.

King Meldryn, a spear in his hand, hastened toward us. Tegid rose and went to him; they talked together and then Tegid turned to me. "Go with the king," he said. "Whatever happens, stay at his right hand."

The king strode to the fire, stooped, and withdrew a burning branch. He offered me the firebrand and took another for himself. We then hurried away to the horses. The king had ordered the horses to be picketed at the edge of our camp in small groups of eight or ten, between the forest and the river; the line stretched from one end of the camp to the other. We positioned ourselves at the head of the first picket. Other warriors quickly joined us, each a few paces from the next, and soon I could look along a line of shimmering torches stretching the length of the camp.

Brushwood had been hastily gathered and heaped at intervals along the rank. As the cries of the wolves drew closer, the brushwood was put to the flame. We waited, gripping our weapons, the forest echoing with the wild wails. This continued for a time and then ceased abruptly. In the sudden silence, the hiss of the torches sounded loud in my ears.

I strained into the darkness. Cold, moonless, black as pitch—the night clung close around us, and I could see little beyond the limited circle of the torch in my hand. The wolves would see us long before we saw them. I heard a rustle in the distance behind me, spun to meet the sound with my spear, and saw Prince Meldron and the king's champion, Paladyr, running toward us. Both held spears and torches and ran through the snow with some urgency.

They proceeded directly to the king. "Father and Lord," said the prince, "allow me to take my warriors to meet the wolves. We could keep them from the camp—they would never reach the horses."

The king listened to his son, watching him in the fluttering torch-light, but made no reply. The prince glanced at Paladyr, drew a deep breath, and pressed on. "Father, a single line makes no sense—it is certain to break. And what will happen when the torches fail? We cannot keep the fires going all night. As soon as the fires begin to fail, the wolves will attack."

The king did not answer. "Did you hear me, Father?" demanded Meldron, his voice rising. "Grant me leave to ride the wolves down. It is our best protection!"

As I stood looking on, Prince Meldron appealed to me. "You will ride with me," he ordered. To the king he added, "But, Father, we must ride now, while we still may." As I had not moved, he turned again to me. "Well?"

"I am honored to be included among your warriors," I answered. "But my place is with the king."

"I have command of my father's warriors," he said angrily. "I say you will ride with me."

"I must beg your pardon, Prince Meldron. Tegid has commanded me to abide with the king."

"And I am commanding you to ride with me!" the prince shouted. "I lead the war band, not Tegid." He railed at me with supreme self-assurance. Paladyr, grim and imposing beside him, did not appear so certain, however. He nervously jabbed the snow with the butt of his spear.

"Again I must beg your pardon, lord," I replied. "I have pledged myself to serve the bard, and Tegid has commanded me to remain with the king."

"Tegid!" the prince cried in frustration. "Tegid is not in authority over me! His is not the place to command! You will do as I bid!" He

335

made to step toward me, but the king held out the shaft of his spear and halted his son.

Perhaps Tegid heard his name uttered, for we heard a shout and turned to see him hastening toward us. "What is wrong here?" he asked.

"You!" the prince snarled. "I command the war band, not you. It is foolish to stand here waiting for the wolves to attack us. I say we must ride to meet them and drive them away."

"The king has commanded otherwise," Tegid replied softly.

"Father!" Meldron spat. "Tell this insolent dog of a bard that I command the warriors!"

Tegid stepped close to the king, and Meldryn Mawr whispered something in the bard's ear. Tegid then turned to the prince. "The king has heard you," he told the prince coolly. "He wishes to remind you that he holds authority over all that passes in his realm. He bids you return to your place and defend the people as you have been ordered."

Prince Meldron stood glaring for a moment, and then, with a snarl of impotent rage, threw his torch into the snow. The firebrand sizzled and sputtered out, whereupon the prince spun on his heel and hurried away.

Paladyr looked first to the king—who watched him without expression—and then glanced at the prince's retreating back. He stood for a moment undecided. Then the champion turned and hastened after the prince.

"So be it," Tegid murmured. "Paladyr has chosen."

I did not fully understand the implications of the event I had witnessed. Nor did I have time to dwell on it further, for someone down the line sounded a warning cry. I looked in the direction of the shout and saw a ghostly flickering among the trees.

I turned my gaze to the forest before us, and at first could discern nothing in the darkness. Even as I watched, however, I caught the faint glint of a golden eye like a spark darting through the trees, and I heard the whisper of swift, almost silent feet.

I did not see the wolf until it was almost on top of me, and it was much larger than I expected. I had imagined a creature the size of one of our hounds, which were far from small. Tegid had warned me that the wolves were big, but this animal seemed nearer in size to one of our ponies!

Long-legged, lean, gray, and swift as smoke on the wind, the wolf came. A more fearsome sight would be hard to describe: narrow eyes like glowing coals burning in his head; long, gaunt snout above slavering jaws filled with jagged white teeth; a bristling coat, dark-striped across the high shoulders and spiked with fury. In all, it appeared an apparition conceived to inspire horror and panic in its prey.

Certainly, I felt the terror of its appearance and quailed within myself as it bounded nearer. I saw the cruel teeth, the burning yellow eyes, the long bones beneath the stiff-bristled fur. I tightened my grip on the spear, couching the ash shaft between my ribs and arm. Less than a dozen paces separated it from me.

If the beast had attacked, I do not know that I could have stood against it. But just as the ghastly thing cleared the last tree with a rush, it turned aside. Given the length of the animal's ground-eating stride, the wolf might have leaped clear over me and into the midst of the horses. Instead, it ran snarling and growling along the king's torch line.

In no time at all, this first animal was joined by no fewer than six others—including one huge black brute that was their lord. I glanced away to the forest for just a moment, and when I turned back there were ten more. An instant later, there were no fewer than twenty. They raced back and forth along the torch line, snarling, snapping their jaws furiously.

The tumult was unnerving, and rightly so. This fierce display was meant to send us into a rout of terror and confusion. Once we broke ranks, the wolves would charge through us and drag us down from behind. That is their way. Wolves lack nothing in courage, but they will not fight if they can more easily gain the advantage through stealth or bluff.

When we held our ground, the beasts howled in black fury. Now and again, one of the wolves would dodge toward the line, teeth flashing; the men would shout, thrust their spears, and the wolf would break off its attack and scramble out of range of the spears once more.

"They are testing our resolve," Tegid observed. "If we show them no weakness, they may leave us."

Judging from the ferocity of the wolves' determination, I thought this unduly optimistic. The harsh cold had made them hungry and bold. Also, they had seen the horses—and the horses had seen the wolves! The frightened animals whinnied and neighed, tossing their heads hysterically, eyes white with terror.

Still, the wolves did not attack. They did not like the torches, and they did not like the gleaming spears in our hands. They could howl and rage, but they could not get at the horses as long as the line remained unbroken.

The king's simple plan had worked. We had only to remain steadfast in our places and the wolves would not attack. Despite their dismaying size, the wolves were neither hungry nor bold enough to risk the fire and weapons in our hands. Harrowing though it was to stand before them, we were safe.

Indeed, I saw that the wolves were quickly tiring; the frenzy of their assault rapidly exhausted them. Soon they were no longer so fleet of foot nor so loud in their challenge. The dodging feints came less frequently. Their tongues hung out and their gaunt sides heaved.

Presently, the black wolflord stopped in his tracks, stood panting for a moment, then turned and loped back into the forest. He was conceding the victory to us. We were safe. No one had been hurt, and we had not lost a single horse. We had won. The wolves were with-drawing.

I was about to say as much to the king. I turned my head and drew breath to speak; Meldryn Mawr was smiling. But before I could even utter a word, I heard a loud battle whoop. The smile disappeared from the king's face as he glanced beyond me down the torch line. I spun toward the sound and saw—far down the ranks where Prince Meldron and his warriors stood, I saw someone dashing after the retreating wolves. He was waving a torch and calling for others to fol-low him.

It was the prince. The defensive line broke as the prince and the warriors of his Wolf Pack gave chase to the wolves of the forest. "They are mad!" cried Tegid. "They will get us all killed!"

The bard made to halt them. "Stay!" he shouted. "Hold the line!"

If they heard him, they paid no heed. The prince and his men were too intent upon catching the wolves. Someone threw a spear, and I saw one of the last wolves struck in the hindquarters. The animal yelped in pain and fell. Whining, the wounded beast began dragging his hindquarters in an effort to dislodge the spear.

The man ran to the wolf. A long knife flashed, and a moment later the wolf lay dead in the snow. The warrior—it was Simon—retrieved his spear and raised a cry of triumph. He turned and lofted his spear, urging others to follow. Inspired by this feat, more warriors broke ranks and hastened after the wolves.

The warriors disappeared into the forest. Their torches flickered through the trees; their shouts and the howls of the wolves rang in the darkness. And then, so suddenly it could not be anticipated, the wolves appeared once more.

Whether they had been hiding nearby or had turned to the attack after drawing the men away, I cannot say. However it was, the wolves simply appeared and without the slightest hesitation streaked through the gaping hole in the rank where Prince Meldron and his men had been standing only moments before.

In the space of two heartbeats all became chaos and confusion: men running, horses rearing, spears flashing, and torches being flung this way and that. The shouts of men and the screams of the horses drowned out all else.

"What are we to do?" I cried, turning to Tegid for an answer.

"Stand firm!" he replied, as he began running down the line to recall the men. "Stay with the king!" he called back to me.

We stood our ground, and the wolves did not attempt to attack us. They centered their attack on our weakest place and ignored the rest of the line. Tegid flew to the place, but before he could close the hole in the ranks, some of the horses broke free of the picket and bolted. Men leaped for the trailing bridle ropes, and threw themselves into the horses' path, trying to turn them back. But to no avail.

The horses, terrified of the wolves, the noise, and the fire, could not be turned. They fled into the forest. The wolves seized the opportunity and gave chase, and as suddenly as it had begun, it was over. The wolves were gone, and a good many horses with them.

We stood waiting for some time, listening to the cries of the wolves and the screams of the horses as they crashed blindly through the forest undergrowth; but the wolves did not return. The sounds of the chase receded, becoming fainter as the pursuit hastened away from us. And then we heard nothing.

When it became clear that the attack was ended, the king threw down his torch and began walking down the line to the place where the prince and his warriors had abandoned their posts. I hesitated for a moment, and then followed. Tegid had told me to stay with the king, after all. Together we hurried to the place of attack.

From the amount of blood I saw splattered in the snow, I was prepared for the worst. Five men had been wounded—savaged and mauled by the wolves, but not killed. Four horses were down, and two of these were dead, their throats ripped; eight more had fled into the forest. The wolves would run them until they dropped. We would not see them again.

The king surveyed the damage without expression. Tegid hastened to meet us. "We have lost twelve horses," he reported. Even as he spoke, the two wounded horses were relieved of their misery; a quick spearthrust behind the ear and they ceased their thrashing.

When Prince Meldron and his warriors returned, the five wounded warriors were having their wounds washed with snow and bound with strips of cloth by some of the women. The prince glanced quickly at the wounded men and strode to where we were standing.

"We have driven them off," he declared proudly, wiping sweat from his brow. His warriors came to stand behind him. In the fluttering torchlight the fog from their breath shimmered like silver as it hung above their heads. "They will trouble us no more!" The prince was expansive in his judgment. "We have put fear in their craven hearts."

"How many did you kill?" asked Tegid sharply. I heard the anger in his voice, cold and quick.

Those gathered close behind the prince heard it, too, and murmured ominously. Meldron smiled and held up his hand to them, however. "Siawn killed one, as you well know," he replied amiably.

"Yes," replied Tegid. "And how many more? How many more wolves did you kill?"

"None," the prince said, his tone going flat. "We killed no others. Neither did we suffer defeat."

"No defeat?" snapped Tegid. "Twelve horses lost and five men wounded—you deem that a victory?"

The prince looked to his father, who stood glaring at his son. "But we drove them away," Meldron insisted. "They will not dare attack us again."

"They have already done so! The moment you broke ranks they doubled back and attacked the place where you should have been."

"No one was killed. We have shown them we will fight." He raised his spear, and the warriors muttered agreement.

"You have shown them, Prince Meldron, that it is well worth coming back: twelve horses, and only one of theirs killed. They will not even notice the loss," Tegid said, his voice thick with fury. "I can assure you they will return. They will harry us from this night forth until we reach Findargad, for you have shown them most wonderfully that the gain is great and the risk is light. They are already laughing at the ease with which they have outsmarted us. The wolves *will* return, Prince Meldron. Stake your life on it."

The prince glowered at Tegid, his eyes narrowed to hate-filled slits. "You have no authority over me," Meldron growled. "You are nothing to me."

"I am the bard of the people," Tegid said. "You have defied the king's command. Owing to your disobedience, five men are wounded and we have lost twelve horses."

Meldron returned a haughty stare. "I have not heard the king say that he is angry. If my father is displeased, let him tell me so himself."

The prince looked to his father. King Meldryn glared at his son but did not open his mouth to speak. "You see?" the prince sneered. "It is as I thought. The king is well satisfied. Go your way, Tegid Tathal, and do not trouble me with trifles. If not for me, we would still be fighting the wolves. I have driven them away. You will thank me yet."

Tegid's face was livid in the torchglare. "Thanks to you, O Headstrong Prince, we will fight the wolves again. Thanks to you, twelve who might have ridden must walk in the snow. Thanks to you, five whose bodies were whole must now endure suffering, and perhaps death."

I thought Prince Meldron would burst. His neck swelled and his eyes narrowed still further. "No one speaks to me like this," he hissed. "I am a prince, and the leader of men. If you value your life, say no more."

"And I am the bard of the people," Tegid replied, once more reminding the prince of his authority. "I will speak as I deem best. No man—prince or king, least of all—makes bold to stop my tongue. You would do well to remember this."

The prince fairly writhed with rage and frustration. He appealed silently to his father, turning angry, imploring eyes upon him. But the king merely stared back in stone-cold silence. The prince, humiliated by his father's lack of support, turned abruptly and stomped away. Those men who deemed themselves the prince's own followed him. And Paladyr, the king's champion, was among them.

30

THE BATTLE
OF DUN NA PORTH

Tegid spoke the cruel truth when he said that we had not seen the last of the wolves. Emboldened by their victory, they followed us—slipping silently through the snow-laden forest by day and skulking just outside the firelight by night. They did not attack us as they had that first night. But neither did they abandon the trail.

"They have eaten well," Tegid said. "They are content for now, but we must remain wary." He pointed to the sharp peaks rising steeply before us, and close. "Soon we will leave the forest behind. When they see that we are making for the high trails, they will strike again."

"But they will not follow us into the mountains," I said optimistically. It did not seem likely that wolves would pursue us once we left the cover of the trees.

"Would you care to make a wager?" the bard inquired slyly. He grew suddenly grave. "I am not lying when I say I have never known wolves like this."

"This determined?"

"This cunning."

I knew what he meant. In the days since the attack, I had felt the eyes of unseen watchers upon us. Time and again, I found myself looking back over my shoulder, or darting a glance to this side or that as we traversed the forest trail. Only occasionally did I see the gliding, ghostly shape of a wolf flickering in the deep-shadowed dimness.

For safety's sake we kept close to the river. And, though the waterway narrowed as the path grew steeper, the high rock bank offered some protection and the swift-moving water did not freeze. At night we banked the fires high and warriors maintained vigil from dusk until dawn. I took my turn at watch on those endless nights: huddled in my cloak, stamping my feet to keep warm, slapping myself to stay awake and alert, peering into the void of darkness for the phantom glint of a feral eye, and then shuffling back to camp and collapsing into a dull, exhausted sleep until the sun rose once more.

Not that we ever saw the sun. So cloud-wrapped and snow-bound had the world become that we lived in a world bereft of light and warmth. It was as if Sollen now ruled in Albion and had banished the other seasons to eternal exile. Each dark day that I awakened, I heard again Tegid's words, *The Season of Snows will not end until Lord Nudd is defeated.*

The trail narrowed to little more than a rock-strewn path. The forest grew gradually more sparse, the trees smaller, stunted and deformed by the constantly battering wind, and the distance between them greater, as if in their misery they shunned one another. The ice-hard sky drew nearer as we climbed toward it. Torn shreds of cloud and tattered squalls of snow obscured the uncertain path ahead. And, when we looked behind, it was into a snow-hazed bleakness of white, relieved by gray slabs of rock and boulders the size of houses. We climbed above the tree line, slowly nearing the mountain pass leading into the rock-bound heart of Cethness.

Each day the way grew steeper; each day the wind blew ever colder; each day the snow flew ever faster. Each day we traveled less far than the day before. And each night my shins and ankles ached from the upward strain of the trail, my face and hands burned from the wind blast, and it took longer to massage warmth back into stiff, half-frozen limbs.

We brought as much firewood from the forest as we could carry; the horses were laden with it. But the nights were bitterly cold up among the bare peaks where the wind wails and moans without surcease, and we burned great quantities of precious fuel each night in a futile effort to keep warm.

If I had thought leaving the forest meant leaving behind the wolves, I was sharply disappointed. The second night above the tree line, as we set about making camp, we heard them once more—high up in the rocks around us, raising their eerie howls. The next day we could see them on the trail behind us. They no longer troubled to conceal themselves. All the same, the wolves did not attack. Neither did they abandon the pursuit, although they were careful to keep their distance.

I began to think that they would not attack again. Why should they? All they had to do was simply wait until, one by one, we began falling by the way. They would take the stragglers, kill and devour any who lagged behind, slaughter those too cold and too weak to go on. So that this would not happen, the king commanded the warriors to walk last in order to aid anyone falling too far behind, as well as to prevent the wolves from drawing too close.

We struggled through the snow, higher and higher, climbing steadily into the fierce, frigid air. Cold, hunger, and exhaustion united against us. Despite the king's precautions, people began to fall away. We found the stiff, gray, frozen bodies each morning as we broke camp. Sometimes we would see someone laboring on the trail ahead; they would suddenly fall, never to rise again. Or sometimes they would simply sink into the snow at the side of the trail and no one would see them again. The bodies we saw, we buried under mounds of rocks beside the trail. Those we did not find were left for the wolves.

We lost fifty before reaching the pass called the Gap of Rhon, a narrow slash between two mountains where the trail clings precariously to the sheer mountainside far above the crashing white-water cataract of a river known as Afon Abwy. The swollen river thrashed its way to the mountain glens, sending up a fine white mist which coated the rocks and froze on them. The whole gorge was encased in ice.

On the day we came through the Gap of Rhon, we lost five to the yawning gorge. The wind gusted and the hapless climbers lost their footing on the ice and were swept to their deaths upon the rocks of the Afon Abwy. I saw this happen but once, and it is a sight I hope never to see again: the broken body falling, raglike, striking the sides of the gorge, tumbling, spinning, glancing off the ice-covered rocks, disappearing into the mists and churning water.

I saw it only once. Yet each time it happened, I heard the short, splintered cries pierce the thin air. The mountains echoed with the scream long after the victim had died. There was nothing to be done. We moved on.

The mountain trail was treachery itself. Sheer, slim, dangerous, twisting unexpectedly. Ice-choked and snow-filled, torturous, winding through the naked peaks with the guile of a serpent. Now we were passing under massive slabs of stone; now clinging to a sheer face of smooth rock; laboring step-by-step up an endless incline one moment, speeding headlong down a precipitous decline the next.

Our sole consolation lay in the fact that if the journey was difficult for us—and it was agony—it was no less harsh for our pursuers. Each day we could see them: sometimes far, far behind us; sometimes near enough to hit with a well-aimed stone. Behind their black leader, they paced our every movement, never tiring, never abandoning their relentless pursuit.

I grew used to seeing them, and I no longer feared them as before.

347

But even as I grew inured to their predatory presence, Tegid became more and more wary and fearful. Time and again, Tegid would suddenly halt in the trail and spin around quickly, as if trying to catch sight of something elusive and unseen.

"What are you doing?" I asked him, when he had done this several times without explanation. I also scanned the trail below us and the ragged line of travelers on it.

Eyes narrowed and shielded from the snow with his cupped hands, he replied, "There is something back there."

"Wolves—as you well know," I replied. "Or had you forgotten?"

He gave his head a sharp jerk. "Not wolves. Something else."

"What else?"

He did not answer but kept his eyes trained on the trail for a time. Then he turned around and began walking once more. I fell into step behind him, but now I, too, felt an uncanny sensation of deepening dread. I told myself that with a determined wolf pack dogging our every step I need look no further for the source of my foreboding— it was as close as the nearest wolf. I told Tegid as much, but the bard was not so easily persuaded. He still scanned the trail at intervals, and I looked too; but we did not see anything except the flickering shapes of the wolves.

Our food supply came to its end. Firewood dwindled dangerously. It became a matter of speculation which would kill us first: starvation, the freezing cold, or wolves. For three days we staggered, weary and half-frozen, before hunger drove us to kill and eat the first of the horses. We stripped the still-warm flesh from the bones and ate it raw. The hides we scraped and gave to cover the children. Little Twrch greedily gobbled unlikely scraps of offal; I saved a bone for him to gnaw later and assigned him to the care of the young girl who, with her mother, rode my horse. The woman had lost her husband to the treachery of a mountain precipice, and in her grief was grateful for some small diversion for her child. Twrch could not have had a better keeper and companion.

Always the king led the way, walking; he would not ride. Sometimes he walked with Tegid, but more often he traveled alone. Each casualty cut him like a knife; he bore the pain of each loss as his own. Yet he could not sacrifice the living for the dead. So he led on, striding stiffly, leaning into the slope, shoulders bowed, as if bearing on his own broad back the weight of suffering his decision to flee into the mountains to Findargad had brought about. As to that decision, King Meldryn remained resolute, despite the grumbling against him. And there was no lack of that. We might have exhausted our meal grain, but we possessed the bread of dissent in perpetual supply. When the last of the grain went, people reached for those ready loaves.

Loudest in reproach was Prince Meldron. He, who should have been foremost in support, filled himself and those around him with complaint and quarrel. I know I got a bellyful of his snide mockery. "Whither now, Great King?" he would call out, whenever he stopped for a moment's rest on the trail. "Speak, Great King! Tell us again why we must hie to Findargad." His taunts were cowardly; Meldron knew his father would make no reply. His geas kept him under vow: the king would not speak—even to defend himself against the unjust charges of his son.

Though it shames me to admit it, much as I trusted the king, I, too, began to doubt the wisdom of his decision. Were there no graves in Sycharth? It is not easy to keep the flame of hope burning in the cold, empty heart of Sollen. The Season of Snows is not the time to make bright plans for the future. One slow foot in front of the other—that was all the future I knew. Just one more step, and then one more . . . I cared about nothing else.

On the day we finally came in sight of Findargad—an immense, many-towered fortress, a magnificent stony crown on an enormous

STEPHEN R. LAWHEAD

granite head lifted high on the shoulders of Cethness—we also caught sight of our true pursuers at last. I say that it was day, but the sky was dark as dusk and the snow swirled around our frozen faces. I saw Tegid stop abruptly and whirl round, as if to catch a thief creeping behind him. I had seen him do this countless times. But this time, I saw his mouth writhe and his dark eyes widen in alarm.

I hurried to his side. "What is it, brother?"

He did not answer but slowly raised the oaken staff in his hand and pointed behind us on the trail. I turned to look where he was looking. I saw what he saw. My heart seized in my chest; it felt as if a giant hand had thrust down my throat to clench my stomach and squeeze my bowels in a steely grip.

"What . . . ?" I gasped.

Tegid remained rigid and silent beside me.

There is no describing what I saw. Words were never meant to serve such a purpose. For lumbering into view was an enormous, yellow, splay-footed abomination dragging a tremendous blubbery gut between its obscenely bowed legs; its splotched, ravaged hide sprouted scraggly tufts of black bristles, and its narrow eyes burned with dull-witted malignance. The thing's mouth gaped froglike, toothless, and slick, and its long tongue lolled, drooling spittle and green putrid matter; its long arms, wasted thin, dangled; its crabbed hands clutched, tearing at the rocks and flinging them as it scrambled frantically over the rough terrain.

Behind this squat monstrosity surged a swarming legion of grotesques. Scores of insanely freakish creatures! Hundreds! Each one as repulsive as the next. I saw skeletal members thrusting, bloated torsos squirming, lurid faces leering, frenzied feet rushing toward us at frightful speed. I marveled at their pace, for the deep snow did not seem to slow them at all. Long-limbed or short, fat-bodied or slat-ribbed and thin, huge and hideous or small and abhorrent, they skittered across the snow, racing toward us in a vile, vomitous mass.

350

They rushed upon us, driven by a gale blast of hate. Their shocking appearance was only part of their paralyzing power—I could feel malice streaming out from them, a potent poison, blighting all it touched. They drove the wolves before them, lashing them to rage. Over the snow, fast and sure as death they came—wolves and demons. Who could stand against such a formidable onslaught?

"It is the Host of the Pit," said Tegid, his words a murmured understatement. "The Coranyid."

It was the Demon Horde of Uffern, whose coming Tegid had silently anticipated for many days. Demons they were, and ghastly beyond belief. Yet to say that I saw the vile Coranyid is tantamount to saying nothing. To look upon them was to behold the face of wickedness and strong evil. I saw abhorrence embodied, malevolence incarnate, putrescence clothed in mouldering flesh. I saw the death beyond death.

My hands grew weak; the strength left my legs. The will to flee deserted me. I wanted only to sink to the ground and cover myself with my cloak. This, of course, is what the demons desired. They hoped to stop us before we reached the king's stronghold—though why they had waited so long, when they might have taken us at any time since leaving Sycharth, I cannot say.

I glanced quickly over my shoulder to Findargad towering above, estimating the distance. "The fortress is too far. We will never make it."

"We must," Tegid spat. "If we can reach Dun na Porth, we have a chance."

We hastened to the king. Meldryn did not seem dismayed, or even much surprised, by the news. He turned his tired eyes toward the mountain pass, then raised the signal horn to his lips. An instant later a shrill blast cut the chill wind with the sharp note of alarm. Even as the first warning echoed and reechoed among the cold rock crags, people instinctively responded. Other warning blasts were sounded

351

down the line, and within the space of three heartbeats everyone was running, staggering, slipping, sliding, floundering through the snow toward the protection of the fortress above.

The pass that Tegid had indicated was just ahead: Dun na Porth, Gate of the Fortress—a steep-sided notch through which the trail passed before rising to the aerie whereon Meldryn Mawr's mountain stronghold perched. I entertained scant hope that we could reach the sheltering walls. Indeed, as the people hurried by, struggling in haste, Tegid—at the king's command—summoned the warriors to arms.

I threw off the cloth wrap protecting my sword and strapped the chill metal to my hip. Wrapping stiff fingers around the cold shaft of my spear, I ran down the trail to join the other warriors at the rear, pausing only to lift to their feet those who stumbled and to set them on their way.

Prince Meldron scowled at me as I fell in with the other warriors, but he was soon too busy to begrudge me a place among his own. Once the last of the stragglers had passed by, we formed a tight wedge, blocking the trail from one side to the other. To reach our kinsmen and the king, Lord Nudd's infernal war band would have to slay us first. I did not know whether demons could be killed, nor even if they could be fought with sword and spear. Still, if a demon could feel at all, it would feel the bite of my blade.

As the battle line formed, I found myself near the center in the second rank of warriors. We held our spears at the ready, over the shoulders of the rank before us. As Tegid and the king led the main body of our people upward into the pass, we advanced slowly back down the trail toward the onrushing enemy. At the sight of our tight-formed ranks the demons raised a weird, unearthly cry: plaintive and furious at the same time, a cry of demented wrath and torment intended to breathe despair into the most resolute will. The numbing wail assailed us on the wings of the wind, yet we stood our ground; and, as the

Coranyid drew near, we welcomed them with taunts, banking our courage high with loud battle cries.

Few of the demon warriors wielded formal weapons; I saw only an occasional sword or spear gripped in clawlike fingers, and some carried fire-blackened clubs. Most came on empty-handed—but not for long. For, as they swarmed nearer, they tore rocks from the trail and from the mountainside and pelted us with stones. We were thankful indeed for the protection of our shields.

The demon battle leader sent the wolves before them. Whether the Coranyid had been using the wolves all along, or whether they had merely turned the beasts' natural ferocity to their own purposes, I do not know. But the starving, fear-maddened animals, driven to frenzy by their inhuman masters, rushed upon us without heed. There was no sport in the killing. We met them with the points of our spears as they leapt, and they died snapping their cruel jaws at the blades that pierced them.

Behind the wolves came the main body of the Coranyid. Warriors hardened to battle, fearing neither pain nor death, trembled to see Lord Nudd's fell war band. Truly, this was a terrible array: skull-headed, swollen-bellied, spindle-limbed loathsome deserters of the grave; misshapen monsters each and every one. Naked, malformed, half-human fiends they were, malicious servants of an even more abhorrent master. More than one man shrank from the sight, and it was not accounted to their shame.

Though I searched the teeming throng, I could not see their loathsome lord. I little doubted that he was near, however, directing the onslaught from some unseen vantage. For I felt the waves of sick dread break over me as the horrid hellspawn advanced. Instinct told me this feeling was more than the repulsion inspired by the enemy's gruesome appearance. Lord Nudd was near. I could feel him, feel the despair and futility his presence inspired.

At the same time, I remembered the hope which Tegid and I had discovered in the ashes of Sycharth: the enemy was not omnipotent. Far from it! Nudd's only weapons were fear and deceit. Surrender to those and he would win. Defy him and his attack would founder. He could not fight against men who did not fear. This was his weakness—though perhaps his only weakness.

The first of the Demon Horde reached us, shattering the air with their appalling shrieks. The forerank of warriors stumbled backward as the screaming battle host threw themselves headlong onto our weapons. Black bile and curdled blood gushed from their wounds and we were suddenly engulfed in a sickening stench. The stink was almost stupefying; a stomach-churning fetor that caused the gorge to rise in our throats. Strong men gagged and puked, tears streaming from their eyes. Vile as the sight and sound of the hateful creatures was, the stench was worse—overwhelming the warriors' mettle. The foreshank faltered, sagged, and then broke, as brave men turned their backs and ran from the fight.

Within moments Meldryn's dauntless war band was in full rout, streaming back up the trail toward the pass, with the demons and wolves in howling pursuit. Prince Meldron strove mightily to turn his men, crying, "Hold! Hold, men! Stand and fight!" But they could not hear him above the drumbeat of panic in their own hearts.

I ran too. Hemmed in on all sides, I could do nothing else, lest I be trampled in the crush. We reached the pass of Dun na Porth. I looked up at the sheer rock face of the stone gate and paused, thinking that here a few might hold the trail against many. I stopped and turned to face the oncoming flood.

One black wolf carried a screaming demon on its back as it leapt, snarling, on the heels of a fleeing warrior. As I thrust through the streaming throng, the animal saw me and veered to the attack, mouth agape and foaming, teeth bared. I let the beast draw near, then lowered my spear and thrust it down its open throat. The wolf reared, clawing the air, choking and gagging on its own blood. The demon made to leap upon me, but Prince Meldron rushed forward and, with a quick downward chop of his sword, parted the demon's skull in a single stroke. Both demon and wolf expired in a heap at our feet.

Another demon skittered close, swinging a gnarled root around its flat, reptilian head. The prince struck aside the club, severing the demon's arm in the same blow. His next thrust pierced the foul creature through; it toppled backwards with a gurgling of exuded gas and pus. Meldron laid low another of the repugnant creatures with a single stroke as it made to leap upon him. And, with as many strokes, I sent two more back to the pit whence they came.

"They slaughter more easily than sheep!" exulted the prince. "There is no skill to it. We will have to work twice this hard to earn our glory."

It was true. The demons displayed no knowledge of warfare, or skill at arms. They could swarm and overwhelm, but they could not stand toe-to-toe against a warrior; they could hurl rocks and swing clubs, they could rip with their tusked teeth and hooklike claws, but they could not present an ordered attack. Still, there were hundreds of the demonspawn and only the prince and myself to hold them. We might quickly succumb to their numbers. We stood in the gap, meantime, hewing at them, stroke on stroke, razing them like weeds before the scythe.

The wolves were more dangerous. Their strength and speed, their ferocity in the fight, made them more than a match for a man. But the demons had roused them to such frenzy, they forgot their natural instinct and simply hurled themselves at us. I had only to let one come close and thrust my spear and the wolf either died or fled— tearing at its wounds in maddened fury.

I heard something behind me and spun ready to strike. "Stay your hand, brother!" came a loud voice. It was Paladyr, leading Prince

Meldron's Wolf Pack back to the fray. Simon—Siawn Hy—stood next to him. They had seen our stand against the enemy and had returned to join the fight.

"Now that the battle is won, you come to claim the victory," scoffed the prince. "Leave us! We are all but finished here."

"Nay, Prince. Did you think we would let you steal all the glory for yourselves?" answered the champion. "Come, there is more than enough for all."

"Prove it, then," replied the prince. "But with your sword—not your tongue!"

"Watch me!" shouted Paladyr. And with a great cry, he lifted his sword and thrust into the midst of a dozen demons advancing in a knot. He was a wonder to behold! Every movement honed sharp, flawless as gold, and lethal as the blade in his strong hand. He slew with every stroke. He was the millstone, and the enemy was the grain he crushed, their tangled bodies heaped around him like shapeless husks.

Siawn gave a piercing, ear-shattering scream and leaped after the king's champion, matching stroke for stroke and thrust for thrust. Wherever Paladyr strove, there was Siawn at his shoulder. Their quick-flowing blades rose and fell as one. Lest we lose place to them, Prince Meldron and I redoubled our efforts. Together we hewed a wide swath through the onrushing demon tide, wading into the battle with reckless courage.

Seeing how accommodatingly the Coranyid perished, more warriors rushed to meet the foe and soon Dun na Porth was filled—not with snow, but with the odious bodies of the Demon Host. We bent our backs to our labor, and a mighty work it was. Despite the cold, the sweat of battle ran from us; our breath clouded the air, and steam rose from our wet heads.

The stink made the tears run from our eyes and flow in rivulets down our cheeks. But the warriors steeled themselves against it and encouraged one another with bold words and shouts of valor. Shoulder to shoulder we stood against the squirming, writhing, noisome onslaught. Stroke by stroke we bettered them. We might have overcome them completely, but there were too many, and darkness was coming on.

As the light began to fail, it became more difficult to see the wretches. Yet they seemed to experience no trouble seeing us. Indeed, their strokes became more accurate as ours grew less so. Their assault strengthened while our defenses began to falter.

The reason was obvious: Darkness was their element. They could see in the dark. They had attacked Sycharth and the other strongholds in the dead of night. They could strike us in the darkness before we knew the blow was coming. Even so, we fought on long after it was foolhardy to do so. And we suffered for it.

As the deep Sollen darkness finally claimed the mountain pass, and the howl of the wind drowned out the cries of the Coranyid, Paladyr turned to the prince. "I am no coward, but I cannot fight what I cannot see."

"Nor can I," Prince Meldron replied. "By all means, let us save some to fight tomorrow."

Retreat on the twisting mountain path in the dark was difficult. We struggled upward, feeling our way toward the stout gates and high stone walls of Findargad. Never was I more grateful for a heavy gate at my back than on that night as I tumbled into the fortress yard, to be met by kinsmen bearing dry cloaks and cups of steaming ale. They pried the weapons from our stiff fingers and pressed warm cups into our hands, helping us to swallow the first gulps of the soothing drink. Those who could not stand, they carried into the hall. Those who could walk, they led.

Findargad was well stocked and provisioned. Those who had gone before us had readied everything, taking all that was needed from the fortress stores. The hall was ablaze with the light of scores of torches, and warm from the blaze of three enormous hearths. The boards before us were laden with food—though many of us were too exhausted to eat. We sat on benches before the hearth, hunched like old men over our ale, clutching our cups to our chests, sipping the life-kindling liquid.

The king moved among his warriors, Tegid by his side, lauding their bravery, praising their skill, offering each the word required to restore strength of arm and renew courage of heart. Meldryn Mawr had not fought beside his men, but he had watched the battle from the rampart until darkness stole the sight from our eyes.

When they came to me, Tegid said, "The king wishes me to tell you that he marked your courage. It was the saving of many lives."

"Great King, I am sorry I could do no more," I answered, for truly I never felt less like a hero than I did then. "Perhaps, if I had not run with the others, we might have prevailed against them. As it is, I did nothing your own son did not do."

King Meldryn whispered something in Tegid's ear, and the bard spoke it out to me. "Though you may not know it, you have done something the prince did not do. You have stood by your king in all loyalty when others did not. Even the prince cannot boast as much. This is accorded to your renown: you have never dishonored your king through disobedience."

They moved on. I was too tired to take in the full meaning of the king's words then, but soon I would have cause to brood long over them. And I would learn to rue every syllable.

31
KING'S COUNCIL

By day and night the Demon Host prowled outside the walls, while we kept watch from the ramparts. Now and then one ventured close and, seizing a handhold among the stones, skittered up the wall. Quick as spiders, the Coranyid could climb. And if we were not alert, the demon might reach the rampart itself. Then the nearest warriors would stab the thing with their spears and heave the obscene carcass over the wall. Usually, however, a vigilant warrior would hurl a rock upon the creature's wicked head and dash out its watery brains before the odious thing had scaled halfway.

Each defeat served to keep the rest of the demons at bay for a time. I cannot say why. They seemed to possess no fear, yet could not bear the loss of one of their number. It infuriated them. Those nearest the incident would shriek and scream, raising the most horrendous din.

Always, day or night, we stood in the cold and wind wrack, keeping vigil lest we be overcome. As the days drew on, more demons joined the battle throng. We could see them toiling along the mountain pathways, summoned by their dread lord's wrath to the place of slaughter. Of Lord Nudd we saw no sign. But we often felt his lurking presence—a sudden laboring of the heart, a pang of nausea in the stomach, a daunting distress, a lingering despair.

Still, we were safe behind the stronghold's high walls. Rage though the demons might, they could not penetrate the stones like spirits, nor float over the ramparts like ghosts. As long as we kept the gates barred against them, they could not gain entrance. If we did not let them in, their rage and fury remained impotent.

The first days after reaching Findargad, we rested; we nursed our wounds and mourned our dead. The flight had exacted a terrible price. Of the six hundred who had begun the journey, fewer than four hundred remained; of these, only eighty warriors and horses enough for sixty. It might have been worse, of course, but that was no consolation. Any loss is lamentable. The fact that we had succeeded in gaining Findargad, against every obstacle, appeared a small thing in our eyes compared to the loss.

On the sixth day of the demon siege, the king summoned those of his chieftains who were still alive—five in all—with the prince, Paladyr, and Tegid, to his council chamber. I, whose duty it was to remain always with Tegid, went too; and, although I had no right, I was included in the council.

Tegid it was who spoke the summons, and Tegid who opened the proceedings. The king sat in a chair of stag horn, lined with rich furs. The others sat on the stone-flagged floor upon brown and white oxhides. A crackling fire flamed in the hearth around which they all sat. Tegid stood at Meldryn Mawr's right hand, his left hand resting on the king's right shoulder, so that there would be no doubt by whose authority the bard spoke. I found a place to sit near the door so that my presence would not trouble anyone.

When all had assembled and taken their places, Tegid began. "Wise chieftains, Boars of Battle," he said, "hear the words of your king, and give him the benefit of your wise counsel."

Tegid inclined his ear to the king's mouth, and Meldryn charged him with the words to say. "Thus says the king," said Tegid, straightening slowly to address his listeners. "Strong are the Llwyddi, and proud in the strength of our arms. In battle we shrink not from any foe, neither do we falter in the defense of our realm. The indignity of defeat was not known among us from the time of our fathers to this."

Meldryn Mawr nodded as Tegid finished, leaned close, and whispered something more; then he raised his right hand and touched the bard on the mouth. Tegid straightened and turned to those gathered around the firepit.

"Thus says the king," he intoned. "Our homes have been destroyed and the land laid waste. Wolves gnaw the bones of the brave, and ravens feast on the flesh of our children. Ashes drift like black snow where once fine halls stood; sheep and shepherd alike are slaughtered; timber walls are broken; stout houses have become tombs; hearthstones have been overturned and sweet mead poured out on the thirsty ground to mingle with the blood of good men. The owl and the fox cry where laughter once sounded. The kite and hawk make nests in the skulls of poets.

"More bitter to me than defeat are the deaths of my people; more bitter than the destruction of my strongholds is knowledge of evil in the land. We are men. But we are not like other men. We are Llwyddi: rulers in this worlds-realm since its beginning. It is not in us to yield our lands to the oppression of usurpers. It is not in us to yield place to murderers. It is not in us to forget the blood debt.

"Chieftains, hear your king! The voices of the slain cry out from their graves for vengeance; the innocent dead require recompense for the lives which were brutally stolen from them. It is the duty of the living to honor the dead. It is the duty of the warrior to slay the foe. It is the duty of a king to protect and defend his people, and to provide for them.

"I am Meldryn Mawr. I provide for my people in life and in death. Though the foe slay me, the sovereignty which I have held will continue; the kingship I have borne will not be extinguished.

"Thus says the king: there is even now an enemy raging outside our walls who seeks to destroy us—a craven who dares not challenge us on the field of honor, but only by stealth, treachery, and deception. And now that we are weak in the strength of our arms this enemy raises siege against us. We are made to endure the indignity of his taunts and the insult of his vile presence before our gates.

"I ask you, Wise Leaders, what is this snow which falls unceasingly from the wounded sky? What is this battering wind which all night long worries us with its howl? What is this ravening cold which every day sinks its teeth deeper into the land?

"And what is this grief which taints the water we drink and turns the bread bitter in our mouths? What is this wrath poured out upon us like scalding oil? What is this terror which grips our hearts and makes our blood run cold?

"Hear me now, Keen of Judgment, and answer if you can: What has silenced the Men of Song? What causes fair Modornn to tremble? What is this abomination among the peaks of Cethness? What drives the boar from the glens and causes the deer to fly from the forests? What is it that vexes heaven and steals the birds from the skies?

"While you are yet deliberating, consider this: Who stretches forth his hand over our realm in conquest? Who wastes our land? Who makes the tears of our people flow more freely than rushing streams? Who raises the outrage of war against us?"

Tegid paused to give his listeners time to ponder all he had said. When he continued, he asked, "Do you yet wonder? Does no one dare to speak the name aloud? Very well, I will say the hateful words. It is Nudd, Lord of Uffern and Annwn, Prince of the Pit, who is answerable for all these afflictions. It is Lord Nudd who has slain our kinsmen and makes of our bright realm a wasteland most wretched. It is Nudd the Accursed who turns our women into widows and our warriors into food for worms. It is Nudd, King of Eternal Night, who directs the demon king against us.

"I tell you the truth, Companions of the Heart, unless we make bold to end Lord Nudd's reign, the outrages practiced against Prydain must soon be known in Llogres and Caledon also. Then will the Three Blessed Realms be united—in misery, not in harmony; in distress, not in peace. And Albion, fairest island that is in the world, will writhe beneath the hateful torment of Nudd's Coranyid."

As these words concluded, brows furrowed and frowns deepened on the faces of his listeners. Meldryn's chieftains peered at one another in despair. At length, Tegid broke the brittle silence. "You have heard. You have pondered. You have considered. Now it is time to share out the treasure of your wise counsel. Your king is waiting."

Prince Meldron, in deference to his rank, was the first to speak. "Father and king, it has ever been our way to repay wound for wound, and grief for grief. Or have you forgotten this along with your ability to speak?" The prince could not resist twisting the knife in his father's heart. "Yet it is worth remembering. I say, let us collect the blood debt which is owed to us. Let us assemble our warriors—and any who will ride with us—and make war on Nudd. Let us take up our weapons and banish him from our lands."

Several of the chieftains, Paladyr the Champion among them, slapped their hands against their thighs and raised their voices in acclaim. The king listened without enthusiasm and motioned for Tegid to step close.

After a brief consultation, Tegid turned and said, "The king has heard you, Meldron. It is in his mind that this evil will not be driven from our realm by force of arms alone. For there is a sickness at the heart of this matter that must be remedied before the land will be healed."

"There is no affliction wrought by enemies that cannot be remedied by the sword," boasted the prince.

Tegid listened patiently to the king's reply and then spoke it out. "Thus says the king: Think you that the tribulation which has befallen us will succumb to the edge of a sword? I tell you that Lord Nudd is not afraid of your spears or swords. He fears one thing only: the True King in his stronghold. The foul lord is bound by one thing only: the Song of Albion."

"As to that," the prince replied haughtily, "I know nothing. It seems to me that this trouble which has come upon us is but the meddling of bards." He turned the accusation toward Tegid. "None of this would have happened if you and your kind had held to your own domain."

Tegid bristled at this. "Do you suggest that the bards of Albion had anything to do with encouraging this horror?"

The prince did not deign to answer but neither did he back down.

"So that you will know," the bard snapped, "so that everyone will know the truth, I will speak plainly. Know you this: the Cythrawl is loosed upon the world." At the name of the Ancient Evil, all gathered before Meldryn's hearth shivered within themselves. "Ollathir, Chief of Bards, faced the Beast of the Pit and was slain, but not before binding it with strong enchantments. Thus bound, the Cythrawl has summoned its servant Nudd to harrow and destroy what it could not possess. That is how this tribulation has come upon us."

Prince Meldron scowled and thrust out his chin. "It is the blather of bards in my ears." He flicked an ear with his fingers. "What do I care how this happened? I care only about reclaiming what is mine!"

"Well said, lord," replied Paladyr loudly. "We have shown that we can kill the Coranyid. Let us send the ogham spear to all the clans throughout the Three Realms and summon all kings and their war bands to a great hosting against Nudd and his Demon Horde."

This plan was heartily approved by Meldryn's chiefs, who, contrary to Tegid's best efforts, would not believe the enormity of the evil facing them, nor credit the cause. For, despite all the hardship we had endured, and all we had seen of the enemy, they still trusted only to the weapons in their hands.

With the king's consent, Tegid dismissed the gathering and everyone withdrew, talking loudly of the great hosting and the glorious war which would be waged. They still thought that trouble could be averted by swordstrike and spearthrust; they still thought Sollen would soon end and Gyd come again of its own.

After they had gone, the king rose slowly from his council chair and stood before the hearth, gazing into the fire's crimson depths, as if searching for the face of his enemy. After a long moment, he departed to his inner room. I saw his face illumined in the firelight as he turned, and it seemed to me the face of a dying man: eyes bright and hard, the flesh of his face stretched tight on the skull, the skin papery and pale. It was the face of a man who watches his life drain rapidly away but is powerless to prevent it.

I approached the hearth and sat down on a speckled oxhide near the fire. Tegid noticed my worried expression. "The king is tired. He needs rest."

"You did not tell them about the Phantarch. Why?"

Tegid prodded the coals with an iron. "You saw how they were. They would not have heard me."

"Perhaps not. Even so, they had a right to know."

"Then *you* tell them!" he shouted in a voice as raw as an open wound. "*You* have the Chief Bard's awen; you tell them. Perhaps they will listen to you." He threw the iron down.

Anger flashed quick and hot through me. "Stop it, Tegid! You say

I have received Ollathir's awen, and maybe I have. But I did not ask for it. In truth, I do not remember it!"

"Then it is lost! It is rich mead spilled out upon dry sand. It is wasted and that is the end of it." And with that, Tegid rose and stormed from the council chamber, and I saw no more of him that night nor all the next day.

⎄ ⎄ ⎄

Two days after the king's council, I took my turn at watch on the wall. I was dismayed to see that there were yet more demons gathered outside our gates. I gazed out into the snow-swirled gloom and saw many hundreds, perhaps thousands, of Coranyid surging around the foundation of the fortress like a restless, angry sea. They grimaced obscenely at us, defecating and breaking wind in crude defiance of our hurled rocks. The din they made with their hideous shrieks was appalling. The stink rising up from their squalor and filth was worse. I retched before I could stop myself, involuntarily adding to the reek.

"There are more each day," a warrior named Hwy confirmed. "No matter how many we kill, there are always more."

It was true, and I soon learned why.

"What is that?" I asked, pointing to a red glow among a cluster of rocks swarming with Coranyid.

"It is their fire," the warrior replied. "They warm themselves at it."

I wondered at this. Where did demons find fuel to feed a fire? Why would Creatures of the Pit require warmth? They seemed immune to cold. They neither ate, nor drank, nor slept—nor required any other human comfort. Why did they need a fire?

The question persisted, so I walked along the rampart to the end of the wall for a better view between the towering rocks. I saw that, indeed, the enemy had made a huge fire. What is more, they had set an enormous cauldron to boil on the flames. The steam from this cauldron flew away in ragged wisps on the blustering wind. Scores of demons labored at the fire, stoking it, banking it. But what was its purpose?

My questions were answered at once. As I stood looking on, a cluster of Coranyid gyrating before the gate suddenly rushed forward, attempting to scale the gate timbers. The alert watchmen hurled rocks down upon them, crushing and killing three instantly and injuring two others. The injured ones were also killed as they attempted to drag their mangled bodies away. It was over in but a moment. The others retreated, wailing horribly, and leaving five dead behind.

No sooner had the would-be attackers scurried out of range, than a dozen more rushed forward. But instead of throwing themselves upon the gate as the first had done, these scampered to the crumpled corpses of their wretched dead, seized them, and dragged them away. A curious thing to do, I thought. And then I saw where they took the bodies and what they did with them. I watched, and the marrow froze in my bones.

I turned at once and ran to find Tegid.

32

THE CAULDRON

F ollow me, Tegid. There is something you must see."

I had found the bard alone, sitting before the fire in the king's council chamber, cutting the ogham letters into the shaft of a spear Prince Meldron and the battle chiefs intended to use to summon the kings of Albion to the hosting. We both knew it to be a vain gesture. There would be no summons, no hosting, and no glorious battle. Meldryn Mawr's chieftains could not even agree on who should take the spear; as to how they meant to pass through the swarming Coranyid at our gates and survive the bitter Sollen journey, they had no idea at all.

"There is nothing I care to see," Tegid growled.

"You should see this," I told him.

"Can it not wait?"

"No."

"Oh, very well," he said irritably, casting the spear aside. It clattered on the flagstones of the empty room. He rose, brushing wood shavings from his breecs. "Show me this thing which cannot wait."

Despite his complaining, he was not greatly upset at leaving his futile task. He followed me readily. We passed from the chamber into the hall, threading carefully among scores of sleeping people, pausing at the door of the hall to wrap our cloaks tightly around us. Opening the door a crack, I pushed aside the oxhide and stepped out into the storm. Blown across the snow-filled yard, the wind tearing at our clothing, we climbed the steps to the rampart behind the wall. There I pointed to the red fireglow flickering against the rocks. Shreds of sulphurous smoke, torn by the wind, scumbled across the snow, staining it a filthy yellow. "Do you see that?" I said.

"They have made a fire," he replied.

"Yes. Why, O Keen of Knowledge, have they made a fire?"

Tegid made to answer, then cocked his head to one side. "Why, indeed?"

"Exactly." I motioned for him to follow me further and led him along the wall to the place where the vessel could be seen. "And there?" I pointed into snow-churned gloom.

"A cauldron," responded Tegid with mounting interest.

"Yes, it is a cauldron. Now watch this," I told him and directed his attention to the gate.

We stood looking on for a short while, the cold wind whipping at us. We did not have long to wait, as there soon came another attempt on the gate. These assaults had been regular occurrences for several days and were growing more and more frequent. Four demons were killed this time; they died hideously, screaming and thrashing in the snow. This time, however, the broken bodies were snatched up and carried away by other demons. Tegid admitted that this was curious, but failed to see the significance.

"Wait a moment," I advised, "and keep watching."

The broken bodies of the four slain Coranyid were borne away to the enormous fire, where they were heaved over the rim of the great iron kettle; the corpses were tumbled in one by one, and the fire leapt higher. "They eat them!" observed Tegid with a shiver of disgust.

"No, they do not eat their dead. Watch."

A swell-bellied hunchback with a face like a rat leapt upon the rim of the steaming vessel and thrust a long black paddle into the seething depths. The bloated creature made a few stirring motions, then stopped and withdrew the paddle.

"What—" began Tegid.

"Watch," I said, not taking my eyes from the fire-wreathed kettle.

The words were no sooner out of my mouth than one of the corpses began to rise from the cauldron: first a hand and an arm, and then the head, shoulders, and torso. The arms moved, and the head. The undead thing clambered to the rim of the vessel, ignoring the flames licking round its gleaming shins, and then sprang to the ground to rejoin the writhing masses of his monstrous companions.

Meanwhile, the second demon had risen from the froth of the massive iron pot, and now scrambled over the rim. The head of the third corpse bobbed to the bubbling surface, mouth open, eyes wide and staring. It grasped the rim with its two horny hands and pulled itself out of the cauldron and fell sprawling onto the rocks outside the circle of flames. The last corpse emerged from the boiling liquid, and rejoined the loathsome horde.

"*Crochan-y-Aileni,*" muttered Tegid darkly, "the Cauldron of Rebirth. This is how they preserve their numbers. We cannot kill them. We cannot stop them." His voice rang hollow with resignation and defeat.

"You said the Song would stop them," I reminded him.

"The Song is lost."

"Then we must find it."

Tegid scoffed. "A fool's errand. It cannot be done."

I threw a hand toward the imposing vessel. "Only a fool would stay here and wait to be starved and overwhelmed by these fiends and their accursed pot. It seems to me, brother, we are fools either way."

The bard glowered at me, and I thought he might tip me over the wall. But then he glanced at the cauldron once more, and at the thousands of teeming Coranyid cavorting obscenely around its shimmering, fire-wrapped bulk. "What do you propose?"

"I propose we find the Phantarch. Maybe he is not dead. We do not know that he is dead. We will not know for certain until we find him."

"Impossible," grunted Tegid. "And futile."

"What have we to lose?"

"Must I say it all again? No one, save the Penderwydd, knows where the Phantarch resides," protested Tegid weakly. "Ollathir knew and—"

"And Ollathir is dead," I snapped. I had no more patience with Tegid's pessimism. "So you keep saying. Well, I say *someone* knows where the Phantarch resides, because whoever killed him knew well enough where to find him."

Tegid, who had been about to object, jerked suddenly upright, his eyes narrow as he sifted the truth of my words.

"It seems to me," I continued, "that we have either to find out who killed the Phantarch or find out how they discovered him."

"It will be difficult."

"Difficult is not the same thing as impossible."

"Now you are talking like a bard." Tegid allowed himself a fleeting smile.

It was meant as a jest, but, even as he spoke these words, I remembered my solemn vow to the Banfáith: *It seems to me a task more befitting a bard*, I had told her. *Yet what may be done, that I will do.*

"It is a task for a bard," I said. "I am no bard, Tegid; we both know it. And yet the Chief Bard's awen was given to me."

The smile faded, and his face clouded with the despair that had dogged him since Sycharth. He said nothing.

"Yes, to me, Tegid. It was given to me! It should have been you—I wish it *had* been you. I know I am no fit vessel. But the fact remains that I was there when Ollathir died, and I was the one who received the awen. That is the way of it."

Tegid's mouth twitched unhappily, but he did not respond.

"I am willing, but I do not know what to do. You do. You are a bard. Tell me, Tegid; tell me what I need to know. I remember nothing of what Ollathir told me. But I would like to remember. And, maybe if I could remember it, it would do us all some good."

Tegid was silent still, but I knew he was considering what I had said carefully. And I could sense that he was even now beginning to put his hurt and disappointment behind him. He stared hard at me—as if I were an untried horse and he a reluctant buyer trying to decide where he could trust me. Finally, he said, "Will you do whatever I tell you?"

"What may be done, that I will do."

Tegid turned abruptly and said, "Follow me."

33

HEART OF THE HEART

We slipped out into the wind-lashed night, the light from the hall spilling like molten bronze upon the snow of the yard. We carried torches, fluttering in the gusting wind with the sound of rushing wings. Pulling a fold of my cloak across my face, I followed Tegid across the dark expanse of snow.

On the walls above us I could see the torches of the watchers. I heard the shriek of the Coranyid as they swarmed without the walls and the shouts of the warriors as they hurled stones down upon the vile brood.

Tegid led us to a small stone house in the shadow of the great hall. The hut was a storehouse for leather, wool, and other supplies, dry and smelling of sheep, with bales of fleeces and tanned oxhides rolled and stacked against the walls. There were also slabs of beeswax and bundles of carded wool for weaving. The roof was thatched with heather and moss; the floor was timber, and there were no windows.

In the center of the room stood a post, and next to it a square opening in the floor. Tegid moved to the opening, handed me his torch, and stepped down onto a wooden ladder. He disappeared into the square of blackness, and a moment later he said, "Hand me the light."

I moved to the edge of the hole and handed down first one torch and then the other. Holding on to the post, I lowered myself into the darkness, feeling for rungs with my toes. Beneath the floor, the constricted hole opened into a narrow passage, almost—but not quite—high enough for a man to stand upright. "This way," Tegid said, handing me a torch.

Two other passages opened off either side, but Tegid, head down and shoulders hunched, moved off along the central passage. It was dry, but cold. Our breath drifted in curling vapors to the stone ceiling above our heads. In thirty paces the passage ended in a larger chamber, where we could stand upright once again. At one side of the chamber there was a stone trough carved in the wall. A thin trickle of water seeping down a groove in the wall filled the basin, and the overflow dripped into a cistern. I could hear the pinging echo of the drips as they splashed into the cistern somewhere below. On the wall opposite the trough a knotted rope hung down into a round hole cut in the floor.

Tegid walked to the hole and gave me his torch. He then seized the knotted rope, stepped to the edge of the hole, and lowered himself down. "There are steps in the wall," he told me when he reached the bottom. "Take the rope and throw down the torches."

Following his instructions and example, I took hold of the rope and dropped the torches down the hole. Tegid retrieved them and held them high, so that I could see the clefts cut in the rock face. Half-dangling and half-climbing, I lowered myself down the vertical steps to find myself in a large, round, vaulted room which was the interior of the cistern itself. A rock ledge bordered the deep, dark pool of water. Without a word, Tegid handed me my torch, turned, and led the way along the ledge. We stopped at an opening halfway around the circumference of the cistern and half a man's height from the ledge.

Two small holes bored into the stone at the side of this larger aperture held our torches, and we clambered up and into the entrance, and into another passage. Recovering our torches, we proceeded—first on hands and knees, then in a cramped crouch, and at last upright as the roof rose away into the darkness overhead. Though outside our small, wavering sphere of light the passage lay in darkness, I could tell that it was leading downward at a slight angle, and also turning slowly inward. The walls of this passage were wet. Water continually seeped, trickled, and dripped from the unseen ceiling. It may have been the exertion of our endeavor, but the passage seemed to me warmer, and I began to feel a clammy sweat on my face and neck.

How long this passage continued, I could not tell. I lost track of the steps and it seemed as if we might walk all night. At times the stony corridor narrowed so that we were forced to go sideways for some distance. Other times, the walls widened until lost to the light from our torches. As we followed the passage further, the way became steeper, and the floor beneath our feet smoother and more slippery— as if the passage had been carved into the heart of the mountain by an underground river. I also began hearing, faintly and far away, the sound of running water, like that of a brook splashing and sliding over its rock-strewn bed.

After some time, we arrived in a huge, hive-shaped chamber—naturally formed, not made by men. Through the center of the chamber coursed a stream, wide but not too deep, and Tegid followed it, making for a crevice in the wall through which the waterflow disappeared. This fissure spanned the height of the room floor to ceiling, and was wide enough at floor level for a man to enter.

"This is the womb of the mountain," Tegid said, his voice echoing in the hollow chamber. "Here is where a bard is born. Beyond this portal the awen is awakened."

He moved the torch to illumine the rock face at the edge of the crevice. I saw that a square patch of the wall had been smoothed and a design incised in the center of the square. It was a design I knew well, a common device seen throughout Albion: the circle maze whose elaborate, hypnotic loops and whorls could be found on arm rings, tattoos, brooches, shields, wooden utensils . . . almost anything. The circle maze also adorned standing stones and was cut into the turf on hilltops.

"That was on the pillar stone on Ynys Bàinail," I said, indicating the carving. "What does it mean?"

"It is *Môr Cylch*, the maze of life," Tegid told me. "It is trodden in darkness with just enough light to see the next step or two ahead, but not more. At each turn the soul must decide whether to journey on or whether to go back the way it came."

"What if the soul does not journey on? What if it chooses to go back the way it came?"

"Stagnation and death," replied Tegid with mild vehemence. He seemed irritated that anyone would consider retreating.

"And if the soul travels on?"

"It draws nearer its destination," the bard answered. "The ultimate destination of all souls is the Heart of the Heart."

Tegid moved to a niche carved in the wall, reached in, and brought forth two fresh torches which he lit from the one in his hand. He gave one of these to me and placed his used torch in a cleft beside the circle maze, directing me to do the same.

He turned and, hunkering down, stepped into the crevice. I heard the splash of his steps and saw the flame-flicker of his torch on shiny walls. Then he called out to me, "Come with me, brother. Here is where memory begins."

I stooped and entered that narrow way, squeezed through a pinched opening and emerged into a high-ceilinged passage, wide enough to stand with hands outstretched to either side. The curved walls of the passage were smooth and shone as if polished. Along the floor ran the water from the stream. The turbulent crash of rushing water was louder here, though still distant-sounding and distorted, as if shunted and reflected by innumerable walls or baffles.

This was, in fact, the case, for we had entered an enormous maze—the likeness of which was carved on the wall outside—and the sound of the waterfall reached us through the many turns and curving pathways of the serpentine structure. We walked in water to our ankles, and soon our feet were wet and numb from the icy flow.

After wading for a little time in silence, Tegid began to tell me about the place and why we had come there. "This is very old," he said, reaching out and slapping the smooth stone with his hand. "Almost before anything else in Prydain existed, this was made. This is the *omphalos* of our realm, the Navel of Prydain. It has been kept and protected by our kings from the creation of this worlds-realm."

I had wondered why Meldryn Mawr required a fortress so far away from his lands. "But I thought the White Rock was the sacred center of Albion."

"This, too, is the center," Tegid replied, apparently unconcerned that there should be more than one sacred center. "And everyone who would become a bard must tread this pathway into the Heart of the Heart."

We walked along the gently curving passageway and came eventually to what I first thought was a blank wall, but which, at closer approach, I saw was actually a close turn, doubling the passage back upon itself. We proceeded along this new corridor, holding our torches high to throw as much light before us as possible.

Despite Tegid's guidance, I found the maze utterly disorienting. As we moved along the curving walls to the sound of rushing water all around, I felt like a lost soul stumbling alone, steering by my fitful light, hoping to reach I knew not what. And the water, swiftly flowing, was like time or the force of life, bearing us along on our journey.

The passage turned abruptly once more and we rounded the bend and started down yet another curving corridor, this one just slightly more sharply curved than the last. It may have been my imagination, but it did seem as if the bend became both a literal and symbolic turning point, a point of doubt requiring a decision. The way ahead was dark and uncertain, the way behind could no longer be seen. To go ahead meant to trust in the Maker of the Maze that the reward sought at the Heart of the Heart would bless and not curse.

The curves of the maze became sharper, the turns more frequent. By this I knew that we were coming to the center of the maze. The sound of rushing water grew louder as well. We would reach the central chamber soon. What would we find there?

The sound of water all around, the darkness, the cold, the hardness of the rock—I felt as if I had indeed entered into an initiation. Here is where memory begins, Tegid had said. Memory begins with birth. Was I being born into something? Or was something being born in me? I could not tell, but I felt the expectation growing with each step.

Tighter became the turns, quicker the steps. I felt my pulse racing and the surge of anticipation rushing through me. Water, fire, darkness, stone—a world of elemental simplicity exerting an elemental force upon me. I could feel the pull in my bones and blood. My mind quickened to a call older than any other, ancient, primeval: the summons to life which had called man forth from the elements.

We rounded the last bend in the maze and entered a circular chamber. It was empty—except for a large hole in the floor where the icy stream which had coursed through the winding pathways of the maze now disappeared. The roar of the water voice, like that of a god, came up through the dark hole as the falling stream shattered on the rocks somewhere below.

"We have reached the Heart of the Heart," Tegid explained. "Here memory is extinguished."

"Memory is extinguished in death," I mused.

"That is so. But to die to one world is to be born into another. Therefore life, like all created things, though it ceases to flow in this world, continues its journey in the place beyond."

The tingling I felt was the hair on the nape of my neck creeping. *In the place beyond . . . the Phantarch sleeps . . .*

Standing in the icy water, listening to the roar of falling water, I felt again the terror of that night on the sacred mound. In the darkness I saw again the looming maw of the Cythrawl and felt Ollathir's arm tight on my neck and his breath hot in my ear. And I heard again the strange words the Chief Bard had bequeathed me with his dying breath.

"Domhain Dorcha," I said, turning to Tegid. "The place beyond."

Tegid's eyes flicked sharp and quick over my face. Interest sparked the bard's voice. "Where did you hear those words?"

"Ollathir told me," I answered and told him what I remembered. "I did not know what he was saying, but I know now. I remember it now. In the place beyond, the Phantarch sleeps. That is what Ollathir told me." I pointed to the hole where the water cascaded out of sight. "And there is where we will find the Phantarch."

"Are you willing?" asked Tegid quietly.

"I am," I answered.

Trembling with awe and excitement, we moved to the hole and held our torches low in an effort to penetrate the darkness beneath our feet. We could see nothing below the rim of the hole, however. The water spilling over the edge splashed into the unseen depths below. We stood for a moment wondering how far the water fell.

Then Tegid dropped his torch into the hole. The firebrand spun end over end, and for the briefest of instants there flashed the glassy walls and floor of a lower chamber before the torch doused itself in a pool. He raised his head and our eyes met and held the glance. "Well? What say you, brother?"

"There is no other way down," I said.

"And perhaps no other way back up," he pointed out.

True. We had no rope, no tools of any kind. We must decide what to do without knowing the outcome of our actions. If we failed there would be no second chance, no delivery, no rescue, no salvation. We were to risk all, to trust the tortured, perhaps confused word of a dying bard.

"If Ollathir was here and told you to go down into that hole," I asked, "would you do it?"

"Of course," replied Tegid, without hesitation. His faith in his leader was simple and direct. Tegid's assurance was good enough for me.

I gazed into the darkness dense as dirt and blacker than oblivion. It might well be our deaths awaiting us below. "Will you go first, or shall I?"

"I will go first," he said, eyeing the round black void before us. "And when I call to you, hold the torch over the hole and drop it. I will try to catch it."

Then he simply stepped into the hole and plunged from sight. I heard the splash as he hit the water and, for a heart-catching instant, nothing . . . and then a coughing, sputtering gasp.

"Tegid! Are you hurt?" I threw myself onto my stomach and lowered the torch through the hole.

"It is cold!" he roared, his voice echoing away into the depths below. I heard him thrashing in the water and then, "Throw the torch. I am directly beneath you."

I tilted the torch fire-end upright as far as I could manage without burning myself. "Here it comes," I said, and let it drop.

I saw it flutter and flare for just a moment, and I was certain it would go out. But, just before it touched the water, I saw a hand swoop out and Tegid was waving the torch and shouting, "I have it! I have it!"

I could see his upturned face in the torchlight, grinning up at me as if from a well. "Now you," he called.

He moved aside, and I sat down on the edge of the hole, letting my legs dangle into the void below. The darkness closed upon me like a physical force; I could feel its pressure on my eyeballs and lungs—a vast, soft, invisible hand, squeezing me, suffocating me. Blind, breathless, cold water flowing all around and over me, I placed my hands on the edge of the precipice and pushed myself off the rim. The sensation of plunging through space in absolute darkness was more unnerving than I had expected. It seemed as if I fell and fell and would go on falling and never stop; I was beginning to wonder if I would ever hit the bottom, when I smacked the surface of the water.

Instantly, the water closed over my head, and I was plunged into the wet, dark cold. I sank until I felt solid rock beneath me. I pushed against the bottom with my feet and shot up, floundering and spewing, icy water pouring down on me from overhead. I dashed water from my eyes and looked toward the light. Tegid stood at the pool's edge holding the torch high so that I could see him. I swam to him; he knelt and grabbed my arm and pulled me from the pool.

I stood, conscious of a subtle change in our surroundings—as if we had indeed passed from one realm into another. Tegid made to turn away, and, at the movement of the torch, I glimpsed a fleeting glimmer of light on the wall, the flash of a spark. "What next?" I asked. My voice did not echo but fell hushed at my feet.

"Let us see what we have found," Tegid replied, and we began exploring. The chamber was round, we discovered, and carved in the living rock of the mountain. Opposite the pool was a low tunneled passage. The walls of the tunnel, like the walls of the chamber, were shot through with veins of silver crystal which sparkled as we passed. We entered the tunnel and began a long descent to a deeper room. Twice along the way I stopped. "Wait!" I told Tegid. "Listen!"

We would stop and listen but would hear nothing. Still, I thought I could hear something—a low rhythmic humming, like a big cat purring or an animal snoring. It sounded alive, whatever it was that we could not quite hear. I imagined tumbling from the tunnel into the den of a sleeping cave bear.

The tunnel wound down and down, our dark, slow way lit by the momentary flashes and sparkles of torchlight in the crystalline walls. Once I grazed the tunnel wall with my fingertips and found it warm to the touch. I imagined that we were descending into the very heart of the mountain, so far down that we were approaching the molten core of the earth itself. And still we moved on.

Then, unexpectedly, the tunnel ended, and we stepped out into a dome-shaped chamber that appeared to have been hollowed from a single gargantuan crystal. The light from our single torch was reflected and magnified in a myriad of facets, blazing like a heaven full of flaming suns. After the darkness of the tunnel, such brightness hurt my eyes. And that is why I did not see the heap of stones lying in the center of the chamber—until Tegid directed my attention to it.

We stepped closer and saw what appeared to be a scrap of white cloth. Tegid held the torch near and we saw a human hand protruding from among the stones. The flesh on the hand was shriveled, the bones sharp through the pale, leathery skin.

"We have found the Phantarch," Tegid said, his voice a choked whisper. I turned to where he pointed with the torch to the crude grave mound. "Cold as the stone that covers him. The Banfáith was right: the Phantarch is dead. And all hope with him. There is nothing for us here."

34

DOMHAIN DORCHA

They have murdered him," said Tegid in a hollow voice. "The Song is silenced and cannot be recovered." He sounded lost and tired and defeated. "There is nothing for us here."

He turned to go, but I stood there stubbornly, staring at the lifeless hand reaching out from the heap of stone.

Tegid started into the tunnel once more to begin the long walk back to the upper chamber. I meant to follow him, but my feet remained firmly planted where I stood. We had found the Phantarch. Yes, but someone else had found him first. They had killed him and entombed him in Domhain Dorcha, the place beyond the Heart of the Heart. Yet, we had come so far . . . and the need was so great. I had to see the battered corpse with my own eyes before I would believe what Tegid knew to be true.

"Are you coming?" the bard asked.

"No—not until I have seen him. I want to see him with my own eyes before I believe he is dead."

"It is over!" he roared. "This is the end. There is nothing for us here."

"I will not leave until I have seen him," I stubbornly insisted. "Go if you wish, but I am staying."

"Fool!" he bellowed angrily. "This is your doing! We have come for nothing!"

I did not blame Tegid for this outburst. At my coaxing, he had allowed himself to hope, and now that last, precious hope had been snatched from him. In the end, we had only proven what he had maintained all along: the Phantarch was dead, and there was no escaping the doom that awaited us and all the rest of Albion.

"Tegid, please," I said, "we have come so far."

He pressed his mouth into a firm, straight line but did not deny me. I stepped into the mound, and, bending down, began to shift the stones one by one. Tegid watched me for a while, and when he saw that I meant to uncover the whole mound, he gave in and came to help me. Propping the torch between two rocks at the head of the mound, we began carefully pulling away the stones.

We worked without speaking, and in a short while I glimpsed a bit of dirty white cloth. I shifted a few more stones, and saw a gray crumpled hand. We continued removing the rocks until the corpse was completely exhumed—then stepped back to view our labor's sorry yield.

The Phantarch appeared to be an old man, an ancient man of years beyond counting, dressed in robes of white with a corded belt of woven gold. He wore a wide, flat neck ring that covered the upper part of his chest. In his right hand he carried a ceremonial knife of glassy black stone; a rod of gold nestled in the crook of his right arm. His left hand was empty, and his feet were bare.

The flickering torchlight gave his face the appearance of life, but the sunken eyes and cheeks told a different tale. And though battered and broken terribly by the stones, that head still held a high nobility; white-haired, with a wide brow and hawklike nose, a strong chin and firm jaw covered by a low, flowing white beard—it was the visage of a prophet. Even in death the Phantarch retained his dignity and something of the reverence his presence must have inspired.

He had been dead some time, but the corpse showed little sign of decay or putrefaction. He seemed to be asleep—as if I might touch his cheek and he would awaken once more. But the flesh was woody and cold when I stooped to touch it. I withdrew my hand as if I had touched hot iron. Until that very moment, until I brushed that cold and waxen skin, I believe I had imagined that the Phantarch would yet live somehow. But I knew now that Tegid was right.

As for Tegid, he did not utter a sound—either of rebuke or scorn. He merely gazed at the broken body before him with mournful eyes. When he had looked his last upon the corpse, he turned and walked to the tunnel, taking the torch with him.

As the torchlight disappeared, I was overcome by a despair so black and hopeless that I fell to my knees before the grave mound. I felt stupid and cheated and abused. If only I had been quicker, I thought, and smarter. My cheeks burned with shame and anger at my sloth and stupidity. But no. The Phantarch was murdered long before I thought to look for him, before Nudd destroyed Sycharth. The night of the Cythrawl was the night the Phantarch died.

So we were doomed from the beginning; before we had even set foot on the trail to Findargad our destruction was sealed. Tegid was right—there was nothing for us here, and I was a fool. I could have screamed with the unfairness of it. We had never had a chance.

I wanted to kill Lord Nudd and the demon Coranyid, to crush them beneath my fury. I wanted to destroy them, to rid the land of their vile presence. I wanted to smash them into the filth and ooze from which they arose. I reached out, seized a crystalline stone in both hands, and lifted it above my head. With a mighty groan, I heaved the stone, smashing it down with all my might as I would have if the Dread Lord's face had been before me at that moment.

I threw it so hard that the jagged rock shattered. Sparks flew from the fractured stone, and all at once the entire chamber exploded with a dazzling light. In that splintered instant, I heard the most incredible sound.

It had a musical quality—like that of a tuned harp struck by the bard's skillful hand. As if an unseen hand had plucked a triumphant chord, the last strain of a joyous song that swelled the heart to hear it. The wondrous sound filled the chamber, rising and swirling and penetrating every crack and fissure, every crevice and corner of the underground caverns, reverberating in the very rocks themselves. The crystals in the walls of the chamber began to glow with a rich and steady light, as if kindled from the sparks of that fractured rock.

And all at once, with the sound of that struck chord filling my ears and the light dazzling my eyes, my mind was engulfed by a sudden flood of bright images. I saw as one drunk on golden mead—through a dizzy, dimly comprehending haze—a magnificent array of images, a sparkling vision of a fantastically rich and wonderful world: a world infinitely alive and full of beauty and grace; a blessed world clothed in green and blue—the matchless greens of grass and trees, hillsides and forests without compare; the radiant blues of fair skies and moving water; a world made for humankind and adorned with every good thing for food and comfort; a world made luminous with peace, wherein every virtue is proclaimed and extolled by the very substance of which it is made—from the smallest leaf to the largest mountain, all things declaring a great and powerful benison of glory, goodness, and right.

My vision became keen and fantastic. I saw shimmering rainbows around each particular I chanced upon: whether tree or mountain, bird or beast. I saw all things clean, clear, and sharp as new spearpoints, burning with the brightness of the sun and arrayed in that dancing rainbowed light. My hearing became acute: I heard the shriek of the hunting eagle as it circled in the airy heights above Ynys Sci; I heard the rustle of a wild sow's feet in dry leaves as she tramped the wooded trackway of Ynys Oer; I heard the low thrumming of the blue whale as it churned the shadowed water trail of the wave-tossed deep.

Above and through all this I heard music—such music! I heard the wild skirl of pipes and the charming enchantment of harpsong: ten thousand pipes, a thousand thousand harps! I heard the voices of maidens blending in sweet, willowy harmonies, too fair and beautiful to bear without heartache. I heard the clarion call of the carynx and the sharp blast of the hunting horn. I heard the rhythmic beat of the drum, the booming bodhran, urgent, compelling. I heard all that passed in this worlds-realm—but high and lifted up, magnified into an exaltation of infinite strains and interwoven strands, ever changing, ever new, ever fresh as its first beginning, preserved in innocence forever.

I realized, even as the wealth of this extraordinary display washed over me, that I was seeing Albion itself, but higher, nobler, and purer than the Albion I knew. It was Albion perfected in unutterable purity, immaculate, without fault or blemish. It was the rarest essence of Albion, distilled like a priceless elixir into a single, shimmering atom of excellence unequaled.

Heady and rich, this marvelous revelation made me swoon. It made me giddy with delight. I opened my mouth to laugh, and my mouth was instantly filled with a surpassing sweetness—not cloying like honey, but delicate and clean—as rare and fine a taste as anything I have ever known. I licked my lips and tasted the sweetness on them. It was in the air itself; it was everywhere.

Sight, sound, and taste combined to unmake me, and I laughed out loud. I laughed until my laughter dissolved into tears, and I do not know which gave the greater release. I felt as if I was caught up into an ecstasy of light and music. I was one with the sound that swirled endlessly around me. I was as a solitary drop merging with the vast ocean of the miraculous sound. Like a fleck of foam swept away by the tiderush, I was borne along by the tremendous, all-sustaining power of the music. It flowed all around me and through me; I merged with it, melded with it, became one with it—as the sound of the flute becomes one with the breath that fills it. I became the sound. I was the sound.

Then, as suddenly as it had begun, the glorious sound ended.

I drifted for an instant, as if falling, then snapped back to myself with a jolt. I heard the echo of the harp-sound fading away as the glowing light of the chamber dimmed. And I understood that all I had seen and heard and felt had taken place in the briefest of instants, the fraction of a heartbeat—the small space of time occupied by the snap of a breaking rock. And yet, in that fleeting moment while it endured, the sound was timeless and whole and eternal. I understood then the meaning of the brilliant vision contained in the ineffable music I had heard.

I had heard the Song of Albion. Not the whole song, not even the smallest fragment of the song; a sliver of a single note only, that is what I had heard. And that tiny fragment had filled me with strength and wisdom and power behind my imagining. I had been touched by the Song, and though it was but the slightest touch possible, I knew myself changed; deeply and profoundly changed.

I knew not how deeply or profoundly I had been changed, nor in what manner the change had been wrought—until Tegid returned with the torch. "What was that?" he asked, stumbling into the chamber. "What happened?"

"Did you hear it?" I turned my face toward him.

He almost dropped the torch in surprise. He fell back and thrust a hand before him in fear.

"What is it, brother?" I asked, rising to stand before him.

But Tegid did not answer. He continued to stare as if he had never seen me before.

"What do you see, Tegid?" I asked, and when he did not answer, I became annoyed. "Stop staring, and answer me!"

He stepped nearer then, but warily, his face half-turned away, as if he feared I might strike him down. The torch wavered in his hand; so that he would not drop it, I took it from him. Tegid cringed and released the torch. "Please, lord!" he cried. "I cannot bear it!"

"Bear it? What are you talking about? Tegid, what is wrong with you?" I made to move toward him.

He shrank away, burying his head in his arms. I stopped. "Why do you behave so? Tegid! Answer me!" I demanded, my voice rising. My shout filled the crystal chamber and rolled through the subterranean halls with a sound like a peal of thunder.

Tegid dropped as one stricken. I stepped toward him, and it seemed that I observed his huddled body from a great height. I began to shake; my limbs trembled and I was seized with a violent shuddering—every muscle and inward organ shivering, twitching uncontrollably. "Tegid!" I screamed. "What is happening to me?"

I fell writhing upon the ground, grinding my teeth and drooling out of the corners of my mouth. Strange words—words which I did not know—bubbled from my throat and touched my tongue with fire. At each utterance, I felt my body melting away. I was a spirit shedding its confining bonds, loosing its gross fetters, expanding, rising within my body as if passing through layers of denser atmosphere, soaring up into higher regions of clarity and light until I was a spirit only, free to fly the peculiar prison of the clumsy and cumbersome earthen vessel that contained it. I was a spirit and I flew—high, high, as high as the highest headlands above the surging sea, as high as the peaks of Cethness, as high as the golden eagle above Ynys Sci . . .

And then I plunged into the soft, dark heart of an all-sustaining silence. And this was to me a blessing more wonderful than the glorious music and light of my previous revelation. For I heard within the silence the enduring stability of creation's solid foundation: eternal and unchanging, unyielding and unassailable, inexhaustible in its wealth of abundance, complete and absolute, upholding all that was or would ever be.

I sank into the blessed silence and let it cover me with its patient, enduring tenderness. I gave myself up to it, and it received me as the great wide ocean receives the grain of sand which falls through its fathomless depths. And I was established within the motionless center around which the dance of life revolves; I became one with the perfect peace which is the wellspring of all existence. I drank deep of the all-enduring solace of the silence I had penetrated and which now pervaded me. I drank, and felt myself gathered in an eternal, infinite embrace—gathered and held by loving arms—like a lost child in the soothing, healing embrace of its mother.

∾ ∾ ∾

I woke, if waking it was, in darkness black as pitch. I had dropped the torch and it had gone out. I lay on the floor on my side, knees drawn up, head tucked to my chest. I raised myself up slowly. At my movement, Tegid called out, "Where are you, lord?"

"I am here, Tegid," I answered. My face hurt, and my head and limbs. I had thrashed around so much I was bruised in a hundred places; I ached all over.

I heard a rustle of clothing in the darkness and then felt Tegid's fumbling hand brush my shoulder as he reached for me. "Are you hurt?" he asked.

"I do not think so," I said, wagging my sore jaw back and forth. "Nothing is broken. I think I can stand."

"I have found the torch, but it is burned out. I cannot light it again," the bard answered and added in quiet despair, "I do not know how we shall find another."

I climbed gingerly to my feet and stood swaying for a moment. Strength returned . . . and sight. I do not know how it was, but I could see. What had been darkness total and absolute was now merely dim—like the interior of one of Meldryn Mawr's storehouses. I could see in the dark. I could see!

However, this did not strike me as anything more than merely remarkable at that moment. Perhaps it was an after effect of the light that had dazzled me. I was grateful for the benefit of sight, but not overcome with amazement. It seemed strangely appropriate that I should be able to see, that my eyes should penetrate the darkness so easily.

"All is well, brother," I said. "There is nothing to fear." Then I told him that I could see well enough to find the way back.

I turned to the heap of stone on which lay the corpse of the Phantarch. He was dead, but the song—the Song of Albion—had not died with him. The wise Phantarch had seen to that. I suppose the murderers, hardly daring to rouse one so powerful, had simply heaped stones upon his inert body, slowly crushing the life from the sleeping Phantarch. But not before the canny bard found a way to save his precious treasure.

With strong enchantments the helpless Phantarch must have bound the Song to the stones that covered and killed him. The Song was not lost. The stones at my feet vibrated with it.

I walked quickly to the far side of the chamber and began inspecting the wall. About halfway round the circumference I discovered what I had not been able to see by torchlight: a low passageway, the entrance of which was littered with stone chippings and broken rock. It came to me that perhaps the Phantarch's murderers had not come to the crystal chamber the way Tegid and I had come. It looked as if they had broken into the chamber from the outside, and then used the loose stone from their tunneling to heap upon the Phantarch and kill him where he lay.

"Tegid," I said, dashing back to the gravemound, stripping off my cloak as I came. "Quickly now, take off your cloak and spread it on the floor."

"Why?" he asked, staring blankly in the direction of my voice.

"I will explain while we work, but just do exactly as I say, and do it quickly. We must hurry, and pray to the Goodly-Wise that we are not already too late."

35

SİΠGİΠG STOΠES

I do not know how long we were in Domhain Dorcha, the place beyond the Heart of the Heart, deep inside the mountain. We made our way to the fortress above as quickly as we could, but the going was torturously labored and slow. Our burdens were heavy, and our way twisted and steep. We followed the path the murderers had used, and each of us carried on our backs a bundle of stones from the Phantarch's gravemound.

A few dozen paces outside the Phantarch's chamber, the tunnel opened onto a natural cavern which had been cut in the softer rock by a swift-running underground river. The river sped by, tumbling recklessly down and down into the depths of the earth, its cascade booming loud in our ears. While the river rushed to its secret destination below, we struggled upward, step by weary step, our cloaks slung on our backs, straining under the weight of the stones we carried.

It was more difficult for Tegid. At least I could see well enough in the darkness to find our way, but he had to trust my directions. He followed blind, holding to the tail of my siarc, placing his feet in my footsteps. Still, we stumbled and fell, bruising already sore muscles, rising each time slower than the last. We struggled, we grappled for every handhold, hauling ourselves and our heavy packs up and ever upward—up from out of the heart of the mountain, as if from out of the pain and darkness of the very Pit of Uffern.

Our hands, gripping the knotted hanks of our cloaks, chafed and bled from the unrelenting abrasion. The rocks battered our shins, elbows, and ribs; the sharp-edged stones in our crude packs pummeled our backs and gouged our shoulders. Our feet slipped constantly on the water-slick rock; our toes were battered, our knees scuffed raw.

"Please," I groaned with every weary aching step, "please, let us reach the end."

But the end did not come—only more shadowed passages and dim tunnels filled with the sense-numbing roar of rushing water, and countless stumbling stones to be dodged, clambered over, squeezed under. Each twist and turn in the cavern corridor brought disappointment; every hump and slab of stone brought pain.

Tegid, bless him, never once cried out in his anguish nor questioned my lead. He bore his pain without a sound; he suffered in silence. He trusted me completely, and I loved him for it. I had heard the Song—or part of it—and I knew what it was we carried with us, but Tegid did not.

Once, when he stopped to rest, I asked him if he had heard the sound I had heard in the Phantarch's chamber. He said he had heard me call his name. I did not remember calling out his name, although I might have. "But you do believe that I heard something?"

"I know that you heard something, lord," he answered. His conviction was unyielding as the rock beneath our feet. I asked him how he knew, but he declined to answer. Besides, talking used up too much energy, and it was difficult shouting over the noise of the crashing water. So we lay in the darkness, weak and exhausted, wondering how much further we still had to go.

When the time came to trudge on, I jostled Tegid gently and we hauled ourselves upright, sore-footed and weak-legged, hoisting the heavy bundles upon our injured backs. Then, slow step by aching slow step, we continued on our way.

It seemed ages, eons since we had left the Phantarch's chamber. It seemed to me as if we had walked in this dim underworld forever—lost spirits, wandering shades, neither completely dead nor fully alive, made to journey between the worlds, bearing the weight of our transgressions on our battered backs until the end of time.

After two more brief rest stops, I noticed the passage we were traversing began to rise under my feet, becoming gradually more steep. Shortly after this—or perhaps days later, I cannot say—we came to a divide. On the right-hand side, the river side, the water frothed from a nearly vertical shaft; the left-hand passage was dry, and this appealed to me. We turned aside from the river and its roaring water, and entered the left passageway.

We had not gone far when I noticed that the walls had begun to narrow, and the cavern ceiling over our heads had begun to lower. Soon I could touch either wall with outstretched hands, and I had to duck my head to keep from bumping it on the rock roof above me.

We were being squeezed into an ever more narrow constriction. The further we went, the closer grew the walls and the more cramped the passage between them. Had I made a mistake in leading us this way? Perhaps I had taken the wrong passage, or had missed the way far earlier on. Perhaps we were simply wandering, lost, through endless underground caverns, aimlessly navigating passages with neither beginning nor end.

Doubts swarmed my mind like hornets shaken from a rotten log. Fool! I cursed myself inwardly. *What are you doing? Where are you going? What makes you think you can do anything? You are doomed! You are lost. Fool, for thinking you are a match for Lord Nudd and the Coranyid! Give up, little man!*

I stopped and stood wondering: should we turn back, or go on? Turning back seemed the wisest thing to do. We could always return here if the other passage proved to be wrong. No one could have come this way. Yet . . . and yet . . .

I could not decide. And I could not bring myself to take another step one way or the other until I was certain. Brute stubbornness would not let me turn back; indecision would not let me proceed. So I stood rooted with uncertainty, and the hesitation was more painful to me than all the wounds I had endured so far. I simply could not bring myself to take another step until I knew beyond all doubt that we were on the right path. But knowing was impossible.

We might have been standing there yet if Tegid had not roused himself and said, "I see light ahead."

I looked and saw that it was so. While I had stood frozen in doubt, the tunnel ahead had lightened somewhat. Tegid's light-deprived eyes had noticed it first. But, even as I watched, the passageway lightened some more. The thin, spidery light was definitely growing brighter.

It was dawn in the outside world. We had traveled underground through the night, and now the passage ahead was becoming brighter because the sky outside was growing light. Had we turned back, we would have missed it, and we might never have found our way again.

It came to me then that my attack of doubt was a trick of Lord Nudd, a subtle attempt at turning us aside. But we had not succumbed to his ruse. We now knew the way before us was the true path and, what is more, that we were very near the end. In all events, we were very near the end of our strength.

"Courage," I said, more to myself than to Tegid, "it is just a little further."

That little, however, turned out to be the most difficult by far. The already narrow passageway was made more so by chunks of rock and boulder-sized slabs protruding from the walls. We were made to go on our stomachs and worm our way under the jutting obstructions; or, faces pressed to the cold rock slab, clamber laboriously over, dragging our burdens.

We struggled slowly ahead, keeping our eyes fixed upon the dim light filtering fitfully down the shaft. The grayed glow neither brightened nor did it fade, but shone steadily, if faintly, from somewhere ahead. On battered knees and bleeding elbows, we advanced. Dogged, determined, but never drawing nearer our destination.

The buskins on our feet had long since become soggy scraps of leather; our clothing hung on us in shreds; our faces were bathed in a grimy mist of sweat and blood. And, when my muscles no longer obeyed, when my blistered feet refused to shuffle another step further, when the very bones beneath my flesh cried out for breaking, we came to the end.

The passageway terminated in a blank wall. The light we had seen issued from a vertical shaft. Snowflakes sifted down from above, and we could hear the wind's shivering shriek as it tore itself against the rocks of the entrance somewhere high above. To look at the climb we must make was to despair. And we were not the only ones whom despair had caught in that desperate place. For, as we lay down our bundles of stones and stood for a moment blinking in the light, Tegid motioned to a heap of cloth partially covered in drifted snow.

"Murder has overtaken one of her own," he said, prodding the heap with his toe. "This one is long dead."

I joined him as he stooped and rolled the cloak-wrapped body into the light. Tegid pulled away the stiffened cloth to reveal that the gray, frozen features, eyes wide and staring, mouth open in an expression of disbelief, belonged to Ruadh, the prince's bard. I had seen him only once or twice but recognized him nonetheless.

"Did he fall?" I wondered, looking up into the shaft above.

"I think not," Tegid said, lifting the cloak. A brown-black stain, now hardened, spread across the former bard's chest. "Whoever was with him let him lead the way out and then killed him here to seal the secret."

We knew now who had killed the Phantarch, and we knew also that Ruadh had not acted alone. "How did they know about this passage?" I wondered.

"That we will learn when we discover who was with Ruadh." He rose and turned his face to the opening above. "Come, we can do nothing more here and we are needed elsewhere."

Stepping beneath the opening, I cupped my hands and boosted Tegid into the shaft. He climbed, bracing his back against one side of the shaft and his feet against the other, then hunching himself upward until he disappeared into the white haze of light above.

And then . . . after an eternity, I heard him call to me from somewhere above. I roused myself and stood. The end of a rope dropped before my face, and Tegid, his voice faintly echoing, shouted, "Tie one of the bundles to the rope. I will haul it up."

I watched as the first bundle swung slowly up. After the longest time, Tegid shouted again and dropped the rope for my second bundle. When that had cleared, it was my turn to climb. Using a loop in the rope, I boosted myself into the crevice. Then I followed Tegid's example and hunched my way up the vertical shaft. Tegid stood waiting to haul me out of the pit, whereupon we both collapsed and lay panting in the deep-drifted snow at the sheltered entrance to the cavern. It was cold, and the wind sliced at our skin. But, after the noxious darkness and fetid underground air, the crisp cold felt like a blessing. It revived us and quickened us to our purpose.

We had emerged from a dry well which had at one time served the kitchens behind the hall. We could not see the gate and eastern rampart from our position, but we lay for a moment listening—above the wail of the restless wind we heard the hideous cries of the Coranyid and knew that they were still swarming outside the walls. We had returned in time.

I looked at the tattered bundles we had, at enormous sacrifice of toil and strength, raised from the Phantarch's tomb. In the cold, dim light of a dark Sollen day those two lumpy bundles of stones seemed pitifully small, an impotent weapon to raise against such a fierce and relentless foe.

Tegid watched me for a moment, shivering. Then, placing a heavy hand on my shoulder, he pushed himself up onto his knees and struggled to his feet. "Come, it is cold out here, and I am beginning to miss my cloak."

I stood on stiff legs and forced stiff hands to grasp the knotted end of my bundle. "Very well," I said, swinging the burden once more onto my back, "let us do what we have come to do."

It was all I could do to remain upright, and almost more than I could do to force my wooden stumps to totter forward. I did not think about the cold, or how wretched and exhausted I was, nor what I would do if my ridiculous plan failed. Inside the hall, the hearthfire burned bright. I held this image in my mind and drove myself toward it. The sooner I delivered myself of my burden, the sooner I could sit before Meldryn Mawr's fire and rest . . . blessed rest. In the end, that was all I cared about; the thought of a warm cup in my hand and dry clothing on my weary limbs, and rest, kept my battered carcass moving.

Step by plodding, weary step we crossed the yard and reached the wall. The warriors on the rampart gaped at us strangely. They gazed down upon us with expressions of awe and bewilderment. No one said a word.

I thought it odd and called them to help us lift our bundles to the rampart, but no one moved. "What is wrong with them?" I asked Tegid angrily. "Why do they stand staring like that? Can they not hear?"

"They heard you," replied Tegid oddly.

"Well, are they frozen up there then?"

"No." He shook his head slightly. "Neither are they frozen."

"What then? Why do they not help us?"

He did not answer. Instead, he shifted the burden on his back and indicated the icy step. "Will you go first, or shall I?" he asked.

Up the icy steps we trudged. A condemned man ascending to the gallows could not know a steeper or more labored climb. Fatigue and lethargy seemed to descend upon my weary limbs like loops of iron chain. My legs trembled to support me. My heart labored in my chest; my breath burned my throat. I wanted nothing more than to release the bundle I bore on my back—how stupid to be carrying rocks! Certainly, a moment's rest would do no harm.

Rest . . . rest and sleep . . .

No. There could be no rest, no sleep, until the work I had come to do was finished. One step at a time, and each step seemed to take a lifetime. Shivering with cold and exhaustion, I placed my foot on the next step and heaved myself up. Oh, but I *was* tired. So tired . . .

I glanced toward the rampart and saw the warriors still frozen in attitudes of amazement. Why did they not help me? Why did they stand looking on like that? Would no one lift a hand to help me?

Black mist gathered before my eyes, stealing the faces from me. I closed my eyes and raised my foot to the next step and missed the edge. I toppled forward and struck the step with my knee. The bundle on my back slipped sideways, almost pulling my arm from its socket. Every nerve and sinew screamed for me to release the knot I gripped so tightly, to let it go, let it fall. It was not worth my life, after all. My stiff hands would not obey, however; dead cold, they held numbly on.

The pain brought tears, which the wind froze, stinging my cheeks where they dried.

And although my knees throbbed, at least the pain drove away the black mist clouding my senses. I could see clearly again. Lifting my bundle of stones onto my back once more, I raised myself up and took the next step, and the next.

And then I was standing on the rampart, standing clutching my precious bundle, surrounded by astonished warriors—astonished by my monumental idiocy, apparently—swaying as the wicked wind raked my ragged clothes, slicing at my flesh.

I lurched to the breast of the wall and lowered my burden. Tegid stumbled to a place beside me, and we looked out over the wall to the swarming mass of Coranyid below. They were more vile and heinous than I remembered: great hulking toad-bodied red monstrosities dwarfing smaller spindle-shanked skeletal subcreatures, whole ranks of scaly reptilian fiends and hosts of naked, squatting, half-human imps with exaggerated genitals and shrunken heads, and more.

I saw the squirming, bloated, misshapen, mangled bodies and mocking, leering faces, and I burned with anger at their profane glee. I fell upon the bundle at my feet and began tearing at the knot, suddenly afraid that I had come too late, that no power on earth could halt the advance of evil that had been unleashed against us.

My hands clawed at the knot. It was twisted tight and frozen with the sweat from my hands and would not give. I whirled in desperation and snatched the spear from the hands of the nearest dumbstruck warrior. I slashed at the cloak with the spear, tearing at the cloth. The rocks spilled out onto the snow, dull and colorless in the foul light. Their drab appearance mocked me. Surely, I was mistaken. Suddenly my plan seemed absurd and pathetic. It could not but fail.

I raised my eyes and found Tegid watching me. He mistook my hesitation for deliberation and said, "Here, brother, allow me." He reached out and selected one of the larger chunks of rock from the pile. "Begin with this one." His confidence was not abated by the ordeal we had endured. If anything, his trust was the greater.

I took the stone between his hands, straightened, and turned to the breastwork of the wall. The wind gusted sharp, as if to tear the stone from my hands. The Coranyid surged like a wind-lashed sea around the base of the fortress, screaming, wailing, grasping with their awful hands. Revulsion and disgust swept through me. In one swift motion I raised the stone and sent it tumbling from the walltop onto the hateful heads of the Demon Host below.

I saw it spin as it fell. The demons scattered, and the stone struck the rocky escarpment below, shattering on impact.

Instantly, the air swelled with the sound—that incomparable sound of the hand-struck harp, that sustaining chord I had heard in the Phantarch's chamber. The extraordinary sound burst from the stone which had contained it, shattering the air with an explosion of vibrant music.

The demon Coranyid scattered. Before they could regroup themselves, Tegid handed me another stone, and I sent that one sailing down after the first. The second stone struck the rocks below and gave forth a ringing, jubilant sound which rose up in shimmering waves, spreading from the point of impact as if to engulf the world.

Tegid had a third stone ready, while the air still reverberated with the strains. I heaved it over the walltop and it struck the ground, splitting into fragments. Each fragment gave forth a shimmering, silvery note of astounding beauty that echoed in the mountain peaks round about.

Those standing with us on the wall heard the sound and were transfixed. From out of the king's hall, kinsmen poured into the yard. They stood in the snow, gazing up at the mountains now reverberating with strange and exquisite music.

I bent down, gathered an armful of stones, and pressed these into the hands of the nearest stupefied warriors. Tegid did the same, and, at my signal, we all threw our enchanted stones down upon the Coranyid. The unleashed sound burst forth in a thunderous peal of chorused exultation.

The demons shrank from the sound, withering before it like flesh before red-hot iron. They squirmed and writhed, howling, shrieking, dancing in their torment, falling over one another in their haste to escape the assault of the singing stones.

The people in the yard heard the marvelous sound and rushed to the wall and climbed to the rampart to see the terrible Coranyid retreating, shrinking away in agony, their hateful presence dissolving like a filthy stain before the cleansing water.

Just as the demon throng seemed on the point of full retreat, a tumult arose among them, and from out of their teeming midst appeared an enormous dark-garbed figure, astride a huge aurochs black as a raven's wing. This chieftain wore a black cloak and carried a black shield; in his right hand he carried a long, curved tusklike sword, black as polished jet—the Wyrm's fang. At his throat he wore a coiled serpent, a living torc with a shiny black skin and yellow eyes burning like live coals. I could not see his face, hidden as it was beneath a war helm of black. But I did not need to see his face to know that this was Nudd, Prince of Uffern and Annwn, dread lord of the Nether Realms, who rode on his strange beast to join battle with us. He had come to stem the rout of his demon war host.

The swart figure of Nudd advanced slowly toward the wall. The Coranyid, halted by the sudden appearance of their lord, scuttled after him, their wails of agony turned to ghastly peals of demented delight. They drew closer in a repulsive, gyrating mass.

Quickly, Tegid and I passed Song-laden stones along the walltop hand to hand—men, women, and even the children—until all who had joined us on the wall possessed a stone.

Nudd raised the Wyrm's fang. The black blade circled in the air. At his command, storm clouds gathered. The wind shrieked to gale force, ripping at the stones in our hands, blasting and buffeting all who stood on the wall. The wind howl drowned out everything else. Snow and ice stung our eyes. Some collapsed under the frigid assault of ice and wind; their places were taken by others. The line remained unbroken.

Nudd advanced. The dread form loomed larger with every step, growing as he neared. I could not see the face hidden beneath the helm, but the dark lord's malice stung me like the prick of a knife. My heart thumped savagely against my ribs.

The enemy was formidable beyond reckoning, powerful beyond imagining. We could not escape his wrath. He would crush us to dust beneath his feet. Already, he was drawing the life from our hands. My fingers were growing numb and slack. I could no longer feel the stone in my hands.

Lord Nudd leveled the black blade, and his eager minions leapt to the attack, tearing at the wall, scaling the vertical heights of the stronghold. I knew that my kinsmen were waiting for me to give the command to throw the stones. They were watching me, waiting for me to lead them. But I could not. Who was I to think I could outwit such a powerful enemy?

I turned away from their expectant faces. I turned away and closed my eyes.

And then I felt the touch of a strong hand on mine. I opened my eyes to meet Meldryn Mawr's clear, confident gaze. I do not know when he had appeared, or from where. Weak with hunger and thirst, gaunt and swaying unsteadily on his feet—yet he was there, standing beside me, steadying my trembling hand. The king did not speak; he would not, but his courage emboldened me, bracing my faltering bravery as his hand strengthened mine.

I turned to see Lord Nudd's head and shoulders cresting the level of the walltop. He was immense in his vast, swelling hatred. In a moment he would overwhelm us. I looked to the king; he inclined his head, allowing me to give the order.

"Now!" I cried. And raising the enchanted stone high above my head, I hurled it into the dark lord's face. With all my might I threw it.

36

THE SONG

All along the wall, stones sailed out into the gale. Spinning, tumbling, careening, smashing, scattering in a thousand sparkling pieces; striking down through the tempest to fall upon the seething enemy masses. And from each splinter and fragment there arose a strain of that matchless melody.

The individual strains twined and melded, swelling full and fair, and striking deep into the ranks of the enemy. Lord Nudd raged to hear it; he raised the black Wyrm's fang, and the wind-wail became a deafening roar. The wind obliterated the wonderful melody, drowning it beneath its horrific scream. Surely we were undone; nothing, not even the Song of Albion could survive the hate-blast of the Lord of Darkness, Death, and Destruction.

The wind swirled, seizing the sound and lifting it high, as if to drive it away. But the sound was not extinguished in the tempest. It rose and intensified, spreading on the wings of the storm, filling the wind-scoured heights with shimmering melody as the gale gave it strength. And suddenly the sound began forming itself into words. The life-giving words of the Song of Albion:

Glory of sun! Star-blaze in jeweled heavens!
   Light of light, a High and Holy land,
   Shining bright and blessed of the Many-Gifted;
   A gift forever to the Race of Albion!
Rich with many waters! Blue-welled the deep,
   White-waved the strand, hallowed the firmament,
   Mighty in the power of One,
   Gentle in the peace of great blessing;
   A wealth of wonders for the Kinsmen of Albion!
Dazzling the matchless purity of green!
   Fine as the emerald's excellent fire,
   Glowing in deep-clefted glens,
   Gleaming on smooth-tilled fields;
   A Gemstone of great value for the Sons of Albion!

The Coranyid could not stand against the power of the Song. The sound struck them and they fell, choking, retching, gagging, and gasping for breath. As the Song coiled around them, the demon war band began to melt away, seeping back into the ground, dissolving like mud before the driving rain. The hateful hell spawn sank down foot, knee, and thigh, liquefying, dissipating, dwindling, retreating into the cracks opening in the earth to receive them. The hard brilliance of the Song drove them down, raining its glad refrain upon them like a fall of bright-barbed arrows. They fled before it, hastening back to the dismal galleries of their underworld home.

   Abounding in white-crowned peaks, vast beyond measure,
     The fastness of bold mountains!
     Exalted heights—dark wooded and
     Red with running deer—
     Proclaim afar the high-vaunted splendor of Albion!

Swift horses in wide meadows! Graceful herds
on the gold-flowered water-meads,
Strong hooves drumming,
a thunder of praise to the Goodly-Wise,
A boon of joy in the heart of Albion!

Higher and higher, the Song rose in sweeping arcs into the clouds, piercing the hard Sollen sky. Sunlight bright and dazzling shone forth, scouring the hidden places where the shadows had grown thick, banishing the darkness. Fair golden light touched the Host of the Pit, and they screamed in pain as they ran—hopping like lizards, scrabbling like beetles, slithering like vipers—fleeing for the refuge of their dank, noisome dens.

Meanwhile, the soaring Song echoed in the air. All Albion trembled with the sound, echoing the Song from mountaintop to mountaintop, filling the glens and valleys. Like the waters of a mighty flood bursting through the seawall and inundating the land; like fountains of sweet golden mead bursting forth from a bottomless vat; like a shining river charged from infinite springs, swelling, spreading, overflowing its banks, cascading over the land, sweeping all before it in a deluge, in torrents of sparkling water. And we cupped our hands and drank as much as we could contain, but the waters—the Song—rushed on undiminished.

We caught but the smallest fragment of the whole, yet that little was life to us. The life-giving words burned themselves into our hearts and into our souls. We wept with joy to hear them.

Golden the grain-hoards of the Great Giver,
Generous the bounty of fair fields:
Redgold of bright apples,
Sweetness of shining honeycomb,
A miracle of plenty for the tribes of Albion!

Silver the net-tribute, teeming the treasure
of happy waters; Dappled brown the hillsides,
Sleek herds serving
the Lord of the Feast;
A marvel of abundance for the tables of Albion!

Nudd, standing alone amidst the floodtide of his retreating forces, raised his spear and uttered a great shout of defiance. But the Song, ringing all around him, drowned out his shout. Instead of the hateful voice of Nudd, we heard the Song.

Wise men, Bards of Truth, boldly declaring from
Hearts aflame with the Living Word;
Keen of knowledge,
Clear of vision,
A glory of verity for the True Men of Albion!
Bright-kindled from heavenly flames, framed
of Love's all-consuming fire,
Ignited of purest passion,
Burning in the Creator King's heart,
A splendor of bliss to illuminate Albion!

The Foul Lord could no longer stand against the exalted majesty of the Song. Deserted by his legion of the damned, weakened by the Song's magnificent and merciless onslaught, the Prince of the Pit, Lord of Corruption, Nudd shrank into himself. He bellowed his frustrated rage to the mountaintops, but the Song covered all, permeated all, saturated all.

Noble lords kneeling in rightwise worship,
Undying vows pledged to everlasting,

Embrace the breast of mercy,
Eternal homage to the Chief of chiefs;
Life beyond death granted the Children of Albion!
Kingship wrought of Infinite Virtue,
Quick-forged by the Swift Sure Hand;
Bold in Righteousness,
Valiant in Justice,
A sword of honor to defend the Clans of Albion!
Formed of the Nine Sacred Elements,
Framed by the Lord of Love and Light;
Grace of Grace, Truth of Truth,
Summoned in the Day of Strife,
An Aird Righ to reign forever in Albion!

Defeated, Lord Nudd followed his demon Coranyid down into the netherworld depths. We watched as his black form grew pale and wispy, dispersing like a dirty mist before the blazing radiance of the sun. The wicked enemy simply disappeared before our eyes, fading back into the abyss from which he had been released. Nudd himself was the last to go, and he took the Cauldron of Rebirth with him. For, when he had gone, it was nowhere to be seen.

I looked out on the rocky plateau below: not a single enemy remained. All had vanished. Sunlight shone golden all around us; blue sky, dazzling and radiant, glowed through the gaping rents in the broken clouds. The siege was ended and the battle was over. We were saved.

We stood gazing at one another, and for a moment the world quivered with the afterecho as the Song of Albion sped on and on. And then the stillness was shattered by a tremendous shout. I whirled toward the sound, to see Tegid leap onto the wall to dance there, arms upraised, his cloak flying around him. An instant later, everyone was crying and shouting—tears of gladness, shouts of joy. Others leapt onto the battlements and joined in the dance. Such delight could not be contained and the whole caer rang with the happy sound.

Above the ecstatic tumult, I heard Tegid's voice, strong and clear, lifted in song. And the song he was singing was the Song of Albion. The words poured forth from his heart, igniting the hearts around him like sparks from a kindling torch. And soon the Song was echoing from the mountaintops round about.

"Listen!" I cried, turning to the king beside me. "The Song of Albion is restored!"

But the king did not answer. His head was bent and his eyes were closed; tears ran down his cheeks, and his shoulders heaved with the sobs breaking soundlessly from his throat. Amidst the great jubilation of victory, King Meldryn Mawr stood and wept.

37

THE KING'S CHAMPION

The gates of Findargad were thrown open wide, and everyone—men and warriors, women and children, dancing in their joy and rapture—streamed out to prove beyond all doubt that Lord Nudd and the Demon Host of the Coranyid were gone. The enemy had indeed been driven back into the nether realms of the underworld, leaving only the filthy snow behind—and that was rapidly melting under the bright-kindled sun. Gone, too, was the oppressive stink and stench, banished by Gyd's fresh winds. The Llwyddi rushed here and there beneath the wall, and the scattered fragments of the song-laden stones were gathered by hundreds of eager, happy hands.

Tegid continued to dance along the walltop to where I was standing with the king. "The enemy is defeated! Your kingdom is free of their defilement. Will you put aside your geas and speak to your people now, Great King?" he asked.

But the king raised his tearstained face and beckoned his bard close. Tegid inclined his ear to the king's mouth, whereupon the bard raised his hands and called out to all gathered on the wall below it. "People of Prydain!" he cried. "Hear the words of your king: This day is our enemy defeated. This night we will celebrate the victory in the king's hall. Three days we will feast and take our rest; but on the fourth day, we will leave this place and return to our homes in the lowlands."

Then the king left the wall and returned to his chambers. I watched as he walked alone across the yard. Prince Meldron and Paladyr approached him as he neared the entrance to the hall. The king stopped and turned stiffly to meet them. The three stood together for a moment. I could not hear what was said, but I saw Prince Meldron make a quick, violent gesture toward the open gate. The king stared at his son for a moment, then turned away without reply and proceeded to the hall. The prince and Paladyr then hastened away; they passed from my sight beneath the wall, and I did not see them anymore.

The preparations for the feast continued all through the day. The sun remained bright and the clouds disappeared, and we began to believe that Gyd, the fairest of seasons, had at last returned to Prydain. After bleak Sollen's endless reign, we had feared the world would never more enjoy the bounty of the sun. Accordingly, we reveled in the warmth as we went about our chores.

I searched for Simon—Siawn Hy—both inside and outside the wall, but could not find him in the general bustle to make ready the celebration. All too soon the sunlight faded to dusk, and the chill of night returned. It was with great reluctance that we kindled the torches in Findargad's hall at dusk, even though it meant that the feast could begin. As I stood in the throng outside the hall, waiting to enter, I thought I saw Siawn standing among the warriors of the prince's Wolf Pack. But by the time I had worked my way over to the place, they had gone inside and I lost him again.

Sweet mead shone rich and golden in the countless cups that circled the king's hall. The hearthfire leapt high and the torches and rushlights burned bright, and we drank to victory and the vanquishing of foes in the shimmering firelight. Everyone—warriors and men, maidens and wives, children and babes—everyone joined in the celebration. We ate and drank and sang. How we sang! The night was transformed into a beautiful praise song, a glittering gem of gladness and thanksgiving to the Swift Sure Hand for our deliverance.

And when we had eaten and drunk enough to make us merry, and sung the songs of liberation, Tegid called for the king's throne to be brought into the hall. A number of warriors hastened to the king's chamber, took up the throne, and carried it on their shoulders into the hall. Whereupon the king, looking more like the Meldryn Mawr I had first encountered—all glittering and golden in his finery—with little evidence of his recent illness, took his place at the head of his hall and, with wide sweeps of his arms, motioned for all the people to gather and draw near.

Because of his vow, the king did not speak outright but directed the gathering through the voice of his bard. Tegid relayed the king's words, saying, "Tonight, while the light of life burns in us, it is right to sing and dance our delight in the victory we have been granted. But let us pause to remember our kinsmen who lost their lives to Nudd."

At this, Tegid began to sing a lament for the dead. It was a well-known lament, and he was not more than a few words into the song when everyone in the hall joined in. I did not know the song, but it was as beautiful as it was sorrowful, and heartbreakingly sad. I could not have sung; just to hear it, my eyes filled with tears and my throat swelled so that I could hardly breathe.

Others wept, too, their eyes shining with tears in the torchlight as they sang. When the song was finished, silence filled the hall. The last notes lingered long in the empty places. After a time, the king leaned again to his Chief of Songs, and Tegid said, "We have remembered the honorable dead as it is right to do. Now let us pay homage to the living who have earned the hero's portion with their feats of courage and valor."

To my amazement, the first name called was my own. "Llyd, come to the throne."

A way opened before me through the crowd, and I stepped forward hesitantly. I was aware, once again, of the stares my appearance provoked and the hushed exclamations of astonishment. But why? Had I changed so much? The king beckoned me to stand before him; whereupon he removed a gold ring from his finger and held it out to me. I reached out to take it, and he grasped me by the wrist and turned me to face the crowd.

"You, above all men, are to be honored this night," Tegid said, speaking loudly so that he could be heard by all. "At great danger and sacrifice, you brought the enchanted stones from their hiding place and conceived the plan by which they might be used to defeat our enemy. Without the stones we could never have prevailed against Nudd and his demon brood of Coranyid. Therefore, receive the gratitude of your king."

The Great King stood and, still holding my wrist, raised my hand high before the close-gathered throng. Taking the ring, he slipped it onto my finger. I saw torchlight glinting in a thousand watching eyes and heard the undercurrent of amazement buzzing through the hall. Again I felt the eerie and unaccountable sensation that people were awed by my appearance.

I had no time to wonder over this. Tegid lifted his hands, palms outward in declamation, and loudly proclaimed, "Let it be known that your king has set a high value upon your skill and courage. From this night you are champion to the king. In recognition of this honor, henceforth are you named Llew. Let all men greet you thus from this time forth: Hail, Llew, Champion to the King!"

"Llew! Llew!" the people cried in fervent reply. Indeed, they seemed eager to respond. "Hail, Llew! King's Champion!" Their voices filled the hall from hearthstone to rooftree, and I trembled within myself: Llew, the name of Albion's savior, was now my name. What the Banfáith had predicted was coming to pass.

Had I known what Tegid was contemplating, I would have prevented him—and I was not the only one. For, as I took my place at the king's right hand, I chanced to see Paladyr standing aloof, clearly furious at the staggering insult that had been paid him. Nor did I blame him. For Paladyr had been deposed as champion without being given the chance to defend his exalted position; he was disgraced before his kinsmen and swordbrothers. A greater humiliation could not have been contrived for him.

Other gifts were given out—brooches and gemstones and armbands of silver and gold. Other names were lauded, other deeds acclaimed. I saw little of it, and heard less. My mind whirled, desperately trying to discover a way to dissuade Paladyr from challenging me to single combat in an attempt at reclaiming his position. He would move heaven and earth to restore his honor—it was worth his life and more. A warrior without honor suffered shame worse than death. Indeed, I entertained no hope at all that he would ignore the slight: his pride was greater than the king's, and Meldryn Mawr's held all Albion in its sway.

So I stood beside the king—in Paladyr's place—frantically searching for a way to disentangle myself from this grim, and likely fatal, predicament. I looked over the throng in the hall, hoping to catch fresh sight of the king's former champion; but I could not see him. Still, I imagined I could feel his seething wrath—like a bonfire fanned by a gale, burning wild, out of control.

When the last warrior had been summoned and the last gift given, King Meldryn ordered the celebration to continue. The instant I saw my chance, I grabbed Tegid by the arm. "Why have you done this to me?"

"I did nothing," he told me flatly. "It is the king's privilege to choose a new champion and to name him. He has done so. And I find no fault in the choice."

"Paladyr will kill me! He will have my head on his spear. You must speak to the king."

"This is a supreme honor. It is your right; you have earned it."

"I do not want it! Take it back!"

Tegid made a sour face. "I do not understand you, Llew."

"I am *not* Llew" I growled. "I want no part of it! Do you understand?"

"It is too late," he said, glancing away.

"Why?"

"Paladyr—he is coming."

Striding toward us through the slowly dispersing crowd came Paladyr. He wore no expression, but his eyes were alive with anger. I braced myself and turned to meet him. He stopped before me, glowering. Before I could open my mouth to offer a word of conciliation, he placed a hand to my chest and shoved me aside. The people saw this and halted where they stood; no one moved, no one breathed. The hall grew instantly silent.

Paladyr continued to the foot of the king's throne and threw himself down before it. Meldryn Mawr gazed upon the prostrate man impassively. Tegid hurried to the king's side and, after a quick consulation, said, "What do you seek by coming before your king in this way?"

The former champion remained facedown before the throne; not a muscle twitched. The king whispered to Tegid, who nodded and addressed the prostrate warrior. "Rise, Paladyr," the bard said. "If you have something to say, stand on your feet and speak it out."

At this, Paladyr rose to stand before the king. He appeared humble, but not altogether humiliated, as he stretched forth his empty hands to the king. "What wrong do you lay on my head that I should be thrust aside in this way?"

"Do you suggest that your king has treated you unfairly?" Tegid asked.

"I demand to know why I have been cast aside," he replied sullenly.

"It is not your place to demand, Paladyr," the bard observed. "It is your place to obey. Nevertheless, the king is mindful of your loyal service, and for this reason he will answer you."

"Answer, then," Paladyr said, barely containing himself. "But I would hear it from the king's mouth—not yours, bard."

Meldryn Mawr inclined his head toward Tegid, who bent to hear him, then straightened and said, "By reason of the king's geas, this cannot be. But hear the king's word and receive it, if you will. Thus says your king: those who serve me must remain true to me, and to me alone. You, Paladyr, were first in loyalty. So long as your fealty remained true, you were champion to the king. But you put your loyalty aside when you chose to follow Prince Meldron. Therefore, I have put you aside." Tegid paused. "Your king has spoken."

These words seemed to have great effect on the man. Instantly, he appeared humble and contrite. "This rebuke is hard, O King," he said. "But I accept your judgment; only allow me to swear again the oath of fealty and pledge again my loyalty."

King Meldryn nodded slowly, and Paladyr stepped forward, his head low, his arms limp. He sank to his knees before the throne and fell upon the king in a great show of repentance and remorse. He placed his head against the king's chest and cried out in a loud voice, "Forgive me, O King!"

Meldryn Mawr raised his hand and seemed about to speak. But the hand faltered and fell away; the king closed his mouth and bowed his head over his once-esteemed champion. It was a most affecting display, touching all who looked on.

After a moment, Tegid said, "Paladyr, speak again the oath of fealty." And he began to recite the words which the former champion was to say.

But Paladyr did not answer. He did not even wait for Tegid to finish. Instead, he rose to his feet, stood over the king for a moment, and then turned his back on the throne. All eyes watched him as the former champion hastened from the hall.

The chorus of murmured astonishment which followed Paladyr's baffling behavior quickly turned to cries of shock and disbelief when someone shouted, "Murder! The king is slain!"

The words were sharp as knives. Like everyone else, I had been watching Paladyr. At the first cry of murder, I whirled back to see Meldryn Mawr still sitting on his throne, head bowed forward, hands in his lap. He appeared in the same attitude as a moment before. He had not moved.

And then I saw it: Paladyr's knife jutting out of the middle of Meldryn's chest, just below the breastbone. Blood, spreading in a brilliant crimson bloom, seeped slowly from the wound. The king was dead.

For the space of three heartbeats, the hall held its breath in a horrified hush. Then everything happened at once.

Tegid shouted, "Stop him! Seize him!"

The crowd surged toward the throne. Someone screamed.

In the crush, I fought to join Tegid. More screams. Cries of outrage. Panic. The door to the hall slammed shut. The sound echoed like thunder. Warriors shouted confused orders. The air shimmered with the ring of drawn weapons.

Prince Meldron materialized from nowhere, holding up his hands and loudly proclaiming, "Peace! Peace! Do not be afraid! I am here! Your king is here!"

And there was Siawn Hy—standing beside the prince, brandishing an upraised sword, as if he would protect his lord from attack. Attack from whom? I wondered. Fortunately, the sight of Meldron in control had a reassuring effect. The panic and confusion subsided at once.

"Wolf Pack!" Meldron called, and the warriors of his elite war band pushed through the crowd at the foot of the throne. "Ride after Paladyr. Hunt him down and bring him back. But bring him to me alive. Do you hear? He is not to be harmed!"

The warriors, all except Siawn, who stayed by the prince, pledged themselves to the task and hurried away. The prince turned to Tegid, who was bending over the king's body. "He is dead?" the prince said, less a question than a statement of an obvious fact.

The bard straightened; his face, drained of color, appeared ashen and grim, and his voice trembled—but whether with sorrow or anger, or some other emotion, I could not tell. "The knife pierced his heart," Tegid intoned. "The king is dead." To me, he said, "Gather some men. We will move the king to his chamber."

Three warriors joined us, and we carefully raised the body and bore it between us. We carried the king to his chamber and laid him in his sleeping place. Tegid removed his cloak and spread it over the king; he then dismissed the warriors and commanded them to guard the door.

I looked at Tegid standing over the body, chin in hand, deep in thought. I hardly knew what to say or think. It seemed so unreal, so dreamlike. Yet there lay Meldryn Mawr . . . dead. And, as his champion, it was my duty to protect him.

"Tegid—I . . . I am sorry," I stammered, coming to stand beside him.

"Did you know what was in Paladyr's heart?" he asked coldly.

"Well . . . no, I—"

"Could you have prevented it?"

"No. But I—"

"Then you have no cause to reproach yourself." Though his voice was soft, his tone was adamant. "Neither do I reproach you."

"But I was his champion!" I insisted. "I stood by while Paladyr killed him. I did nothing. I—I should have . . . done something. I should have protected him."

The bard stooped to smooth the cloak over the corpse. He straightened abruptly and took hold of my arm. "Hear me now, Llew," he said quietly, but firmly. "The king's life belongs to his people. If one of his own determines to take that life by treachery, no force on earth can prevent it."

Tegid spoke a hard, hard truth. I understood him, but it would be a long time before I could accept it.

"What are we to do now?"

The bard turned once more to the king. "The body must be prepared for burial. Once we have observed the death rites, a new king will be chosen."

"Prince Meldron said—"

"Prince Meldron has overreached himself," Tegid replied coldly. "Meldron must submit to the will of the bards."

In Albion the Derwyddi chose the king, and the kingship did not routinely pass from father to son. Rather, any worthy member of the clan could become king if the bard chose him. They valued the kingship more highly than to hand it down like a used garment. Instead, the king was chosen from among the best men in the clan.

"I see," I told him. "But you are the only bard left among the Llwyddi—the only bard left in Albion, for all we know."

"Then I alone will choose." He offered a bleak smile and added, "I hold the kingship now, brother. I bestow it where I will."

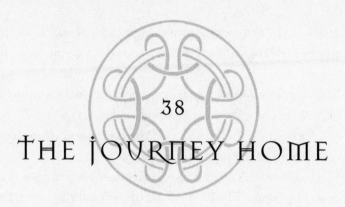

38

THE JOURNEY HOME

The body of the Great King lay in Findargad for three days, as the days of feasting turned instead to mourning. During that time, Tegid prepared the body for its eventual burial and directed preparations for the journey home to Sycharth. The king would not be buried in the mountain fortress, but would be laid to rest in the Vale of Modornn, in the gravemound of the Lwyddi kings. The body was washed and clothed in his finest garments. His sword and spear were burnished bright; his shield was painted fresh, the circular bosses polished so that they shone like suns.

On the fourth day, the corpse was carried from the king's chamber and placed on a wagon piled high with furs. Then, when all who had survived Lord Nudd's onslaught had assembled in the yard, Tegid led the wagon out through the gates, and we began the long journey home. Six warriors walked on either side of the funeral wagon carrying spears. Prince Meldron rode behind the wagon, dour and mournful, and all the rest of the Llwyddi followed after.

Thus we left Findargad. At Tegid's behest, I walked at the head of the horse, opposite him. The first day we did not speak at all. Tegid, eyes fixed on the trail ahead, stumped along lost in thought, his brow creased in a reflective frown. I do not know what occupied him, and he did not say.

In the days that followed, however, he began to share the substance of his ruminations with me. Solemn and somber, his musings formed a bleak assessment of the future he saw stretching before us: the future described in the Banfáith's terrible prophecy.

"The Golden King in his kingdom will strike his foot against the Rock of Contention. The Wyrm of fiery breath will claim the throne of Prydain," he said gloomily. We were standing beside a mountain stream, waiting for the retinue to cross so that we could continue. "Look at them." He indicated the long lines of people splashing through the water. "They are lost and do not know it. There is no one to lead them. A people without a king are worse than sheep without a shepherd."

"They have Prince Meldron," I pointed out. The prince sat his horse in the center of the stream while the people crossed before him. It was as if he were indeed watching over his flock. Siawn, I noticed, stood nearby, leaning on his spear. In the last days he had never been out of the prince's sight, so I had not been able to speak to him alone.

Tegid cast me a sidelong glance, his mouth twisted in a bitter grimace. "Prince Meldron will never sit his father's throne."

I asked him what he meant, but he gave me to know that it was not something he cared to voice aloud at the moment. And he warned me: "Speak of this to no one."

I considered this to be the end of the matter, until a little while later, when we were on the trail once more. "The king will be buried properly." The bard spoke so softly, I thought he was speaking to himself. "I may not be able to prevent what is to come, but at least I will see my king laid in his tomb in a rightwise manner. We are not sunk so low that the ancient rites are to be abandoned."

"Tegid, tell me. What do you think is going to happen?"

He raised his head, gazing into the cloud-wrapped distance. "That you already know," he replied.

"If I knew, I would not ask." I was growing tired of his evasive manner.

"You know," he repeated, and added, almost as a challenge, "*Llew* would know."

Before I could wheedle any more out of him, we were halted by the return of the Wolf Pack. The warriors under Prince Meldron's command had ridden hard and traveled far by the look of them. Their clothing was dirty, and their horses were lathered and muddy. The prince saw them approaching, left his place behind the funeral wagon, and rode ahead to meet them.

"I wonder what they found," I remarked, watching the prince and his warriors conferring a little way ahead of us in the trail.

"Why do you wonder?" Tegid asked tartly. "Are you blind?"

"I suppose I must be," I snapped.

"Open your eyes! Must I describe what is before your very nose?"

"The Wolf Pack has returned," I said in exasperation. "The prince is talking to them."

"Is Paladyr with them?" Tegid asked snidely.

"No—no, he is not."

"Well?"

"Well, they did not find him. Paladyr must have escaped."

"Paladyr escaped." Tegid rolled his eyes. "These men can track a boar through the depths of the darkest wood. They can run a deer until it drops from exhaustion. They can follow an eagle in flight and find its eyrie. How is it, then, that Paladyr has escaped?"

"They let him go? But why would they do that?"

"Why indeed?"

That was all I got out of him before the prince turned his horse and trotted back to his place behind the funeral wagon and the cortege continued on its long, difficult way. I sifted Tegid's insinuations carefully in my mind as we traveled, weighing each word before adding it to the others.

Clearly, he was preoccupied with the Banfáith's prophecy, and he was determined to see it fulfilled through me. That was unsettling enough, but even more alarming was his intimation that Prince Meldron had caused his father's death. Because if Prince Meldron was involved, Simon surely was as well. The two were rarely apart! It was unlikely the prince could plan something so treacherous, and so devastating, without Simon knowing about it. Perhaps Simon had participated . . . perhaps he had done more than that . . .

The thought chilled me to the marrow. What had Simon done?

I pondered this, turning it over in my mind for a long time. But the day was bright and good, and the sun warm where it touched the skin. Despite my apprehension, I was slowly drawn once more to the clear vistas before me. The snow still lay deep on the mountainsides, and the trail was mostly snow-covered. It had begun to melt, however; brown and gray stone poked through the white, and occasionally even some green could be seen.

As if to soothe the Sollen-ravaged land, Gyd was quickly reasserting its gentle claim. The streams and freshets ran with melting snow, and water dripped from every rock. The sky remained clear for the most part, and the sun warm. The nights were chill and the ground wet, but we built fires high and slept on ox skins. A complement of warriors stood watch over the king's corpse, taking it in turn through the night.

On the night I took my turn with the first watch, it chanced that Simon was also in the group. I waited until our replacements came to relieve us, and then went to him. It was the first opportunity I had had to speak to him privately in a very long time.

424

"Siawn," I said, using the name he preferred. I touched him on the arm.

He whirled around, his fists ready, his face hard in the light of a rising moon. His eyes played over my face, but he betrayed no sign of recognition. Neither was he awed by my presence, as so many seemed to be. "Llew," he said, and his lips formed a sneer. "What does the mighty Llew want with me?"

His sneer angered me. "I want to talk to you," I replied. He turned away, but I followed, falling into step with him.

"Simon, what is happening? What are you involved in?"

He swung toward me, angry once more. "I am Siawn Hy!"

"Siawn," I said quickly, "what do you know of Paladyr?"

At mention of the fugitive's name, his eyes narrowed. "Nothing," he said, his voice bristling with menace. He made to turn away, but I caught him by the arm and held him fast.

"I am not finished," I told him.

"I have nothing to say to you," he spat. "Go your way, Llew." He put his hand to my wrist and removed my hand. Keen, virulent hatred flared in his eyes. Anger flowed from him in waves. He stepped slowly away.

"Wait!" I said, desperate to hold him. "Siawn, wait, I want to join you."

He halted, rigid. "Join us? What do you mean?"

"You know what I mean," I told him, and, though my heart raced, I heard my voice cool and insinuating. "Do you think I am stupid? I can see what is happening. I want to join you."

Suspicious, he glared at me, trying to discern the intent behind my words. "The prince listens to you," I persisted. "I have seen the way he depends on you, Siawn. He would be nothing without you."

He stiffened, and I thought he would turn away. But he was intrigued. "Speak plainly," he said. "I am listening."

"Meldron wants to be king," I said. "I can help."

"How?"

"Tegid will not allow it. He will prevent it."

"Tegid is not important. If he stands in our way, we will kill him."

"No," I said, "you need him alive."

"Bards!" The word was a curse on his lips. "Meldron would be king now if not for the meddling of bards. Things will change when Meldron takes the throne."

"The people would rebel," I pointed out. "They would never support a king who killed their bard. But there is an easier way. If Tegid were seen to deliver the kingship to Meldron outright, the people would not question it."

"You could do this?"

"I could help. I have Tegid's trust; he tells me things. I could help you a great deal," I said. "But I want something in return."

Simon understood that. "What do you want?"

"I want a place with Meldron when he is king," I said simply. "I want to join the Wolf Pack."

"It is true the prince listens to me," he said, for he could not help boasting. "I will speak to him for you. I will tell the prince of your interest." He lowered his voice. "It may be that Meldron will require some assurance of your loyalty."

"What might that be?"

He thought for a moment, eyes sly and glinting in the moonlight. "Find out what Tegid plans to do when we reach Sycharth."

"That will take time," I lied. "I will have to coax him without raising suspicion."

"It should not be difficult for mighty Llew." The sneer of contempt was back in his voice.

"Very well, I will do it."

Simon reached out and gripped me by the shoulder. My flesh

crawled under his touch. "Good," he said. "The prince will be pleased."

He lifted his chin arrogantly, and then turned away. I peered through the darkness at his disappearing form; he swaggered as he walked.

The next morning, as we readied ourselves for the day's march, I went to Tegid and asked him, "When is Beltain?"

The bard thought for a moment—as well he might, for the unnaturally long Sollen had played havoc with the regular observances of sun and season. "It is"—he paused again, rethinking his calculations—"the third dawn from this one."

"We will not reach Sycharth in time," I reflected.

"No," Tegid agreed, "we will not reach the caer in time for Beltain."

"Where will we hold the celebration?"

"At one of the sacred places along the trail," he replied, "and there are several. There is a mound and standing stone near here. We should reach it the day after tomorrow. That will serve."

Yes, I thought, that will serve. For the next two days, I watched the prince and his coterie closely—and knew that I was being watched in turn. In the early evening of the second day as we set about making camp for the night, Simon approached me while I watered the horses.

"What do you have for me?" He was too eager. Ambition burned bright in the prince and his champion. I knew I had them.

"Not here! Tegid is suspicious. He must not see us together," I said harshly, glancing nervously over my shoulder. "There is a mound and standing stone just ahead of us on the trail. We will pass by it tomorrow. Meet me there at dawn."

He was accustomed to such secrecy and accepted it without protest. "Dawn, then," he agreed. "At the standing stone."

"And come alone," I warned. "The fewer people who know about this, the better."

"Do not give *me* orders!" he growled.

We parted then, and I walked back to my place at Tegid's campfire. We ate our meager meal in silence and unrolled our oxhides upon the damp ground when we finished. I was unsettled in my mind and in my heart, but Tegid seemed not to notice; no doubt he had more than enough on his mind.

That night, well before dawn, I rose from an uneasy sleep, took up my spear, pulled my cloak around me, and crept away. I stayed well away from the other campfires, skirting the sleeping places of the prince and his warriors until I struck the trail once again. With a setting moon to guide me, I hastened along the path. I dared not think about what lay ahead, nor what I must do.

I followed the twisting path, dodging low-hanging branches and the dark boles of trees. As I made my solitary way through the forest, I began to fear that Simon would not come alone, that he would bring the prince with him. If he did, my plan would fail. Eventually I came within sight of the meeting place. As the sun lightened the east, I walked impatiently around the large, grassy mound with its slender finger of standing stone jutting from the top. Now I began to worry that Simon would not come at all.

He did not disappoint me. Simon's ambition was great enough to ensure that he would do exactly as I said. I saw him approaching through the dim predawn light and forced myself to draw three deep, steadying breaths. I raised my spear in greeting.

He smiled his sly, superior smile when he saw me. "Well, I am here. What do you have for me?"

"Have you spoken to the prince?"

"I have," he replied, striding confidently nearer. "He will show his gratitude when the time comes. You will see."

"Good." I glanced quickly skyward. It was the time-between-times. "Walk with me," I said.

I could see Simon thought this an odd request, but he obeyed.

"This has not been easy," I began slowly, moving around the base of the mound. "Tegid can be very difficult, as you know. He is not one to openly discuss what he is thinking. He is a bard—you know how they are."

He made a derisive sound low in this throat. "Go on," he said.

"I just wanted you to know that it has not been easy to get information from him. There were certain difficulties."

"I told you Meldron stands ready to give you the reward you deserve," Simon said, suddenly suspicious. "What else do you want?"

"We will come to that. Now listen, this is what I found out: as soon as we reach Sycharth, Tegid is going to summon a gathering of bards to help him decide what to do."

"Why? Does he not know what to do?" He halted, his brow lowering skeptically.

"You do not understand," I said bluntly. I kept walking; Simon followed, and we completed the first circuit around the mound. "Meldryn Mawr must be buried first. It takes time to choose a new king."

"How much time?"

"That is not important." I kept walking.

"How much time?" Simon demanded.

"Twenty days at least," I said, choosing a number from thin air. "Once the bards have assembled—and we do not even know how many are left—there are preparations to be made, rituals and ceremonies that must be performed."

"We know all this," Simon replied in a clumsy attempt to bully me. "What else?"

I stopped and turned to him, gripping my spear tight between my hands. "If you know so much," I growled, "why accept my help at all? Do you want to learn what I found out, or not?"

"I am here," he replied tersely. "I am listening."

I started walking once more, feigning a sullen silence. The ruse worked. He followed. "What else did you learn?" he asked in a mollifying tone.

"Well," I replied slowly, "I think that Tegid will wait until all the bards have assembled, and then he will delay the choosing."

"Delay? Why would he delay choosing?"

"There is an ancient law," I answered, drawing out my words, "which allows the bard to gather all the men of the clan to a hosting for the kingship."

"What manner of hosting?" This intrigued Simon, as I knew it would.

"That is for the bards to decide," I bluffed, completing the second sunwise circuit of the mound and beginning the third. "Usually, there are numerous martial contests—trials of strength, skill at arms, horsemanship—and tests of courage and mental agility." I paused to let these words sink in, and then said, "The king will be chosen from among those who fare best in the competitions," I told him, "not just the princes and chieftains."

Simon bristled. "Why should a new ruler be so chosen when there is an heir with royal blood, one who is prepared to take the crown that is his by right?" He set his jaw in defiance of my words, and I knew I had read him right. I knew what he had done, and I could guess how he had done it.

Simon had inflamed Prince Meldron's ambition with talk of birthright succession: kingship passing from father to son, through bloodlines rather than through the merit of the individual. Simon, whose entire life was a testament to unmerited privilege, would champion the idea. And he would have no trouble at all convincing the weak and greedy prince that he was entitled to his father's throne.

Yet this is not the way of Albion: kings are chosen from among the clan's best men; and the bards, who retain the power to confer sovereignty, do the choosing.

Had he won over Prince Meldron with his easy talk of a kingship that could be gained without merit, without the blessing of the bard? A kingship that came through the blood of birth, not the blood of sacrifice?

I did not know who killed the Phantarch; indeed, I could not guess how he had even been found. But I was absolutely certain of one fact: Simon, who had forced his way into this world, had brought with him alien and deadly ideas. His heresies had caused the deaths of Ollathir, the Phantarch, the king, and countless thousands who had been destroyed by Nudd and his hordes. He had blithely and selfishly sought to take what could not be his, to create an order that would serve his selfish interest.

He knew and cared nothing about true kingship. He knew nothing of the Song or the Cythrawl. Or of the host of powers and forces loosed by his words of treachery—even now! He cared only for himself. His greed had almost destroyed Albion, and it had to be stopped. It was time for Simon to leave.

We walked a bit further, completing our third sunwise circuit of the mound. The sky lightened to sunrise, glowing softly pink. He was silent for some moments, thinking through what I told him. "Tegid's hosting," he said at last, "when will it begin?"

"It must take place in the space between one new moon and the next, sometime after Beltain and before Amhain," I told him.

"Beltain is soon," Simon observed.

"It is," I confirmed. "Very soon."

I stepped quickly to one side, leveling my spear upon Simon in the same swift motion. He glanced at the blade and made to push it aside. "Stand easy," I told him. "It is over, Simon. You are going back."

"Going back?" he wondered in genuine bewilderment.

"Home, Simon. You do not belong here. This is not your world. You have done great harm here, and it has to stop." He drew breath to protest, but I did not let him speak. "Turn around," I ordered, motioning toward the mound with the tip of the spear.

"You would not dare hurt me," he scoffed, throwing back his cloak and reaching for his sword. With a quick flick of the spear, I nicked his upper arm. He looked at the blood welling from the scratch and became angry. "You will die for that!"

"Turn around, Simon," I commanded.

Simon glared and hesitated. "You want it for yourself! You think yourself a king."

"Move!" I jabbed at him with the spear and stepped closer. "I am right behind you."

"You will regret this," he spat with cool menace. "I promise you will die regretting this."

"I will take that chance," I said, stepping near and pressing the sharp blade of my spear into his ribs. "But you are going back where you belong. Now move!"

He turned and stepped stiffly to the dark cavelike entrance yawning open at the base of the mound. With a last murderous look at me, he bent his head and entered.

I did not spare a moment celebrating my success. The Otherworld portal would not remain open long. Simon was right, I was already regretting what I had done—but not for the reason he suggested. I glanced around fair Albion one last time and realized how much I had come to love it, how much I would miss it all. Sadly, and with extreme reluctance, I leaned my spear against the mound. Then, breathing a silent farewell, I bent my head and stepped into the dark entrance.

39

THE RETURN

The interior of the mound was dark as a womb and suffocatingly close. I could not see Simon, nor could I hear him or sense his presence. He had already crossed over. Fearing the portal would close at any moment, and that I would miss my chance to return—and, having missed it, that I would not be able to make myself go through with it the next time—I took a deep breath and stepped into the howling void that separates the two worlds.

A wild blast of wind tore at me, and I teetered upon that narrow span—the sword bridge. I flung out my arms for balance and slid my foot forward over the blade's edge, ignoring the wind's heart-tearing scream and the dizzying sensation of balancing above an infinite and invisible void.

The sword-blade bridge beneath me bit into the soles of my feet as I slid them carefully along. The merciless wind ripped at me from every direction. I fought to breathe, fought against the paralyzing fear swimming at me out of the wind-blasted darkness. Gathering the last of my quickly failing nerve, I took two more sliding steps along the sword bridge.

I felt as if my clothing was being rent to shreds and stripped from my body, as if my flesh was being pared to the bone by the searing wind. *Courage,* I told myself, *it is soon over.*

I took another step.

My foot trod empty space, and I fell . . . weightless, stomach-wrenching, plunging into endless night, my lower lip clamped between my teeth to keep from screaming . . . falling through time and space, spinning through multilayered realms of possibility, through Earth ages that never were and potential futures that never would be, plunging through that unspeakably rich, elemental reservoir of the transcendent universe. I fell, landing hard on my left side. I lay on the packed dirt floor for a moment—until my head stopped spinning—and then opened my eyes on a dim, gray limestone interior.

I flexed my arms and legs experimentally but detected no broken bones. I raised myself up slowly and climbed to my feet. A thin, cold light entered the hive-shaped interior of the cairn. Simon was nowhere to be seen. Stepping to the low entrance, I gripped the cold stones at the edge of the hole and pulled myself out into the manifest world once more.

It was a winter dawn, and freezing. The sun was new risen in the east. A grainy pall of snow covered the ground. The sky through the trees above the glen showed ashen and pale. I emerged from the cairn into a world immeasurably forlorn and futile. My first thought was that I had come to the wrong place, that I had crossed over into a shadowland, a slight, sickly reflection of the world I had left behind. But then I saw it: the canvas tent of the Society of Metaphysical Archaeologists.

And there, sitting on a camp stool, drinking steaming coffee over a small fire before the tent was a man I recognized—in the way one recognizes someone from a dream—his name . . . his name . . . Weston. It was Weston, the director of the excavations, and across from him Professor Nettleton. I saw them and knew I had come home.

The realization settled on my shoulders like a dead weight.

For the world was no longer the same. Frail, colorless, weary, the world before me displayed a tentative, temporary appearance. Everything—trees, rocks, earth, and sky and dull winter sun—seemed not to exist as much as merely to linger—like a fast-fading memory. There was no feeling of import or solidity, nothing at all substantial about the world I saw. Ephemeral, impermanent, it looked as if it were a transitory phenomenon—a mirage that might dissolve at any moment.

And I could see that Weston and Professor Nettleton had changed as well, subtly but perceptibly: their features were coarser, their bodies smaller and more ungainly. They appeared slighter, less physically present somehow. There was a peculiar ghostlike quality to them, as if they clung to corporeal existence by the slenderest of threads, as if the atoms making up their bodies might relinquish their cohesive attraction and go flying apart at the least provocation.

Even as I stood looking on, the man Weston rose abruptly and ducked into the tent. As soon as he was out of sight, I lurched forward and the movement caught Nettleton's eye. His gaze shifted. An expression of frank amazement appeared on his owlish face.

"Oh, no!" he whispered sharply.

He clearly did not recognize me. Why should he? I was dressed like something out of the *Mabinogion*—from the silver torc at my throat to the leather buskins on my feet, breecs, siarc, and bright-checked cloak. He was waiting, yes; but he was obviously not expecting a Celtic warrior to come shuffling out of the cairn.

I stepped cautiously forward, aware of the disturbing effect my appearance was having on him. "Do not be afraid," I said.

Nettles gaped at me in uncomprehending shock. Thinking he had not heard me, I repeated myself, and only then realized that I was speaking ancient Celt. It took me a moment, and not a little effort, to find the English words.

"Please," I said, "do not be afraid." My voice sounded harsh and clumsy in my ears.

If my Celtic speech puzzled him, my native tongue terrified him. Professor Nettleton, trembling like a terrier, put out his hands as if to hold me at arm's length away from him.

"It—it's all right," I said. "I have returned."

The professor peered at me through his round-rimmed spectacles in the wan, uncertain light. "Who are you?"

I cannot describe the devastation wrought by those three innocent words. Sharper than spears, they stabbed me through. The gorge rose in my throat. I gasped and pressed the heels of my hands to my eyes.

"*Who . . . are . . . you?*" the professor repeated slowly, adopting the carefully exaggerated speech one would use in speaking to a foreigner, or a madman. Then he said the same words again, in Welsh, which only made me feel more of an alien being.

It was a moment before I could utter a sound. "I—I am . . . I am . . . ," I stammered. The words clotted on my tongue. I could not make myself speak my name.

In dawning realization, the professor edged forward. "Lewis?" he asked softly. "Is that you?"

Indeed, the professor's question was better than he knew. Who was I? Was I Lewis, the Oxford graduate student who had been sucked into an impossible Otherworldly adventure? Or was I Llew, the changeling who stood with one foot in both worlds?

Nettles crept closer, darting a quick glance to the tent behind him. "Lewis?"

"Y-yes . . . it is Lew—Lewis," I said thickly, stumbling over my own name. Wrapping my tongue around the language was an effort.

"I have been watching," Nettles said. He stepped closer, his eyes taking in my appearance—he gazed at me as if at a wonder. "I have been waiting."

"I've returned," I told him. "I've come back."

"Look at you," he breathed in an awed voice. His eyes glowed like a child's at Christmas. "Look at you!" He raised a trembling hand to touch my cloak. "Why . . . it—it's miraculous!"

I had encountered astonishment before, and the same expression of awestricken disbelief—on the faces of the warriors on the wall and in the eyes of the gathering in Meldryn Mawr's hall. I knew my sojourn in the Otherworld had changed me; and judging from the reactions of so many, my contact with the Singing Stones in the Phantarch's chamber had changed me still more. But standing in the chill, thin light of this shabby, pathetic world, I understood at last: I was not simply changed, I was transformed.

I spread my arms and looked down the length of my body. My hands were hard, my arms muscled and strong; my legs were straight, powerful, my torso lean, tight, and my chest broader, my shoulders heavier. I reached a hand to my face and felt a straighter nose, a stronger chin, and more forceful jaw. But the change was more than physical. There was the aura, the glory reflected from my encounter with the Song.

Lewis was gone. Llew stood in his place.

"What has happened?" Nettles asked, an eager light animating his face. "Did you find Simon? Did you stop him? What was it like?"

How could I tell him what I knew? How could I even begin to describe the Otherworld, let alone put to words all that had happened?

I stood gazing at my friend, a welter of emotions swirling inside me. He looked so weak, so fragile, and so insignificant. Embarrassed by the visible poverty of his crabbed, miserable existence, I wanted to raise him up, to make him see what I had seen, to know what I knew. I wanted him to sleep under Albion's undimmed stars and to feel the fresh wind of virginal green valleys on his face; I wanted him to hear the soul-stirring melody of a True Bard's harp, to smell the salt sea air of Ynys

Sci, and savor the exquisite sweetness of honey mead; I wanted him to feel the firm rock of Prydain's matchless mountains under his feet, to see the bright fire-glint on a king's golden torc, to exult in the glory of the good fight. I wanted to show him all these things and more. I wanted him to breathe deep of the higher, richer life of the Otherworld, to drink from the cup that I had tasted . . . to hear the incomparable Song.

I longed to show him the paradise I had discovered in Albion, but I knew that I could not. Try as I might, I could never make him understand. The gulf between us was too great. Words alone could never span the distance, nor describe the cruel destruction yet threatening that fair world.

But I was spared the need to answer, for Professor Nettleton laid his hand to my arm and leaned close. "Unfortunately, we do not have much time. The others"—he jerked his head in the direction of the tent, and I knew who he meant—"will return at any moment. They are very close to a breakthrough—they know about the portal here. I have contrived to join their excavations so that I can stay close at hand. But we cannot let them find you here like this."

"Where is Simon?" I asked, my tongue awkward and clumsy in my mouth.

"Simon?" The professor seemed mystified. "But I have not seen Simon. Only you have returned."

Even as I stood there, struggling to understand, I noticed that the feeble light had dimmed yet further; it was darker now than just a few moments ago . . . odd.

I glanced over my shoulder toward the cairn . . . the glen was sinking into darkness, shadows deepening. A crow circled slowly overhead, silently watching . . . Then I realized that it was not dawn at all—but dusk. In this world the day was rapidly approaching twilight and the time-between-times. Soon the portal inside Carnwood Cairn would open.

And if Simon had not returned . . .

I saw the signs and felt the elemental tidepull of the moment in my blood and in my bones. And I heard the Song—streaming across the blinding distance between the worlds. I heard the Song and knew that the war for paradise extended to this world and to this very moment. And I had, now, to choose.

Nettles was watching me. I swung towards him and raised my hand in a simple farewell. Then I turned and walked to the ancient cairn. I heard Professor Nettleton call out behind me: "Good-bye, Lewis! God go with you!"

And then another voice—Weston's voice, excited, alarmed, shouting, "Wait! Stop! Stop him, quick!" I heard frantic footsteps on the frozen earth behind me. "No! Please! Turn back!"

But I did not stop. I did not turn back. For I had heard the Song of Albion, and my life was no longer my own.

ALBION FOREVER!

BY STEPHEN R. LAWHEAD

Sean Connery has a tattoo on his forearm that is rarely visible in any of his films: a small blue banner bearing the words *Scotland Forever*—a slogan that expresses the fierce pride and patriotism of so many of his countrymen. The meaning goes well beyond mere words. It is at once a defiant battle cry, a poignant expression of love for the auld country, and (as in that memorable scene from *Braveheart*), a flip-of-the-kilt to the hated English and all would-be foreign occupiers.

Since the first volume in the Song of Albion series was published in 1991, I have received hundreds—thousands?—of letters and e-mails from readers who have found in these books some articulation of a related sentiment: *Albion Forever*. I cannot claim credit for those who have decided to engrave the words indelibly on their bodies' can-vasses, but I do take great pleasure in knowing that the story of Llew Silver Hand has resonated so strongly with Britons of all back-grounds, North Americans, Europeans, and readers in many far-flung lands. More than any other book or series I've written in the past twenty-five years, these volumes have the most stalwart following—including the publisher of this new edition, who read them in his twenties and was determined to publish them himself when he had the chance.

If any author knew why certain books succeeded where others

failed, he would apply the magic formula without deviation, and reap the benefits of a sure thing. But this is not the case, so I have had years to ponder the enduring appeal of these books, whose readers sometimes report reading them yearly, incorporating certain passages into marriage or funeral ceremonies, naming their children after characters in the story, and making pilgrimages to the real and imagined sites in the manifest and Otherworld of Albion.

I have concluded that the potent emotional charge many readers experience derives from three interwoven factors, the first of which is the "story vehicle," or the means by which the reader moves through the tale. Here we have a first-person narrative—which I enjoy writing—by an everyman named Lewis who is, at the outset, sufficiently ordinary to seem familiar to any reader, male *or* female. He is a person from our own here-and-now world with the sort of frustrations and problems most of us can relate to, and who inhabits a recognizable niche in modern society: an American graduate student in Oxford who should be getting on in life, but has yet to settle. Our viewpoint character, Lewis, hasn't yet found his joy, his passion, his meaning and role in life.

This vehicle allows Lewis's thoughts and feelings to become *our* thoughts and feelings. We know him, because he is us. And, since the narrative is written in the first-person voice, we are inside his heart and head on every page. Instead of reading *about* a legendary hero doing heroic things in a legendary kingdom, Lewis's exploits become our own.

This strong identification proved to be a powerful conduit for the underlying substance of the story, and the second important factor: Celtic myth and legend.

I—a Nebraskan, whose native myths revolved around cowboys and Indians—had virtually stumbled upon and into the whole grand universe of Celtic myth and legend while researching and writing my King

Arthur series, The Pendragon Cycle. While writing the first three books in that series, I was picking up numerous references to various ancient tales peculiar to the British Isles which, while not specifically about Arthur or Merlin, nevertheless informed the spirit and background of the various tales and legends. Upon completion of *Taliesin*, *Merlin*, and *Arthur*, I was eager to turn my attention to what I considered the raw material of the Arthurian legend: its Celtic roots.

Deeply impressed by the imagery of Celtic folklore and the ancients' love of beauty and ostentation, as well as the solid sensibility of the voices I heard speaking to me across the centuries, still fresh and still potent after so many years . . . it was my ambition to write something that would honor this tradition.

Of course there were problems—and opportunities. The myths themselves were broken: fragments only. Although it is almost miraculous that anything at all survives from a culture that stubbornly refused to write down anything (for most of their history, the Celts distrusted the written word), still I had to deal with the fact that there are but a handful of even partially complete stories surviving from the past fifteen or sixteen centuries. The rest are mere incidents, story segments, and shards of larger works now lost; nothing like a whole cycle of interconnected tales existed. However, there were some recurring characters and tantalizing clues to suggest tenuous connections to other stories, and even intriguing references to incidents in tales now forgotten but previously well-known.

It would never work to patch together the diverse pieces in hopes of re-creating a plausible whole. Rather, it was obvious from the beginning that my approach would be to create a new myth out of the old—basically, to fashion a brand-new suit of clothes using those ancient scraps. Of necessity, I became something of a scavenger, picking up bits of this and that with which to work: names, incidents, odd bits of lore. And I set about capturing the Celtic mythos in a contemporary story, but one that used the characters, settings, and culture the ancient Celts themselves would have recognized.

I determined that the story would move through all the stations of a traditional heroic myth tale and complete the cycle, because I wanted it to be a whole myth, not a broken one. This meant that certain constraints would be present and certain elements needed to be present. I studied the way mythic stories moved and the various component parts to be acquired or supplied—either by myself or lifted from one or another of the various Celtic tales, building up a ready working knowledge of not only the necessary shape of the story, but the characters, devices, and objects that populated Celtic myth and legend.

So The Song of Albion rests on a solid foundation of Celtic myth and is, in its construction, also a mythic story. A viewpoint character with whom we identify closely—the everyman, Lewis—creates resonance. And for the final factor, the language of the story touches the heart of the reader.

By language, I refer not to the modern language in which it may be read—English, French, Greek—or even the Gaelic words and names that are found sprinkled throughout the books. Rather, I refer to the means that the story uses to express itself, and that language is fantasy.

In fantasy, the author echoes the creation of this manifest world, in which we live, with the fashioning of a subcreated world, in which the story's characters live. A common feature of such literature is a portal—C. S. Lewis's wardrobe must surely be the most well-known—through which the reality-bound protagonist travels into a more stylized imaginary, yet somehow more *true*, world. Stripped of much of the clutter of the mundane world and its often trivial preoccupations, more important matters of life stand in higher relief—good and evil, loyalty and betrayal, hope and despair, love and hate—can be better appreciated as they are played out in the story and, consequently, better understood.

J. R. R. Tolkien, undisputedly a most fluent speaker of this language, was criticized in his day for indulging his juvenile whim of writing fantasy, which was then considered—as it still is in many quarters—an inferior form of literature and disdained as mere "escapism."

"Of course it is escapist," he cried. "That is its glory! When a soldier is a prisoner of war it is his duty to escape—and take as many with him as he can." He went on to explain, "The moneylenders, the know-nothings, the authoritarians have us all in prison; if we value the freedom of the mind and soul, if we're partisans of liberty, then it's our plain duty to escape, and to take as many people with us as possible."

It is a difficult thing—perhaps also a foolish thing—for an author to analyze his own work, attempting a rational explanation of what is essentially and necessarily intuitive and mysterious. If these words have diminished your sense of wonder in any way, I apologize. If they have helped you better appreciate what you have just read, I am glad.

All told, I am pleased to have written a book that has struck a cord with so many readers, and happily join those who have escaped into the world of Llew Silver Hand, Goewyn, Cynan, Tegid, Scatha, and all the rest, and gladly proclaim: "Albion Forever!"

iNTERVIEW WiTH THE AUTHOR

Publisher Allen Arnold read the Song of Albion books when they were first published fifteen years ago. He has re-read them a few times since, and recently was able to ask Stephen Lawhead some questions about this exceptional trilogy and the world of Albion.

Arnold: What was the catalyst for this epic trilogy? Do you remember a moment in time when the concept first crystallized for you?

Lawhead: The Song of Albion was gestating throughout the time that I was writing my Arthurian series—*The Pendragon Cycle.* I had discovered the Celtic foundations of the King Arthur tales—which was new to me, and fascinating to me. This was in the 1980s. So, while I was researching and writing about Taliesin, Merlin, and Arthur—I kept encountering this rich, complex and, to me, exotic material—tales and legends of the ancient Celts which, although they didn't have anything directly to do with Arthur, were nevertheless influencing the Arthurian tradition in a profound way.

I began scheming a way to use this wonderful material directly—in a story that reflected all the elements of Celtic myth, and that moved through the complete mythic cycle, beginning to end. The Song of Albion was the result.

A: *The Paradise War* uses a cairn as a gate to the Otherworld. Why is this?

L: In Celtic legend, almost anything can be a gateway. I simply chose cairns because they are ubiquitous in the Celtic lands. They're every-where, these curious heaps of stones. Whether simple or elaborate, they all mark significant places--yet we usually don't know what that significance is.

Like most writers, I often ask myself, 'What if . . . ?' What if a particular cairn was raised to mark a gateway to the Otherworld? What if someone in the present day stumbled through?

A: Nettles is such an eclectic, memorable character. Who served as your inspiration for him?

L: I live in Oxford, remember! These guys are all over the place. Professor Nettleton is my idea of the ideal and archetypal academic: agreeable, approachable, enthusiastic about his area of expertise, and formidably knowledgeable.

A: This trilogy works together so well as a whole—partially due to the intricate foreshadowing you plant in this first novel. Yet you have remarked that you allow each novel to flow organically as you write it. Can you describe how this balance works since it seems you have to have the end in mind—as well as a million connected details—from the start in order for the trilogy to build as it does.

L: The story grew from the ideas carefully seeded throughout the book and, while it is true that I allowed it to grow as it would, its cre-ation was not an open-ended process. I had a definite ending point in mind, a specific destination. As the story unfolded and moved through each section it always had to be checked against that final destination.

This is not the same thing as knowing the end of the story; I didn't know how the story would end. I only discovered the ending as I wrote. The balance, then, lies in allowing the story to develop as it would while making sure that what developed was moving toward the final destination.

A: The spiritual quality of your books is distinctive, and something I resonate with very strongly. How does all that work?

L: The way it works is, you write what you know.

The world I live in is a spiritual world. I have certain beliefs that include a creative God; a 'manifest' or temporal and broken world that is bracketed by an 'otherworld' which is eternal and perfect; the need for, and existence of, redemptive possibilities. Basically, I believe in the life and teachings of Jesus Christ.

Naturally, these beliefs inform my writing, just as a person with other beliefs—a naturalist, nihilist, humanist, or hedonist, for example—will write books that express his or her point of view . . . whether they intend to, or not! It's unavoidable. And, the more subtle it is . . . the more compelling it is.

I suppose there's a parallel here with the book, eh? In the world of Albion, what happens in the Otherworld effects what happens in the manifest world . . . and my contention is that what is going on in any author's own belief system effects what happens in his or her books.

A: Each book in this series has thirty-nine chapters. Is that important?

L: In Celtic numerology, thirty-nine is a highly symbolic number. To the ancient Celts, three was the sacred number, and what is nine but three times three—which is to say thrice sacred, which is three times more holy, and so on. Thus, in a series about divine kingship, I thought it might be interesting to keep each book to thirty-nine chapters as a way to reinforce this ancient holy concept.

ROBIN HOOD.

THE LEGEND BEGINS ANEW

STEPHEN R. LAWHEAD

HOOD

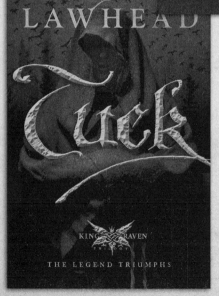

STEPHEN R. LAWHEAD

Tuck

KING RAVEN
TRILOGY

THE LEGEND TRIUMPHS

STEPHEN R. LAWHEAD

Scarlet

KING RAVEN
TRILOGY

THE LEGEND LIVES

KING RAVEN
TRILOGY

EXCERPT FROM *HOOD*

The pig was young and wary, a yearling boar timidly testing the wind for strange scents as it ventured out into the honey-coloured light of a fast-fading day. Bran ap Brychan, Prince of Elfael, had spent the entire day stalking the greenwood for a suitable prize, and he meant to have this one.

Eight years old and the king's sole heir, he knew well enough that he would never be allowed to go out into the forest alone. So rather than seek permission, he had simply taken his bow and four arrows early that morning and stolen from the caer unnoticed. This hunt, like the young boar, was dedicated to his mother, the queen. She loved the hunt and gloried in the wild beauty and visceral excitement of the chase. Even when she did not ride herself, she would ready a welcome for the hunters with a saddle cup and music, leading the women in song. "Don't be afraid," she told Bran when, as a toddling boy, he had been dazzled and a little frightened by the noise and revelry.

"We belong to the land. Look, Bran!" She lifted a slender hand toward the hills and the forest rising like a living rampart beyond. "All that you see is the work of our Lord's hand. We rejoice in his provision."

Stricken with a wasting fever, Queen Rhian had been sick most of the summer, and in his childish imaginings, Bran had determined that if he could present her with a stag or a boar that he had brought down all by himself, she would laugh and sing as she always did, and she would feel better. She would be well again.

All it would take was a little more patience and . . . Still as stone, he waited in the deepening shadow. The young boar stepped nearer, its small pointed ears erect and proud. It took another step and stopped to sample the tender shoots of a mallow plant. Bran, an arrow already nocked to the string, pressed the bow forward, feeling the tension in his shoulder and back just the way Iwan said he should. "Do not aim the arrow," the older youth had instructed him. "Just *think* it to the mark. Send it on your thought, and if your thought is true, so, too, will fly the arrow."

Pressing the bow to the limit of his strength, he took a steadying breath and released the string, feeling the sharp tingle on his fingertips. The arrow blazed across the distance, striking the young pig low in the chest behind the front legs. Startled, it flicked its tail rigid, and turned to bolt into the wood . . . but two steps later its legs tangled; it stumbled and went down. The stricken creature squealed once and tried to rise, then subsided, dead where it fell.

Bran loosed a wild whoop of triumph. The prize was his! He ran to the pig and put his hand on the animal's sleek, slightly speckled haunch, feeling the warmth there.

"I am sorry, my friend, and I thank you," he murmured as Iwan had taught him. "I need your life to live."

It was only when he tried to shoulder his kill that Bran realized his great mistake. The dead weight of the animal was more than he could lift by himself. With a sinking heart, he stood gazing at his glorious prize as tears came to his eyes. It was all for nothing if he could not carry the trophy home in triumph.

Sinking down on the ground beside the warm carcass, Bran put his head in his hands. He could not carry it, and he would not leave it.

What was he going to do?

As he sat contemplating his predicament, the sounds of the forest grew loud in his ears: the chatter of a squirrel in a treetop, the busy click and hum of insects, the rustle of leaves, the hushed flutter of wings above him, and then . . .

"Bran!"

Bran started at the voice. He glanced around hopefully.

"Here!" he called. "Here! I need help!"

"Go back!" The voice seemed to come from above. He raised his eyes to see a huge black bird watching him from a branch directly over his head.

It was only an old raven. "Shoo!"

"Go back!" said the bird. "Go back!"

"I won't," shouted Bran. He reached for a stick on the path, picked it up, drew back, and threw it at the bothersome bird. "Shut up!"

The stick struck the raven's perch, and the bird flew off with a cry that sounded to Bran like laughter. "Ha, ha, haw! Ha, ha, haw!"

"Stupid bird," he muttered. Turning again to the young pig beside him, he remembered what he had seen other hunters do with small game. Releasing

the string on his bow, he gathered the creature's short legs and tied the hooves together with the cord. Then, passing the stave through the bound hooves and gripping the stout length of oak in either hand, he tried to lift it. The carcass was still too heavy for him, so he began to drag his prize through the forest, using the bow.

It was slow going, even on the well-worn path, with frequent stops to rub the sweat from his eyes and catch his breath. All the while, the day dwindled around him.

No matter. He would not give up. Clutching the bow stave in his hands, he struggled on, step by step, tugging the young boar along the trail, reaching the edge of the forest as the last gleam of twilight faded across the valley to the west.

"Bran!"

The shout made him jump. It was not a raven this time, but a voice he knew. He turned and looked down the slope toward the valley to see Iwan coming toward him, long legs paring the distance with swift strides.

"Here!" Bran called, waving his aching arms overhead. "Here I am!"

"In the name of all the saints and angels," the young man said when he came near enough to speak, "what do you think you are doing out here?"

"Hunting," replied Bran. Indicating his kill with a hunter's pride, he said, "It strayed in front of my arrow, see?"

"I see," replied Iwan. Giving the pig a cursory glance, he turned and started away again. "We have to go. It's late, and everyone is looking for you."

Bran made no move to follow.

Looking back, Iwan said, "Leave it, Bran! They are searching for you. We must hurry."

"No," Bran said. "Not without the boar." He stooped once more to the carcass, seized the bow stave, and started tugging again. Iwan returned, took him roughly by the arm, and pulled him away.

"Leave the stupid thing!"

"It is for my mother!" the boy shouted, the tears starting hot and quick. As the tears began to fall, he bent his head and repeated more softly, "Please, it is for my mother."

"Weeping Judas!" Iwan relented with an exasperated sigh. "Come then. We will carry it together."

ABOUT THE AUTHOR

Stephen R. Lawhead is an internationally-acclaimed author of mythic history and imaginative fiction. His novels include, *The Skin Map*, the King Raven Trilogy (*Hood*, *Scarlet*, and *Tuck*), *Patrick*, the Dragon King trilogy, and the Pendragon Cycle series. Lawhead makes his home in Oxford, England, with his wife.